THE TEARS OF THE
❈ DIVINE ❈

THE AP'LYDIN CHRONICLES

The Heirs of Lydin
The Slaves of the Horned God
The Tears of the Divine

THE TALES OF AELZANDAR

The Grey Mage
The Errant Princess

The Tears of the Divine

Book 3 of the Ap'Lydin Chronicles

AIDAN HENNESSY

Published by Atallas Publishing 2024

Copyright © 2024 Aidan Hennessy

Cover Design by James, GoOnWrite.com

Cartography by Sebastian Breit

ISBN: 0648186490

ISBN-13: 978-0-6481864-9-6

For Jan.
Every step of the way, you have been this book's biggest supporter.

SKURI

Liderial

Harralin

MOUNTAINS
OF
SORROW

Dilmun

Port
Jemesch

Emperor's Palace

Lerid

Port Nikolaus

Oldharbour

LERIDIAN PLAINS

Teagleberg

GORUNCHIA

CARUILLIN

Georgeton

Qar Arrid

Socorific

Gorin

QARLD

Gorlion

EMPARIA

Selvarial

NECROMANCER'S
PEAKS

VALLISTIAN MARCHES

Ralom

Vallanzik

N

Dracacoilis

W   E

Nefencoilis

S

Jagoncoilis

Anacoilis

MACRODONIA

CARURLONIA

0 60 120 180
· SCALE IN MILES ·

Kieocoilis

YEAR 234 OF THE THIRD EPOCH

SOTAR
MOUNTAINS

Aderial

ADERILUND

THE LANDS OF
EMPARIA AND GORIINCHIA
SCALE IN MILES
0 25 50 75
· YEAR 234 OF THE THIRD EPOCH ·

PROLOGUE

Year 222 of the Third Epoch

Wulfric couldn't help but smile.

He'd been in a good mood ever since they left Oldharbour. Even the soaking rain and muddy conditions had done little to dampen his spirits, much to his companions' dismay.

"You're still bloody smiling, Wulfric?" Alusine asked. "I thought you'd have soured by now." The men had known each other for decades, but Alusine still found himself surprised by his friend's relentless optimism. They'd been riding for days, yet Wulfric was as fresh as a daisy. Even his horse throwing its shoe a few days back hadn't affected his mood.

"If that tumble he took didn't wipe the smile off his face then nothing will." Haakon de Morcor was the youngest of the trio, but as the King's nephew, technically of higher social status. Despite this he never received, nor expected any deference from his two closest friends.

Wulfric let out a chuckle. "Well, my lords, yes the journey may have been an absolute nightmare, but it is nearly at an end. Hotar Citadel is in sight and tomorrow the celebrations begin." He looked at Haakon and

Alusine. "Ten years."

"Seems like yesterday," Alusine said.

"For us old men, certainly," said Wulfric. "But for some of these young men with us?"

He called out to the squire riding close by. "You there, squire –"

"Geoffrey, my lord."

"Yes, Geoffrey, of course. How old are you?"

"I have seen eighteen summers, my lord."

"Of course. Do you know what happened tomorrow, ten years ago?"

The squire looked nervous. "Of course, my lords, the Battle of Silverwater Bay. The end of the war. No one would forget that. It's legend."

Wulfric gave the others an impressed look. "Do you see that, my lords? It appears we have already passed into the realm of legends. I guess that settles it."

The spires of Hotar Citadel were already coming into view. It appeared a small group of individuals had gathered for their arrival.

Alusine looked pleased. "Well, it looks like they knew to expect us. The messenger must have arrived in good time."

Wulfric scanned the crowd and saw at least one face he wasn't happy to see. "Look, Alusine, your favourite jester is here to greet us as well."

"Enlim is a valued member of my court, Wulfric," Alusine chided. "You should treat him with respect. I've always found his advice both wise and insightful."

Wulfric screwed up his face. "He looks like a dried-up prune." He glanced at Haakon who seemed disgusted. "I see you agree with me."

Haakon waved him away. "No, my stomach has just taken a turn, my lords."

"I'm not surprised," Alusine said. "My trail rations tasted a bit queer. Why don't you head on up first, Haakon? Take some rest and settle your stomach. I won't be long."

Haakon gave the rest of them a quick nod and spurred his horse forward.

"Never had the strongest stomach, our Haakon," said Wulfric, as he watched the other noble depart.

As they came closer to the castle entrance, Simon Enlim stepped forward. Wulfric noted that the rest of the crowd had given the cloaked figure a wide berth. There was a palpable sense of dread surrounding Alusine's advisor, and few spoke of him in anything but hushed tones.

"Lord Alusine," Enlim said, his voice a hoarse whisper. "You have returned, and not a moment too late. We must speak."

"Then speak, Enlim."

"Alone."

"In a moment," Alusine said. He didn't look Enlim directly in his eyes and seemed irritated and impatient. "Let me rest, gather my strength and attend to a few matters first."

"This will not wait," Enlim said.

Alusine let out a sigh. "Nothing ever can with you, Enlim. I'll see you in a moment, Wulfric."

Alusine and Enlim entered the castle together, speaking to each other in hushed tones. Wulfric could make out none of it, but knew it was bad counsel, no matter how Alusine protested.

"Have you heard the stories about Enlim, Squire?" Wulfric asked Geoffrey.

"Yes, your grace," Geoffrey said. "But I don't know how much to believe. The stories make him out to be impossibly old."

"He certainly looks it. Twisted face, too. I believe them when they say the old earl dragged him from a raging inferno."

"I've heard other things too. That he's a murderer. What stock do you put in that?"

Wulfric's mouth turned into a grimace. "I don't know the truth of it. But I know a killer when I see one." He looked around. "Enough waiting, I'm not leaving Alusine alone with that lunatic any longer. Come with me, Geoffrey."

The two men entered the castle together, climbing the stairs, their conversation turning to idle matters.

A scream interrupted them.

"What was that?" said Geoffrey, alarmed.

"That was Alusine!" Wulfric called out, his hand moving instinctively to the sword on his belt.

There was another scream, a woman this time, and from a different direction.

"Lady Eleanor!" Geoffrey said.

"Treachery!" yelled Wulfric. "Squire, go to her Lady's aid, rouse any help you can find. I'm going to help Alusine."

Geoffrey ran off as quickly as he could, weapon drawn.

Wulfric steeled himself. "Enlim, you bastard. I'm coming for you."

Adrenalin and rage fuelled Wulfric as he raced to Alusine's chambers, desperately hoping he was not too late. When he reached the room he almost kicked the door off its hinges. His heart nearly leapt out of his chest at the scene before him.

Alusine's corpse lay on the floor, blood pouring from wounds and pooling about the body. There crouched over the body was Simon Enlim, his robes smeared with blood. A trail of blood led from Alusine across the room.

Enlim turned to face Wulfric and stared at him with that monstrous face of his. "Don't do anything rash, Highcrown. You must listen to me, there is —"

The red mist descended on Wulfric. "Devil, I'll slay you where you stand before I let another lie come from your mouth." He lunged at Enlim, sword drawn, but his enemy easily sidestepped it. Wulfric was not finished though, and he let loose a flurry of blows. Not all connected, but it was enough to throw Enlim off guard, allowing Wulfric to place him in a grapple hold and shove him towards the open window.

"You are making a mistake!" Enlim called out, but Wulfric slammed his fist into Enlim's mouth. As his enemy toppled from the window, Wulfric exulted in his victory too early. Enlim grabbed and pulled Wulfric towards him, and the pair tumbled out of the castle and onto the ground far below.

Wulfric's last conscious vision was of Enlim's cold, dark eyes boring into his soul, and the words that came from the misshapen wretch's lips.

"True justice is elusive this day."

CHAPTER 1

Autumn, Year 235 of the Third Epoch

Polnygar's teeth chattered. Pulling the cloak tighter over her shoulders and wrapping it around her body, she attempted to keep some of the warmth from escaping. It did not seem to work, and her teeth continued to chatter.

"You didn't tell me it was so cold here," she said to Aelzandar.

"Well, my dear," the archmage said. "Why do you think they call it the frozen north?"

Augustin and Hebu looked like they were not handling the cold any better than Polnygar. For months they had journeyed through the sunny pastures of Lerid, making good time as they made their way through the Grand Duchy. Sir Holger Keller, their guide, had insisted they kept to the main roads for safety, even though some of the less travelled routes might have been quicker.

Eventually the weather had changed, and the weakening of the sun's light seemed to mark their entrance into Skurj, the perilous and forbidding northernmost province of the Empire of Caruillin. It was here that they would find their quarry: the rogue spellweaver Ivellios.

Aelzandar turned to Hebu. "Are you all right down there, Hebu?"

The Nemoi, wrapped head to foot in fur, made no real response. He concentrated on keeping his legs moving through the heavy snow.

"Worse than I remember," said Augustin, trying to yank a foot from the snow. "Though I guess last time I came here I had two hands. The cold is hell on my arm." Augustin rubbed the metal arm, his teeth chattering. As he did so Polnygar felt self-conscious. She had sudden flashbacks to that day in Ralom where she had been forced to mutilate Augustin to free him from Ivellios' magical control. She still blamed herself for the Baron losing his hand, even if the others, including Augustin himself, had told her not to. Hebu and Aelzandar had constructed Augustin a replacement in Qar Arrid, but it was not the same.

"We will be there soon enough," said Aelzandar. He matched his pace with Sir Holger ahead, his staff making tracks in the snow.

"Sir Holger, you still haven't told us who we're looking for," said Augustin, trying to catch up to the knight and Aelzandar. He threw a look over his shoulder to Polnygar. "By the gods, they move fast."

"The town is a few hours journey north. We are meeting with the Lord Mayor," said Sir Holger.

Aelzandar gave Augustin a look. "Does that satisfy your curiosity?"

"Well, somewhat," grumbled Augustin.

Polnygar realised with elation they were nearing their destination. It had been just over a year since they had left Ralom, and after months and months of travelling through the interior of Carurlonia, Polnygar would be glad to reach somewhere that they could stay for at least overnight.

Augustin spoke. "Looks like someone's come out to meet us."

Polnygar peered ahead, shielding her eyes from the snow and wind. She could see a vague silhouette some distance ahead.

As they moved forward, the figure became clearer. It was a tall, brawny man, dressed in furs and armour. He wore a thick moustache, greying with age.

Once they came near, Holger called out. "Grand Master!"

"Sir Holger." The newcomer embraced the knight. After they parted, the older man dropped to one knee, on the snow in front of the archmage. Aelzandar, seemingly unsurprised, offered a hand to the man, who kissed it reverently.

"My Lord Archmage." The man spoke with a distinct accent. "It was my missive to the King-Emperor that brought you here. I sent my nephew here to ensure no one delayed the archmage."

"You know me then?" Aelzandar said.

The older man stood, rising back to his full height. He was taller than even Augustin, towering over Polnygar and Aelzandar, and bore himself with a quiet, weary sort of dignity. "Only by reputation and name, my lord, but I would recognise you anywhere. You are just as my grandfather told me." The man seemed to remember something, and his expression changed. "Oh, forgive me, my lord, I did not introduce myself. I am Sir Agmar Keller, Grand Master of the Knights of the Crux Caruillin."

Aelzandar smiled, and there was recognition in his eyes. "Ah, of course. I remember a Keller who was Grand Master here. What was his name? Wulfgar?"

"My grandfather," Agmar said.

"How is he?" said Aelzandar.

"Long gone," Agmar said. "He passed away many winters ago."

Aelzandar frowned, "Oh, of course, I am sorry. I sometimes forget the human lifespan is so short." He clasped the knight's hand. "He lives in my memory. He was a good, brave man, and I'm sure you are the same."

"Thank you, my lord." Agmar looked at Polnygar and the others. "These are your companions?"

"Indeed," said Aelzandar. "This is Polnygar, my apprentice; Hebu, my scribe, and Baron Augustin Bauer of Emparia."

Agmar nodded to each in turn. "I am pleased that Sir Holger has been able to convey you here safely. I had worried that the temptations of Lerid might delay you."

Augustin raised an eyebrow. "Temptations?"

"You were right uncle," Sir Holger said. "Lerid is as base and sinful a land as you said, but I remained strong, and let nothing stray me from the true path."

Agmar smiled. "My trust in you was well placed, then." The Grand Master turned to Aelzandar. "Archmage, the Burgomeister is awaiting you in Harralin. He sent us here to greet you, to make sure you found your way."

"The Burgomeister of Harralin?" Augustin asked.

"Yes, Freiherr Gerd von Genio," Agmar nodded. "He could not be here personally, as he had urgent matters to attend to, but he has instructed me to take you to Harralin immediately."

"Very well," said Aelzandar. "Lead the way. We can discuss these matters more as we walk."

With Agmar in the lead, the travellers continued up the path, moving steadily across and over the snow-covered hills towards the faint glow of Harralin in the distance.

"Grand Master," Aelzandar said to Agmar. "We have heard things from Sir Holger about the troubles plaguing Harralin, but perhaps you can give us a more complete account, particularly about the temple."

"It was a few months ago that it all began," Agmar said wearily, trudging through the snow. "The temple had stood just outside Harralin for generations, but it had been abandoned for most of that time. I don't think there is a person alive who remembers it when it was last occupied."

"But things have changed, I gather," said Aelzandar.

"Yes, Lord Archmage," Agmar concurred, his voice grave. "The temple seems to be occupied again. We've seen it lit by torch glow at night, and strange noises echo from the earth below. They have returned."

"Who has returned?" asked Polnygar.

Agmar sighed. "About a century ago, a vicious cult launched an attack on Harralin from the temple. We defeated them thanks to Aelzandar's assistance, destroyed to the last man. We thought them gone forever. We were wrong."

"The cult has reformed?" Aelzandar raised an eyebrow.

"Strangers arrived in the area, drawn by some new leader taking power," Holger said. "All of them took themselves to the temple without as much as a word."

"You should gather some men, Grand Master," said Augustin. "Launch an assault on the temple before this new cult can attack."

"We wanted to," Agmar said. "But the Burgomeister forbade it. He thought it far too risky, that it would leave Harralin vulnerable. Better to wait for the cultists to come to us."

"Pah," Augustin scoffed. "Cowardice."

Aelzandar smiled. "No, Baron. Prudence. There is more going on here than meets the eyes."

"You always say that," Augustin said tersely.

"Ah, but I am always correct, am I not?" Aelzandar said with a smile.

11

"It is good you have arrived now, archmage," said Agmar. "As I have said, you are needed now more than ever. This is an uncertain time."

"Have you sent emissaries to Liderial, to inform the elves?" the archmage asked.

Agmar shook his head. "We are not on the best of terms with Alfheim, and I doubt they would come to our aid even if we asked."

"Let us not be that pessimistic, Sir Knight," said Aelzandar. "I shall talk to my brethren as soon as the opportunity arises. I have some influence there."

"I hope so, my lord," Agmar mumbled. "They won't talk to us. Not anymore."

"That seems odd," said Aelzandar.

"They refuse any messenger we send them. You are welcome to try your own luck, but I have little confidence that you'll do any better. Not if they know you come in our stead." Agmar stopped at a ridge, shielding his eyes from the glare of the sun. "Here we are. Harralin."

Nestled in the valley below was a small town. Smoke rose from the chimneys of rustic, thatched houses. Polnygar's eyes were drawn to the centre of the town, where an imposing stone structure stood.

"That is the Fortress of the Knights Crux Caruillin," Agmar said, noting Polnygar's interest. "It is also where we will find the Burgomeister."

"He lives in the fortress?" said Augustin.

Agmar nodded. "Harralin is small. Our fortress serves as the centre of the entire town. Besides, it is to our benefit that he remains close."

Polnygar looked towards the knight curiously, but Agmar did not elaborate. Aelzandar, however, flashed a knowing smile.

***

Awfully quiet place. Polnygar thought as she and the others walked through the town square on their way to the fortress. Polnygar did not see a single person and the air was still and silent. She surmised that everyone was indoors, away from the biting cold. Polnygar glimpsed the occasional flickering flame through the windows she passed. "You seem so isolated here," she said.

"The town grew from the fur trade," said Agmar. "For generations, it wasn't much more than a tiny village. Skurj was never really the most hospitable place, and there was little interest from any powerful lords in seizing this frozen waste. But then, things changed."

"That's right. I remember stories about a pair of dark wizards hereabouts," Augustin said. "Or was it a trio?"

Agmar nodded brusquely. "Yes, there were three wizards who once dominated these lands. But that was a very long time ago. Many lifetimes."

"Two hundred years," said Aelzandar. "A lifetime even for me."

"They made an alliance with some usurper in Alfheim. Harralin became their main base of operations. They built some castle outside of town, up on the mountain. The settlement here had doubled in size by the time they were defeated."

"I suppose even dark wizards need a place to buy food," Polnygar mused.

"So it would seem," Agmar said. "Come, let us get inside before we all die of cold. Sir Holger, you are dismissed. We shall speak later."

Sir Holger bowed to his uncle and then nodded at the others. "It was a pleasure to travel with you, friends." After exchanging a few more pleasantries he left the rest of the group to enter the fortress proper.

The Grand Master escorted them through the main thoroughfare. Having noted the structure's Spartan interior and the grave-faced soldiers that patrolled its halls; Polnygar was pleasantly surprised when they came to a comfortably furnished, heated room. A well-stocked fireplace blazed in one corner, and standing next to it was a neatly dressed, if a somewhat unremarkable looking man.

"Finally. There you are." The man came towards them. He was of average height, middle-aged in appearance, his brown hair thinning, and well-manicured beard flecked with grey.

"My Lord Archmage, and companions," said Agmar. "May I present Freiherr Gerd von Genio, Burgomeister of Harralin."

Aelzandar made a half bow and Polnygar, Augustin and Hebu did likewise.

"Archmage." grinned Gerd. He spread his arms wide. "So, the stories are true. You have returned."

"I trust you understand why, my Lord?" Aelzandar asked.

The smile left Gerd's face and he nodded silently. Grasping his shirt at the neck, he carefully undid the fastenings, exposing his chest. "Just as you instructed my ancestor, archmage."

Polnygar gasped. Hanging around Gerd's neck was a thin golden chain. Attached to that chain was a small piece of metal, unmistakeable to Polnygar's eyes. It was another piece of the Tears of the Divine. "And just as he told his own son, who then told his son, and so on down the line. We have kept it safe, all these years, just as you asked."

Aelzandar exploded in anger. "You fool. I also told your ancestor to keep it secret. And yet here you are, exposing it to all of us here. Or did that part of my message not travel down the line?"

Gerd looked wounded and, eyes wide with shock, quickly closed his shirt again. "I'm sorry, Lord Archmage."

"No, no," Aelzandar's tone softened. "That was unfair of me. I'm sorry, it has been a long journey."

"Perhaps you should take a seat, my lord," Agmar gestured towards a nearby chair. Aelzandar slumped into the chair with plain relief.

"Well," said Gerd. "I think you're all a little tired and hungry by the sounds of it, so let's take care of that." He nodded to Agmar. "Grand Master Keller, have the servants lay the table in the dining hall. Tell them we have four guests."

Agmar nodded. "Not a problem, mein Freiherr."

As Agmar left, Gerd turned to the others and said, "I hope you all like goulash."

***

It was roughly an hour later when they sat down for supper. The serving staff of the fortress had prepared a rather unexciting but filling meal, consisting mainly of bread, cheese, and a thick broth that the Burgomeister called goulash. Beer was on hand to wash down the meal.

"I hope this simple fare is to your liking," Gerd said. "We have few visitors here in Harralin."

"It looks delicious," Aelzandar said. "Give my compliments to your chef."

"I will," Gerd said. "So, Aelzandar, your companions are both Emparian, are they not?" He smiled at Augustin and Polnygar.

"How did you know?" Augustin asked.

"Your accents have given you away, I'm afraid," said Gerd. "I am of Emparian descent myself. My ancestor was the younger son of an earl."

"Ah, of course. You are of House Genio." Augustin tore off a piece of bread and added it to his plate.

"Indeed," Gerd said. "You have heard of my family?"

"I know your family once held the Earldom of Genio, but I heard

House Genio had died out during the civil war."

"Well, Lord Bauer," Gerd made a sour face. "Some of us survived here, away from the usurper's reach and the reach of those traitors who backed him."

"Who are you calling a traitor?" demanded Augustin.

"I make no accusation," Gerd said. "Only the observation that House Bauer prospered from its betrayal of the true king."

Aelzandar coughed. "Lord Genio, if instead of trawling through history long past, we might turn to other matters?"

"Suits me," said Augustin.

"Very well then, archmage," Gerd leaned back into his chair. "Let us see if we can be useful to each other. You are here to help me with my problem with the temple, and I am here to help you with your fugitive. What was his name, Agmar? Vallios?"

"Ivellios," Agmar corrected.

"Right. Tell me of this Ivellios."

"Ivellios is a bigoted psychopath," Augustin said.

"Is that all?" Gerd stretched his arms. "I would have thought he'd be no trouble for an archmage then."

"Ivellios is canny and experienced," Aelzandar's tone was grave. "He is not an opponent to be underestimated. He never was. We were acquaintances when we both were young, and we have seen each other occasionally in the centuries since. Despite my friend here's bluster, Ivellios is no fool. The spellweaver thinks ahead. He knows what he's doing."

Gerd looked unconvinced. "Why would he come here, then? If it is Liderial he wishes to visit, he could have done so openly."

"He comes seeking something I hid here a long time ago." Aelzandar's eyes stared straight at Gerd's chest, where the piece of the Tears was hidden under the burgomeister's clothes.

Agmar caught his breath. "You think he comes for the Tears?"

Augustin scoffed. "We *Know.*"

"He said as much himself," Polnygar said. She felt all eyes come to rest on her. "Well, not explicitly. But the intent was clear."

"Perhaps you are mistaken," Gerd said. His tone was dismissive, and Augustin seemed to take note. He cut off the burgomeister with a brusque interjection.

"Look, the way I see it, he already has one piece. He said he knew what the archmage had hidden here, and that he was going to find it. Putting two and two together..."

Aelzandar looked thoughtful, tapping his fingers together. "Yes," he said, after a moment. "That would seem to be the logical conclusion."

"Do I understand this correctly?" Gerd said, "This man..."

"Elf," Hebu corrected.

"Sorry, this elf. He already has one piece of the Tears?"

"That is correct," said Aelzandar.

"How did Ivellios acquire it?" asked Agmar.

Polnygar suddenly felt embarrassed and tried to avoid the knight's gaze. In doing so, she inadvertently found herself staring at Augustin instead. He looked awkward and ashamed, his head hanging low. His lips moved, silently attempting to form words.

"How Ivellios stole the Tears is unimportant," Aelzandar cut in before Augustin had a chance to speak. "It is enough to know that they are securely in his grasp, and he comes here to obtain the final piece."

"You don't think he's already here, do you, archmage?" said Gerd, alarmed.

"Ivellios was well ahead of us the entire time. Unless he was significantly delayed, which seems unlikely, he must be here now."

"You haven't seen him then?" Augustin said to the Grand Master.

Agmar shook his head. "He is not in Harralin, of that I am certain. We have no elves here and if one were to arrive, he'd stick out like a sore thumb. The people of Skurj, good-hearted though they are, can be a superstitious lot. If I were to hazard a guess, I would say he has gone to Alfheim."

Gerd nodded. "It would make sense for him to go there, amongst his own kind. Wouldn't it?"

Aelzandar said, "Probably. That is merely another reason for us to contact the Eldara. We must send a messenger to Liderial."

"I told you," Agmar said with weary resignation. "The elves will have nothing to do with us."

"I understand that," said Aelzandar. "But they will not refuse me, I can assure you of that."

"You plan to go to Alfheim?" Gerd asked. "Alone?"

"I will take Polnygar with me," Aelzandar said.

Augustin nodded. "Makes sense. What about the rest of us?"

"I'm afraid that Hebu and you may have to wait here, in Harralin. If what Grand Master Keller has told me is correct, then it seems the Eldara of Liderial will be reluctant to admit anyone not of their blood."

"Fair enough," said Augustin. "Anyway, I had about enough elves for a lifetime after Aderial, thank you very much."

Aelzandar chuckled. "Somehow, I thought as much." He turned to Hebu. "And I know you'll relish the chance to amuse yourself for a change,

Hebu."

The Nemoi turned to Aelzandar, feigning a look of shock. "Why master, you know that serving you in any capacity is enjoyment enough for me."

"Liar," Aelzandar said good-naturedly.

"Well now," said Hebu with restrained glee. "What way is that to treat your humble and ever-loyal scribe?"

"If you don't mind, Baron," Agmar said to Augustin, "I would appreciate it if you would accompany me to the training grounds while the archmage is in Alfheim. I don't know what will happen in the coming days, but it pays to prepared, and though the Knights are well-trained, the militia of Harralin is woefully under prepared. Sir Holger is drilling them, but we could use another well-trained soldier to help get them into shape."

Augustin was clearly flattered. "It would be no problem at all. A pleasure."

"Then it is all decided." Gerd clasped his hands together. "We shall attend to these matters early tomorrow. For now, though, I shall leave you to rest. Servants will show you to your quarters. Good night."

Polnygar found her room to be comfortable if a little sparsely furnished. Her hosts had supplied the bed with plenty of linen and blankets which, judging from the freezing temperature outside, she knew she would need. Sighing, she dropped her travelling clothes to the ground, changed into her sleeping garments and settled into bed.

As she lay there, Polnygar wondered what the morning would bring. She was to accompany Aelzandar to the Eldara city in the north, and she did not how the elves would receive her. The Grand Master had repeatedly spoken of the Eldara not being on good terms with their human neighbours and it seemed Aelzandar agreed with the knight, judging by his decision to leave Augustin and Hebu behind. Would the Eldara welcome her? The Eldara in Aderilund had never truly accepted her, even in Aderilund, and the people of her mother's homeland sounded positively cosmopolitan in compared to the elves she was about to meet. They would know she was a half-breed. Most elves could tell just by looking at her. Would they hate her for her mixed heritage? Or merely pity her? She rather wished they could bring Augustin along somehow. She'd feel less out of place then. If nothing else, she enjoyed his company and humour.

With these thoughts billowing around her mind and eventually dissipating, Polnygar slowly drifted into sleep.

CHAPTER 2

They left early the next morning, sparing only the time required for a quick breakfast before they departed. Servants packed food into parcels for the pair, enough to last them the trip to Liderial and back. With Aelzandar in the lead, the duo made good time. The archmage seemed to know the route almost instinctively, even picking out paths through the hills that had long since disappeared under snow.

"When was the last time you were here, Aelzandar?" Polnygar said.

"Oh, a long time now," said Aelzandar. "It has been a hundred years since I was last in Skurj and even then, I hadn't taken the chance to visit Liderial while I was here."

"Will they still remember who you are?" Polnygar said.

Aelzandar smiled. "They will. Eldara have long memories. They never forget." He sighed. "Nor forgive."

"Forgive?" said Polnygar, coming up next to the archmage.

Aelzandar's shoulders slumped. "There are matters between myself and the city of my birth, mostly too complicated to explain now. To put it plainly, my dear, the Eldara of Liderial and I did not part under the best circumstances."

"They will let us in, won't they?" Polnygar said. The timbre of her voice betrayed her concern. She hated to think they had come all this way only to be locked out.

"Without a doubt," said Aelzandar. "They must do so, regardless of their personal feelings. It is an ancient law that the gates of Liderial are never shut to any Eldara born within its walls."

"And what about me?" said Polnygar. "I wasn't born here. How am I going to get in?"

"I doubt very much they will bother to bar you, my dear," said Aelzandar. "They'll be too preoccupied with my perceived crimes."

A few moments later they crested another hill and came to a rocky outcropping. Below, the ground sloped abruptly downward into a large, open valley. Aelzandar tapped the ground with his staff, as if to announce that they had reached their destination.

From their vantage point, Polnygar could see the whole spread of the Valley of Liderial, or as the Skurjans knew it, Alfheim. In the distance, at the centre of the valley, stood an awe-inspiring city. Towers with spires of pure white stone reached into the sky, nearly invisible against the snow. The entire city was encircled by a wall, built of the same white stone as the rest of the city.

"Marble, my dear," said Aelzandar. "Mined from the area over the course of five thousand years. When the first Eldara king, Lideros the Great, founded this city, your father's ancestors were savages on an unknown island."

"I see no farms," Polnygar said, her eyes sharp. "Where does Lideral's food come from? Do they magic the food out of thin air?"

The archmage chuckled. "I doubt there is enough energy in the entire Ether for that sort of trick. The truth is a little more mundane. Eldara rangers harvest the bounty of the forests and plains here in the warmer months. For the rest, they supplement what they produce with imports from elsewhere. But enough of the lectures, we have things to attend to."

Polnygar followed the archmage down the path into the valley. As they approached the city, its smooth white walls towered before Polnygar, silent and impregnable. A massive gate, twice as tall as she was and twenty times as wide stood before her.

"Let's see if anyone's home." Aelzandar banged loudly and firmly on the gates with the end of his staff.

At first, nothing seemed to happen, but with the creaking and groaning of unseen mechanisms, the massive gates began to open. Through the space between the opening gates, Polnygar got a first glimpse of the grand, pristine streets of Liderial.

A figure dressed in fur and robes stepped through the gap. With his pointed ears and chiselled features, he could only be an Eldara. He looked at the pair expectantly. Polnygar noticed a pair of armoured Eldara guards approaching them, coming up to stand either side of the first Eldara, their polearms at the ready.

"Travellers," the middle Eldara said, his voice calm, and without emotion. "Your faces are not known to me. Strangers are not welcome in this city. State your names and ancestry."

Polnygar opened her mouth to speak, but Aelzandar waved her off, and she closed it again without saying a word.

"I am Aelzandar, son of Ellthiros, son of Geihnos. This is my pupil and companion, Polnygaranna, daughter of Saegralanna, daughter of Saegras."

Aelzandar recited the names quickly, though it seemed to Polnygar that he was doing so by force of habit more than anything else. She also noticed that when reciting her lineage, he neglected to include any of her non-elven ancestors. Was that shame? Or something else?

The Eldara looked from Aelzandar to Polnygar and then back again, eyeing them both critically. "Your name is familiar to me, Aelzandar, son of Ellthiros, though I do not know your face. You are not welcome in Liderial. You should return to your human friends." The Eldara's tone was calm as ever; Polnygar could not tell whether the statement had been intended as a threat or a warning.

"My human friends can carry on without me for now. I have come to visit the place of my birth," Aelzandar said.

"You should plan your trips better in future," the Eldara said. "This is not a suitable time for you to return."

"That may be, my friend," Aelzandar said. "But I am Eldara, of pure blood and born within Liderial's walls. You cannot deny me." The Eldara looked to the guards on either side and smiled knowingly, causing Aelzandar to speak again. "It is the law of Lideros."

"Indeed, it is, Aelzandar, son of Ellthiros," the Eldara replied. "And I will not detain you. But again, I remind you, you would be foolish to expect a welcome here."

Aelzandar responded forcefully. "I do not intend to stay for long if that is any relief to you. I have come here merely to speak with King Talan."

"Then I am afraid you will leave disappointed," the Eldara's voice was cool. "His Majesty has fallen ill and is not taking visitors."

Aelzandar persisted. "Then I shall speak to the queen."

"She is with the king, and likewise seeks no disturbance."

Polnygar looked at Aelzandar but the archmage stood silent, his eyes staring straight ahead, betraying nothing.

"Enjoy your stay in Liderial, Aelzandar," the gatekeeper said. "Make it a short one."

Nodding to the two guards, the gatekeeper departed. After they were out of earshot, Polnygar turned to Aelzandar, speaking Emparian in an attempt to not be overheard.

"What's going on?" she asked. "Do you think the king is really ill?"

"Perhaps," said Aelzandar. "But not by coincidence, I wager. There is something lurking beneath the surface here. Things are not as they appear."

"Well, what can we do then? It doesn't sound like they will let us see the king."

"I agree. But no matter. There are others who may be sympathetic to our plight." Aelzandar was already moving through the paved streets of Liderial as if he had never left. "Come along, my dear."

"Where are we going?" Polnygar followed the archmage, turning into one street and then into the next.

"To visit an old friend – left here." They turned into another street.

"I don't like it here," Polnygar whispered to Aelzandar. "The Eldara. They're all staring at me. It's not like Aderilund."

Aelzandar concentrated on the task at hand, not moving his eyes except to pat Polnygar on the shoulder reassuringly. "Liderial is a little more isolated than Aderilund, my dear. Few of the Eldara here have ever seen one of mixed blood before. They're curious, intrigued with your exotic looks." He smiled. "I'd take it as a compliment."

Polnygar flushed, feeling a little self-conscious.

"Ah, here we are." Aelzandar stopped in front of an elegant building. Constructed of white marble, like most of Liderial's structures, it stood at least three stories tall, yet had only a small, nondescript door for an entrance.

"I do hope he is home," Aelzandar muttered. He rapped on the door, then stood expectantly.

"When did you last visit your friend?" Polnygar asked as they waited.

"Oh, I missed him when I was last in Skurj, so it would have been two hundred years or so."

"Two hundred years." said Polnygar. "What makes you think he still lives here?"

"These are Eldara we are talking about, my dear," Aelzandar said. "Change is not our strong suit."

The door creaked open, and a pair of eyes peered through the crack. "Who is it?"

"Vaerath. It's me."

The eyes blinked and then, after a moment's hesitation, the door opened wider. An Eldara, stooped with age, stood in the doorway eyeing the pair of them with wonder. "Aelzandar? What in the name of Mother Hydria are you doing here?"

"It's a long story, my friend," Aelzandar replied, "But it is enough for you to know I returned out of necessity."

"Why have you come to me?" Vaerath blinked in the sunlight.

"I need your help, Vaerath," Aelzandar said. "There are serious matters to attend to."

Vaerath's eyes darted from left to right. Then, with a sigh, he said, "You'd best come inside then. Come, come." He ushered both Aelzandar and Polnygar through the doorway and looked up and down the street to make sure no one had seen them, before closing the door behind him.

Polnygar found the interior of the house to be warm and comfortable, if a little old-fashioned. Despite its large size, it exuded a certain homeliness. The main entrance opened up into a short hallway. On their left an archway opened into a well-stocked library and on the right, a secluded sitting area.

"This way, this way," Vaerath urged them down the hallway. They came to a large room, dominated by an immense table that stood in the centre, surrounded by half a dozen chairs.

"Sit, sit, both of you," said Vaerath. Aelzandar and Polnygar complied, as Vaerath watched warily. Once they were seated, he seemed to relax and sat down himself. He looked at Polnygar curiously and then turned to Aelzandar, saying with a whisper "She's not yours, is she?"

"I'm sorry?" Aelzandar said.

"I know you have many human friends that you feel close to, I just never imagined how close."

Aelzandar laughed. "No, no, nothing of that sort. This is my apprentice, Polnygar. Her grandfather was Lord Saegras."

"Lord Saegras," Vaerath said, almost wistfully. "Now there's a name I miss hearing." Vaerath took Polnygar's hand in his, kissing it softly. "Charmed, my dear. Though your face and form may be human, your name is pure Eldara. It means 'Dark One', I expect in reference to your beautiful hair."

"Thank you," Polnygar said. "You knew my grandfather?"

"Of course. He was Lord Spellweaver when I was a newly minted spellweaver. I was with him at the Sunset Isles during the incident with Cassian and Vanaja. Have you heard the tale? Aelzandar saved my life, but without Saegras, we would have all perished. He was a great man. You should be honoured to have his blood." Vaerath fidgeted with his clothes nervously.

"You seem a little agitated my friend," Aelzandar said.

Vaerath let out a strangled laugh. "I have reason to be, Aelzandar. These past few months haven't been the most tranquil of my life." He leant in towards Aelzandar and Polnygar, and whispered, "It is an uncertain time for Liderial."

Aelzandar leant back, frowning. "Yes, I was told something at the gates.

About the king's illness. Are the rumours true?"

"For the most part, yes," Vaerath said. "He fell into a deep sleep a few months ago. No one's been able to talk to the king since. The Council of Ancients forbade it."

"Well then, perhaps the Crown Prince can help me."

Vaerath waved his hand. "He's not here, I'm afraid. Prince Caerunos left many months ago to escort his younger sister to her wedding in Fudarial. This was before the king fell ill, and the prince is not expected to return anytime soon."

Aelzandar nodded. "We saw him on our way through Selvarial. I had hoped he would have returned by now. Who rules in the king's stead?"

"In Caerunos' absence, and the king's infirmity, the Council of Ancients and the Lord Protector are acting as regents."

"In the past Queen Talina has acted as regent herself. Why not this time?"

"You've been away for a long time, Aelzandar. Things have changed," Vaerath said. "Now, would you like a drink? It must have been a while since you've had some good wine, my friend."

"That is true," said Aelzandar. "Polnygar?"

"Sure," Polnygar said. "I'll have some wine."

"Laerosanna." Vaerath called out and a young Eldara woman approached them, her head bowed. "Be a good girl and fetch some wine for our guests, would you?"

Laerosanna nodded and went off to do as asked.

"Laerosanna is my pupil," Vaerath said. "I hope to make a spellweaver out of her one day."

"Is that so?" Aelzandar said. "I didn't know you were training anyone these days."

"I have decided to take it up again," he said. "I've always enjoyed teaching."

Laerosanna returned with a bottle of wine and three crystal glasses. She poured Vaerath, Aelzandar and Polnygar a glass each. Then, nodding to Vaerath, she returned to her duties.

Vaerath took a deep sip of the wine. "Now, where were we? Ah yes, the king's illness. Terrible shame. His Majesty is a most wise and charismatic ruler. The sudden turn seems to be quite unfortunate."

"Yes, a few months ago, you said. Do you remember when exactly?"

Vaerath scratched his chin, deep in thought. "It was shortly after the arrival of the Lord Speaker of Aderilund. Yes, that's right. Fairly soon after that."

Aelzandar took a sharp intake of breath.

"Ivellios," Polnygar said.

"I told you he would have arrived before us," said Aelzandar.

Vaerath looked perplexed. "What do you mean? You're not saying he might have something to do with this, are you?"

"Let me share something with you, Vaerath. You deserve to hear the entire story." Aelzandar began to outline the events that occurred in the past year and a half, beginning with Polnygar's arrival in Macrodonia to Ivellios' enthrallment of Augustin Bauer and his theft of the Tears and the subsequent flight to Ralom, and then on to Skurj. When Aelzandar had finished his tale, Vaerath shook his head in disbelief.

"I had no idea, Aelzandar." Vaerath rubbed the sides of his head. "If you're telling the truth, then Liderial is in greater trouble than I thought."

"Liderial is not the only place in danger, Vaerath. The temple near Harralin has been reoccupied. The people of that town fear that the cult has reformed. They know if it has, its eyes will turn to Harralin first."

Vaerath shrugged. "Don't the humans have those knights down there to protect them?"

"It won't be enough, Vaerath. That's why I came here. A few spellweavers might help the people of Harralin."

Vaerath chuckled. "I'm sure they would but I'm afraid you won't find many takers."

"What do you mean?"

"You won't like to hear this, old friend," Vaerath's voice trembled, "but Lord Ivellios would never consent to it."

Aelzandar scoffed. "I'm long since past caring about the opinions of Lord Ivellios."

"You should care, Aelzandar. Ivellios is popular here, especially with the younger Eldara." Vaerath said. "I'm afraid that you won't get a good hearing. They are unlikely to believe you, especially with your own less than stellar reputation. With the king incapacitated, Ivellios wields great power over the Council. Most of them whether they agree with him or not, are too awestruck to contradict any decision he makes. He is effectively ruling Liderial."

"How could this have happened so quickly?"

"After everything you've told me, I have no doubt Ivellios planned this for some time. Do you remember Keras, Aelzandar? The fool boy came to me last year, just before the king and queen departed for Aderilund. He seemed agitated and nervous, and told me there was something he wished to share with me about Ivellios when he returned."

"Keras," Aelzandar said. "I don't recall his name, but it appears he may have known something. Perhaps I should speak with him, Vaerath"

Vaerath's response came quickly. "He died in Aderilund, under mysterious circumstances. Since then, I have seen no one speak out against the Lord Spellweaver."

Aelzandar persisted. "Is there none here that can be counted on? Surely not every Eldara in Liderial follows Ivellios."

Vaerath shook his head. "If they don't, fear of him will keep them silent."

"And what of the queen?"

"She is preoccupied with her husband's illness. She will not intervene, not now."

Aelzandar slumped in his chair. "Then it seems I've wasted my time."

"I'm sorry I couldn't be more help," Vaerath said. "It is a delicate situation we face here."

"That I can see," said Aelzandar. He paused before venturing. "Can I count on you, Vaerath, when the time comes?"

Vaerath looked nervous. "Aelzandar, it is difficult. I must consider my position."

Aelzandar scowled. "Then I suggest you do so, quickly Vaerath. There are lives at stake here, not just your own reputation. I will bid you farewell and leave you alone to think on this. Come, Polnygar. It's time to leave." Aelzandar turned to Vaerath. "I know you will make the right choice, in the end, my friend."

Vaerath frowned and didn't meet his gaze.

"Well, my dear, that certainly didn't go as well as I'd hoped," Aelzandar admitted later, as he and Polnygar left Vaerath's house.

"He seemed like he wanted to be helpful," mused Polnygar.

"I agree," said Aelzandar. "He did desire to assist us, despite his anxiety. His hesitation was driven by fear. The king's illness has complicated matters. Ivellios has become more powerful than we expected."

"Then what do we do now?" said Polnygar, her shoulders slumping. The situation seemed hopeless. She could not see how they would get any help from the Eldara as the situation currently stood.

"We will have to return to Harralin empty handed."

As Aelzandar sighed, Polnygar noticed a trio of figures watching them from the shadows. From their gait, she guessed they were trying to be inconspicuous

"A disappointment, to say the least. I had hoped that – "

Polnygar tugged on Aelzandar's sleeve, "I think we should go."

Three Eldara guards walked towards them deliberately. They were outfitted in fine chain mail shirts and white tabards emblazoned with the emblem of the Aspen Throne and carried swords in their hands.

Polnygar whispered to Aelzandar, "I don't like the look of this."

"We'll be fine, my dear," Aelzandar said. "Just let me talk to them. Blessed be, and honour to your Houses. Fine day, is it not?"

One of the guards looked the pair up and down before speaking in the elven language. "Are you Aelzandar son of Ellthiros?"

Growing up in Aderilund, Polnygar had always thought the voices of the Eldara sounded for the most part like her mother's – soft, calming and with a slight, almost musical, lilt. This did not seem to be the case in Liderial. Almost every Eldara she had heard so far seemed to speak in the same unpleasant, staccato tone.

"I may be," Aelzandar responded. "Why does it matter? Has it suddenly become appropriate for guardsmen to question free-born Eldara on their identity as they go about their business?"

The guardsman's voice was tinged with disdain. "Do not play games with us, Mal-halyth lover. You have been named by the Lord Protector as a disruptive influence."

Aelzandar raised an eyebrow.

"Do you deny these charges?"

"Am I under arrest for being a disruptive influence?" Aelzandar seemed amused. "I wasn't aware that was a crime."

As Aelzandar continued to stall, the other guards gripped their weapons, and Polnygar did likewise, her fingers curling in anticipation. As one of the guards moved his right arm, Polnygar's eyes were drawn to a mark on his skin. It was the same mark she had seen many times before. The mark of the Horned God. Panicked, Polnygar looked to Aelzandar to see if he had noticed, but the archmage seemed oblivious.

"If I were you, friend," the words dripped off the guard's tongue like a threat, "I would depart from the city as soon as possible. Your kind is no longer welcome here."

"Then, I shall take my leave," Aelzandar said, bowing.

"See that you do." Signalling to his fellows, the guard pointed to a nearby street, and the three continued on their way.

Once they were gone, Polnygar turned to Aelzandar. "Did you see? One of them had the mark of the Horned God."

"Are you sure?" said Aelzandar. "Absolutely sure?"

"There's no mistaking that symbol," Polnygar said. "Cultists in Liderial. What does this mean?"

Aelzandar did not respond immediately, looking as if he was taking time to digest the information. "I'm not sure. But it is certainly not a positive development. If the cultists of the Horned God have infiltrated Liderial, then there's no telling what mischief they could cause."

"Why would Eldara want to join a cult founded by humans?"

"I don't know, my dear," Aelzandar said. "There have always been many unanswered questions about the Horned God and his worshippers, even as far back as to their first appearance. What troubles me most is why cultists seem to be serving Ivellios."

"It could be a coincidence," offered Polnygar.

"In my experience, there's no such thing."

"So, what's the connection then?" Polnygar asked.

"None that springs to mind," Aelzandar said, "But I'm sure the answer will present itself." He rubbed his forehead, muttering under his breath.

"Is something wrong?" Polnygar asked.

"Yes, very wrong. I think it's time to get to the bottom of things." Aelzandar raised his eyes with renewed purpose, looking towards the centre of the city. "Come, Polnygar, let's go."

"Where are we going now?"

"To visit the king."

CHAPTER 3

They moved through the city streets quickly, and Polnygar did her best to avoid the furtive, suspicious glances of the Eldara they passed. Polnygar did not care for the way they looked at her. Their glares were cold, full of understated menace. She wondered just what they were thinking. Vaerath had said there were stories going around the city about them. Just what did these stories say? She suddenly felt a pang of homesickness. In Aderilund, she may have occasionally felt out of place, or distant from the Eldara there, but never in her years there had she felt the hostility that she was now feeling from the Eldara of Liderial.

Aelzandar brought the two of them to the central district of the city. As they approached the urban core, the houses grew larger and grander, and ever more opulent. Eventually they reached a large open area, where a forested hill rose above the rest of the city. A sparkling clean cobbled road wound up the hill towards their destination.

Pointing to a structure ahead Aelzandar announced, "That's the great palace of Liderial, my dear, built by Lideros himself thousands of years ago."

"It's beautiful," Polnygar said.

The structure was magnificent, a palace of marble and gold, dominating the central district of Liderial. The focal point of the palace was a set of massive gates, decorated with glyphs and sigils. A tree-lined boulevard led to these gates, alongside which stood white marble statues of various heroic-looking Eldara. Stern of eye and void of emotion, the stone faces seemed to stare into eternity.

"These are the kings and queens of the Eldara, Polnygar. You may not recognise them all, but you surely know of Lideros, of Laeral, of Karn-Raka…"

As they continued towards the gates, Aelzandar identified the statues they passed. Some of the names were familiar to Polnygar – she could remember her mother telling stories of the ancient kings – yet others were unknown to her. The Eldara of Liderial seemed to be much more interested in their history than those of Aderilund were. She wondered idly if such interest in the past had led them to become disdainful of the present, and fearful of the future. As if to illustrate that point, the stern guards standing either side of the gates eyed Polnygar and Aelzandar with contempt as they approached.

"Will they let us in the palace?" Polnygar said. "They seem to want us to leave."

"Yes and those Horned God worshippers seemed to want to encourage us to leave as well," Aelzandar said.

"Encourage? They all but threatened us."

Aelzandar shrugged. "Perhaps they don't know the difference."

To Polnygar's surprise, the soldiers did not turn the pair away. Upon remarking that he wished to see the king, the guards simply nodded at Aelzandar, opening the gates, and escorting the pair through.

"I am honoured that you have permitted us to enter," Aelzandar said.

"It is not our doing, spellweaver," the guard said. "The Lord Protector

36

expected you. He commands that you be escorted to him without delay."

Aelzandar affected a droll tone. "How gracious of him."

The guard ignored Aelzandar's tone and moved them forward. Inside, the palace was equally awe-inspiring. However, with its cold marble walls, its huge, vaulted ceilings, and bare-bones furnishings, it also seemed cold, austere, and unwelcoming.

"Not the warmest of places," Polnygar said quietly, shivering in the frigid surroundings.

"Liderial never was," Aelzandar said to her in Emparian.

The guard glared at them but said little else. They reached a set of large and ornate doors guarded by two more soldiers as stern and humourless as the others. Their soldier escort whispered a few hushed words to his counterparts and in short order, the doors were opened, and Aelzandar and Polnygar allowed through.

An elderly and sour-faced Eldara met them, her thin lips twisted into a semi-sneer. "The king is expecting you, Aelzandar son of Ellthiros. You and your…" She looked at Polnygar with disdain, her lips struggling to form the word. "…companion. This way, both of you."

Polnygar tried to ignore her words, even though they had been calculated to be offensive. It was with a certain dread that she had expected this treatment in Liderial, so when it came, she was not really surprised. It was just how things were.

The Eldara herald led them forward into a great hall. Even more ornate than the rooms and hallways before, the hall was dominated by an enormous podium at the other end, atop which stood an inspiring throne of gold. For all its grandeur, however, the throne was empty.

Polnygar and Aelzandar were led past the podium, past the throne, and through a doorway to the left of the podium. Another grand and stately room awaited them. This one, judging by its furnishings, was a bedroom. A large, four poster bed was the room's main feature around which stood a group of richly attired Eldara nobles.

"Aelzandar, son of Ellthiros, your eminences," the herald announced, before taking a few steps back. Her duty done, she would take no more part in the conversations and, as a result, left the room to stand outside. The remaining Eldara turned towards Aelzandar, their expressions hardly changing. Of the four there, only one – the female – smiled at Polnygar.

"Your Majesty." Aelzandar bowed at the woman, "It is a great pleasure to see you again."

"We are, as always, indebted to you, Aelzandar," She offered her hand to Aelzandar who took it in his and kissed it softly.

"Your Majesty," Aelzandar said. "I was saddened to hear of His Majesty's sudden illness. It seems a quite unfortunate turn of events."

The queen nodded, "I thank you for your concern. These are trying times, as you can imagine. I must be by my husband's side."

"You are the nation's heart, my queen," Aelzandar said.

"Fine words, Aelzandar," said one of the Eldara, a spellweaver named Pallios. "But who are you to speak of the Eldara nation? You have no part in it. You abandoned your birthright years ago."

"That was your judgement, not mine," Aelzandar responded. He stiffened. "I wish to see the king. You cannot deny me."

"Why, I have no intention of doing so, my friend." From behind the bed stepped Lord Ivellios, grinning from ear to ear. Polnygar always felt unsettled by the way Ivellios smiled. It was as if he was enjoying some private joke at everyone else's expense. With the events of recent months, Polnygar was beginning to think that perhaps the joke was on her.

"Ivellios," Aelzandar said through gritted teeth. Polnygar could see the frustration and restrained anger on the archmage's face. She knew he was trying to keep down the urge to throttle Ivellios right there and then.

Lord Ivellios was attired in white and gold robes of state and bedecked in jewellery, befitting his position of Lord Protector. He smiled again, indicating the bed. "You may approach His Majesty."

Polnygar and Aelzandar approached the bed, the archmage in front, bending down as he came closer. Polnygar had never met the king or queen, nor ever seen them in person, but she had seen portraits and sculptures made in their likeness. Her mother had kept busts of the royal couple on the mantelpiece in their home. The queen looked much as her bust did, but the thin, pale figure that lay on the bed in front of her was as different from the strong, proud face she had seen as night was from day.

"My liege," Aelzandar said quietly. "I'm here." He reached out, holding the king's pale hand in his. The king did not react, nor even move in the slightest. The only noise was the slow wheeze of his breath, and the irregular beat of his heart.

"What's wrong?" Polnygar said to Aelzandar. "What's happened?"

"It is as they told us. The king is gravely ill. He sleeps but does not dream."

"When will he wake?" Polnygar asked.

"I cannot say," Aelzandar said. "Perhaps never."

Polnygar frowned. "Mother never told me the king was ill."

"That is because until now, he wasn't. King Talan was the very epitome of vigour and fine health. Something has changed that. Something or, more likely, someone."

Pallios stood face to face with the archmage. "You still have not told us why you have returned, Aelzandar."

The queen approached Pallios, placing a hand on his shoulder, and smiling gently. She glanced at Aelzandar briefly, nodded, and then turned her gaze to her husband. Aelzandar placed the king's hand gently back onto his chest and then turned to face the Eldara who had spoken. "Does one need a reason to visit the place of their birth and childhood, Lord Pallios?"

"Only when one has never shown the desire to do so before," Pallios said. "You are hardly someone given to moments of sentiment."

"Very well," Aelzandar said. "I come with a plea for assistance from the people of Harralin."

Another Eldara noble cut into the conversation. "The affairs of humans are not our concern, Aelzandar. You know this."

"Well, whether you like it or not, Lord Retharus, the affairs of humans are about to become your concern. I've learned that the temple has been reoccupied. Someone is trying to reform the cult here. Skurj, and by extension, Liderial, is in very real danger."

The Eldara lords looked taken aback, and some started to mutter to each other.

"Come now, Aelzandar," Ivellios said. "This is all rumour and hearsay, surely. The temple has been abandoned for a hundred years. Why would someone want to reoccupy it now? And why would they want to draw attention to themselves with some sort of foolish attack?"

"There is much here that does not seem to make sense yet, my lords," Aelzandar addressed the Eldara as a group, yet kept his eyes fixed on Ivellios. "But I assure you: what I say is true. War is coming here, whether you believe it or not."

"Do you have any proof of your claims, spellweaver?" Pallios phrased his words as a question, but the tone of his voice indicated he had already decided in the negative.

"I have no proof but my own word," Aelzandar said.

The Eldara lords all laughed, Pallios loudest of all. "You know your word, of all things, is worth nothing here anymore."

Aelzandar turned towards the queen, who was preoccupied with her comatose husband. "Your Majesty, please. You, of all people, must heed my warning."

The queen rose and looked towards Aelzandar, her expression sympathetic. Frowning, she looked from Aelzandar to Ivellios and then, her head bowed, said quietly, "I have faith in the Lord Protector. I will heed his wisdom."

"A most cautious and wise decision, Your Majesty," Ivellios turned to Aelzandar. "Will that be all, my friend?"

Aelzandar, his eyes hard, looked at the queen as she resumed her ministrations. "It appears I've wasted my time here."

"Perhaps you have," said Pallios.

"We shall not hold you any longer, Aelzandar," Ivellios said. "May your journey back to Harralin be swift."

After they were safely out of earshot, Polnygar turned to Aelzandar. "Why didn't you tell them?"

"Tell them what?" Aelzandar said. It was about half an hour later, and they had left the palace district and were now heading back towards the city gates.

"About the cultists, about the mark," Polnygar said. "They wanted proof, and we had some. We saw it, with our own eyes, right here in Liderial."

"It wouldn't have helped in the slightest," Aelzandar remarked. "The Eldara lords had made up their minds long before we arrived. Ivellios saw to that. Besides," he added, "They wouldn't have believed us anyway. It was a waste of time coming here at all, I should have listened to Agmar."

"Well, what do we do?" Polnygar said. "Return to Harralin empty handed?"

"It's all we can do, my dear. I wish the situation were different, but that's the truth of it. We will have to do without the assistance of the spellweavers of Liderial." He looked about the city coldly. "I have no desire to spend another moment here."

"You did your best, Aelzandar," Polnygar touched the archmage gently on the shoulder.

"Thank you my dear, but I have misjudged my own people, and this troubles me. My reckless optimism was of no help to us. It's time we left."

The journey back to Harralin was uneventful. Aelzandar led the way in silence, barely looking back at Polnygar, who trailed behind him, except for the occasional glance to make sure she was still following. He seemed deeply affected by the disappointing experience in Liderial. Polnygar wondered if it was because he felt let down by his own people, or that he was disappointed in himself for having ever believed the Eldara might help them at all. By early the next day they were both warming themselves by the fire in the fortress of Harralin.

"Please tell me you have good news," said the Burgomeister.

"The Lords of Liderial have declined my invitation," Aelzandar said. "They don't wish to involve themselves."

"Is that it? They don't wish to involve themselves?" Gerd yelled. "I guess they would rather we all die quickly, to save them the effort of getting off their noble backsides." He thumped the table with a fist. "Damn those pointy-eared nuisances."

Muttering under his breath Gerd rose from his chair and started to pace about the room. "Of all the ungrateful, low-down —" He searched for the right word. "Curs. For centuries this city has protected their precious lands from all manner of threats, and this is how they repay us?" He pointed a finger at Aelzandar accusingly. "You. You didn't do enough to convince them."

"I did all I could, Burgomeister," Aelzandar said calmly, without rising from his seat, "But it wouldn't have matter what words I used. They made their decision long before I arrived."

"Bah." Gerd's face was blood red. "You can dress it up however you like elf, but you've failed. Failed."

"Aelzandar tried his best," Polnygar said.

"Not hard enough." Gerd closed his eyes and sighed. "What do we do now?"

"We must rely on ourselves, Burgomeister," Aelzandar said.

"Don't be ridiculous." Gerd spat. "This is Harralin. We're hunters and trappers, not soldiers."

"You have the Knights to help you," Aelzandar said.

"Bah. They won't help. Agmar doesn't respect me, and if he doesn't respect me, how can I be sure he'll do what I tell him?"

"Do what you tell him?" Aelzandar said. "I don't see what that has to do with it. I thought the issue was whether they would help defend Harralin, not whether they would obey your orders. I am sure the Grand Master and his knights are perfectly capable warriors even without direction."

"That's just it, though, archmage," Gerd said. "They must realise who is in command here. Gerd von Genio, not Agmar Keller. There is only room for one leader here."

"With all due respect Burgomeister —"

"I must have complete control archmage, do you understand me? Complete control." Gerd said firmly. "I cannot rely on the plans of others for my own safety."

"Ah." Aelzandar gave a brief smile. "Would it be possible to have a brief discussion somewhere more private, Burgomeister?" Gerd, looking surprised, nodded, dismissing his servants with a few words.

Aelzandar turned to Polnygar. "My dear, if you don't mind, perhaps you might like to take a brief stroll around the town? There are a few things that the Burgomeister and I need to discuss alone."

Doing as she was asked, Polnygar left the fortress. From there it was a short walk to the town. Once there Polnygar strolled through the streets of Harralin, pulling her cloak tightly around her body to avoid the freezing winds. Before she arrived in Skurj, it would have impossible for her to ever imagine that it could be this cold anywhere. The frigid air cut through her light travelling clothes with ease, so she had since abandoned the Qardleean-made fabric for the sort of thick, woollen outfit that the Skurjans favoured. Still, even as she shivered, she was beginning to suspect that a lot of it was merely a matter of perspective. All around her, the people of Harralin went about their daily duties and most, though less warmly dressed than she was, seemed to barely notice the cold. She slowly shook her head, amazed at their resilience.

"Don't worry. You'll get used to it eventually, friend."

Polnygar turned her head and saw a young man chopping wood nearby. He was lean but muscular, and, despite the cold weather, stripped to the waist, wearing only a pair of trousers and a set of leather boots. He looked at Polnygar and smiled, leaning on his axe. "The name's Odo. Odo Aelfling. You must be new here."

"Hello," she extended a hand. "Polnygar."

"Guten Morgen." He placed the axe against the wood and grasped Polnygar's hand firmly. "Wilkommen, Polnygar. I hope you are enjoying Skurj."

"Aren't you cold?" she remarked. "It's absolutely freezing."

Odo stretched his arms, shaking his feet. "You get used to it. Besides, wood chopping tends to keep you warm." He walked closer to Polnygar. "You're a southerner, am I right?"

"Aderilund," Polnygar said, nodding again.

Odo looked surprised. "That is further south than I thought. But I knew you were an Alfkin when I first laid eyes on your pretty face."

Polnygar smiled, brushing back a piece of stray hair. "Alfkin? You mean Half-Elf?"

"Takes one to know one." He tapped his clearly pointed ears. "If you notice, my pa also left my mother something to remember him by. Oh, don't tell me you didn't notice? No one ever does. Is it the beard?" He tugged on the scraggly blonde beard he wore for emphasis, and Polnygar couldn't help but laugh.

"You speak Caruillani well for an outlander, pretty girl. Where did you learn it?"

Polnygar was about to mention she didn't know a word of Caruillani when she remembered the bracer Aelzandar had given her, the bracer she was still wearing. This wondrous magical artifact gave its wearer the ability to speak and understand any language spoken to them. Understanding everyone who spoke to her, no matter how foreign was so effortless for her for so long now that she'd almost forgotten she had been wearing the bracer constantly since Macrodonia. "My master," she hastily said. "My master taught it to me."

"He must be a well-travelled man then."

"You might say that."

"So why come all the way here from Aderilund then? Can't be for the weather, surely."

"I'm with my master," Polnygar avoided any specifics. "He's here to find something important."

"Oh, so you came with that elf mage?" Odo said. "Well, you're both wasting your time here. I'll tell you right now, there's nothing important here in Harralin unless you're talking about that old temple on the outskirts."

"No, it's not that," Polnygar said. "Really, I don't know exactly what it is anyway."

"Well, it was only a guess," said Odo. "The temple's the only thing anyone comes to Harralin for anymore. I see all sorts of people ending up there these days."

Polnygar stared at the young man in shock. "What? Wait. You see people go inside the temple? Where is it?"

Odo looked at Polnygar, a little surprised. "Me and my friends used to hunt game up on the western ridge. I used to go there with my friend Keras when he came down from Alfheim. The temple's not that very far away."

Polnygar was intrigued. She recalled Vaerath having mentioned an elf named Keras. "Isn't it dangerous to be this close to it? The way people talk about that temple around here, I would've thought no one would want to get within five miles of it."

"Well, there was some sort of conflict here with the worshippers of the temple some time ago," Odo said, offhandedly. "But that was a century ago. Keras used to tell me that he saw people there recently. So, I went there myself to see, and since then, there have been new people arriving all the time. I've been staying out of their way, just to be safe. I figure if they don't know I'm there, they won't look for me. Good for me, good for them." He picked up the axe and idly ran his fingers across the handle. "Besides," he said, shaking his head and putting down the axe again. "They're far too busy with whatever's going on inside that temple to care about anyone else."

"Just what is going on in there?" Polnygar said with a raised eyebrow.

"That would be telling." Odo grinned.

"Oh, come on. You can tell me. What did Keras see?"

"I don't know, but the last time I saw him, he seemed shook up about something."

"He didn't tell you anything else?"

"Not really. But maybe you'd like to see for yourself," Odo said, "I could take you if you'd like."

"Take me there? I don't know…" She looked behind, wondering if she should leave without telling Aelzandar where she was going. The archmage certainly wouldn't want to hear that she was going anywhere near the temple. "Are you absolutely sure it's safe?"

"I've been there dozens of times and no one has bothered me yet," Odo said. "We won't go too close. And if there's any sign of any trouble, we'll turn back immediately."

"I'm not sure," Polnygar said, but she was wavering. She really did want to know what it was Odo's friend Keras had found there.

"Should be back in a few hours, it won't take long," Odo said. "Come with me." Placing his axe down near the wood, he picked up a shirt that had been haphazardly thrown on the ground nearby. After putting it on swiftly, Odo grabbed Polnygar by the hand and led her down the path. They had only gone a few dozen feet when Polnygar heard a voice from behind her.

"Going somewhere, Polnygar?"

Stopping in her tracks, Polnygar turned around slowly, as if almost guiltily. "Um, yes Hebu."

"Oh really? Where in particular?" The Nemoi approached her, a patronising smile on his lips.

"Oh, just for a walk. Just outside Harralin," Polnygar said.

"There're some interesting things to see just outside of the town," Odo said, his eyes wide at the small creature before him.

"I'm sure there is," Hebu peered up at them. "And I'm sure that Aelzandar is well aware that you're going somewhere."

"Um, yes," Polnygar said. There was a moment's silence. "You won't tell him, will you?" Polnygar pleaded.

"Well, I will need to eventually," he rubbed his chin. "But I could, of course, delay the message, and if you were to return after not too long a delay, then well, as far as the archmage is concerned you would have never left. Hypothetically speaking, of course." He added the last few words under his breath.

"Understood," Polnygar said.

"Now get out of here before I reconsider. *Hypothetically.*"

CHAPTER 4

Bellaydin shivered.

It was not fear that chilled him. It was anticipation, the same sense of thrill that he felt every time he entered battle, the fire of overcoming seemingly insurmountable odds, of following one's force and gumption to the final accomplishment of a cherished goal.

He had no need to glance up. He knew the sword was there, hovering just above his head, ready to come down upon his shoulder, as if to cleave him in twain. The hand that gripped the blade waited, almost hesitated, and the sword seemed to be almost stuck in the air. Bellaydin's mouth went dry, his breath rattled in his chest. And then, without warning, the sword came down.

"In the name of the Unconquered Sun; the Queen of Light and Life, and Kytilas, the Divine Martyr, I dub you, Bellaydin Ap'Lydin, knight of the realm." The point of the sword gently touched each of Bellaydin's shoulders as Bellaydin heard the words. "Rise, Sir Bellaydin Ap'Lydin."

Bellaydin rose to the sounds of cheers, as the Great Hall of Emparia erupted into applause. It appeared that every duke, earl, and knight from the entire kingdom was here today, but Bellaydin managed to pick out a few familiar faces in the crowd. Sir Talthas li'Lyros stood out, his elven features making him easy to identify. Next to Talthas, Bellaydin saw Sir Geoffrey Keslin clapping enthusiastically, and some distance away, a grinning Haakon de Morcor, Duke of Alariat, with a sour-faced Wulfric Highcrown, Duke of Oldharbour.

Queen Amaryllis looked him in the eyes, nodding and smiling at him. Returning the gesture, Bellaydin bowed to her once more, before taking his place with the other newly named knights. He was greeted warmly, with most of those already assembled shaking his hand, or patting his back reassuringly.

"Welcome to our little fraternity, brother knight," Geoffrey winked. "I'll be the first to say that you deserve it, and not just for saving our lives half a dozen or so times."

"Seven," Bellaydin corrected. "But I guess that last one doesn't count since it was from your own horse."

Geoffrey feigned innocence. "*I* wasn't the one that scared it."

"Your horses are difficult for me," said Talthas. "They look like farming animals."

Bellaydin laughed, and, almost as an afterthought, shifted in his armour. "Still trying to get used to this armour. I'm not sure how you'd ever fight someone in this tin suit."

"Breathe easy, Bela. There's a reason they keep this armour for ceremonies like this. Looks nice and shiny, and impresses the ladies of the court, but no good for anything else. Besides," Geoffrey gave the polished surface of the armour an approving tap. "You wouldn't want to get this stuff dirty or dented, it costs a fortune."

"Bellaydin," said Talthas. "I think I see a few of your old friends."

Bellaydin watched as a few familiar names were called. Kurth Bauer, of

Tyronsville, whom Bellaydin considered a friend, and Edgar de Morcor, of Alariat, whom he decidedly did not. The new knight from Alariat obviously noticed Bellaydin's attention and shot a smug smirk in his direction.

"Don't let him get to you," Geoffrey cautioned. "No good could ever come from a feud with the royal house."

Bellaydin tried to shut out Edgar and looked about the remaining squires. "I don't see Otto anywhere."

"He was the youngest of all of you, wasn't he?" Geoffrey said. "I wouldn't be surprised if he's a few years off his own knighthood. If he ever gets there…"

"Are you saying he's not good enough?" Bellaydin said the words louder than he expected. He felt rather protective of Otto Mainstream.

"No," Geoffrey said. "But not all squires are suited to the life of a knight. He might decide to choose another path. There's no shame in it, not in my view."

Bellaydin gave a silent nod and turned back to watch the queen dub the remaining knights. Most were unfamiliar to him, but he remembered the newly named Sir Xavier de Cheltenham from a recent battle and applauded him as the queen touched the sword to each of his shoulders in turn.

"That was the boy who took on three Goriinchians and came out unscathed, was it not?" Talthas asked. When Bellaydin responded in the affirmative, Talthas gave a hearty cheer.

The knighting ceremony was ending, and the last new knight, a young man from Warding that Bellaydin did not recognise, came to join his new companions. He was offered similar congratulations and encouragement.

The queen, her duty finished, climbed the steps, and took her seat on the throne. She nodded to her cousin, Haakon, who took his place in the centre of the Great Hall.

"My lords and graces, Your Majesty. Knights of the realm. It is both an honour and a privilege to address you all here, on this glorious day, now that victory is in sight in the Third Goriinchian War. It has been almost a year to the day that the savages from the south invaded us without warning at the Battle of Wishapton. The Goriinchians had numbers unsurpassed, while we were depleted, weakened by the civil wars that had raged throughout our lands. Defeat seemed almost a certainty."

There were cries of "No" and "Never" from the assembled knights and lords. Haakon smiled, and held up his hands, waiting for the audience to be quiet enough for him to continue.

"But Emparians are taught never to accept defeat, taught never to forget that a good cause is worth fighting for. And what cause could be greater than to fight and die for one's homeland?"

Haakon stopped, and grimaced, clutching his chest. Concerned, Bellaydin stepped out to help the Duke of Alariat but within an instant, the look of pain was gone from Haakon's face and, smiling, he indicated to Bellaydin to remain where he was. Without missing a beat, Haakon continued with his speech.

"And so it was that one man exemplified the best and finest qualities of freeborn Emparians that day. Though William Ap'Lydin may have fallen in battle, his example meant that the city of Wishapton would not fall to the invaders. It was then that we knew, though the fighting would remain hard, and the casualties high, the Goriinchians would never triumph and conquer this land, not while any single Emparian man still stood."

The room erupted into cheers. "Hail Emparia. Hail Queen Amaryllis," Haakon shouted. The room resounded with knights and lords echoing his chant. "And hail William Ap'Lydin, Earl of Genio, Scourge of the Goriinchians, Hero of Emparia."

"Hail William Ap'Lydin, Earl of Genio," Bellaydin and Geoffrey chanted, joining the rest of the hall in showing appreciation for Bellaydin's fallen cousin and Geoffrey's former lord

"The Earl of Genio's grandfather, Sir William Ap'Lydin, was himself a hero and martyr of the Second Goriinch War, so it is perhaps fitting that today sees the opening of a new chapter in the history of that great family, with the crown recognising the service of Bellaydin Ap'Lydin, the new head of the Ap'Lydin family."

Bellaydin Ap'Lydin suddenly found himself the centre of attention again, as the assembled knights and lords shouted and cheered out his name. Feeling a little awkward, and his cheeks flushing, he quietly nodded to thank them for their applause.

"Now, now," Geoffrey whispered in his ear. "No need to be so modest. Can't be anything you learned from me."

"Not bloody likely," Bellaydin gave a quiet chuckle. Geoffrey laughed loudly and slapped the younger man on the back.

"After a long, bloody year," said Haakon. "The Goriinchians have been defeated. Their war chiefs are dead, and their Prophet-King slinks back across the border like the honourless cur he is. Some may regret that we do not have the strength to follow them and finish them off, but I say this is of no concern. Let them crawl back to their lairs and hide. Let them lick their wounds while they curse the name of all Emparians. Let their Horned God fume and rage, wherever he may be. He can do no harm." Haakon's eyes suddenly widened, and he cried in pain, clutching his chest. Panting and sweating profusely he slumped to the floor, his ending words choked off.

"Haakon!" Alarmed, Bellaydin ran to help the older man. Geoffrey and Talthas followed, and together the three knights grabbed the duke and hauled him to his feet. There were gasps and muttered whispers from the crowd and some of the assembled knights came to offer their assistance.

"I'm sorry, my young friends," said Haakon, smiling faintly. "Sometimes this old body of mine just can't stay on its feet."

"You must have overextended yourself, your Grace," said Talthas.

"You need some rest, Haakon," Bellaydin said gently.

"Yes, yes," Haakon said, clutching his head. "I believe you may be right."

"Come on, old man," Geoffrey said affectionately, wrapping Haakon's arm around his shoulder.

At the queen's insistence, a few of the palace guards assisted in helping Geoffrey and Bellaydin take Haakon outside the great hall to a waiting carriage.

"Would you two put me down?" Haakon said testily once they were outside, "I'm not dead, damn you."

"Haakon, you need rest, you've been on your feet all day." Bellaydin protested.

"What do I always tell you when you get like this, my boy?" said Haakon. "I'm fine."

"Yes, and I never believe you," Bellaydin said.

"That's your right, but I still want you to put me down," Haakon said.

"Better do what he says, Bela," Geoffrey said. "Never a good idea to get an old man angry."

The two of them carefully eased the older man to his feet. "You're lucky that the party inside was nearly over anyway," Geoffrey straightened out the duke's clothing.

"I apologise to you both for the disturbance I caused. My heart's not as well as it used to be. All part of getting old, boys."

"All the same, you should get some rest." Bellaydin was not as easily convinced. These spasms Haakon experienced had become far more frequent in recent months. To Bellaydin Haakon's problems had started very suddenly one day, for no discernible reason.

"Just like your cousin," Haakon scowled. "I suppose Willy will always be with us as long as you are, my boy."

Bellaydin smiled. "Maybe, but I think we'd all prefer to have the real William back."

Haakon sighed. "We cannot change the past, Bellaydin. We must learn to live with the present."

"Speaking of learning to live with the present," said Geoffrey, looking from Talthas to Bellaydin, "I think it's time for a few drinks. Bela, care to join us?"

"No, no," said Bellaydin. "I have to get back to Wishapton. I've got a lot of work to catch up on."

"You mean more studying?" Geoffrey said, with an easy smile. "I swear, Bela, you're turning into a scribe. Is it true you speak Goriinchian fluently now?"

"Well, I wouldn't say fluently," Bellaydin stammered.

"Fluent or not, it's only been a year since you arrived, so you can be assured we're all impressed by the achievement. Still, don't overdo it. I mean, it's bad enough what they call you."

"I don't care what-Wait, what do they call me?" Bellaydin said.

"Bela the Swot," Geoffrey scratched his ear.

Bellaydin flushed, while Haakon chuckled softly.

"My boy, if that's the worst you ever get from him, consider yourself lucky," Haakon said.

"Not my doing," Geoffrey protested. "I would have come up with something better."

"Good night, Geoffrey," Bellaydin said.

"You too, Bela. Don't stay up too late with those books of yours." Geoffrey winked at Bellaydin, then left with Talthas, laughing loudly.

"Don't mind him, Bellaydin," Haakon said as they watched Geoffrey depart. "He's never really thought much above his belt. Walk with me, Bela. I feel the need to work some of the stiffness out of these old bones."

The two men started to stroll side-by-side through the outskirts of the palace. A pair of statues had been erected in the open square outside the gates, as a monument to the war; a knight in armour holding an adolescent boy in his arms. Both figures had beatific expressions on their faces, despite their wounded conditions. Carved underneath the statues was an inscription.

"To the martyrs of the Third Goriinchian War, from their grateful queen and her Privy Council. May the Triune bless the lives of William Ap'Lydin, Earl of Genio, and Squire Tancred Zalltor."

Bellaydin felt a horrible twisting sensation in his stomach. Tancred Zalltor. The traitor. What right had he to be memorialised next to Bellaydin's cousin, a man who had risked his life to defend others? All Tancred had done was try to get others killed for his own family's gain. But the Privy Council had woven a lie around Tancred's death, a lie that Bellaydin had to support to protect his own cousin, and William's daughter, Maria.

"Sometimes the truth is too dangerous to be set free, Bellaydin. Sometimes it must be caged for the common good."

Bellaydin did not respond but nodded silently. Haakon gave him a reassuring smile and squeezed the younger man's shoulder. "It's been quite a year for you. From squire to knight. Your cousin would be proud."

"I certainly hope so," Bellaydin said. "I miss him."

"We all do, Bela," Haakon said. "William was taken from us in the prime of life. There was so much more of his life to live. The fortunes of the House Ap'Lydin are now firmly on your young shoulders. Perhaps it is time you started to think about the future."

"What do you mean?" Bellaydin eyed Haakon suspiciously.

"Bellaydin, Bellaydin, my boy, no need to sound scared," Haakon said, putting his arm around the younger man's shoulders. "I just think it's time we started to raise your profile at court."

"And just why would we want to do that?" Bellaydin said.

"Well," Haakon said, taking a breath, "Now that your cousin's daughter has been married off, we must look to you to see the continuation of your family's line."

"I can see where this is leading," said Bellaydin wearily.

Haakon smiled. "Bela, please, the queen is still unmarried, awaiting a suitable match. I am her cousin, and I could have great influence in deciding any match."

"I sure wouldn't have let William pick someone for me to marry." Bellaydin said.

"It could be a great chance for the Ap'Lydins to achieve the greatness they've always deserved."

"You seem awfully enthusiastic about this idea, Haakon, give you have no real stake in the matter." Bellaydin turned to him, smiling cheekily. "Or maybe you're planning on changing your name to Ap'Lydin?"

Haakon licked his lips nervously. "No, no. I'm just looking out for your interests, Bellaydin. Just like your cousin was, you're like a son to me. I want you to succeed in life."

"What I really want is for you to stop pestering me about it."

"Very well, Bellaydin," Haakon said. "But do promise me that you'll think about it."

"Cross my heart," Bellaydin traced a finger over his chest, "I'll give you an answer soon enough. Just give me a few years or so."

Haakon sighed. "Just keep it in mind while your head is buried in those books."

"Anything to keep you off my back," Bellaydin said.

Haakon smiled widely. "One more thing, Bela, if you will indulge me for a moment," Haakon leaned closer. "Have you spoken to Wulfric recently?" His voice was scarcely more than a whisper.

"Well, in the last week, yes. Why do you ask?"

"Did you notice anything strange about him?" Haakon said.

"Strange, how? What do you mean?"

"He didn't seem at all agitated to you? I mean, more than normal, as if he were preoccupied with something?"

"Well, that's understandable. The growth in the Cult of the Horned God's has him deeply concerned."

In the year since its legalisation in the lands of Emparia, the Cult of the Horned God had grown with remarkable speed, despite its connections to the hostile nation to the south. Rare now was the town which did not contain a temple dedicated to the god. In fact, Bellaydin had noticed that in some of the border settlements, the worship of the Horned God outstripped that of the true Emparian gods.

"I don't know if that's it, not entirely," Haakon said. "I think there's something else."

"What do you mean?"

"Well, it's a little difficult to explain properly. Remember how I said Wulfric was quite different as a young man? This coldness he displays only existed after our friend – your father – was murdered by the mad cultist Simon Enlim."

"Yes," Bellaydin said. He was unsure as to where the line of discussion was headed.

"Well, in recent months, he seems to be descending even further into that frigid abyss of despair. I can barely talk to him these days. It's as if he's feeling the death of Alusine all over again. Next time you see him, talk to him for me, would you? Maybe discussing these things would be easier for Wulfric if they came from one other than me. I think he tires of the interference of old Haakon. He may listen to someone younger."

Bellaydin nodded. "I'll do my best."

"I know you will, my boy," Haakon sighed. "Well, I'd better be on my way. Take care, Bellaydin, and look after yourself."

"Same to you, Your Grace," Bellaydin said.

He watched Haakon depart. The old Duke was frailer now than he had ever been, and with Haakon's heart spasms becoming much more frequent, Bellaydin wasn't sure how much longer the old man would last. He hardly spoke of it, but Bellaydin knew that Haakon had taken William's death hard, just as much as Bellaydin himself had. In fact, it may have affected Haakon even more. The Duke of Alariat seemed distant, distracted and more paranoid than ever. His ailments, both physical and mental, were beginning to consume him.

Bellaydin's thoughts quickly dissolved when he suddenly felt a clawed hand on his shoulder. He turned around swiftly, coming face to face with the Ahktarran warrior Kahlaf el-Lahn.

"Congratulations on your knighthood, Ap'Lydin," the Ahktarran said gruffly, observing none of the proper protocol or etiquette. Bellaydin always admired the way that Kahlaf was able to cut straight through the confusing and often arbitrary strictures of society and get straight the point. It spoke of a sort of self-effacing honesty that Bellaydin found refreshing.

"Thank you, Kahlaf," Bellaydin said.

"It was well deserved," the Ahktarran said, before pausing for an intake of breath. "If you are free, the Duke of Oldharbour requests a moment of your time."

Bellaydin frowned. He couldn't fathom there being any good reason for Wulfric to want to see him now. "Well, I was just on my way back home."

Kahlaf's expression was unreadable. "I am sure his Grace would be happy to ride with you. It will only take a moment."

"Very well," said Bellaydin. "Just let me get a few things."

Half an hour later, Bellaydin was riding next to the Duke of Oldharbour. "I trust Kahlaf was not too demanding." The duke's lips barely moved.

"Not at all," said Bellaydin.

They rode slowly down the road, their horses moving at a leisurely and relaxed pace. Kahlaf walked a few steps behind them, keeping pace with his long strides. As they moved through the semi-rural hinterlands of the capital, they passed groups of people kneeling, chanting, and praying to the Horned God. Even here, outside the capital, various villagers had assembled crude shrines and altars so they could make offerings in between their labours.

"Things are changing, Bellaydin," Wulfric said. "Changing before our very eyes."

"That's what happens," Bellaydin's eyes passed over the scene only briefly before returning to Wulfric's face.

"I hear you were talking with the Duke of Alariat," Wulfric said coolly.

"I was. Why do you ask?"

Wulfric did not respond immediately, but his eyes drifted over the chanting peasants. As he looked at them, his face turned sour. "Did Haakon seem any different to you?"

Bellaydin moved his horse a little closer. "I suppose he's sicker than I've ever seen."

"There is that," Wulfric said. "But something else, too. I see it, in his eyes. He is frightened of something, something terrible."

"It's nothing much," Bellaydin said. "He's just worried about you."

Wulfric narrowed his eyes. "And what have I done to earn the deep and no doubt abiding concern of the Duke of Alariat?"

"Well, I suggested it was just the growth of the Horned God's cult that was occupying your mind."

"Don't be foolish, Bellaydin," said Wulfric. "The gullible masses swayed to this sort of nonsense do not concern me in the least. It is not the numbers here that are important; it is the cult's existence. Just how far do you trust the Duke of Alariat?" Wulfric's eyes, cold and penetrating, caught Bellaydin in their gaze.

"What does that have to do with the Horned God?" Bellaydin said.

"Answer me," Wulfric said, looking straight ahead, his voice strong but calm.

"Haakon is a good man," Bellaydin said firmly.

"Do you know that for certain?" said Wulfric. "How long have you known him?"

" How can you even ask me that? You know he's a good person. You and he were childhood friends."

"Our childhoods were a long time ago. We were both different people then. But that is no matter. I was asking how much you trust him, not whether you think I do."

"He's always been kind to me. He's my friend, just as he was a friend of my father's."

"Your father was a fool," said Wulfric coolly.

Bellaydin clenched his jaw and turned to Wulfric. "My father was a great man."

"You say that, yet you never knew him," Wulfric deadpanned, while Bellaydin felt his face burn crimson. "A time is coming, Bellaydin, when choices will have to be made, when you, when all of us, will have to decide where we stand. I wonder, Bellaydin, if you will make the right choice in the end."

Bellaydin screwed up his face at the old man's words. Wulfric seemed to be speaking in riddles, and the casual manner in which he had dismissed Bellaydin's father stung. His head hot with anger, Bellaydin found it difficult to arrange his thoughts. "I will do what's right," Bellaydin said finally, after some thought.

"So I hope," Wulfric said.

Nodding to Kahlaf, the duke pulled his horse away from Bellaydin's. "Good day, knight. Have a pleasant journey home."

CHAPTER 5

During the long journey back to Wishapton, Bellaydin reflected on Wulfric's words, and those of Haakon. Both men seemed agitated, worried about something they would not reveal, and were increasingly suspicious of each other. It seemed to Bellaydin that whatever remained of the two men's friendship had dissolved completely. They barely spoke to each other anymore, and sometimes, at court, they did not even acknowledge each other's presence. Despite Wulfric's denials, Bellaydin did not doubt that their friction was because of the Cult of the Horned God. Wulfric blamed Haakon for the religion's spread, and Haakon resented shouldering that blame.

Bellaydin shook his head ruefully. Old men and their quarrels would have to wait. He had more important things to worry about. In the year since William's death at the siege of Wishapton, Bellaydin had divided his time almost evenly between fighting the Goriinchians and learning their ways and customs. With some effort, and the resources of the Ap'Lydin family, he had taught himself Goriinchian, and obtained a valuable collection of Goriinchian holy artefacts which he kept along with the holy book of the Horned Good given to him by Morgan Culainn.

Morgan – there was a name he had not thought of for quite some time. Though it had been many months since he last saw her, he could still picture the girl's face in his thoughts. Bellaydin remembered ever so clearly that, were it not for Morgan, he would not be alive this day. She saved his life, even though it meant risking her own. Her father, her sole protector and provider in Goriinchian society was dead, and his death left Morgan to the tender mercies of her uncle, the high priest Cathan Culainn, whose sneering disdain for his niece was obvious even to Bellaydin. Bellaydin wondered how Morgan fared. He made a silent prayer to the gods to watch over her and keep her safe and free from harm, wherever she was now.

His thoughts drifting, Bellaydin continued on his way. It was not long before the familiar sight of the gates of Wishapton came into view.

"Welcome home, sir," said the guard as Bellaydin's horse neared. "You've done the Ap'Lydin name proud."

Bellaydin brought his horse to a halt so he could speak to the guard. "I see word spreads quickly,"

"Yes, sir," the guard nodded. "The proclamation arrived just before you did. I suspect a noble title won't be far off."

Bellaydin laughed. "Let's not get ahead of ourselves."

Pulling the reins, he urged his horse forward to the main keep. Accolades could wait. All Bellaydin wanted right now was a hot meal and a soft bed. Once he had got within feet of the stables, he practically jumped from his horse, handing the reins to the waiting groom, and bounding up the stairs.

"It is good to see you again sir," said the steward, as Bellaydin approached.

"Thank you, Carfel," Bellaydin said. "It was a long journey."

"Of course, sir," Carfel said, taking Bellaydin's travelling cloak and boots. "We have prepared your meal, sir, once we knew you were close. If you take a seat in the dining hall, I will have one of the servants lay the table."

Bellaydin sighed with relief. "Thank you, Carfel. I'm famished."

"Without a doubt sir."

Moments later Bellaydin had taken a seat at his table and was enjoying a meal of mutton, beets, carrots, and cheese. "So, Carfel, fill me on what has been happening while I've been away." Bellaydin reached for the pitcher of beer.

"It has been fairly quiet, sir," Carfel said. "We have continued with the restoration work around the keep. As you suspected, there is a lot of damage to take care of there. Work is ongoing."

"And how is Maria?" Bellaydin had not seen or spoken with his cousin's daughter for many months.

"The Countess of Genio is well, by all accounts, sir," Carfel said. "I understand plans for her betrothal are well underway. I believe they're keeping her in Hotar Citadel, in Genio, for the time being."

Bellaydin took a gulp of beer. He still felt uneasy at the haste with which Maria's betrothal was being organised. It didn't seem like what William would have wanted for his daughter.

"This also arrived for you while you were away, sir." Carfel passed a scroll to Bellaydin.

"What is this?" Bellaydin said.

"A gift, my lord, from the Duke of Alariat," Carfel said. "I will leave you to read it."

As Carfel departed, Bellaydin pondered the scroll. It was written in Goriinchian, and immediately a few choice words stood out: "Broffwyd-Brenin", the Goriinchian title for Ygarak, translated in Emparian to "Prophet-King". He also noticed another familiar name: "Mael".

Mael the Apostate.

He had heard that name before. The High Priest, Cathan Culainn, had used the fate of Mael the Apostate to taunt Bellaydin's cousin William before the Battle of Wishapton. In Bellaydin's months of study, he had read any piece of Goriinchian literature he could get his hands on, and despite a few vague mentions of Mael the Apostate – the so-called "Enemy of God" – he had found little real, tangible information on such a figure. It was as almost as if the mystery surrounding Mael was by design, and that the Goriinchians desired to obliterate Mael's shadow from history.

Excited, Bellaydin grabbed some bread and meat from the table, and clenching the scroll in his other hand, retreated to his private library to study the manuscript in closer detail. Lighting a candle, Bellaydin placed the scroll down on the table, smoothing out its edges so he could read it better.

In the last days of the heathens of Karlicia, before the great Prophet-King, Ygarak – beloved of the Horned God, King of Kings, Chosen of the Heavens – ruled over these lands, Karlicia was held by the barbarian warlords, savage and wicked, whose depravities tore apart the land and left it raw, bleeding, and easy prey for the Enparran infidels of the north. In those days, all things that are holy and moral were abhorred, and all those things that are wicked and sinful were embraced. The land was sick with depravity.

The Horned God had sent prophets and guides to draw the people from their sinfulness and evil but the people of the world, ignorant wretches all, had spurned them, murdering the Horned God's chosen with little hesitation. But the Horned God did not abandon his children, wicked though they were. He searched the land until he found one being, pure and untouched by depravity, to deliver his word. That man was Ygarak, and he became the Prophet of Prophets, the final and perfect messenger of the Horned God.

With righteous fury, Ygarak soon went about bringing the lands of Karlicia under the guidance of the Horned God. One by one the mighty heathen lords surrendered to Ygarak and the Horned God. One by one they fell, either surrendering to the Horned God and joining the faithful under Ygarak or dying without repenting their heathen ways, preparing them for the torments of the Underworld.

The Tears of the Divine

In the end, only one remained, and truly, he was the most corrupt and degenerate of all. Mael, Lord of the North, had been born into the Horned God's faith but, led astray by the lies of those wicked heathens who remained, he spurned the Horned God's love and became Mael the Apostate, one so vile as to have been given the grace of the Horned God and to have heard the truth, yet to have denied it like a base infidel. The Apostate drew evil to his side – a warlock, a slave of demons and fey, advised him in his folly and a witch, steeped in the decadence of the old faith, shared Mael's bed. He made war on the children of the Horned God and defied all of creation with his unholy crusade.

But the Horned God's children prevailed, and Mael the Apostate fell before Ygarak and disappeared into the north. Never again did the forces of darkness challenge the rule of Ygarak, and never again was Mael the Apostate seen in the lands of the believers. Thus, did peace finally come to the lands of southern Karlicia, with the faithful safe and awaiting the coming of the Heir of Lydin, who would spread the Horned God's name to all corners of the world.

Bellaydin rolled the scroll up, and leaned back in his chair, his blood running cold at the unsettling nature of the text. He was not sure how much of what he had read could be taken at face value. The Goriinchians rarely differentiated between allegory and actual history. Nevertheless, it was a useful piece of information to add to his Goriinchian knowledge. He suspected, at the very least, that Mael the Apostate was an actual historical warlord of Goriinchia, but he was unsure as to how much of the damning portrait he had just read was accurate.

He took the scroll to the bookshelf and added it to his other tomes and scrolls, his fingers shaking as he did so. The mention of the Heir of Lydin had again rattled him. For a year now, that title had become so firmly fixed with the events surrounding his cousin's death that Bellaydin had taken it upon himself to uncover every aspect of its meaning, hoping to discover why the Goriinchians had tortured William Ap'Lydin so terribly. Such a quest had been the impetus for Bellaydin's pursuit of knowledge about the Goriinchian religion and culture. Deep down, he felt he owed it to his cousin to discover why he had suffered so horribly in his last moments.

Answers were not as forthcoming as Bellaydin had hoped. In fact, all the information he had been able to gather on the Heir of Lydin seemed to reveal nothing that would merit the Goriinchians wishing to torture such a figure. Lydin was an ancient Goriinchian folk hero who, according to Goriinchian myth, was the leading figure in defeating the so-called fey lords who used to reign over Goriinchia and Emparia. Sometimes referred to as "General Lydin" – although "Marshall Lydin" or even "Lord Lydin" might be a better rendering the figure was an important part of Goriinchian myth. Despite Lydin's death in battle, Goriinchians believed in his return, reincarnated as a figure named the "Heir of Lydin" to herald a new golden era. Despite this legend predating the worship of the Horned God, it had become entwined in the modern Goriinchian religion so much that Goriinchians believed that the Heir of Lydin would also be a devout and pure follower of the Horned God.

If this was the case and they had believed William to be such a figure, why then would they torture him? Several possibilities came to mind, none of them particularly convincing. Perhaps Ygarak and his generals were not as religious as they outwardly appeared and wanted to remove William for purely strategic goals. Or perhaps, it was the other way around. Perhaps Ygarak, though devout and religious, saw the messiah-aspect of the Heir of Lydin as a threat to his position, and wished to eliminate him to secure his own hold on the Goriinchian state. Where exactly did Cathan Culainn fit into all this then? It was a bit of mystery.

Bellaydin sighed. Trying to think his way through this muddle made his head hurt. Perhaps there was no great answer buried underneath it all. Perhaps, just as the others had said, the Goriinchians were simply insane fanatics, and Bellaydin was wasting his time looking for reason in madness. Rubbing his forehead wearily, he took a bite of the bread and meat he had with him, chewing slowly.

The legendary fey so feared and reviled by Goriinchians were another curious facet of their mythology. From the small, tantalising mentions,

Bellaydin had begun to believe that perhaps the mentions of such fey were garbled, centuries old references to the Eldara, but that explanation seemed unsatisfactory. If elves had indeed ever lived in the lands of Emparia or Goriinchia, they had long since vanished, and left no trace of their passing. Perhaps there was a simpler explanation – the fey may have been human, nothing more, and once they were defeated by the people who eventually became the Goriinchians they were retrospectively transformed into inhuman monstrosities through the power of oral history and myth.

There was one piece of evidence as to the truth: the piece of mosaic in the ruins Bellaydin had stumbled across when he travelled through Goriinchia with Kahlaf and Geoffrey. He wished he had kept it, since months later the memory of what the mosaic had depicted was beginning to fade from his mind. He did seem to recall the mosaic depicting a vaguely elven figure, but he could not be sure without looking at it again. It may have just been an exaggerated artistic interpretation.

He rapped his fingers on the desk in irritation, frowning. With a glance to the scattered portraits of various Ap'Lydins he muttered, "Any of you come up with any answers then? William? Father? Grandfather?"

The assorted members of the Ap'Lydin clan continued to stare at Bellaydin blankly from their canvas prisons. As Bellaydin gazed back, he was momentarily surprised to see something his eye had not caught before. There was something odd about one of the paintings of his father Alusine. Curious, he moved towards the painting for a closer look and noticed that portions of Alusine Ap'Lydin's body in the picture seemed to have been painted over.

"Excuse me, sir."

Bellaydin turned around in surprise.

"I bring a message from the labourers at the base of the castle," Carfel said. "They say they've found something you might be interested in."

"Oh really?" said Bellaydin. "What exactly?"

"Well, they're not quite sure. They claim it's some old ruin underneath this castle."

Bellaydin's interest was piqued, and he followed Carfel downstairs, and out of the castle to where the workmen had been busy repairing the castle's foundations.

"Right, who's in charge here?" said Bellaydin.

"I am, sir," said a man. "Foreman Foril, at your service."

"Show me," Bellaydin said simply.

"This way, sir," Foril replied.

Bellaydin followed Foril down a dozen or so feet around the side of the keep where the works had excavated a large amount of the ground near the keep's base. Crouching down above the hole, the foreman pointed down, indicating something in the freshly dug pit.

"Looks like a kind of old masonry," Bellaydin's eyes adjusted to the gloom.

"It's more than that, sir," the foreman said. "We looked at that stonework buried there, and our engineer estimates that it would have to be over two hundred years old. That predates not just this keep, but the entire town."

"Are you sure?" said Bellaydin.

"From all accounts, sir, yes."

"Fascinating." Bellaydin added. He turned to Foril and said, "Get some more men here. I want as much of these ruins uncovered without damaging the keep."

"Very well sir."

Foril gave the signal, and other men joined him, shovels in hand, to start overturning the dirt covered ruins. Bellaydin stood by, watching. A slight thrill went through his body as he contemplated what they might discover. He had heard the town of Wishapton was built on land that had once been deep inside Goriinchian territory. Perhaps some remnants of that time lay buried here.

One of the worker's shovels struck something solid, causing a loud clang.

"Sir, I think we've found something." Foreman Foril and the other workers scrambled to help uncover the find. Hands scrabbled in the dirt, brushing off the last loose pieces of dirt and rock, until a rusted metal object was pulled from the hole.

"Looks like an old helmet, sir," Foril said. "There looks to be a few other pieces of metal here. Might be the rest of the armour."

"Uncover the rest." Bellaydin took the helmet from the foreman.

As the workers continued, Bellaydin examined the helmet. It was obviously of great age, predating Wishapton, and heavily corroded. At first Bellaydin agreed with the foreman's assessment and recognised it as a helmet, but after a closer examination, he began to doubt that identification. While it was of a shape that suggested it would be worn on the head and possessed a noticeable grill for the mouth and two holes for eyes, there was a problem. The helmet did not seem to have enough volume to fit even a small human head inside. In fact, even after Bellaydin scooped out the remaining dirt and rocks, the helmet seemed to be filled with various pieces of rusted metal fixed inside small depressions in the interior of the helmet. These were situated alongside curious raised nodules on the metal. There would be no way for anyone, even a small child, to wear this helmet on their head. Perplexed, Bellaydin turned the helmet over and over, wondering who exactly had built it. His eyes caught sight of a faint, runic inscription near the top of the helmet. It was only just legible, but Bellaydin knew immediately that the script was Eldaric, though it was too faint to be read properly. Was the helmet of elven make? Was this tangible proof of the existence of the legendary Fey of Goriinchian myth? He stood contemplating the helmet for a few more moments, until a voice snapped him back to reality.

"Sir…"

"Yes, Carfel?"

"A message for you. It just arrived from the city of Genio, sir." Carfel passed a scroll to Bellaydin who nodded his thanks as he unfurled it. As Bellaydin's eyes scanned the text on the parchment, his face sank. "Not good news then, sir?"

"No, Carfel, no," Bellaydin stuttered and feigned a smile. "It's good news. It is. My cousin Maria. She is to wed."

"Congratulations, sir," Carfel said. "You must be very pleased for her."

"Of course, Carfel." Bellaydin tried to ignore the sinking feeling within. "The wedding is to be organised without delay, so it looks like I won't be staying here too long. Make the preparations for my journey."

Carfel bowed his head, "Yes, sir."

CHAPTER 6

"Are you sure we're going the right way?"

Polnygar pushed through the wall of thick, thorny bushes. Snow and pine needles crunched beneath her feet as she followed Odo into the thicket.

"Yes, this is it, alright," Odo said. "Shouldn't be too much further." He stopped, allowing Polnygar to catch up with him. "You alright?"

Polnygar panted, catching her breath. "I think I'm having second thoughts. Let's go back. It's getting late anyway."

"Oh, come on," Odo placed a hand on her shoulder. "We're almost there. It'd be a waste to turn back now. Don't you want to see this temple?"

Polnygar looked at Odo, and then over her shoulder, and then back again, indecision playing on her features. Odo looked at her expectantly.

"Well, I would like to see it," she said. "Are you sure it's safe?"

"Absolutely," said Odo. "We'll keep our distance, get close enough just to see it."

Polnygar was still unsure but felt slightly reassured by Odo's words. He seemed calm and collected, with little of the fear that had begun to grip Polnygar.

"You sure you're alright?" Odo asked.

"Yes," Polnygar said. "Let's keep going."

Odo led Polnygar a little further and before long the pair was on the edge of a steep ridge, which tapered into a cliff overlooking a valley. Odo knelt into the snow, crouching behind some rocks, and motioned for Polnygar to do likewise.

"Is that it then?" Polnygar stared into the fog.

"That's it, alright."

Polnygar looked ahead, and, as the fog slowly subsided, a set of tall, white minarets poked through the mist. Pillars of marble stood at all four corners of the temple, topped with grotesque, snarling gargoyles. A massive set of ornate gates stood at the temple's southern end, and in front of the gates, Polnygar saw a small group of figures dressed in white arranging themselves into a half-completed circle.

"What's going on?"

"Those are the cultists," Odo said grimly. "They wear those white robes every time I see them here. Send shivers down my spine, those creepy bastards."

"Where do they come from?" Polnygar said, fascinated.

"Close by, I'd guess," Odo said. "I don't know for certain. I don't think they travel far to get here."

"What are they doing?" Polnygar said.

"Some sort of religious ceremony is my guess," Odo said. "I never get close enough to know for sure."

"Maybe we could get a bit closer without them seeing us," Polnygar said.

Odo looked at her, furrowing his brow. "Get closer? That's not what you said just a few minutes ago. What about all that danger?"

"Changed my mind again," grinned Polnygar. "Come on." She edged closer to the cliff face, taking each footstep slowly and carefully. Odo came up beside her, his feet trailing in the snow and dirt.

"Careful now," said Polnygar. "It looks a long way down."

"It's not the fall I'd be worried about," Odo frowned. "Is this close enough?"

"Maybe," Polnygar said. "They're chanting something. What exactly are they saying though? I can't quite hear."

"Let me," Odo said.

He raised himself slowly from the ground and crept towards the very edge of the cliff. Steadying himself with one hand, he leant over ever so slightly, pointing his ears towards the chanting cultists. Polnygar knew that like her, Odo would have a sense of hearing far keener than that of a human. As a young girl, Polnygar had often teased her younger brother for what she saw as his half-deafness. It had become a favourite game of hers to stand some distance away from him, calling his name in such a way that he would have trouble working out the direction she was calling him from.

"Anything?" she ventured, noticing Odo frowning with a look of concentration on his face.

Odo extended himself a little further. "Just a bit closer –"

The next few minutes unfurled before Polnygar's eyes like a dream. Odo reached over the edge of the cliff with one side of his body. His other hand fumbled for something to grab on to, and losing his balance, he toppled over the edge.

Polnygar acted on instinct, lunging forward. She tried to grab Odo before he plunged out of sight but was too far away to reach him in time. As panic set in, she instead turned inwards, remembering what Aelzandar had taught her of magic, what they called the Art. The words of a spell formed in her mind, and quickly came to her lips. She could feel tendrils of energy, like cobwebs touching her fingertips, and tried to control and master the power that was beginning to well inside her. She reached out over the cliff edge, extending her hands as if she meant to catch a snowflake. Then, with firm purpose and steeled resolve, she clenched her fist tightly, speaking a few words of the arcane tongue of the Art. Looking down, her heart skipped a beat – Odo was a few feet below, suspended in mid-air, his face showing a mixture of terror and sheer bewilderment.

"Hang on, Odo," Polnygar looked down towards him with as reassuring an expression as she could muster. Once again, she turned within herself, grasping the threads of magical energy, and weaving them into a new incantation. She moved her hands as if she were pulling Odo towards her on an invisible rope. She had only ever cast this spell once, and that was some time back in Macrodonia, and she had only used it to pick up a book from the floor. She prayed that she had remembered how to do it properly.

As she moved her hands back and forth, pulling the invisible hoist, Odo, his face white with shock, rose towards her, ever so slowly. As she continued the spell her shoulders started to relax as she recovered from the shock of seeing Odo tumble over the cliff. Alarm set in again, however, when she felt resistance to her spell. It was almost as if someone else – another wizard – was pulling her spell in the opposite direction. She lost her grip on the spell, and Odo started to plummet in the other direction. She heard shouts and yells, and looking down, noticed with alarm that the cultists below had noticed her. Some of them were facing her, hands in the air, chanting something of a different nature.

Panicking, Polnygar doubled her efforts, trying to pull Odo back with twice as much power, but the cultists below were far too strong, and they heavily outnumbered her. Sweat beaded on her forehead and she struggled to hold onto the spell, even as the magical energies slowly seep out of her grasp. Burning pain shot through her head and she felt her spell unravel totally. She screamed in frustration, as every bit of magical energy fizzled and dissipated from her body. She stumbled to her feet, nearly tipping over backwards. Trying to right herself she leant too far in the other direction and tipped over the cliff, joining Odo in the short, sharp trip to the ground.

***

Polnygar awoke lying at the base of the cliff, her skull feeling as if it had been bashed in with a hammer. She tried to stand up, but as she did, a sharp pain ran through her leg. She looked down and noticed that her leg was twisted at an odd angle. She did not know if she had broken it in the fall but the rest of her, though bruised and bloodied, did not seem to have suffered any additional injuries.

Turning her head, she saw Odo lying next to her. His body was still, and Polnygar's heart sank when she realised he had not survived the fall. She closed her eyes, trying to shut out the pain which was compounded by the guilt that had set in. Polnygar heard voices, shouts and yells, and the shuffling of feet as people approached.

The first voice was deep. "They're just eavesdroppers from the village. They're dead now, just leave the corpses."

Another voice, raspier than the first, cut in. "This one's not dead, brother,"

Polnygar felt a harsh prodding and opened her eyes to see one of the cultists poking her with the butt of his staff.

"She's awake," said a third cultist, coming up to stand behind the first one.

Now that she was closer to the men, she could see their features clearly. They bore high cheekbones, angled features, and pointed, lobeless ears that could mean only one thing. These cultists were Eldara and judging from the strands of blonde hair she could see poking out from under the hoods, they were from Liderial. They seemed to be as surprised by her appearance as she was by theirs. What on earth were Eldara doing here, worshipping a foreign god? Considering the usual attitude of the Eldara to human culture, it did not make much sense. The more Polnygar tried to think about it, the more her head throbbed.

As the first cultist looked over Polnygar critically, others arrived, looking at the prone girl with malicious interest.

"Is she the one we were told to seek?" one of the newcomers said.

"She is of the Eldara, as we were told," said another.

The first cultist raised his hand, silencing the others. "There is only one way to know for sure."

He used the end of the staff to move Polnygar's arm to the ground, turning it so the palm faced up. Then, with a smile, he traced the end of the staff over the scar that was still clearly visible on Polnygar's palm – the scar that had been formed from touching a piece of the Tears of the Divine in Macrodonia, more than a year ago. Polnygar flinched with pain. As she did, murmurs passed through the crowd of cultists.

"She is the one we seek," the first cultist said. "Praise the Horned God, for he has delivered victory to us this day."

As dozens of cultists swarmed towards her, their eyes glinting with cruelty, Polnygar slumped into unconsciousness.

***

Polnygar opened her eyes and found herself staring at an unfamiliar ceiling, decorated with strange and lurid glyphs and sigils. The grotesque and horned faces of gargoyles leered back at her from the corners. Still groggy, she tried to move, only to find that her arms and legs were securely lashed to her sides. She tried to speak, but her voice was hoarse, and her throat sore and cracked when she finally found the words.

"Let me go."

A cultist came towards her, still wearing his hooded cloak. "You cannot leave, Heir of Lydin. You belong to the Horned God, body and soul."

"Let me go!" This time she was more forceful. She swore at the cultist in the Eldara tongue, and he flinched in return. Polnygar knew that the Eldara themselves considered cursing to be irredeemably offensive, and an affectation of "barbarian" human nations.

"Again, I tell you, you may not leave," the cultist said again. "It is not my decision to make."

"Then whose is it?" Polnygar said, "Who is in charge here?"

"The Hierophant is master of this temple, Heir of Lydin." The cultist stroked Polnygar's cheek. His hand was cold, almost lifeless. "Don't worry. You'll be meeting him soon enough."

Polnygar felt a sickening sense of dread. This did not bode well. As the cultist walked away, she tried to turn her head to see, but her restraints prevented her neck from moving all the way, and she was barely able to glimpse a fleeting vision of the cultists – dozens of them – assembling in the centre of the great hall. The cultists began to chant, their voices droning as one, just as they had at the temple earlier. They were clearly building up to something, and it did not take long for Polnygar to work out that they were welcoming the entrance of a new figure, who began to approach her. This new one dressed like his peers, but he wore a much richer looking robe, trimmed in black and decorated with sigils and glyphs like those on the temple's ceiling. The figure, who could only be the Hierophant that the cultist had spoken about, carried with him an ornate staff, topped with a grisly looking skull.

"Heir of Lydin, you are the Horned God's slave," the Hierophant said.

Even in her current state, Polnygar's mind suddenly reeled. There was something very familiar about that voice.

"Mal-halyth," the Hierophant added. "I see that recognition dawns."

As the Hierophant pulled down the hood of his cloak with dramatic flair, Polnygar gasped, and her eyes widened. The face that looked back at her was that of Ivellios, Spellweaver and Lord Protector of the Eldara.

"Ivellios…how?" Polnygar felt weak, and not just from the fall down the cliff, and the uncomfortable imprisonment in the temple. She felt she was in a nightmare, and desperately hoped that she would soon awake.

"In time, those questions will be answered, little one," Ivellios said. "But for now, you should revel in the thought that the Horned God himself has picked you out for a special destiny."

Polnygar did not like the sound of that. She wondered why this special destiny seemed to involve multiple attempts on her life.

"I didn't think you would be the kind to follow a human god," Polnygar said.

For a moment, there was only silence, but it was soon broken by Ivellios' distinctive low chuckle. "Humans are just the most numerous of the many slaves of the Horned God," Ivellios said. "I am His voice and the mailed fist that enforces His commands."

"Traitor," Polnygar muttered, avoiding Ivellios' gaze.

Ivellios looked unperturbed. "That charge does not carry much force when it comes from your mongrel lips. I lead this group of true-born Eldara towards the hope for a better future for our people. One where corrupting influences are removed and the Children of Hydria once again seize the glory that is their birthright. In fact, you might say I'm a patriot – the last true Eldara."

"Corrupting influences? Like humans?"

"Amongst other things," Ivellios muttered. "You have vexed me with you very existence. Do you know, girl, that your mother should have been mine? Our parents had arranged the match, many decades ago. But then your grandmother died, and your grandfather kept delaying his final assent to the match. And then he took your mother with him to Emparia…"

Polnygar knew where Ivellios' thoughts were headed. In spite of herself, she couldn't help sniggering. "Is this jealousy, Ivellios?"

Ivellios' face twisted in disgust. "Saegralanna let that human have his disgusting way with her, and when he eventually cast her aside, I went to her father. I offered to go ahead with the marriage, to spare his family the loss of face and the blow to their honour. Do you know what the old fool told me? He said that I did not understand honour, and that I was not fit to kiss the ground below Saegralanna's feet." Ivellios laughed. "But see how I was right, Mal-halyth. With your birth no Eldara would ever take your mother as his bride. And so Saegras' line will end."

Polnygar struggled again with her bonds. "What are you going to do to me?"

"Why, it all depends on the decisions you make, my dear," Ivellios said, his words both sarcastic and patronising. "You are both a Mal'halyth and the Heir of Lydin, after all."

"Why do you keep calling me the Heir of Lydin? What makes you think it's even true?"

Ivellios approached her, a smile still on his face, and grabbed her by the wrist, pulling her hand up so she could see her palm. Polnygar cried out in pain as Ivellios bent back her wrist, but Ivellios did not relent. Instead, he smoothed out her palm and traced a finger over her scar.

"The mark, girl, you bear the mark. Just as was prophesied. The Horned God's triumph is near, and you will play a part in it. For decades, I heard the Horned God's voice, speaking to me in my time of need, bringing me visions of a new world, a future where the Eldara are triumphant, pure, and safe. All I needed was to find the Heir of Lydin. The Heir…and this…"

81

He reached into his robe and withdrew a gold chain, dangling it just above Polnygar's face. From the chain hung the very object that had occupied Polnygar's mind for over a year. The broken piece of the Tears of the Divine, stolen by Ivellios from Aelzandar's quarters in Macrodonia.'

"Your master should never have been so careless with this. His foolishness will be his undoing, for within the Tears is power unimaginable, power that will seal the fate of the Horned God's enemies."

Smiling, he pulled the Tears back and placed the chain around his neck, nestling the Tears beneath his robe again. Ivellios moved his face even closer, so close that Polnygar could feel his breath on her lips. "Victory is in sight, but not quite yet, my little Mal'halyth. The Tears are not yet complete. There are still two pieces to recover. I know your master has hidden one here. He will once again regret his carelessness, I can assure you. After the Tears have been reunited, all that remains is for the Heir of Lydin to accept their place as a slave of the Horned God."

"Do you seriously think I would ever willingly be that god's slave? Ever?"

Ivellios frowned. "Oh foolish child, I have ways of persuading you. Voluntary submission on your part would be easier, not to mention painless, but there are other ways your obedience can be guaranteed. You are strong, Mal-halyth. I will give you that. But I will break you." A smile once again spreading across his face, Ivellios stepped back from the bound Polnygar and turned towards his fellow cultists. "Untie her and bring her to the circle."

Within moments, half a dozen hands were all over Polnygar, removing her restraints quickly, with no consideration to her own comfort. When the last rope gave way, they grabbed her, holding her arms tightly so that she could not escape. Polnygar struggled briefly, kicking her legs, and flailing her arms in an attempt to escape, but the cultists were too strong. Eventually she stopped resisting, feeling resigned to her fate.

The cultists dragged her to just in front of Ivellios, carefully placing her directly on top of a black, horned symbol that formed part of the mosaic that made up the temple's floor. They ignored her screams of pain as she was forced to stand on her injured leg, though Polnygar continued to struggle.

"Hold her still," Ivellios said, and the cultists complied. He looked towards her, his face stern and serious, his eyes set. "You were born of sin, Mal-halyth. The impurity of your father's blood means you will never be of the Eldara."

What a shame, Polnygar's thoughts dripped with the sarcasm she dared not vocalise.

"But the Horned God is merciful, and absolution is a path open to you. The sins of the fathers need not carry on to the children. Abjure your mother. Scorn your father. Submit to the Horned God, become his favoured slave, and you will have a part to play in the new world to come."

"And if I refuse this generous offer?" Polnygar said, as the cultists' grips tightened on her arms.

Ivellios smiled slightly, looking Polnygar up and down. "Then I'm afraid we will have to send you to meet your misbegotten father."

The euphemism was not lost on Polnygar and in truth, she had expected that killing her was exactly what they planned to do if she did not cooperate. A sudden chill went down her body as she realised the situation she was in. Despite the panic that threatened to overwhelm her, she tried to keep calm.

"You're bluffing." she said, almost spitting out the words. "You need me for something. If you were going to kill me, you would have done it already."

"You are clever for a Mal-halyth, aren't you?" Ivellios said. "But I'm afraid your conclusions are ill-founded. You have your uses to us, and indeed, we would prefer that you obey so that we do not have to use force. But know this, you are not irreplaceable. The position you hold can easily be filled by another."

"I don't believe you." The defiance was still in her voice, though it had dissipated somewhat. At heart, she suspected he was telling the truth, or at the very least, a half-truth. She tried to avoid his gaze, but Ivellios' eyes seemed to bore into her very soul.

"What is your answer, Heir of Lydin? Submission or death?"

Polnygar made to answer, but her voice died on her lips, her tongue going slack in her mouth. She did not want to die, but she knew that choosing submission would likely lead to death anyway. It would just take a longer time to get there.

"Choose." Ivellios yelled.

The cultists tightened their grip on her once again. Images flashed through her mind, the past year and a half since she left Aderilund winking past in an instant. She wondered if this was what people meant when they talked about their life flashing before their eyes. Then, something stirred inside her. A whisper of energy, a sliver of power.

Polnygar felt a tingling at the base of her spine and immediately recognised the sensation. Just as in Macrodonia so long ago, arcane power was beginning to bubble up inside her, driven by fear, stress, and the turmoil her mind was going through. The question was, would she be able to control it this time? The many months of training, the lessons Aelzandar gave her, the knowledge at her fingertips. *Yes*, she thought. This time she could control it. This time she could – she would – shape it as she willed.

Ivellios looked at her suspiciously, clearly still expecting an answer. Polnygar decided she would give him one.

"Ignis."

There was a massive whoosh of air as flames exploded from Polnygar's person. Ivellios seemed to realise what was happening, gesturing with his hands and shielding himself from the exploding inferno, but not before the force of Polnygar's spell threw him back several feet, smashing him against a wall. The cultists that held Polnygar screamed in agony as their clothes caught fire, and instinctively released her, running off in a vain attempt to save themselves. She flung sheets of fire in every direction, setting everything in her sight aflame.

Wasting no more time Polnygar, still ablaze, turned on her heels and fled. She ran, ignoring the piercing pain she felt every time her leg hit the ground. Ahead of her, the cultists scrambled in terror as she ran towards them, leaving the way out clear. As she escaped, she heard pandemonium behind her; the roar of the fire spreading throughout the temple, cultists screaming and shouting in pain and confusion. Somewhere, above it all, she could hear Ivellios screaming out in fury and frustration, trying to restore order. The Spellweaver-turned-Hierophant abandoned his usual calm tone of voice. "Get her, you idiots. NOW!"

Polnygar didn't linger. She didn't look back. There was no need; she knew what was behind her.

The flames surrounding her had died down by now, and Polnygar felt sapped of energy. Casting the spell had exhausted her, and she could barely find the willpower to keep running. Her legs felt like they were about to fall off, and every step was pure agony. It was sheer fear that drove her now, a fear constantly reinforced by the shouts and cries behind her. There seemed to be dozens of cultists chasing after her, a veritable mob, though she did not look behind her to confirm their numbers.

Panting, she clawed her way up the cliff face, her feet slipping on loose rocks and gravel. Her scorched clothes did nothing to ward off the frigid air, and she felt faint. She tried to push through the exhaustion, through the terror that was consuming her, and through the pain that sliced through her flesh like a knife through hot butter, but it was too much. Her vision blurred and her remaining strength left her. Polnygar toppled from her feet, darkness coming to claim her. But just as she expected to hit the cold, hard and rocky ground, she instead felt strong, warm arms.

"Easy there girl," said Augustin. "I got you."

CHAPTER 7

Polnygar opened her eyes. She was in her room in Harralin, safely back in bed. Her head was pounding, her body still ached, but she felt better than she had before.

"You're awake."

Polnygar looked towards the doorway and smiled weakly. "Augustin."

"How are you feeling, Polnygar?" he said, sitting down in a chair next to Polnygar's bed.

"Terrible," she admitted. "But I'm alive, thanks to you."

Augustin smiled. "The person you should really thank is Hebu – he told us where to find you. Looks like we got there just in time. Just what possessed you to run off like that?"

Polnygar flushed, feeling embarrassed about everything that had happened. She just imagined the lecture she would have got from her mother. In hindsight, going off by herself sight-seeing with a stranger was an incredibly reckless thing to do, and she only had luck to thank for her continued survival.

"I don't know," Polnygar said, her voice still faint. "I wasn't thinking. Please don't be angry."

Augustin leaned forward and patted her hand gently. "You're safe now. Really, that's all that matters. You might want to apologise to Aelzandar though."

"Is he angry with me?" said Polnygar. She wanted to crawl back under the covers and stay there.

"A little, but mainly with himself, and I'm sure he'll get over it," Augustin said. "He's an elf. They're not as hot-tempered as us humans." Augustin's glanced at Polnygar's ears, and seemed to backtrack slightly. "He's older than either of us. I'm sure he was more reckless when he was young."

Polnygar nodded. "I'm just glad you found me. I thought I was going to die. The cultists were going to kill me."

"Don't worry about them," said Augustin. "With Agmar and his knights, we managed to defeat most of them. We well and truly soaked the snow red saving you; I can assure you. Those we didn't kill fled. We never caught the leader, but we can send another patrol out in the morning to mop up."

He got up to leave, but Polnygar grabbed his arm. "Listen, Augustin. You need to know what I saw inside the temple –"

She tried to stand, but wobbled on her feet. She suddenly felt dizzy, and Augustin looked at her with concern, gently easing her back on to the bed.

"Save it for now," he said. "You can tell us at supper. What's important now is that you get some rest."

"But –" Polnygar said.

"I'll see you in a few hours."

Polnygar opened her mouth to speak again, but Augustin had already gone. She felt frustrated that he would not stay and listen to what she had to say, particularly when she was trying to warn them that Ivellios was now in the charge of the Cult of the Horned God.

She lay in bed for a few minutes, soon drifting into sleep, though muddled and distressing dreams soon woke her. It was evident that despite her aches and exhaustion she could not rest any further, so she got out of the bed, wincing as she stood up. Her leg, though better than it was before, was still sore. At the very least it seemed she had not broken it at all, which was something she was grateful for. Most of the rest of her aches seemed to have subsided, leading Polnygar to wonder how long she had been asleep for before Augustin woke her.

She limped towards the wash basin, and washed her face gently, wiping the sweat and grime from her face before pulling on the clean set of clothes laid out on her bed. The dress was plain and with little in the way of embellishment, but it was comfortable, and preferable to walking around in her bed clothes. Polnygar made her way to the dining hall, giving the occasional curt nod and mumbled greetings to the servants and pages she met along the way. The fortress was quiet, not the hive of activity she had expected after the incident at the temple.

"My dear, you should be resting," Aelzandar said to Polnygar as she entered the dining hall. His voice was laced with concern.

"I'm hungry," Polnygar said.

"Well, sit, sit," said Gerd von Genio, sitting to Aelzandar's right. "We are just about to eat."

Augustin, Agmar Keller and Hebu filled some of the remaining seats at the table, along with a few other knights whom Polnygar did not recognise. There was an empty place next to Augustin, which Polnygar took.

"Master," she said to Aelzandar, trying to avoid his gaze, "I'm sorry, I didn't realise how dangerous the temple was."

"Apology accepted, my dear," Aelzandar said, his face expressionless,

"I need to tell you something else as well, about the cultists –"

Gerd cut her off. "I have heard from Agmar that they were all elves. Are the lords of Alfheim preparing to march against us? It figures. No one ever prospered trusting an elf's honour. Present company excluded, of course, Lord Archmage."

Aelzandar coughed, his voice tinged ever so slightly with displeasure. "Polnygar was speaking, Freiherr Gerd."

Gerd stammered and shot Polnygar a guilty glance. "Ah yes, of course, I'm sorry, do go on."

"The cultists are being led by Ivellios."

For a few moments no one spoke. Some looked shocked, others angry, and a few of the knights looked confused, probably unaware of whom Ivellios even was. Aelzandar's face fell; he shook his head sadly. "I had feared as much."

"I'll tell you what; a lot of things start to make sense now," Augustin said. "Should've guessed that bastard would have his finger in every pie."

"There's more..." Polnygar went on to detail exactly what had happened at the temple, describing Ivellios' interest in the prophecy of the Heir of Lydin, and his belief Polnygar was the Heir. She also confirmed that Ivellios had the stolen piece of the Tears on his person and that he was planning to obtain the remaining pieces.

"He's gone mad," Augustin declared.

"Perhaps he was never quite sane in the first place," Hebu said, scratching his chin.

"It will not avail us to treat Ivellios as irrational, my friends," Aelzandar cautioned. "He seeks the Tears, and he has the resources to take them by force. Our worst fears are realised."

"Take them by force?" Gerd sounded more nervous than he ever had before. "But surely you managed to destroy the cult when you rescued the girl, did you not?"

"My lord," said Agmar. "Ivellios is now king in all but name of Alfheim. He can send the armies of the Elf-lords against us. Infantry, cavalry. Let's not forget their wizards, either."

"Wizards?" Gerd squeaked. He started to shrink back in his chair.

"Let's not get ahead of ourselves, shall we?" Aelzandar said. "We don't yet know whether Ivellios's authority extends to the spellweavers. Even if it does, there's no guarantee that they would follow him into battle without good cause."

"And just what might these elf mages consider a good cause?" Gerd demanded.

"Traditionally the spellweaver corps is never sent into battle unless there is a direct threat to the Eldara homeland itself. That is why it is very important that we tread carefully from here on, and not give Ivellios an excuse to fight what he will pass off before the Council of Ancients as a defensive war."

"You really think it will come to war with Alfheim?" Gerd said.

"Let us hope that it does not, my friend." As Aelzandar finished speaking, the servants arrived with the meal, a traditional Skurjan feast of three courses, complete with fruit – rare and expensive in the cold climate of Skurj; and four types of meat spiced with onion and garlic. They also brought out mulled wine, a popular local drink during the frigid Skurjan winter.

Polnygar watched Gerd as he picked up his goblet. His hand shook noticeably, and he looked nervously from Aelzandar to Agmar, and then back again.

"Armies, wizards, elves…" he muttered under his breath before hastily gulping down his drink, "By the gods." He continued to murmur to himself for a few minutes, before slamming the goblet back down on the table with surprising force. Gerd seemed to cough and stutter, unable to find the words he wanted to say. "It is not safe for me here," he said finally. "I must leave Harralin."

"My lord," Agmar sounded weary.

"I always knew that one day those elves would destroy us, I just never thought it would be in my lifetime," Gerd's words came quickly. "You shall secure my retreat south, Agmar. I will take the Tears with me, along with three battalions of your troops. I will be safer under the protection of the Count von Sterrenberg."

"That would not be a wise action on your part, my friend," Aelzandar cautioned. "As long as you hold the Tears, you are in danger."

Gerd's eyes bulged. "Is that so, wizard?" he twisted the last word with scorn. "I think I'm beginning to see what this is all about." The Burgomeister pointed a finger at Aelzandar accusingly. "You want them for yourself, don't you? I should have known. Just like an elf. Well, I tell you that I won't stand for your nonsense anymore. Your advice has been noted, wizard, but my mind is made up."

"My lord, if you would just listen to him, then perhaps –"

"That's enough from you too, Agmar. You obey me, understand? And it is my decision that I leave south with the Tears. You will remain here and cover my escape."

"At least let one of us travel with you, my lord," Aelzandar said, calmly. "I could be of assistance."

"And have you stab me in the back and take the Tears? Not a chance, elf." Gerd stood, waving a hand over the table. "I think I've just lost what remains of my appetite. Agmar can entertain you for the rest of the evening. Good night."

The Burgomeister stormed off, returning to his private quarters, leaving the rest of those at the table in silence. Agmar looked pained. "I'm sorry, my lords. The Burgomeister is upset."

"He's an idiot," Augustin said bluntly, chewing on some pork crackling.

Aelzandar cast a disapproving glance at Augustin. The Baron ignored the look and continued eating.

"Maybe we should let him go," Polnygar suggested. "If he can get the Tears away from here before Ivellios finds out, that would be good, wouldn't it?"

"In theory, yes," said Aelzandar. "The further we can get the Tears away from Ivellios and the cult the better. But I have my doubts about how safe it is for Gerd to leave alone with the Tears. If Ivellios finds out where it is, the results do not bear thinking about."

"My Lord Archmage," Agmar said, "I'll send the best of my knights to protect him. They can face any challenge sent against them."

Aelzandar regarded Agmar dolefully. "I have no doubt that your knights would acquit themselves splendidly in any battle where steel is pitted against steel, but against spellweavers? I'm afraid they may be out of their league."

"I understand," Agmar said. "Though I may not comprehend the power that wizards wield, I've seen it with my own eyes, and know that only wizards can defeat other wizards. I'll see if I can convince the Burgomeister to change his mind."

"You are a man of truth and honour, good knight," Aelzandar said, "And I know you will do what is right."

Agmar stood, bowed stiffly, and then left, the other knights following him.

"I don't like his chances," Hebu said. "I know stubbornness when I see it. Humans and their egos."

Aelzandar sighed. "We must hope that Agmar is successful, my friends. For I see nothing but disaster coming from Gerd's rash decision."

"You're not the only one," Augustin picked up his goblet. "I think he's let his cowardice get the better of him."

"Perhaps," Aelzandar attempted a conciliatory tone. "But we must do what we can to protect him, and the Tears." He turned to Polnygar. "And let us not forget you, my dear. It is clear now that the followers of the Horned God now believe you to be the Heir of Lydin, Ivellios included. Though we may not understand the full significance of this, it is of utmost importance that we make sure you don't fall into their hands again. It was mostly luck that led to your escape, and next time we may not be so fortunate."

Polnygar blanched. The situation was her fault, she knew that. She resented the embarrassment she felt and now she felt as if she was being treated as a child – patronised, protected, wrapped in cotton wool. She suddenly felt angry. "I can take care of myself," she frowned.

"I'd agree with that," Augustin rubbed his hand over his metal arm.

"I would never suggest otherwise," Aelzandar said. "But perhaps we should move a little carefully from now on, yes?"

Polnygar still felt she was being patronised, if ever so gently, but she nodded and said nothing in return.

"We should probably all retire for the night," Augustin said

"Agreed," said Aelzandar. "There is nothing that can be done until tomorrow. Once we know Gerd's decision, we'll know the situation that faces us."

***

Sometime later, Polnygar was back in her bed, attempting to sleep. Unfortunately, it was still proving somewhat difficult for her. Her mind was

94

a mess, still full of the images and events of the past few days. She rolled over, trying to blank out her mind, but to no avail.

Odo's death still gnawed at her. She had barely known the young man, yet now she found herself at least partly responsible for his death. He did not deserve to die in the way he did, and she realised that, in the hectic period of her escape, she had forgotten completely about him. Had Augustin and the others recovered the poor boy's body? Odo needed a proper burial. It was the least she could do, especially after how she had acted. She had panicked, made the wrong decision, and Odo paid for that with his life, while Polnygar escaped to live another day. Polnygar knew it was not fair, but privately she wondered if it happened as such because she was meant to survive.

She had never asked for some grand, prophesied destiny, so why had the gods suddenly decided she needed one? Especially since said destiny seemed to have brought her nothing but trouble ever since she left Aderilund, with the followers of the Horned God apparently unsure whether they wanted to kill or convert Polnygar. Perhaps it was both.

Polnygar had never been a particularly religious child growing up. Her mother Saegralanna was a devout believer in the Transcendent Court and had tried to instil that same belief in her daughter. As a result, Polnygar had been taken to the temple daily by her mother, and even to this day could recite the Four Transcendent Prayers from memory. Despite this, Polnygar had found the services of the holy men of Aderilund so boring, and unlike the typically sedate and well-behaved elven children, had run riot nearly every time she was taken to the temple. It was probably her human side coming out. The other elves had obviously thought so, as they scolded her mother time and time again, and shot disapproving glances every time Saegralanna was out in public with her daughter. Saegralanna nearly fainted once when Polnygar – then thirteen years old – had managed to break the arm off the statue of Great Mother Hydria that stood in the Great Temple of Aderilund. The adolescent Polnygar helpfully offering to stick the arm back on did little to remedy the situation.

As she remembered Aderilund, Polnygar suddenly felt a pang of homesickness. The feeling came as a bit of a shock to her, since she had never been too fond of the place. It was probably her mother that she missed, more than the place, Polnygar reasoned. After all, no matter how much of an outsider she was in Aderilund, her mother had always been there to make sure she was never truly isolated.

Memories of her mother made her think of her brother. They had been so close growing up, the two of them against the world. Constant companions. The feeling in her chest worsened, and she felt like her heart might break. She wondered how Bellaydin was. Indeed, she wondered where he was right now. Ivellios had taunted to them back in Macrodonia that Bellaydin had been expelled from the elven kingdom, a piece of news she did not entirely trust. If it was true, Polnygar had no doubt that Ivellios had engineered the whole thing, especially now that she knew the spellweaver was capable of much more nefarious plots.

She tossed around a few times and then, deciding that she would never get to sleep at this rate, threw back the covers and got out of bed once again. *Perhaps some fresh air will do me good,* Polnygar thought. She made her way to one of the balconies that overlooked the town below and saw that Augustin already there, standing with his arms on the wall, looking out towards the night sky.

"Lovely night," she said.

Augustin turned to her and smiled. "Couldn't sleep," he said, shifting his gaze back to the sky.

"Me neither," she came up to stand next to him. "I used to watch the stars at home, with my brother."

"You miss him, don't you?" Augustin said.

Polnygar nodded.

"I wish I'd been close to mine," Augustin said quietly.

"I didn't know you had a brother."

He shrugged. "Well, we were never particularly brotherly, even as children. There're twelve years between us, and we were effectively raised separately. We never saw eye to eye on a lot of things – he always thought I was reckless. When our father died, Alfred got the hereditary title and barely spoke to me ever again. I always wanted to patch things up with him, but I guess it's too late now." Augustin sighed. "I've got a bad feeling about what's coming for us, Polnygar. It's funny, you know. When I was a boy, I always dreamed of one day being fortunate enough to see the famed elven armies in battle. I just never guessed that I'd be the one fighting them. I suppose that's the sort of ironic fate the gods dole out to us."

"Aelzandar says we shouldn't give up hope yet," Polnygar looked out to the town below, glancing at Augustin only briefly.

"I know when I've got a hope of changing a man's mind, and I can tell you that nothing in this world or the next is going to make that Burgomeister reconsider. He's a coward. Running away is all he knows how to do."

"He's going to get himself killed," Polnygar mused.

"You don't have to tell me that. As I said, the man's an idiot."

"He's just afraid," Polnygar argued. "I can't blame him."

"Don't worry," Augustin said with a teasing smile, "I'll look after you." He put a hand on her shoulder, squeezing it gently. It felt surprisingly pleasant, so Polnygar smiled in return.

"Look," she said, "Thanks again for saving me yesterday."

Augustin chuckled. "I'm a big damn hero. That's the sort of thing I do, don't you know?"

"Do you now?" Polnygar said.

"Only for people I like."

Polnygar laughed, then, noticing Augustin looking straight at her, suddenly flushed. She felt herself move closer towards him, almost as if she had no control over her body.

"You must like me a hell of a lot then." The words tumbled from her lips and the next few minutes happened so quickly that Polnygar did not know if she was dreaming or not. She embraced him, and before she knew what was happening, their lips met, and the pair kissed deeply. A tingle went through her entire body, not quite the same as that which she felt when using the Art, but just as exhilarating. Polnygar felt Augustin's arms wrap around her, and she did the same to him, surrendering to the desire that had been building within her.

She had waited a long time for this.

CHAPTER 8

Bellaydin pulled on his tunic.

For the second time in as many months, he was eschewing the serviceable gear of his day-to-day life for what seemed to be extravagant finery. This time, however, it was not the ceremonial armour of a knight he was wearing, but the opulent garments of the head of a noble house. The tunic was dark green, finely stitched, and embroidered with a white decorated cross, the emblem of the Ap'Lydin family.

As the eldest surviving male of his family, it was Bellaydin's duty to give William's daughter away in marriage. Since Maria herself was still not of age, the marriage itself was more of a betrothal, a promise that Maria would wed the noble in question when she reached adulthood. Having grown up amongst the long-lived, Bellaydin was still not comfortable with the young age at which Emparian nobility married off their daughters. Maria was not yet fifteen, an age at which an elven girl would still have many years of schooling ahead of her. It seemed somehow perverse to put Maria through this when she had not yet even reached her fifteenth year.

Then again, as he always reminded himself when such thoughts came to his mind, he was only a few days shy of his nineteenth birthday, and yet here he was, a knight of the realm, the head of his family, and the feudal lord of over a thousand subjects. The only reason the whole prospect did not terrify him completely was that he tried to avoid dwelling on it. The last time he had thought too deeply on it, he chewed his fingernails almost down to the quick. Shaking his head, Bellaydin pulled on his boots and went for a stroll around the castle to empty his head.

Hotar Citadel was an ancient castle, centuries old, and built long before the city was named Genio. An overly ambitious earl of the past had turned the small, existing keep in the city into a grander and more imposing residence, perhaps to stake his own claim amongst the feuding noble families of the time.

Today the whole place was in festive form, and banners and pennants festooned the walls. It had been a long time since Genio had celebrated such an event and the city intended to put on quite a show. It was a pity that William was not here to see it.

Even a year after it happened, his cousin's death still played on his mind. Thoughts of William and his final moments had a troubling tendency to come unbidden into Bellaydin's head at the most inappropriate moments as if he still harboured some unconscious guilt at not being able to prevent William's painful torture and murder. Never mind, he steeled himself, he would instead honour his cousin's memory and carry out his final will. He would do as William asked and protect Maria's life and future. Today would be the culmination of that duty, his final gift to a man he admired more than any other.

As Bellaydin stood deep in his own thoughts, soldiers marched past him, armed with crossbows, and wearing the coat of arms of the Earldom of Genio. They would soon take their positions up on the walls, ready to protect the wedding procession. Bellaydin knew none of the guards personally but looking at their grim faces, he knew they would perform their duties with accustomed skill and determination.

"There you are." came a voice. "Lost in your own world, as usual."

"Hello Geoffrey," Bellaydin said, without even turning around.

Geoffrey tousled Bellaydin's hair affectionately. "How you been, boy? Haven't seen you for months."

"I've been busy," Bellaydin said.

"Let me guess. Books, again?"

"Something like that," Bellaydin said curtly.

"Blessed be, Bellaydin," came the traditional Eldara greeting as Talthas came to stand next to Geoffrey. The Eldara was resplendent in his surcoat, emblazoned with a wolf's head.

"You've chosen your own sigil finally?" Bellaydin asked.

"It was time," said Talthas. "'Lyros means wolf in Eldaric, so I thought it was appropriate."

"You know, this could've been your wedding today," Geoffrey teased. "Instead, you're letting some other man steal her away."

Bellaydin groaned. "Oh gods, please don't start with that again."

"Ha. Just a little joke, Bela," Geoffrey said, "Don't take it too seriously."

"Geoffrey," Bellaydin said, putting a hand on the older knight's shoulder, "With you, the word serious wouldn't even come to mind. Luckily, Talthas here is sensible enough for both of us."

The Eldara looked askance at them. "This is a change for me. The other rangers used to call me Talthas the Child, on account of my age and immaturity."

"How old are you?" Bellaydin asked.

Talthas looked around and then leaned in close and whispered. "Fifty-five. But I tell everyone I'm sixty."

Bellaydin and Geoffrey looked at each other. "Yes, barely out of swaddling clothes," Geoffrey jested.

Talthas looked confused, and Geoffrey guffawed, looking over the ramparts to the square below. "It's going to be a good show, you know. Hope you're ready for the ceremony and the celebrations afterwards." He suddenly looked towards Bellaydin and frowned. "And don't you dare think about getting out of it this time."

Despite his mood, Bellaydin found himself laughing. He raised his hands as if in surrender. "I won't, I promise."

"Good boy," Geoffrey slapped Bellaydin on this back with some enthusiasm. "Let's go and see if the others are ready."

Below, guests and dignitaries were already milling about the square, watching as the final preparations were being made for the ceremony.

"Bela, my boy," the Duke of Alariat exclaimed, spreading his arms wide once he spotted Bellaydin approaching him. "What a pleasure to see you again. Come, embrace me."

"It's good to see you too, Haakon," Bellaydin gave the older man a hug, and shaking his hand firmly. "Where's Wulfric?"

"Oh, he's around somewhere," Haakon said dismissively. "No doubt sniffing out any secret worshippers of the Horned God hiding around here."

"Careful," Geoffrey rubbed his chin, "You never know when he might be listening."

In fact, Wulfric Highcrown was only a few steps away, deep in conversation with the Ahktarran Kahlaf el-Lahn. It appeared, however, that he had not heard any of the conversation. If he had, he did not react to it. After a few moments, the old duke noticed the group and paused his conversation to address them. "I see you are all here. And ready, it seems. I am surprised, especially with you, Keslin. Isn't there a tavern open anywhere?"

"I thought I'd make an appearance," Geoffrey said.

"Well, it is the polite thing to do," Wulfric's tone was caustic. "Though I very much doubt politeness was ever top of your concerns."

Geoffrey looked confused and a little hurt. Bellaydin was about to say something, but Haakon managed to cut in first. "Wulfric, enough of this. We're all friends here. Or perhaps you are begging to suspect us of being secret Horned God cultists?"

Wulfric said nothing, so Bellaydin changed the subject "There are a lot of soldiers here today." The guards were at their posts now, dozens standing above Bellaydin in the ramparts, crossbows at the ready. Just as many patrolled the square below, weapons at their side.

"His Grace is taking no chances," Wulfric noted. "I admire your caution, Haakon."

"Yes, well," Haakon stuttered. "After all that has happened, I believe that the House Ap'Lydin deserves to avoid any further tragedies. The precautions I've taken, I believe, are well founded."

Wulfric nodded. "The Horned God's followers are persistent, and their vendetta will not end until they believe they have destroyed the remnants of William Ap'Lydin's legacy."

"I wasn't talking about the Cult of the Horned God, Wulfric," Haakon said testily. "There are other threats in this world, even if you don't see them."

"I would advise caution, nevertheless."

Bellaydin swore under his breath in frustration. Every time Wulfric and Haakon were together these days they seemed to squabble and fight like a pair of unruly children. Whether Wulfric – and his obsession with the Horned God – was entirely to blame or not, Bellaydin was beginning to tire of it.

"Your Grace," Kahlaf muttered towards Wulfric. "If we could finish our discussion…"

Wulfric glanced around momentarily and then turned back to the Ahktarran, "Yes, Kahlaf, indeed we should. Would you please excuse me, gentlemen?"

Bellaydin nodded as Wulfric took his leave, walking off with his Ahktarran retainer to talk somewhere else, presumably away from the ears of others.

"He's getting worse," Geoffrey said once Wulfric was out of sight.

"Sir Geoffrey, please," Haakon said. "You know the stress and pressure the Duke of Oldharbour has been under."

"So I've heard," the knight said dismissively.

"I have to see Maria," Bellaydin said.

"Well, Bela," Haakon said. "We'll see you later."

"Don't forget now, first drinks are on you," Geoffrey reminded before he and Haakon disappeared into the crowd.

Bellaydin smiled to himself and made his way up to meet his cousin in her room. Judging by her surprise when he opened the door, she hadn't been expecting him.

"Uncle Bela." Maria came towards Bellaydin at full force, laughing.

"Maria," Bellaydin said as the girl crushed him with a hug. "How are you?"

"Happy to see a familiar face," she said. "I don't know *any* of these people."

Bellaydin laughed. "They're supposed to be your soldiers and servants, my dear Lady Countess."

Maria went red. "Uncle Bela, don't call me that. It still seems so strange."

"You'll need to get used to all of this, Maria," Bellaydin said.

"I don't know how I'm going to get used to being married," Maria said. "I only met Edgar once."

Once is more than enough, Bellaydin thought.

"You know him better than I do," she said. "Mayhap you should go and say hello?"

Bellaydin's face turned a shade of green as he contemplated having to speak to Edgar de Morcor.

Maria laughed uproariously. "Your face! If only you could see it. It was just a jape, you know." Her jovial demeanour gave way to a graver look. "Though I would like to know what you consider the good points of this match."

"Edgar is the queen's cousin," Bellaydin said, trying to sound supportive. "You're marrying into royalty."

"He's fine, I suppose," she said. "Even if he is a little dim. I just don't know if Father would have liked the Earldom leaving our family when I marry a de Morcor."

She smiled at him, her eyes wistful. "I'm glad you're going to be the one to ride next to me."

Bellaydin looked at his cousin. Maria wore a white and blue dress, the traditional garment for an aristocratic Emparian bride, but it was her face which held Bellaydin's attention. She looked more beautiful today than he could ever remember, her blue eyes clear and bright, her soft brown hair elegantly curled. There was something about her nose and about the shape of her face, even her ears that reminded Bellaydin of William. He felt another pang as his heart lurched. He wished William could have been here to see this day.

"I'm going to miss you," Bellaydin said to her.

"Oh, shush," Maria chided. "You make it sound like we're never going to see each other again. I'll only be in Alariat – it's not that far. You'll come visit me, won't you?"

"Of course," Bellaydin said.

"Hurrah." Maria embraced Bellaydin.

She reached to her hair and took off one of her ribbons. "Here," she said, wrapping the ribbon around Bellaydin's wrist. "Something to remember me by."

Bellaydin blushed, as Maria took him by the hand. "Let's go and see the horses, Uncle."

The wedding procession would be a grand affair, in the traditional manner of Emparian nobility. Usually, the bride would ride alongside her father, who would bring her to her future husband. Since Maria's own father was dead, she was instead to be escorted by Bellaydin, her closest living relative. The horses that the Ap'Lydins would ride were fine, strong, and healthy geldings, well-trained and even-tempered. Embroidered saddle cloths bearing the Ap'Lydin coat of arms covered both, white for Maria and black and purple for Bellaydin.

"My lady countess," a page greeted Maria, and led her away to be put on her mount.

Bellaydin smiled, not really concentrating until he was startled by the sound of a horse's neigh. A guard stood next to him, holding a horse by the reins. The guard looked at Bellaydin expectantly. "My lord Ap'Lydin," he said, saluting Bellaydin, "We're ready for you."

With the guard assisting, Bellaydin climbed onto the horse and urged it down to the end of the hall, ready to begin the ceremony.

Trumpets blared, signalling the beginning of the wedding procession.

Bellaydin spurred his horse forward and rode through the square with Maria at his side, as rose petals rained down from the townsfolk above. All around him, people were cheering and shouting out the Ap'Lydin name, and Bellaydin could not help but wave in response. During the procession, the guards at the sides of the square and atop the ramparts above still stood with the same, passionless expression. Amidst all the cheer and goodwill their stern faces seemed a little strange but understanding that they were probably just taking their duties seriously, Bellaydin pushed any suspicious thoughts out of his mind. That was when, out of the corner of his eye, he saw it. One of the guards at the very centre of the ramparts seemed to be signalling, raising his hand up and down almost unnoticeably. Bellaydin barely had time to shout a warning before the first crossbow bolt whizzed past his head. His horse whinnied and reared, nearly throwing Bellaydin to the ground. Another bolt flew towards him, and it was only a quick instinctive movement on Bellaydin's part that prevented the bolt from impaling his skull.

"Assassins! There are traitors among us." Bellaydin shouted frantically, "Protect Lady Maria!"

To Bellaydin's dismay, it seemed that the guards below had also been infiltrated. Half of the honour guard assembled nearby ran towards him with murderous fury, their weapons drawn and their horrific battle cries assailing Bellaydin's ears. The rest of the guards, as startled as Bellaydin, hesitated for a moment before they too charged forward, meeting their former comrades in battle. As Bellaydin watched in horror, the wedding procession turned into a nightmare. Soldiers fought against soldiers, with nothing much to distinguish friend from foe. Those without weapons tried to flee.

"Go, go, go." Bellaydin urged his startled horse forward. Grabbing the reins of Maria's horse, he ensured it followed him as he forced the animals into a gallop. More crossbow bolts rained down from above, whistling past Bellaydin's head with terrifying velocity. The citadel square had descended into total chaos, with dozens of soldiers trapped in a confusing melee, the sound of blades smashing against armour and the cries of wounded and dying men ringing in Bellaydin's ears.

Wulfric was right. That was Bellaydin's first thought as he galloped through the scene of carnage. How did the old man know that this would happen? Dark thoughts entered Bellaydin's mind. Suppose it was not just a coincidence. Just how well did he know Wulfric Highcrown anyway? Haakon had said that the Duke of Oldharbour had changed.

Suddenly Bellaydin's horse jerked violently, throwing Bellaydin off the saddle. A crossbow bolt protruded from the horse's neck, a rivulet of blood trickling down the gelding's body.

"No, no." Bellaydin cried as he hit the ground, the fall knocking the wind out of him. Maria's horse, startled but unharmed, galloped past him, Maria still holding on for dear life. The girl was clearly terrified, screaming for someone to help her. Bellaydin tried to grab the reins of Maria's horse as it sped past, but the animal was moving too fast, and his reach was not far enough. As Bellaydin's hand slipped through the horse's reins fruitlessly, his own horse finally lost its remaining strength and collapsed. Bellaydin barely moved away in time to avoid being crushed by the dying horse's bulk. With a primal scream, someone attacked him, but the blow was weak and Bellaydin leapt to his feet, dodging the man's blows.

"It will not avail you, Heir of Lydin. Soon you will be the last." the man growled.

A giant of a man towered before him, clad in armour, sun glinting off his shaven scalp. He held a tremendous sword with both hands and swung again. Bellaydin dodged and the blade cut through the air just above his scalp. The attacker laughed. "You don't remember me, do you?"

Bellaydin tumbled out of the way, rolling to the ground as he mouthed an answer in the negative. Even as he did so, his thoughts changed. Despite the cold white eyes of his assailant, despite the unfamiliar cobbled together armour or the mark of the Horned God on the man's face, Bellaydin did recognise him. It was the renegade knight Dallen Withers, the murderer of the Duke of Emperor's Palace. The rumours were right – he had escaped his prison. But how was he here?

"Dallen Withers," Bellaydin gasped, coming to his feet. "Murderer! I should have known."

The man's mouth twisted in an unsettling grin when he realised Bellaydin's revelation. "I see I made a larger impression than I thought. No prison can hold me, Heir of Lydin." He looked to the horizon. "Many will fall today. As was commanded."

Bellaydin, still unarmed, stood warily, watching Dallen for any sudden movement. "So, you are not the leader, you are just a weapon. Who is the wielder? Is it the duke? Has he sent you here to kill?"

"Oh yes," Dallen said. "But the duke and I serve a higher purpose." He touched the mark on his forehead. "As you can see."

"The Horned God," Bellaydin said. His jaw became firm. "Then Oswin Zalltor is a traitor, just like his grandson."

Dallen laughed. *"Wrong Duke."* Dallen hissed, sheathing his sword, and shoving Bellaydin to the ground. Dallen looked around before turning on his heels and fleeing in the direction of the gate. Bellaydin tried to follow, but more traitorous guards surrounded him. He backed away from their swords, looking for somewhere, anywhere, to escape.

He heard Geoffrey's voice. "Bellaydin!"

"Over here," Bellaydin shouted. One of the traitors attacked him, and Bellaydin swung to the right, his assailant's sword smashing into the ground. Geoffrey engaged the soldier, their swords clashing, allowing Bellaydin time to get to his feet again. Geoffrey dispatched the soldier with a quick thrust of his sword, leaving the dying man's weapon clattering to the floor. Geoffrey kicked it towards Bellaydin before moving on to engage another soldier. Bellaydin, lacking his own weapon, took the fallen sword up eagerly. He had to find Maria. He had to make sure she was safe. He had to keep his promise to William.

Above them, in the castle ramparts, Talthas was surrounded by men, but he was making short work of them, so Bellaydin dragged his attention back nearby, where several more guardsmen were emerging from the shadows, weapons drawn.

"Where are the others?" Bellaydin yelled to Geoffrey as he parried the attacks of another treacherous guardsman.

"Haakon? I don't know. But I think I saw Wulfric and Kahlaf chasing your little cousin's horse." Geoffrey said between sword blows. The pair was fighting back-to-back now, shielding each other from enemy attacks. Dead bodies of both the devoted and traitorous littered the blood-stained ground.

"Where are they all going?" said Geoffrey.

Twisting his body as he fought, Bellaydin risked a quick glance around the square. Apart from the two soldiers still engaged in combat with them, the other turncoats were escaping the melee, running off in the same direction as Maria's galloping horse.

"It's Maria," Bellaydin said, the realisation dawning on him. "She's the target."

"But that doesn't make sense." Geoffrey kicked a man in the chest and sent him toppling backwards. "What would they want with her?"

"I don't know," Bellaydin said. He deflected another blow and taking advantage of his enemy's attempted feint to the left, swung to the right and thrust his sword into the man's belly. The soldier crumpled to the ground, the palms of his hand facing the sky. Though smeared with blood, one of his palms bore the unmistakable mark of a worshipper of the Horned God.

"But there's a clue," he said grimly. "Come on. There's no time."

Bellaydin and Geoffrey ran. All about them was the clash of steel and the pandemonium of death, as the battle raged relentlessly.

"This way." Geoffrey pointed to the main gate of the keep. A trail of blood, interspersed with the prints of men and horses, led them towards it. Bellaydin's heart pounded as they ran. He had no idea what would be waiting for them when they found Maria, but he prayed to whatever gods were listening that she was not harmed.

The gate mechanism was broken, smashed into pieces, so the traitors had obviously wanted to keep the citadel gates open, probably to aid in their escape. Bellaydin dashed through the mighty stone gates, Geoffrey following close behind.

The trail of blood led from the citadel's gates out into the open. There was no indication whose blood it was, but the sight of it sent shivers down Bellaydin's back regardless. Bellaydin said nothing, trying to prepare his mind for whatever they were about to find.

A few feet further they came across Maria's abandoned horse. There were signs of a struggle – the saddle was stained with blood, and the reins had been torn off.

"She was on the horse, somebody stopped it, pulled her off," he deduced, his words coming quickly and frantically. He looked around, confused, anxious and frustrated. "Where is she?"

"More blood," Geoffrey pointed out. "Fainter, but you can still make it out. This way."

They followed the blood marks down the ridge, over a hill, and down a steep incline until finally, panting with exhaustion, they reached a sheer cliff overlooking the ocean.

"Die!"

Dallen appeared from nowhere, his sword slicing down Bellaydin's shoulder. Bellaydin retaliated with an elbow jab, then brought his sword up against the knight. Another guardsman engaged Sir Geoffrey, keeping him from coming to Bellaydin's aid.

"Who commanded this?" Bellaydin demanded of Dallen as they exchanged sword blows. "Tell me!"

Dallen simply snarled and hurled himself towards Bellaydin with a shoulder charge, sending the younger man toppling into the dirt. As Bellaydin scrambled to recover himself, Dallen's twisted face loomed over him; the knight's voice was cold and without feeling.

"If you knew who planned this, your heart would break," Dallen taunted. "So, imagine how difficult it is for me to not tell you. But alas, I swore an oath."

"You swore an oath to your queen, too. Didn't stop you betraying her, now did it?"

Dallen pointed a sword at Bellaydin's throat. "Some oaths are to men. Others are to gods. Those cannot be broken."

"And what of those to false gods and liars?"

Bellaydin could tell his response had not pleased Dallen. For a moment Bellaydin thought the blade might come down through his throat. Instead Dallen raised his head and brought up his sword just in time to stave off an attack from Geoffrey. As the two traded blows, Bellaydin reached out for his own sword. Once his fingers had closed around its pommel, he rolled to his right, leapt up to his feet and thrust forward with the blade, skewering Dallen through the belly. Dallen's face crumpled with surprise as the blood trickled from his lips. He took a few shaking steps before collapsing to the ground, the blood pooling around his corpse.

"Good riddance," said Geoffrey.

"It was as much me as you. If you hadn't distracted him, I'd be dead." They hardly had time to breathe before Bellaydin spied a towering figure. He grabbed Geoffrey's shoulder. "Wait, who is that?"

"I'd know that snout anywhere," said Geoffrey. It was Kahlaf. As Bellaydin and Geoffrey hurried closer they saw the Ahktarran was crouched over a body, a torn piece of blood-stained white cloth in his claws.

"What in the –" Geoffrey said.

"Kahlaf," yelled Bellaydin, his voice hoarse, "Kahlaf! Maria, where is she?"

The Ahktarran did not respond. Fearing the worse and gripped with panic, Bellaydin ran full pelt to Kahlaf, trying to get close enough to the body to identify it. When he was within a foot, he suddenly pulled up short. The body was not Maria's. It was one of the guardsmen, presumably one of the treacherous ones who had turned on them. The corpse was almost unrecognisable and looked like it had been mauled by a wild animal. Noting the blood and gore dripping from Kahlaf's clawed fingers, Bellaydin suddenly felt sick.

"No…" The words on Bellaydin's lips were drenched in dread. Kahlaf's gaze seemed to purposefully avoid Bellaydin's.

Geoffrey's face had turned white. He came towards the Ahktarran. "Where's Maria?" His voice was strangled with tranquil rage.

"Gone." The voice came from behind them. Bellaydin wheeled around in surprise. Approaching from some distance was Wulfric Highcrown. His clothes were torn, bloodied and filthy.

"Where is she?" Bellaydin demanded.

"This filth," Wulfric kicked the dead guardsman. "He threw her over the cliff, to the waves below. Kahlaf attempted to save the girl, but he was too late."

Bellaydin was stunned. He felt as if he had been hit with a tremendous physical blow. "You're lying – how can…" The words died on his lips. He tasted the salt of his own tears as they ran down his cheeks.

"Kahlaf knows, don't you, Kahlaf?" The Ahktarran was silent, his head still bowed.

"Yes, master." The Ahktarran sucked in his breath, uncharacteristically Bellaydin thought, before droning, "It is my fault that Lady Ap'Lydin fell. I failed to reach the traitor in time. But I have avenged her." He held up his claws, and the red-tinted ends glinted in the sun. It was a chilling sight.

Bellaydin tried to speak, but his throat seemed to have tightened up, and made no sound. He turned to Geoffrey, but the knight was missing his usual jovial appearance. Instead, Bellaydin could see only despair on the man's face. Geoffrey's eyes were red with tears. Bellaydin screamed, something inside him breaking. He lunged towards the end of the cliff, and it was only Geoffrey's quick reactions that stopped him plunging off. Bellaydin sobbed as he looked over the edge, searching for any trace of Maria.

"Where is she? What's happened?" Talthas had finally reached them. He looked about at the others and his expression changed. He did not need the answer.

"No. No." Bellaydin shouted, a sense of helplessness enveloping him.

"I told you, Ap'Lydin. She is gone," Wulfric said.

Bellaydin turned to the man, suddenly furious. He could not understand how Wulfric could be so cold and unfeeling amidst this tragedy. "What is wrong with you? Do you feel nothing over the death of others? Have you no compassion?"

Wulfric did not flinch. "Ap'Lydin, I am old. I have lost many that I care for in my life. I have learned to grieve impersonally, and then move on – as should you."

Chastened, Bellaydin turned his head away. He did not want to hear words like that. Not now.

"Don't mistake my feelings, though," Wulfric said, almost as an afterthought, "I am sorry for your loss."

"Why her?" Bellaydin sobbed quietly. "She was just a child. She was innocent."

"It's monstrous," Geoffrey said through his tears.

"I had to kill Dallen Withers," said Bellaydin. "It might have been the Duke of Georgeton, who sent him to get revenge on my family."

"It doesn't make sense," said Geoffrey. "We covered up for that old bastard. He thinks his grandson died a hero. And Edgar was Tancred's best friend, yet he almost died here today. Do you believe that Oswin Zalltor could be behind this, your Grace?"

The Duke of Oldharbour shook his head. "This is the work of the Horned God and his followers," Wulfric turned the dead man's hand over and traced a finger over the unholy symbol tattooed on the corpse's palm. "They hate the Ap'Lydin family, Bellaydin, for reasons of their own."

"She was an innocent. It's not right."

"There will be more innocents who suffer before this ends, Bellaydin. Mark my words."

CHAPTER 9

Polnygar awoke to the morning light. Beside her, Augustin slept soundly. Polnygar briefly wondered if she should wake him but then thought better of it. She smiled as she remembered the night before. Everything seemed to have moved so quickly. He had been gentle, which endeared him further to her. She rolled over, shifting closer to his warmth.

"Lord Bauer."

Polnygar jumped up with a start. *Hebu.*

"Lord Bauer, I – oh, hello, young Polnygar," The Nemoi's brown lips twisted into an amused smile, while Polnygar tried to cover herself with the blankets.

"Have I stumbled into the wrong room, by chance?" he asked.

Augustin stirred, mumbling something under his breath. He raised himself on one elbow and wiped the sleep from his eyes.

"What do you want, gnome?"

Hebu looked annoyed for a moment and then approached Augustin's side of the bed. "Well, far be it from me to disturb your fun here, but Aelzandar wants to speak with you in the square outside. There's been news from Liderial."

Hebu frowned, his eyes darting from Augustin to Polnygar's blanketed form and back to the Baron. Augustin instinctively placed a protective arm over Polnygar. "Fine. We'll be right there."

"I'll see you in a bit," Hebu bowed. The Nemoi slipped in a final smirk before he disappeared.

Augustin leant back on his pillow. Turning to Polnygar, he let out a great sigh. "I guess we'd better get up then."

A short while later both Augustin and Polnygar, freshly awake and dressed, were outdoors in the citadel square.

"Sorry we're late," Augustin said as he approached. He shot a knowing smile to Polnygar, his eyes tender. In spite of herself, Polnygar blushed deeply.

Two Eldara newcomers approached, and Aelzandar introduced them to Augustin. "Baron Augustin Bauer, I would like you to meet Spellweaver Vaerath and his apprentice, Laerosanna."

"Pleased to meet you," Augustin extended his hand.

Vaerath looked at the hand with a pained expression and then looked at Aelzandar. After a reassuring glance from the archmage, Vaerath took Augustin's hand and shook it gingerly.

"Uh, did I do something wrong?" Augustin asked Aelzandar.

"I'm sorry, Baron, but my friend has little contact with humans, so he finds it difficult to feel comfortable with them. It's nothing personal, you must understand."

"I'll try not to get offended," Augustin said carefully. "The Nemoi said

118

there is news from Liderial." Augustin changed the topic.

"My Emparian is a little rusty," Vaerath said. "So, you will forgive me if my meaning is a little unclear. My apprentice and I rode at speed to arrive here in time, Aelzandar. The king still lies ill, the queen has been, how shall I put it, *removed* from power. Lord Ivellios controls all."

The others were silent as the Eldara spellweaver spoke, and Polnygar felt her mouth go dry.

"You were right, Aelzandar," Vaerath continued quietly. "Ivellios is mad. He arrived with the mangled corpses of many Eldara, and claimed they were murdered by the humans of Harralin."

"The cultists," Polnygar said.

"That was self-defence." Augustin protested.

"There were some, like me, who questioned the circumstances in which our brothers had died, but Ivellios' words won out. The Council was outraged. They gave him the backing to put Liderial on a war footing."

"Oh, gods," said Augustin, crestfallen.

"The army of Liderial marches towards Harralin," said Vaerath. "I am sorry. There is nothing I could do."

"Yet you came, Vaerath. You did as I asked. That is brave, old friend."

"Aelzandar, you saved my life once. All those years ago, at the Sunset Isles. It is only fair that I do the same. Ivellios will have many spellweavers under his command. Laerosanna and I will assist as best we can."

"How many spellweavers?" Augustin asked.

"Humph," Hebu snorted. "Dozens, at the very least. Against what, three wizards of our own?"

"Four," Polnygar said.

Aelzandar gave her a warm smile. "Quite right, my dear. And I would be proud to fight at your side."

Polnygar felt cheered, despite the uneasy feeling she had underneath about what was to come.

"Well, I'm sure we'll welcome any help," Augustin said. "But if you change your mind, it's not too late to back out –"

"I'm afraid I cannot," said Vaerath.

"Why not?"

Vaerath did not respond and tried to look away, seemingly ashamed.

"What Vacrath means is that as a spellweaver who has countermanded the orders of the Lord Protector, his life is now forfeit," said Aelzandar, speaking plainly.

"Oh," Augustin said, embarrassed, "I didn't know."

Vaerath nodded understandingly.

"We need to inform the Knights and the Burgomeister," Aelzandar said to the others. "Harallin's defences must be seen to."

Augustin's shoulders sagged. "Well, let's get to it."

They returned to the citadel. Polnygar felt her stomach knot in fear. She had been in many battles since she left Aderilund, but it had never felt like this before. Every other time she drew her sword she had been sure of the outcome, undoubting that she would survive. As she pondered on this, she realised why she had possessed such confidence – because Aelzandar had shown the same. Now that the confidence had left Aelzandar, and Polnygar found it had left her as well.

She saw Gerd and Agmar from a distance as they reached the Great Hall. Gerd looked terrified, his face pale, his hand twitching nervously. Agmar stood with his shoulders hunched, his head bowed. The knight clearly expected the worst and was allowing his fear to consume him. His nephew, Holger, trailed some distance behind. The younger knight's face betrayed a similar dread to his uncle's. However, it briefly shifted as his eyes took in the newly arrived elves, and Polnygar noticed Holger's gaze lingered on Laerosanna for a moment before snapping back to his uncle Agmar.

"So, do you have good news for me, or not?" Gerd sniffed.

Aelzandar folded his hands, his voice grave. "I'm afraid not."

"Pah." Gerd said. He was shaking noticeably. "Who are these elves with you? Spies? Traitors? Infiltrators?"

"Friends," Aelzandar corrected as he introduced Vaerath and Laerosanna again.

Polnygar noticed Laerosonna's eyes regard Holger with some interest.

The burgomeister was scornful. "Friends. As if we should expect friendship from the lords of Alfheim. You are a fool, Archmage."

"Better a fool than a coward," Augustin said.

"Courage is a much-overvalued commodity," Gerd spat back. "And often confused with stupidity. I gather the elvish army marches towards us, and you have nothing to halt its advance?"

Aelzandar simply nodded.

"Then our worst fears have been realised," Gerd said quickly, "Time is running out."

"We need to prepare for a siege," Augustin said, gesturing around him.

"There will be no siege, Emparian, for the elves will never reach Harralin." Gerd pointed to Agmar. "You will take the army of Harralin outside the city walls and meet this elvish host in the mountain pass to the north. You and your knights will do your duty."

"But my lord, they outnumber us two to one. We would be walking into a charnel house. Let us remain here where we might withstand an attack behind these strong walls."

"You will do nothing of the sort." Gerd waved his finger as if Agmar was an insolent child. "I require you to cover my escape. If you fail, I wish to be far from Skurj when the elves reach this city."

"My lord," Agmar's voice sounded weary. "I would ask you to please, in the name of the Holy Three, please reconsider."

"I agree with the Grand Master," Aelzandar said. "There is nothing to be gained by such a rash gesture. Stay in Harralin with us. I give you my word that you will come to no harm."

"You've failed me already, Aelzandar," Gerd said. "Why should I trust your word again?"

"If you leave the city, I cannot guarantee your safety. Please, stay here."

Gerd dismissed Aelzandar's imploration with a curt wave of the hand. "Enough of this. Agmar, you have your orders. Prepare your men."

Looking absolutely defeated, Agmar bowed his head, and his eyes closed, nodded silently as Gerd left the room. Once the burgomeister was out of earshot, Augustin turned to Agmar. "What he is proposing is suicide, you know that."

"I have no choice," Agmar said. "He is my liege and the heir to the line of Genio. I must follow him, even into death."

"We can help," Polnygar cut in. Aelzandar nodded with approval.

"I thank you all," Agmar said. "But this is my burden to bear, and I bear it willingly."

"That may be true," Aelzandar placed a hand on Agmar's shoulder. "But one should never bear such a heavy weight alone. We stand with you, Agmar."

"I see that I will not be able to convince you otherwise, my friends," Agmar said. "So, I will just say, that it will be an honour to have you fight by my side."

"Show us your enemies, and leave the rest to us," Augustin touched the hilt of his sword. "You've been quiet, Sir Holger. Do you stand with your uncle?"

Holger nodded; his eyes fixed on Laerosanna. "To the end."

***

A short time later Polnygar and the others left the citadel to join the rest of the soldiers. As they walked, Polnygar looked at Agmar. The knight barely spoke, and with his eyes downcast and his shoulders slumped, presented a melancholic sight. Polnygar thought he looked like a man going to his own funeral. For someone who had fought many battles over his life, the knight did not seem to be confident about his chances of surviving this one, and that worried Polnygar. The fear, dread, and anticipation she felt about the upcoming battle only intensified. If Agmar, a veteran of war since his adolescence, was pessimistic about his own survival, where did that leave Polnygar?

Holger stayed close to Laerosanna, shadowing her with a quiet strength. He had barely spoken since he had laid eyes on the Eldara girl, but he treated her deferentially and protectively.

Augustin's face was one of grim determination. The Emparian tended to first decide upon one course of action, and after the decision was made, push out all doubt and uncertainty from his mind. Polnygar wished she could do the same, but she could not stop thinking of what was to come. This was not like the bandits or small assassin bands they had fought in the many months they travelled between Ralom and Skurj. This was a powerful army, one of the most feared in the known world, and Polnygar did not expect they would be merciful.

Agmar rode towards them, having mounted his horse. He drew his sword, and raised it above his head, moving towards the soldiers under his command. "Knights. Attention." His voice commanded strength. "You know what awaits you. All I ask is that you fight with honour and do justice to the name of the Knights of the Crux Caruillin. In the Divine Martyr's name!"

"Kytilas!" the knights cheered back.

Behind the knights, the infantry militia stood, looking uneasy. Unlike the well trained and disciplined knights, the men in the infantry were green and untested. Many had never fought in battle before, let alone against the feared and legendary elven army. Polnygar could see their faces – equal part fear and terror in their eyes. She guessed they too knew exactly what they faced.

Under Agmar's orders, the knights, their horses braying in the cold air, led the way out of the gates of Harralin. They formed three columns – the left wing to be led by Augustin, the right wing by Sir Holger, and the centre column by the Grand Master himself.

"This is suicide," Augustin muttered as a page brought him his own horse. "Damn that Genio fool. We should be staying in the city where we have a chance. Going out in the open like this, it's, well..." He looked around, then with one motion, climbed onto his steed. "It's the sort of stubborn foolishness that costs lives. With any luck, it won't be ours. I'll see you once the battle is over, Polnygar." He leant down from his horse, kissing Polnygar on the forehead before riding off to join Agmar and the knights.

"Are you ready, my dear?" Aelzandar said, approaching with Vaerath and Laerosanna. "The four of us have an important part to play. We are the only ones fighting for Harralin that have the skill necessary to counter the spellweavers fighting for Ivellios."

"I don't know, Aelzandar. How can the four of us hope to fight the dozens of spellweavers that Ivellios will have under his command?"

"It will be difficult, my dear. I don't doubt that, but it is our only chance to avoid defeat. Without our help, Agmar and his knights – no matter how brave or skilled they may be –stand no chance against the power that

Ivellios and the other Eldara spellweavers can bring to bear."

Vaerath turned to Polnygar. "I have known Ivellios for a long time. Even longer than Aelzandar. I know his ways. We shall work in a defensive role only. Focusing all our strength on that will give us the best chance against Ivellios. We shall produce an arcane shield to protect the soldiers from the Art. If we are lucky, we can sustain it long enough to protect the knights from the full might of the spellweavers, giving them time enough to bring the spellweavers down in battle."

Polnygar's head spun. She knew how to create an arcane shield. She had done so many times in the lessons Aelzandar had given her in Macrodonia. She had also managed to refine it enough to produce a small, temporary one over herself during a battle with bandits on the way to Skurj. But a shield large enough to cover a whole army, and strong enough to withstand the attacks of a whole battalion of spellweavers? It did not seem remotely possible.

"I'm not sure I can do it," Polnygar said.

"This is no time for modesty, my dear," said Aelzandar. "Vaerath and I will lead. Laerosanna and yourself will support us. We must succeed, for I fear that our lives and the lives of many others depend on us."

"I'll do my best," Polnygar promised.

"That's all we can ask for," Aelzandar turned to Hebu. "Fetch us our horses. We shall ride out after Agmar until the army stops and then take position on the closest hill."

The Nemoi nodded and did as asked, without the requisite grumbling. Surprised, Polnygar decided that the gravity of the situation must have finally impressed upon Hebu.

"And let's pray to the heavens, that the Gods smile on us today, friends," said Aelzandar looked towards the horizon. "For we need a miracle."

"What about Gerd and the Tears? Will they be safe?"

Aelzandar turned to Polnygar with a smile and rested a hand on her shoulder. "As long as Ivellios does not notice that neither Gerd nor the Tears are with us, we should be able to give the Burgomeister and his guard sufficient time to escape to the south. Once they reach Lerid, they will be out of the Horned God's reach. I hope that we can join them after the battle."

"If we survive," Polnygar said softly.

For once, Aelzandar said nothing.

***

The four of them rode in silence. Aelzandar's face was stern, set, and totally focused on what was to come. Vaerath's eyes looked forward wearily as if he had seen this moment coming for decades. Laerosanna looked frightened, her eyes darting from side to side, seeming as if at any moment, she might turn her horse around and flee for safety.

Polnygar wondered how she must look herself. Did she seem grim and determined like Aelzandar? Exhausted, emotionally, and physically, like Vaerath? If anything, she knew she would be probably the same as Laerosanna. Petrified and wanting to escape. The horrible churning sensation returned to her stomach.

"This way," Aelzandar pointed to a hill that overlooked much of the valley, "We shall make our stand here."

Polnygar saw the army of Harralin ahead, fortifying their position as best they could. Ranks of foot soldiers and crossbowmen jostled for position, while nearby knights organised their horses into the best positions for an inevitable charge. The Eldara army was nowhere to be seen, and Polnygar allowed herself a moment of hope that perhaps it would not come at all, and the battle they feared would never eventuate. But within less than a quarter hour, the sound of trumpets blared from the other side of the valley, and the clanging and stomping sound of an approaching army assailed Polnygar's ears.

"Quickly my dear," Aelzandar picked up his pace. The five of them reached their destination a few minutes later and, upon dismounting, moved to the very top of the hill where they had a good vantage point over the entire force sent from Harralin. Polnygar could see Agmar and Augustin in the front vanguard of the knights, encouraging some of the less experienced troops to find their courage and hold the ground as the elven army approached.

The banners of the Aspen Throne fluttered above the marching ranks of the Eldara soldiers, a large force comprised of cavalry, infantry, and several archer divisions. With King Talan confined to his bed and the queen marginalised at court, Polnygar knew that it would be the first time for hundreds of years that the Eldara had marched to war under the royal banner without the king himself leading them into battle. Instead, it would be the so-called "Lord Protector" – Ivellios the Spellweaver – who would be at the head of the first charge.

Bringing up the rear and identified by their bright and colourful robes were the spellweaver divisions. Their own banners came with them, and there were dozens of them, the spellweavers comprising all the most important noble houses of the Eldara. Polnygar recognised each one of the banners, even though her childhood in Aderilund was fast fading into a distant memory. There was no attempt at subterfuge or trying to hide their most valuable battle resources – the spellweavers stood out as clear as day to even the most ignorant enemy soldier. Even though they comprised some of the most influential and powerful nobility in Liderial, the spellweaver ranks were so confident of their own power that they didn't see their lack of camouflage as a problem.

After all, if you can kill men with a word, and rain fire down from the heavens, what do you fear from a spear or sword?

"Hebu," Aelzandar said. "Keep an eye out. When they give the signal, we shall begin the incantations. Remember too that once we begin the spell, you must do your best to keep us safe."

Hebu nodded and pulled the knife from his belt. Once Polnygar would have found the sight of the Nemoi so-armed an almost comical sight, but after her experiences in Qar Arrid, she knew Hebu's hidden depths.

***

In the valley below the forces of Harralin also waited with bated breath.

"What are they waiting for?" Augustin grumbled as he and Agmar waited.

The elven army had assembled at the other end of the valley, with banners waving in the wind, armour glinting in the sun and blasting trumpets announcing their arrival.

"They're trying to unsettle us," Agmar stroked his moustache. "They know we fear them."

"News to me," Augustin scoffed.

A lone horseman emerged from the lines of the elven army. Riding his horse towards the army of Harralin, he held the white flag of parley.

"Here they come now," Agmar said.

"Humph," Augustin remarked. "About time."

The horseman wheeled about in front of Augustin and Agmar and then, bringing his horse to a halt, greeted them with an open palm salute. Agmar returned the gesture, while Augustin just looked ahead with disdain.

"Greetings Mal-halyth," the emissary said, dismounting his horse, "I bring terms from the Aspen Throne."

"We are listening." Agmar stepped to the ground to meet the emissary. Augustin did likewise, coming to join the knight.

The emissary removed his helmet, revealing the smooth, unlined face of an Eldara lord. His fair, almost white hair was fixed in a top knot. "A terrible crime has been committed in the lands of your people. The crime has resulted in the deaths of many Eldara of noble and upright character. The complicity of the entire settlement of Harralin in this crime has been noted, and so death is a fitting punishment, and well-warranted." The elf's expression was overly proper and haughty. Then, as if realising that the appearance of arrogance would not help his cause, the elf tried to smile, though the smile was like the rest of his appearance, cold, distant, and devoid of warmth and feeling. "And it is a punishment that the Aspen Throne is entitled to carry out. However, the Lord Protector wishes to be merciful. If the representatives of Harralin merely hand themselves to our custody, along with the original instigator, Polnygaranna li'Saegralanna li'Saegras, then Lord Ivellios is willing to let the rest of your forces here return to Harralin, unharmed."

Well, that's awfully considerate of you now, isn't it? Augustin wondered.

Agmar spoke up, responding to the terms. "I'm afraid, my lord, that I must refuse the Lord Protector's offer. I could hand myself over to you, but I have no authority to do so about any others, and they will not surrender themselves willingly."

"Consider your actions, Mal-halyth," the emissary cautioned. "I have heard you are a man of peace. Surely you wish to avoid all this pointless bloodshed?"

Agmar looked pained. "I would. But there is also the matter of my own honour. I cannot agree to such terms when I have been ordered otherwise by my own lord and master."

"Your honour has long since left you, Mal-halyth." The emissary's tone was firm, but without anger, as if he felt he was reprimanding a child. "It died when your people murdered their Eldara betters."

Augustin knew when he was being patronised. "Betters." He gave a mocking laugh. "Is that what you call the sort of people who set up shop in some gods-cursed shrine, and kidnap innocents for perverse rituals to the Horned God?"

The emissary looked taken aback, his face twisted in disgust as if he'd just heard something so revolting as to be beyond the limits of civilised discussion. "The Lord Protector had warned us that you were lying serpents, Mal-halyth. But I was not sure whether he was speaking true. Now I see, if anything, he was far too generous to describe your true nature. Such slander and terrible falsehoods about true, noble sons of Hydria I will never accept. If it was your intention to insult me then you have succeeded. I suggest you prepare yourself for battle." With one last curt salute, the emissary put his helmet back on, and, climbing back on his horse, rode back to his own side.

"You know," Augustin watched the departing rider. "It's a shame I don't have a crossbow with me. He'd make a great target."

Agmar ignored Augustin and instead turned to the soldier next to him. "It seems negotiations have failed. Give the signal."

***

"I see it," said Hebu, from atop the hill, as he watched soldiers lighting the signal fires, "That's the signal."

"It is time," said Aelzandar.

Aelzandar held Vaerath's hand in his own, and the other spellweaver then grasped the hand of his apprentice, and so on, until the four of them were joined together in a chain, facing the army below. Vaerath chanted in Draconic, speaking secret, arcane words of power.

Polnygar felt the familiar surge of mystical energy coursing through her body. This time it was more intense than she could remember – no doubt Aelzandar and Vaerath were using their own skill, to amplify hers many times over.

The feeling intensified, and for a moment, Polnygar felt as if she might explode, and release the arcane energy in one bout. Closing her eyes, she heard Aelzandar's voice in her mind. *Remember your training, my dear,* he said. She willed the energy back under control and stretched forth with her mind to shape it. As she did, she could feel other presences alongside her, doing the same. Aelzandar, Vaerath and Laerosanna took part in the shaping, and together they formed the shield. The strength of their combined willpower was exhilarating to Polnygar, and she felt as if there was nothing she couldn't do.

***

Augustin drew his sword. "Steady," he said to the knights around him.

Augustin commanded the left flank of the cavalry, with Agmar leading the centre and Holger the right. The battle plan was to outflank the elven army before they had a chance to break human morale altogether. If Aelzandar and Polnygar could get the shield functioning in time they might have a chance. Otherwise, they would be incinerated alive by the spellweavers before they'd even charged halfway.

"Come on, damn you, what's taking so long?" Augustin said under his breath. Every moment that passed saw the chance of victory slip even further. If the elves took the initiative before the shield was ready the results would be devastating. As Augustin watched, the spellweavers were moving to the front lines, ready to unleash their barrage. "Come on archmage. Don't let us down."

The spellweavers arranged themselves in a line facing the army of Harallin. Augustin saw Ivellios, the spellweaver as haughty as ever in his robes of gold and white.

"We have tried to be merciful, Mal-halyth." Ivellios called out, astride a magnificent white stallion. "But your barbarism and lack of grace has ruined any chance for peace. Instead, just as with children, you must be punished, and we shall not shirk from that duty. Spellweavers!" Ivellios raised his staff to the sky, and chanted words in the arcane tongue. Following his lead, the

131

other spellweavers did likewise, and with unnatural poise and concentration, they summoned sheets of flames to throw at the army of Harralin.

One moment Augustin and the other knights were looking ahead in horror, waiting for the fire to engulf them and the next the flames vanished in a puff of smoke just moments before it reached them. "The shield!" Augustin yelled. He made a silent prayer to the gods as the militiamen cheered.

The spellweavers seemed astonished at the development and attempted to cast more spells, bringing down more fire, lightning, and arrows of arcane energy at the army, but none of their attempts could penetrate the shield. "What is this?" Ivellios sneered, rearing on his horse.

"Treachery!" shouted another spellweaver, "No Mal-halyth could have done this."

Cries of "traitor" and "betrayed" rose from the elven army, and the spellweavers, noting their attempts to be futile, dispersed, and returned to the rear of the troup. Ivellios remained at the front of his forces, eyeing the human army with disdain.

"Archers," the Lord Protector yelled. "Destroy them."

The elven longbowmen, feared throughout the known world for their deadly skill, snapped to attention and marched to the front of the lines. Once in range, they loosed a volley of arrows into the air, shouting war cries in the Eldara tongue.

"Archers! Archers!" Augustin yelled. "Take cover."

A few militiamen fell to the ground, skewered, but the majority took head of Augustin's warning, bringing their shields up, protecting themselves from the deadly barrage. The archers let loose with another torrent and once again the humans scattered, trying to shield themselves. Again and again, the arrows came, and men fell with every volley, the blood staining the snow.

"Return volley." The militia of Harralin, wielding crossbows, marched to the front and crouched in the snow as they prepared to let off their own barrage. Within moments, the still winter air was punctuated with the sound of dozens of bolts being loosed at the enemy. Despite their best efforts, the crossbowmen could not match the range or power of the elven archers, and they too fell when the archers let loose their next rain of arrows.

Augustin looked at their rapidly depleting numbers. They would have to act soon. He strained his head, looking across the battlefield, trying to find Agmar's face in the crowd, but it was hard to see the Grand Master in the confusion. Even without their spellweavers, the elves were foes to be reckoned with. The battle was slipping away from Augustin's grasp. It was either now or never. Augustin drew his sword. "Alright men. Let's show these elves what us Mal-halyth can do."

They charged into battle.

***

"Grand Master." a knight yelled, "Lord Bauer has taken leave of his senses and engaged the enemy."

Agmar looked over to the other side of the army where Augustin was leading his wing of soldiers into an attack on the elven army's flank.

"That reckless fool." shouted another knight, a warrior named Sir Ulrich. "That is suicide."

Agmar did not speak but looked at the situation before him thoughtfully.

Sir Ulrich's voice came again. "Grand Master, we must act. We are in danger of being overwhelmed."

Agmar looked towards the elven army, squinting from the sunlight reflected on the gleaming armour of his foes. "Destiny approaches."

"Grand Master," Sir Ulrich said, his voice urgent. "What are your orders?"

"*Destiny…*" The words disappeared from Agmar's lips. His throat went dry, and he felt his guts twist in despair. He turned from Augustin to his right, where Sir Holger stood with the militia, awaiting his command. Agmar drew his sword. "It is too late to pull back. Lord Bauer's attack must be supported." Agmar held his sword above his head. "For Harralin."

His knights drew their swords and did likewise. "For Harralin."

Sir Holger caught Agmar's signal and rode in front of the militia, his sword aloft, and the soldiers responded, shaking their weapons, and yelling in response. "People of Harralin! The time has come. Let us drive these elves back to Alfheim and show them that the men of Skurj have no masters, and we will never bow and scrape to those who despise our very race." The militia cheered again. "Forward! For Kytilas. For Harralin. For Skurj."

"Where are we to attack, Grand Master? At the spellweaver centre?" asked Sir Ulrich as the militia charged, raising their voices.

"There is a path, not often followed, that may serve us. If I am right, the elves do not yet know of it. All of you - follow me."

***

"More arrows! Keep up the attack." Ivellios exhorted the archers to continue the barrage. "Until your fingers bleed, Children of Hydria. Don't let any of them get away."

Nearby, the spellweavers rode around in frustration, all their attempts to pierce the magical dome surrounding the human army having ended in failure. "Lord Protector, their shield still holds."

"Forget the Mal-halyth sorcery - we will deal with that in time. We can beat the animals with sword and bow alone. Support the archers. Make their arrows fly true."

"Your will be done, Lord Protector." The spellweavers moved behind the ranks of the archers.

Ivellios turned his horse back to the battle. As his archers continued to harry the frontlines of the human forces, the spellweaver noted with amusement that one of their cavalry flanks was beginning to give way. *Were they fleeing already?*

No, he realised, as he continued to watch. They were not fleeing. They were readying themselves for a charge, an incredibly foolhardy attack that would achieve nothing, except to kill them all, once Ivellios moved his own cavalry in to perform a counter charge.

Sure enough, the Knights of Caruillin attacked, charging forth and yelling battle cries at the top of their lungs. With a few hand signals and guarded words, Ivellios ordered Eldara infantry to reinforce his own flank, and for the cavalry, he was holding in reserve to prepare themselves. The army of Caruillin was about to be crushed because of one stupid act of bravado.

How very foolish, Ivellios thought, as a smile crept across his lips. *How very human.*

***

Augustin is in danger. Polnygar felt a sense of panic as she nearly lost her grip on the slender threads of the Art that they were weaving together.

Concentrate. Aelzandar's unspoken message appeared in her conscious mind without warning.

They're going to die, Polnygar protested, grabbing the tendrils of ethereal energy before they dissipated, and reknitting the fabric of the spell.

Aelzandar turned towards her. *You don't know that. The outcome of the battle still hangs in the balance.*

We need to help them. We must do something.

We are doing something, Aelzandar remonstrated; *it is only due to our work that they are alive at all. If we did not create this protection, the wizardry of the spellweavers would have killed them without any effort at all.*

We can't just stand here and watch them die!

Listen to me Polnygar, Aelzandar's words pulsed through her thoughts. *If we don't continue the spell, their cause is lost. They will die and Ivellios will be one step closer to taking the Tears. If you care for them at all you must concentrate.*

Pushing her fear deep down inside her, Polnygar did as Aelzandar instructed.

***

Onward rode Augustin, the knights alongside him. Onward they rode towards the army of Alfheim, towards the army that stretched before them, towards death or glory.

While the knights of Caruillin called out to Kytilas as they rode, Augustin's thoughts were on what was to come. The elves were assembling to meet the knight's charge, arraying a line of elven infantry on their flank, shields interlocked, ready to meet the attack, and sap it of its energy. Augustin clenched his teeth as they came closer to the elven line. Whatever the outcome, it was too late to pull back now. It was do or die.

With a deafening roar and clash of steel, the knights smashed into the elven line, the force of their charge sending elven soldiers flying, though most of the line held firm. Several knights toppled from their horses, their momentum to weak to break through the elven shield wall.

Augustin pushed forward, ignoring the failed charge, and slashed his sword downward, slicing through the helmet of an elven soldier, cleaving his foe's head in twain. More soldiers came rushing to plug the gap, and soon Augustin found himself engaged with infantry and newly arrived cavalry. His sword swung back and forth as he fought with enemies that rapidly surrounded him.

"You are a fool, human. Like all of your kind." Ivellios unleashed a torrent of magical energy, killing one knight instantly.

"Damn you, elf." Augustin attempted to interpose himself between the spellweaver and the knights. Ivellios pushed his horse towards Augustin's and then rode close enough to Augustin that the Emparian could hear the spellweaver's steady breathing above the din of the battle. Ivellios swung at Augustin with his staff, but the Emparian caught the blow with the blade of his sword.

"You know what I want." Ivellios sneered. "This could all be over in moments. Where are the Tears, Mal-halyth?"

"You'll never find them," Augustin parried another blow. "By the time we've finished with you, the Tears will have left Skurj forever."

Ivellios' face turned sour, and he pulled his horse around and moved away from Augustin. More infantry moved in to fill the gaps and engage the Emparian.

"Regroup. Regroup." Augustin yelled as he tried to disentangle himself from his foes. The elves pushed forward themselves, driving Augustin and the other knights back. Augustin heard excited cheers from the elven side, who obviously believed victory was at hand.

Then, just as things seemed dire, Augustin's unspoken prayers were answered, and the wing led by Sir Holger smashed into the elven army's weak front lines. With most of the stronger infantry withdrawn to counter Augustin's charge, Sir Holger's militia, inexperience notwithstanding, smashed their way into the elven army, nearly causing a rout, until the elven spellweavers ordered their troops back into line. The battle fell back into the blood and noise of hand-to-hand fighting, but the pressure on Augustin's force was lowered enough for them to pull back, ready for another charge. He looked at the knights. Despite the fierce carnage, only a few of them had fallen, though many of the survivors were battered and bruised, their tabards torn and bloody.

"We gave them a good battering, men," Augustin hoped to raise the spirits of the knights, even though he knew that the effect of their charge had been minimal. "But we must attack again, once more, and drive those pointy-eared bastards back to Alfheim."

"My lord Bauer," one of the knights protested. "The elves have our measure, such a charge would be suicide, even if we attacked while they are still occupied with the militia."

Augustin was silent. He knew the man spoke the truth, but he also knew that if they didn't support the militia, then all would be lost.

"Gods damn it, Agmar, where are you?" he said. In the heat of the battle, he couldn't see the Grand Master or his knights anywhere.

***

"We have them, Lord Protector," one of the spellweavers told Ivellios.

Their spells and enchantments influencing the course of the battle, the spellweavers steadily pushed their infantry forward. The human militia was outclassed and their morale near breaking point.

"Good," Ivellios said, peering intently at the faltering line. "Don't let any escape. Kill them all."

"It shall be done," the other spellweaver said.

Ivellios looked towards the enemies. He knew that the Tears were not with them. They had been hidden, but where? Surely, they were not foolish enough to leave them in Harralin. The words of that Emparian, Augustin Bauer, suddenly sprang into focus. Ivellios collected his thoughts and finally, everything started to fall into place. "Keep the archers and cavalry in reserve, pursue them when they turn tail and flee. I am placing you in command Lord Pallios. Do not disappoint me."

"Of course, my lord, I will do as you wish," said Pallios. "But where are you going?"

"To claim something that has long been mine." The Lord Protector turned his horse away, moving out to the flanks. The battle was won, now it was time to find those Tears. And he knew exactly where they would be.

***

A voice cried out in pain.

Polnygar, deep in her thoughts, at first thought it was in her own imagination, but as the careful web of incantations unravelled, she realised that one of the other three with her had been injured.

She opened her eyes with a start and released her grip on the energies, her concentration fading as she returned to the real world. Aelzandar and Laerosanna still stood, chanting the words to keep the shield active, but Vaerath knelt in the snow, a hand clutched to his stomach. His robes were soaked in blood.

"They've found us," he muttered.

"Gods." Polnygar said, rushing to support the injured spellweaver.

"It's too late for me, girl," Vaerath said. "Help...the others...the shield...it's failing."

"But you'll die." She tore off parts of his robe, attempting to staunch his wound.

The spellweaver waved her off weakly, but irritably. "My life...is done...save the others..." Vaerath's eyes rolled back in his head, and he slumped to the ground and did not move.

Frantic, Polnygar returned to her position, and attempted to grab the tattered remnants of the spell that she saw in her mind, and re-knit them, but the strands eluded her, slipping through her fingers like gossamer thread. Without Vaerath's assistance, she despaired at having any hope of keeping the shield alive.

We are losing control of the spell. Aelzandar's voice said in Polnygar's mind.

I'm trying.

Laerosanna' voice echoed in her thoughts: *It's too late.*

Concentrate. Aelzandar's voice nearly screamed in Polnygar's mind.

As the last pieces of the spell disappeared, Polnygar felt her strength fail and, pain ripping through her thoughts, she fell backwards into the snow. Aelzandar, snapping from his trance, reacted only a moment too slow to catch her.

"Vaerath is dead." Polnygar panted, as she looked up towards Aelzandar.

"I know," the archmage said softly. "I felt his passing as the spell failed."

"I'm sorry, master," Polnygar said. "I broke the chain."

Aelzandar gave her a sympathetic look and, extending a hand, pulled her up from the snow. "It is not your fault, Polnygar. Once Vaerath lost his concentration the shield would have failed no matter how hard the rest of us tried. Let us just hope that we have given our friends enough time. With the shield down they will be forced to retreat and Ivellios will be free to pursue the Tears. I just pray that Gerd is far enough away from Skurj to make Ivellios' pursuit of him fruitless."

***

Augustin watched the confusion unfolding around him. The battle raged on, as men and elves fought desperately for supremacy. In the bloody clash of wills, neither side seemed to have yet claimed victory, yet the militia of Harralin seemed perilously close to breaking under the pressure. He wrestled with whether he should help them, even though another charge would be total suicide. Even when he noticed Ivellios leave the ranks of the elven army with only two guards, Augustin still felt unable to decide. Perhaps the elves meant to draw Augustin into a trap and surround the remnants of their force. It certainly seemed overly convenient. As Augustin delayed his decision, Ivellios and his two guards quickened their pace, until they had pushed their horses forward into a gallop, heading south, to Harralin.

Suddenly there was a thunderous brought on by the galloping of horses and the clanging of swords. Agmar's knights finally arrived, catching the elven army's rear unawares. The knights, led by their Grand Master, smashed into the back ranks of the elven army, trampling the ranks of archers before the spellweaver lords knew what was happening. By the time the spellweavers had sent troops to defend against the cavalry charge, the militia had rallied and was beginning to fight back with ferocity.

"Right on time, Grand Master" Augustin breathed. "Thank the gods."

Augustin turned to the knight next to him, sizing him up. "Sir Erich, can you lead?"

The knight blinked. "Of course, my lord."

"Keep the pressure on the elves. Don't let them get away."

"My lord, what do you mean? Where are you going?"

"Going after the source of all this," Augustin said. With a triumphant yell, he turned his horse around and went off in pursuit of Ivellios.

***

"Ivellios is escaping." Polnygar pointed at the fleeing figure of the spellweaver and his attendants.

Aelzandar and Polnygar, having left Laerosanna to watch over her master's body, were riding to join the army of Harralin. Aelzandar had hoped to perhaps assist in ensuring the humans might escape the Eldara army with their lives, but now that they were close, he held out a faint hope that perhaps they could win the battle after all.

"I don't think he's fleeing my dear," Aelzandar said. "I think perhaps he's decided that the time is right to seize his prize."

"The Tears."

"Yes, we must hope that we've bought enough time for Gerd to escape," Aelzandar said.

"And if we haven't?" Polnygar said.

Aelzandar gave no response but only looked towards the battle with a steady eye. Polnygar followed his gaze and noticed the unmistakeable figure of Augustin Bauer galloping out from the army of Harralin, pursuing the escaping Ivellios.

"It's Augustin." she gasped. "He's chasing Ivellios."

"Put him out of your mind, Polnygar," Aelzandar cautioned her. "We must return to the battle."

"But he'll need help –"

"Put him out of your mind," Aelzandar repeated, a little more forcefully. "He will be fine."

Polnygar looked towards the figure disappearing over the horizon, then to the frowning Aelzandar, and back to Augustin. Then without so much as a moment's thought, she rode off after the Emparian baron, leaving the archmage Aelzandar able to do little more than call after her in vain.

***

"Can we not pick the pace up a little?" Gerd asked his attendants nervously.

The Burgomeister rode at a gentle pace, his attendants riding by his side and a wagon full of valuables being pulled behind them.

"We're going as swiftly as we can, Burgomeister," said one of Gerd's guards, a bull-necked, solid man named Lothar.

"Gods damn it," Gerd swore, as his horse trudged slowly through the snow and icy mush. "We need to be past Skurj before sunset."

142

"We'll do our best, Burgomeister," Lothar said. "But the wagon can only go so quickly."

Gerd frowned, Lothar's words taking the wind out of any petulant response the Burgomeister might have wished to give. Besides, Gerd's thoughts were still elsewhere, specifically, for his own safety. *Had Agmar done his duty?* Gerd wondered. He supposed the Grand Master was dead by now, along with the rest of his knights and the strangers – that boorish Emparian, the mad old elf mage, and the half-breed girl. The knowledge of their likely fates stirred little emotion in Gerd, except for a slight easing of his anxiety – perhaps they had bought him enough time, even if he didn't make it to the Leridian border until tomorrow.

Gerd was brought back to reality as his horse suddenly came to a total stop, nearly throwing the burgomeister from the reins. "What in the name of the Triune is going on?"

Gerd kicked the sides of his horse in frustration. The animal refused to move forward at all and tried to take a few steps backwards. The horses of Gerd's companions seemed to be behaving similarly. The soldier named Lothar dismounted and grabbing the reins of one horse after another, trying to pull them forward. Nothing the man did seemed able to move any of the animals even a single foot.

"What has got into the stupid beasts?"

"I don't know, my lord," Lothar said. "The animals seem to have gone mad. They've picked up some sort of strange scent or something. We can't move them."

"Then try again." Gerd felt uneasy by the turn of events. The cold air, framed by fog and falling snow, seemed to obscure the horizon and the sky itself, making it impossible to see into any distance at all. The road out of Skurj was disappearing under snow and ice, and the weak, cold rays of the sun struggled to shine through the clouds above. It was the perfect place for an ambush.

Lothar barked orders to the other soldiers, who dismounted as well, and attempted to move the horses forward. They were no more successful than he was and if anything, the horses seemed even more skittish and agitated. Some reared, bellowing loudly as their riders attempted to calm them.

The wind howled. Gerd, still seated on his braying horse, wrapped his fingers around the piece of the Tears nervously. A deep, unsettling feeling gripped him, almost as if there was a great source of danger nearby, one that he couldn't quite put his finger on.

"Who is it?" Gerd called out. "Who's there?" He heard hooves. "Show yourself, rider." The sound drew closer, and a vague shadow emerged from the fog and mist. Lothar and the other soldiers grabbed their weapons in anticipation.

"You." Gerd exclaimed as Augustin Bauer appeared, an exhausted look on his face, "You were supposed to be securing my escape."

Augustin rode towards Gerd, trying to catch his breath. "My lord, you must flee. Now."

Gerd was confused. "What? What do you mean? What's here?" The soldiers looked alarmed, and the horses still seemed spooked.

"No time to explain. You're in danger. Quickly, come with me."

"What have you done, Emparian?" Gerd's eyes flashed with anger. "You've led them straight here, haven't you?"

Suddenly one of the soldiers cried out in pain as an arrow shot out of the mist and punctured his neck. He slumped to the ground, lifeless, his blood turning the snow and ice red.

Lothar drew his sword. "At arms!"

Augustin once again extended his arm to Gerd, but the man was already gone. He had leapt from his horse and was now running on foot, rapidly disappearing from Augustin's vision as the mist enveloped him. "Gods damn his stubbornness."

More arrows tore through the air. One went straight past Augustin's ear, and another went straight into his horse's leg. The animal reared in pain, throwing Augustin from the saddle and onto the snow with a thud.

Three horsemen emerged from the mist. Ivellios, his robes and staff ornate, was flanked on either side by elven horse archers, who quickly reloaded their bows and dispatched more of the soldiers with amazing efficiency. Augustin, took one look at the battle taking place around him, grabbed his sword, and ran in the other direction, taking off after the fleeing Gerd von Genio.

"Gerd. Stop. They'll kill you if you don't let me help you." Augustin called through the fog.

Gerd didn't slow his pace. "They'll kill me if you do help me, you thick-skulled clod. Go and die with honour. It's all you're good for."

Augustin ran in the direction of the voice and almost collided straight into the staggering Gerd. He grabbed the burgomeister, and shook him hard, almost violently. "Listen to me, you gods-damned fool. We need to get out of here, or Ivellios will kill us both. Can you get that through your addled wits?"

Gerd whimpered a little as he tried to escape Augustin's grip. "You were supposed to have secured my escape."

"We did the best we could. Agmar has probably paid with his life. But I've taken enough orders from you to last a lifetime. You will come with me – now."

Gerd looked panic-stricken and was shaking in abject terror. At first, Augustin thought the Burgomeister was overreacting, but then, ever so slightly, he felt a tingle at the back of his neck, and he knew that there was someone else nearby, watching.

Turning, Augustin came face to face with Ivellios.

***

Polnygar rode through the mist as fast as the horse would take her. It was difficult under the foggy conditions to see Augustin, and the falling snow was rapidly erasing his horse's hoof prints. Nevertheless, Polnygar knew she was travelling in the right direction. She could feel it – almost as if she could see Augustin's route perfectly in her mind.

As she rode on further, she glimpsed a pair of figures through the mist, locked into close combat. As she came closer, she saw a third figure, crouched in the snow nearby.

"Stay back, Polnygar." Augustin was fighting fiercely, but Ivellios seemed to have the upper hand, and the Emparian Baron was being pushed back. Polnygar briefly contemplated using a spell to assist the Baron but realised that her own fatigue from the battle, and Augustin and Ivellios' proximity, made it far too difficult.

"So, the little Mal-halyth has come to watch her bed mate die?" Ivellios said. "How convenient. Perhaps she would like to share his fate?"

"Leave her alone, elf. Your quarrel is with me."

"Give me the Tears and I'll leave all of you alone," Ivellios sidestepped Augustin's blade as he spoke.

Polnygar noticed Gerd's expression change. The Burgomeister was clearly considering Ivellios' words. He reached beneath his clothes.

"No. Gerd, don't." Polnygar dismounted from her house and ran over to him.

"Don't tell me what I can and can't do little girl. The Tears are mine. To do with as I will." Gerd grabbed the gold chain from his neck, and held the Tears in his hand, turning it over and over. Polnygar tried to grab them from Gerd, but the Burgomeister knocked her out of the way. "If giving him this will save us, it's what we should do."

146

Gerd trembled as he dangled the Tears from his fingers. Ivellios' eyes met Gerd's, and the spellweaver smiled, a sense of satisfaction spread on his face. Ignoring Augustin, who stood nearby in pained resignation, Ivellios reached out for the Tears.

Polnygar, lying in the snow where Gerd's blow had sent her, opened her mouth to scream, but it was not her voice she heard.

"No." Augustin yelled, lunging forward. He caught the golden chain with his sword, and with a swing of his arm, flung the Tears over Ivellios' head into the snow. As he did, the expression on Ivellios' face turned dark. The spellweaver chanted a few words, moved his fingers, and Augustin toppled back into the snow, clutching his throat, and making gurgling noises.

Sensing an opening, Gerd leapt from where he stood and ran towards where the Tears lay, but Ivellios snarled a few more words in the arcane tongue, and the Burgomeister suddenly erupted into flames. Screaming as he burned alive, Gerd was transformed into a human torch, his body sizzling with such heat that even the snow and ice did nothing to extinguish it.

Polnygar, stunned by what she had witnessed, found herself frozen, unable to even move. She watched as Ivellios stepped over Gerd's smouldering corpse and as he bent to pluck the Tears up from the snow.

Augustin staggered to his feet. "You'll have to do better than that, turncoat!" The baron drew his sword, holding it in both hands, flesh, and metal. He charged towards Ivellios.

Polnygar called out to him. "Augustin, no!"

Ivellios held out a hand sending torrents of fire towards the baron. As quick as she could manage Polnygar countered the spell, leaving the tendrils of fire to dissipate on the hastily constructed arcane shield.

"You're out of tricks, elf," Augustin said. "Time to balance the ledger."

With a triumphant cry he swung his sword upwards. Ivellios vainly attempted a spell, but it was too late, and Augustin's blade connected with Ivellios' wrist, severing flesh and bone. The spellweaver cried out in agony as his hand swung through the air, an arc of blood following it. Augustin caught the piece of the Tears as it flew past him.

Ivellios grovelled before Augustin. "Don't kill me. Please."

Augustin reacted with scorn. "Begging for your life. Pathetic. But I think you're going to be worth more alive than dead." The baron turned his head to Polnygar. "You should call Aelzandar with your far-speaking, he'll want to be here for this."

With Augustin's attention drawn from Ivellios, Polnygar noticed the spellweaver's other hand move in the snow. She realised too late what the gesture portended. She felt a cold, clammy grip tighten around her ankles. She looked down with alarm and screamed in shock. A hideous, half-burned corpse had grabbed her ankles. It was Gerd von Genio's corpse, even if the soul that had once animated that body was long since gone.

"Don't move Polnygar, I'm coming." Augustin turned.

Polnygar tried to call out for him to stop, but it was too late. The corpse was a distraction. As Augustin moved to come to Polnygar's aid, Ivellios drew back with his remaining hand and with barely a twitch of his fingers conjured a spear of arcane energy and flung it towards Augustin. The baron never had a chance. The spear penetrated through his back, erupting from his mouth. Green sparks flew from his lips, followed by blood and he slumped to the ground.

"No!" Polnygar sent flames to the ground around her, incinerating what remained of Gerd's corpse. She rushed to assist Augustin, but Ivellios held up a hand and flung her back with tremendous arcane force. She went to stand but couldn't. Ivellios had her held in place with the Art.

"Foolish to the end," Ivellios said, snatching the piece of the Tears from Augustin's slackening grip. The spellweaver reached inside his robes and withdrew the piece stolen from Aelzandar in Macrodonia. Breaking Gerd's piece from its chain, he joined it with the piece he already had. Before Polnygar's very eyes, the two pieces fused together, as if they had both been freshly plucked from the forge. Then he waved his hand over the stump of his other arm and the bleeding instantly stopped.

Ivellios turned the newly rejoined Tears over and over in his hand and, turning to Polnygar, regarded the girl with disdain. "And so, we come to the end, girl," Ivellios said. "Alone, and trapped in the cold, desolate north. You and your master have both failed. The Tears are mine, as they always were meant to be, and now I take them to my own master. Aelzandar's failure will be complete."

"Are you going to kill me?"

Ivellios chuckled. His laugh was cold, humourless. "Of course not, my little Mal-halyth. I need someone to bear witness to the events of today. So, you will live on, and scurry back to your master. We are finished here, and I have my victory."

He rubbed his thumb over a ring he wore on his remaining hand. In an instant, Ivellios vanished before Polnygar's astonished eyes. As he disappeared whatever arcane force holding her in place dissipated.

Polnygar remained where she was for a few moments, still in shock at both the events she had witnessed, and at Ivellios' sudden disappearance. Then, her eyes red with tears, she crawled through the snow to Augustin.

"Ah," Augustin managed to croak out as he saw her.

She grabbed him, trying to staunch his wounds but he pushed her away as best he could. His hands were so weak now. He stroked her cheek with a finger, blood staining his lips. "I'm glad you stowed away on my ship."

His hands touched her gently, his fingers pointing at her heart and then, with a final jerk of his head, Augustin went still. Polnygar knew he had passed. His body was rapidly losing its warmth in the frigid air and his head lay slack on his side, neck broken by Ivellios' powers. The wound smouldered with emerald energy. Polnygar's tears splashed down on Augustin's pale, lifeless face and she knew that loss of the Tears was not the loss she cared about.

For a while she did not move, cradling Augustin's body with her hands. Her chest heaved as she sobbed, her tears falling onto Augustin's cheek. This was not fair; it was not right. This was not how things were supposed to end. She felt empty as if her heart had been torn out. Anger and hurt swirled within her.

Ivellios would pay.

CHAPTER 10

It had seemed that nothing would end the battle between the elves of Liderial and the men of Harralin except for the total annihilation of one side or the other. The Eldara certainly did their utmost to make good on Ivellios' promise to wipe out anyone who dared to defy him, so much so that, despite the Lord Protector leaving the battle before its conclusion, total victory over the humans seemed inevitable.

But fate had another hand to play.

Trumpets had signalled the beginning of the Battle for Harralin, and appropriately now they would signal its end. Across the crest of the hill a new army emerged, again bearing the banners of the elven royal house. However alongside the royal banners were those representing parley, peace and, most ominously, treason. The household guard of the royal house of Liderial had arrived and with them, King Talan himself.

Aelzandar, having taken command of the remnants of Harallin's forces, allowed himself a small note of optimism as he noticed Ivellios' own army hesitate, and pull back. Aelzandar did the same with the troops under his command. Ivellios's followers may have feared and respected their Lord Protector, and were willing to die in his name, but to go against the king himself? That would be something different altogether.

The king and his army rode between the two opposing forces. As the monarch drew closer, Aelzandar noticed that he looked tired, sick, but remarkably improved from the bedridden invalid Aelzandar had seen in Liderial.

The king's herald planted the flag of capitulation between the armies, followed by the one representing treason. It was clear to any elf what the king's orders were – end this battle now or face his royal wrath.

The elven host hesitated for a moment but then, one after another, the Eldara – spellweaver, archer, swordsman dropped their weapons and threw themselves to the ground, bowing before His Majesty's august presence. As the humans noted the actions of the elves, they gave out a mighty cheer, relieved at a reprieve that they had never thought possible. Following Aelzandar's lead, the humans too dropped the weapons to the ground.

The Eldara herald strode forth. "His Majesty requests that Aelzandar li'Ellthiros li'Geihnos come before the royal person." Aelzandar, ignoring the worried murmurs of the men around did as commanded, and approached his sovereign lord with confidence.

"His Majesty also requests the presence of the Spellweavers who lead this army in His Majesty's name." Pallios and the other spellweavers, their faces not betraying any emotions, went to join their monarch.

Aelzandar came to stand next to the king's horse and, bending down on one knee, showed the king the respect he was due. King Talan nodded in return, and his gaze went to rest upon the approaching spellweavers. As their King stared at them, they flushed, and bowed before him.

"So, you are the ones who fight in our name, then?" Talan said, his voice still weak, but not without authority.

"Your Majesty, it was the Lord Protector's will," Pallios said.

"And where is the Lord Protector? Where is Ivellios?"

The other spellweavers looked to each other nervously before Pallios responded. "He is no longer here, your Majesty. We do not know where he has gone."

"He shall be found and dealt with in time. Now all that remains is to deal with those of you who have failed us."

"Your Majesty, we thought we were carrying out your will."

"What part of our will involves making war on our neighbours?"

"My lord, Ivellios told us –"

"Silence," the king thundered. "You have spilled innocent blood in our name, spellweavers. You have committed treason."

"But we fought for your Majesty." Pallios pointed at Aelzandar. "He is the traitor. He fought against the Aspen Throne."

The king waved a hand. "He fought for the values that our throne represents, values Ivellios and those of you who blindly followed him seem to have forgotten."

Pallios flung a contemptuous glance to the men of Harralin. "They have murdered our people, your Majesty. Your people. Ivellios showed us the truth."

The king was silent for a moment. "He showed you the truth as he would have it be. But waging war requires more evidence than one man's word. You believed him because you wanted to believe him."

Pallios opened his mouth to speak again, but King Talan raised his palm, and signalled that he had heard enough. "This is my judgement. For usurping my power and waging war on the innocents, the spellweaver known as Ivellios is hereby stripped of his rank and privileges. He is to be exiled from the Aspen Kingdoms forever. His name shall no longer be spoken amongst our people. Those spellweavers who allied themselves with him are hereby also stripped of their rank and privileges, though that will be sufficient punishment for their treason, and they may remain within the Aspen Kingdom's borders."

Pallios and the other spellweavers bowed their heads in shame. "Your Majesty is wise," Pallios said, subdued.

"You may leave my presence," the king remarked. The spellweavers, bowing, left Aelzandar and the king alone.

"Down," the king commanded once the spellweavers had gone. The royal attendant helped King Talan from his horse and, after a few words from the monarch, the attendant departed, taking the horse with him. Talan turned to Aelzandar. "Now old friend, give me your arm. Let us talk."

Aelzandar held out an elbow, and the king grasped the archmage's arm firmly. "Your Majesty seems much improved. I'm glad the illness was not permanent." Aelzandar said as the two of them walked together. They moved slowly, as the king was unsteady on his feet.

"Illness. Hah." The king scoffed. "I was poisoned. That's what the queen tells me. And I have few doubts over who the culprit is."

Aelzandar nodded. "You suspect Ivellios."

"He certainly took advantage of my illness, didn't he? A rather convenient turn of events for the former Lord Protector." The king sighed. "I admire your courage, Aelzandar. One spellweaver against so many. That was brave."

"I had help." Aelzandar said.

"So I heard. You managed to recruit Vaerath into your little act of defiance." The king's eyes twinkled. "I am in a mind to reward the both of you."

"Your Majesty, Vaerath fell during the battle. He is dead. I am sorry."

The king slowed in his step. "I will honour his memory, do not doubt that. I hear he brought his apprentice with him."

"Laerosanna, yes. Why do you ask?"

"I think I will make her a spellweaver. I have need of new blood in their ranks, ones not so tied to the old ways, or sympathetic to the ideals of Ivellios."

"I am sure she will serve you proudly, your Majesty."

"Yes, well I think it's time I removed the chaff from the wheat. All these old men, sneering and strutting about, see where they have led us."

Aelzandar chuckled. "But, your Majesty, I remember when Pallios there was a babe on his mother's knee. You and I are older than any of those spellweavers of yours."

Talan laughed. "But younger in spirit."

Aelzandar sighed. "What happened today was a tragedy, your Majesty. To see such division between our people and the humans. It was a long time coming. I wonder if this divide can ever be bridged."

"Oh, I don't know, Aelzandar," the king said. "I have a feeling the divisions will heal quicker than you think." Talan held up a hand, gesturing to some distance away, where Sir Holger and Laerosanna stood close in conversation, smiling at each other.

"The future may very well be in good hands, after all," Aelzandar mused.

The conversation was interrupted by the arrival of one of King Talan's attendants, rushing forward to meet him. "Your Majesty, Your Majesty!"

"Yes, what is it?"

"Your Majesty, we've received some new arrivals. Quite a number are badly injured, some are carrying the dead."

"Oh?" said Talan. "Eldara or Human?"

"Human, mostly. But I believe one of them looks part Mal..." The attendant swallowed his words before they came out, and then tried again. "Half-Elf, she's a half-elf."

"Polnygar." Aelzandar and the king followed the attendant to the newcomers. Polnygar had arrived with the surviving soldiers of Gerd's honour guard and had brought with them the bodies of the deceased: Augustin, whose peaceful form might almost be sleeping, and Gerd's blackened and incinerated corpse, only identifiable because of the scorched signet ring that was still visible on the finger. The bodies of murdered soldiers lay on either side.

"Oh, my dear girl," Aelzandar embraced the weeping Polnygar. "I am sorry."

The king looked grave. "So many dead. I never imagined such brutality from one of my own subjects."

"He took the Tears." Polnygar's face was wet, and her eyes swollen. "He's gone. I don't know where to. He said he was going to his master."

Talan's eyes widened with surprise. "His master?"

Aelzandar drew a breath. "Your Majesty, Ivellios has turned to the Horned God. For what reason, I cannot say."

The king looked sceptical. "It's been over a century since we last heard from that cult here. Why would they emerge now?"

"I can't say for sure, but they seem to be drawn to the Tears of the Divine."

"It is vitally important that they don't find them." His words rang with alarm. "Where would Ivellios be going?"

Aelzandar considered the question "If he has gone to his master, there is only one place he could have gone. Goriinchia."

"Then he must be pursued," the king mused. "We can discuss this later. First, let us deal with the rites of the dead."

The Tears of the Divine

***

The dead were interred with the proper respect and ceremony. Since the Eldara would not accept a human ceremony for their dead, and the humans would never dream of entombing their own deceased in the manner of the elves, the Nemoi Hebu presided over the ceremony, calling upon the great Celestial Architects of his people to speed the path of the dead into the afterlife. The humans were cremated, as was customary, while the Eldara dead were embalmed in preparation for their journey back to the catacombs of Liderial.

Polnygar watched as the flames claimed Augustin's pyre. Her eyes were red and sore from crying, and she felt a curious emptiness inside as if all the meaning from her life had suddenly been wrenched away, leaving a gaping hole. She made a private vow that she would avenge his death, no matter what it took. She would find Ivellios and make him pay for what he had done here in Skurj.

Aelzandar lay a comforting hand on her shoulder, and she squeezed the hand in return.

"I can't believe he's gone," Polnygar said quietly.

"It hurts now, my dear. And it will continue to do so for a long time yet. But you will survive, you will endure. In my life, I've seen many loved ones taken from me, and each time it happens I felt that pain anew, as if for the first time. But I have survived. I've grown stronger with every loss, as will you. The names of those I have seen die still haunt me: Vanaja, Donal, Pedr, Beran, Ellinda, Cassian, friends and allies both."

Polnygar nodded, but in truth, she didn't feel stronger. She felt weaker than she ever had – more alone than ever. "What is to happen now?"

"Ivellios must be stopped. We must pursue him to wherever he flees. It is of dire importance that the power of the Tears of the Divine is never wielded by someone with a heart as dark as his."

"Ah, Aelzandar," came the king's voice. Polnygar and Aelzandar, turned to the elven monarch as he approached them, both dropping to a knee.

"There's no need for that," Talan said. "Rise, my friend."

"Your Majesty," Aelzandar gave an appreciative gesture.

"Young Polnygar." The king examined her critically, but after a few minutes, his face relaxed. "I had heard the stories of Saegras and his half-elf grandchild, but I scarcely believed it. But I see his features in your face, child. You are most striking." The king took Polnygar's hand in his own and raised them to his lips, kissing the top of her hand. Polnygar was taken aback. After the prejudice and snide comments, she endured through her entire life about her parentage, she'd never have expected the Eldara king himself to compliment her on her appearance.

"Thank you, your Majesty," Polnygar attempted a sort of half bow or curtsey.

"And so polite too," the king smiled. "Your mother has raised you well."

"Your Majesty," Aelzandar interjected. "It is of paramount importance that Polnygar and I secure speedy passage to Goriinchia at the earliest possibility. Perhaps there is a harbour town somewhere nearby – I seem to recall a fishing village to the northeast."

"That's certainly one possibility," Talan had a thoughtful look on his face, "But I have a better one. The Aspen Throne has access to something that might be exactly what you need. An ancient gate, of Soldara design, stands in the oldest portion of the city of Liderial and has been little used for thousands of years."

Aelzandar's interest was piqued. "I do recall this gate from my childhood, but my understanding was that the Soldara gates were all dormant."

"That may be an oversimplification. In the time since your youth our

158

spellweavers have made a breakthrough of sorts, and we have learned to reactivate it. They tell me that it is keyed to Emparia, and it could transport you, and any companions you wish, to the place in a blink of an eye."

For once, Aelzandar seemed lost for words. "Your Majesty. This is indeed a fortunate turn of events. I thank your graciousness in making this possible."

"It is I who should be thanking you, Aelzandar. You fought for my ideals when the rest of my subjects discarded them like table scraps."

"I am, as always, your most loyal subject, your Majesty," Aelzandar bowed. "I'll have Hebu fetch our things."

***

It was much later in the day by the time they arrived in Liderial. The humans of Harralin had returned to their own homes, so it was only Aelzandar, Polnygar and Hebu who accompanied the elven king back to Alfheim. Aelzandar and Polnygar rode on either side of the king, at the monarch's specific request. Despite the status of their host there seemed to be little fanfare at their arrival. Polnygar suspected that the king himself had requested that his army's return not be celebrated as a victory. Once they had entered the city, the army was disbanded. Polnygar, Aelzandar and Hebu headed on to the portal with the king and his chastened spellweavers. The Nemoi was not pleased to be once again loaded down with Aelzandar's books and scrolls.

The Soldara gate was in the royal district of Liderial, right near the Palace of Karn-Raka, but sealed off from the public with a tall wall and large, ornate bronze door. The king, taking a polished gold key from his attendant, unlocked the way to the Soldara gate.

"This is it, the last legacy of Dasarius, Lord of the Soldara," Talan said in awe. Dasarius was the legendary spellweaver who had led the Soldara departure from Liderial many thousands of years ago, "It has stood idle for millennia, but today it shall be quiet no more."

The great, crumbling arch of stone towered over them, more than thirty feet tall. Glyphs and sigils decorated its stonework, along with faded murals depicting the history of the Soldara and their leaders.

"Spellweavers, activate the portal. Your king commands you." As the king spoke, the spellweavers went to work, taking up their positions around the Soldara gate. "Now, you three. If you would just take your position under the portal."

"I hope the advice concerning the destination was accurate, your Majesty," Aelzandar said wearily, as he led Polnygar and Hebu under the arch.

The king nodded and raised his hand, signalling for the spellweavers to begin the incantations. Within moments the air filled with the sound of elven chants. A low humming followed; then with an explosion of light and colour, the portal flared into life.

The king, the spellweavers and the city of Liderial began to disappear from Polnygar's sight and in an instant the three of them had left Skurj completely.

***

Polnygar's eyes took a while to adjust. The white marble buildings and fluttering banners of Liderial had given way to the lush greenery of a temperate forest.

"Are we here?" Polnygar's head was spinning, and she felt slightly ill, a sensation she put down to the operation of the Soldara gate.

"I believe we are, my dear," Aelzandar said.

"It certainly seems warmer," Polnygar loosened her fur cloak.

"What a horribly primitive looking place," Hebu said. "Makes me look back fondly on Macrodonia."

"Well, they may not be great monument builders like the Macrodonians, Hebu, but I believe Emparians have a certain charm of their own."

Hebu sniffed. "You always were inordinately fond of dumb animals, Aelzandar."

"Ouch." Polnygar cried out. "The bracer, it's hurting my arm. It's as if it's, I don't know, shrunk."

She showed her wrist to Aelzandar, who examined the magic armband carefully. "So, it has – most peculiar. It may be a side-effect of the Soldara gate. A sort of magical feedback."

"Can you take it off?" Polnygar said. "It stings."

Aelzandar ran a finger over the bracer and whispered a few words. Instantly the bracer opened with a snap and fell to the ground. He picked it up. "I'd best hold on to it now. When I get a moment, I can probably fix it. For now, let's continue."

"Where are we exactly?" said Polnygar.

"Hard to say," Aelzandar said. "I wasn't even aware of a Soldara gate in Emparia, let alone where exactly it'd lead."

As they looked around, Polnygar spotted a nearby road, winding through the forest. It seemed to be well-travelled. "Over here."

"Excellent." Aelzandar said. "A road. This means we're not too far away from civilisation. We'll be able to find a nearby village."

"What? Are we going to walk there?" Hebu did not seem pleased by the idea.

"Oh, Hebu, do try to at least feign an interest. And don't drop those books."

"Yes, master," Hebu juggled the two tomes before finding a way to carry them comfortably.

Polnygar heard something. "Someone's coming."

Aelzandar nodded. "Yes, I hear them too. Move off the road."

The three of them moved to the side of the road, just as a wagon came around the bend, a horse leading it at a steady pace through the forest.

"Looks like a merchant," said Aelzandar. "Perhaps he can point us in the right direction."

The wagon came closer, and Aelzandar shouted out a greeting. "Hail, my friend. Perhaps we might trouble you for directions to the nearest town?"

The wagon came to a stop, and the man in the front of it, looked at the strangers sceptically. "These are the Goriinchian marches, friend. You'd do well to get yourself somewhere safe. It's never a good idea to dally here. The Goriinchians are vicious. I'm on to Wishapton, you should get moving."

Aelzandar responded in kind. "Your advice is well taken, my friend. I am Aelzandar, and these are Polnygar and Hebu. Perhaps we might accompany you to Wishapton? We have no transportation of our own, and there would be strength in numbers."

The merchant looked them over and seemed to think about the offer for a few minutes. Finally, he nodded and motioned for them to climb into the wagon. "You're right. I would appreciate some help in case I encountered a few Goriinchians on the way there. Keep alert."

"We will strive to do our utmost." Aelzandar helped Polnygar and Hebu into the wagon.

After a few minutes they were off on their way, and Polnygar soon relaxed in time with the gentle rocking of the wagon as it navigated the bumpy and rocky road through the forest. "So, I take it you gentle-folk aren't locals then." The merchant kept his eyes on the road after addressing the trio.

"It must be the ears," Hebu said dryly.

The merchant laughed. "Well, I don't take you for Saldarri. You don't sound like them, and you don't look the part, really. Hair is too dark."

"We're travellers," Aelzandar offered. "Here on business."

"Strange place to be doing business, friends. Out here in the marches."

"Let's just say we're trailing someone."

"Bounty hunters, eh?" the merchant said. "Well, I know better than to pry where I'm not wanted."

"Wise choice," Aelzandar said.

"The name's Egbert, by the way. Don't believe I'd introduced myself properly."

"What do you sell?" Polnygar looked at the darkened back of the wagon.

"Oh, silks, wool, cloth. Quite a demand for these sorts of things in Wishapton these days. The Lord Ap'Lydin's done quite a lot for that town."

"Ap'Lydin?" Polnygar found herself shocked at the sound of a familiar name. "There are Ap'Lydins around here?"

"Aye, this is the southern-most shire of the Earl of Genio's lands. The Earldom goes all the way from here, up the coast to Genio."

"I see." Aelzandar grimaced as the wagon bumped over a hole in the path. The wagon buckled, nearly sending the archmage's head into the wooden beam at the roof. "Does the earl travel this far south?"

Egbert chuckled. "Not likely these days. The earl's been dead for a year, or thereabouts. Died during the siege, or so I heard."

"What siege is this?" asked Aelzandar.

Egbert looked at them sceptically. "Huh, you fellows are definitely new here, aren't you? The siege of Wishapton – those Goriinchians came up from the south, destroying anything that they could find. They were stopped right here, the earl himself leading the battle. He won the day but lost his life." Egbert was silent for a moment. "Poor bastard. Anyhow, the earl had no sons, so his daughter ended up heiress in the north, while they gave the southern lands to some cousin. -One of the queen's new knights, I think."

"What's his name?" Polnygar tried to hide her eagerness.

"How in the name of the Underworld should I know?" Egbert sounded peevish. "He's an Ap'Lydin, that's for certain. Beyond that, I'm not exactly on first name basis with him."

"You'll have to forgive my friend's curiosity," Aelzandar used a soothing tone. "But she does have a good reason for her questions."

"Oh? What's that?" Egbert turned to Polnygar expectantly.

"Well," Polnygar said. "I'm an Ap'Lydin myself."

Egbert laughed. "Hah, and I'm the Grand Duke of Lerid." The humour drained from his face when he realised Polnygar was serious. "You're telling the truth?"

"She wouldn't lie about that. I can vouch for her," Aelzandar said.

"And who are you to vouch for anyone?"

"He is the archmage," Hebu declared. "Lord of the Nine Orders. Grand Master of Wizardry."

"Truly?" Egbert looked Aelzandar up and down.

"Surely you recognise the staff, my good man," Aelzandar said.

The merchant shook his head. "The ways of mages are not any of my business, and I know little of their leader save his reputation. But I know enough to know that you wouldn't dare claim to be that man if it wasn't true. So, she is truly an Ap'Lydin? Well, I'll be. Now I can see the true reason for your journey."

Aelzandar waved aside the man's suspicions. "Truth be told, it is merely a coincidence. And what we told you in the first instance was accurate enough. But perhaps if this Ap'Lydin in Wishapton is truly kin of my young friend here, then we shall find our mission itself to be much easier."

"Well, I'm happy to be of help." Egbert whipped the reins and urged the wagon onwards.

CHAPTER 11

Bellaydin drifted in a sea of stars.

He knew he was dreaming, despite how real the scene in front of him seemed and how each one of his senses was inflamed, stimulated and burning with energy. A landscape drifted in like mist in front of him. Even before it fully could materialise, Bellaydin recognised where he was. Since the vision granted to him by the Seeress of Goriinchia, he had dreamed of this place with increasing frequency. Now, it recurred every few days.

The ground solidified beneath his feet, and the sky took shape, and Bellaydin knew that once again he was once again standing in the hills of southern Goriinchia, overlooking the site of a battle between the ancient Goriinchians and their enemies, the Fey. Other things took shape before him, and Bellaydin's heart skipped a beat. He saw William's body, bloody and mangled, as clear as on the day he had died over a year ago. Only now, in his cousin's cold arms, he also saw the corpse of Maria Ap'Lydin, William's daughter, similarly bruised, bloody, and still.

Behind the dead stood Polnygar, looking straight ahead and right through Bellaydin, as if he didn't exist. Her face was taut, drawn, her eyes filled with tears. Yet she did not move, she did not speak. She looked almost as lifeless as the corpses in front of her. Bellaydin knew better than to try to catch her attention or try to get any reaction at all. In all iterations of this dream, Polnygar had never responded to his calls.

"The blood of Lydin thins," Bellaydin heard himself say, but it was not his voice that came out of his mouth. Someone else, some other being, spoke through him. Every time he dreamed, he was aware of this presence, but its identity still remained unknown to him.

"Those who burnt the topless towers of Seldaria will soon be no more," Bellaydin said again, the alien words springing to his lips with no warning. "That which is broken will soon be whole again." The words came rapidly now, building to a crescendo. "And you will be the last."

An unsettling feeling came over Bellaydin. *The last.* Dallen Withers had taunted him with that exact phrase. He kept hearing it in his dream. But what did it mean? The last of what? And what was broken? He tried to speak, to ask questions, but he seemed to have no control over his own body. He was trapped, a prisoner in his own mind.

***

He awoke with a start; his breath ragged and sweat dripping from his forehead. Rising from his bed, Bellaydin went to the washbasin, splashing water on his face, and wiping his head down with a cloth. Another night of interrupted sleep, of rest plagued with vivid dreams and terrible nightmares. He wondered if he was losing his mind and cracking under the pressure.

He still grieved deeply for Maria. Losing his cousin's daughter felt like losing William all over again. Bellaydin's grief was particularly reinforced by the guilt he felt; he had failed to keep the promise he made to his dying cousin. The consequences of that terrible day had echoed around Emparia.

Haakon de Morcor, Duke of Alariat, suffered greatly, feeling responsible for not foreseeing the treachery of the soldiers he had hand-picked. Wulfric Highcrown, Duke of Oldharbour, had become even more fanatical in his hatred towards the faith of the Horned God. He was openly persecuting such worshippers, detaining them without cause and trying, in vain, to extract information from them about alleged plots and conspiracies. There was even talk that Wulfric was trying to convince the queen to reinstate the ban on the worship of the Horned God. Bellaydin didn't put much credence in those tales. In truth, the faith was too widespread to stamp out now, especially in the south of Emparia, along the border with Goriinchia. Wishapton itself seemed to have a small, but growing community of the faithful, but Bellaydin had not yet seen any sign that they were anything but loyal to the Emparian crown.

Sighing, Bellaydin entered his study. He hoped some of his research might help take his mind off current affairs and relieve some of the awful stress that was obviously leading to his nightmares.

The excavation of the ruins under Wishapton had been going for many weeks now, and the workers had uncovered more of the supposed Eldara armour. In fact, amongst the twisted pieces of rusted metal, Bellaydin now had what he estimated to be a complete set of armour. Excited by the development, he had mounted the armour in his study so he could examine it further at his leisure. He had since discovered that the armour parts were not hollow. Instead, strange pieces of metal filled their interior, broken and snapped off in various sections. The metal pieces seemed intended to join the bits of armour together, though this felt ridiculous to Bellaydin. How was anyone supposed to wear the damn thing then? Although another thought quickly came to him. Perhaps the armour was never intended to be worn. Perhaps, instead, the armour could be suspended and animated solely using the Art, without a living human inside. This would certainly fit in with a probable Eldara origin – the elven people were known for their use of the

Art, and based on what Bellaydin remembered from his youth in Aderilund, a magical, walking man of metal would not be beyond their talents.

Walking men of metal – something about that notion seemed familiar, almost as if he had seen something like that before. He looked about the study, examining each of the paintings in turn until he came to one labelled "The Last Citadel". It was a stylised depiction of a large group of men attacking a tower. Just as Bellaydin had expected, the tower was shown to be defended by a vast array of bronze men, or more correctly, animated bronze armour, just like the set that hung in Bellaydin's study. As he studied the picture closer, it dawned on him that he had witnessed this scene many times before – in the recurring dreams that had been plaguing him. This was the battle the Seeress had shown him back in Goriinchia, in what seemed like a lifetime ago. What had she called it? *The War Against the Fey.* The Goriinchians had fought the Fey Lords of ancient Karlicia, and the same Fey had sent their own minions against the primitive humans who had dared defy them. It now seemed likely that these minions were the bronze men of metal that Bellaydin had uncovered under Wishapton. Bellaydin felt a sense of elation as this ancient puzzle was finally coming into shape. It felt like he had a secret, eldritch mystery that was about to be solved. He felt a sudden compulsion to touch the picture, to feel the texture of the canvas. He traced his fingers over the outline of the painted tower and to his surprise; he found that he could depress the part of the painting depicting the tower. Instinctively, he pushed the tower and as he did so, he heard stone scraping against stone behind him.

Bellaydin turned to find that a section of the study's wall had slid open, revealing a previously hidden section of Wishapton castle. Bellaydin was taken aback – no one had ever told him anything about hidden passages within the castle. Had William known about it? Had Bellaydin's parents known?

Cautiously, Bellaydin entered the newly revealed antechamber, unsure of what he might find. The interior was a clutter. Two large bookcases dominated the small and claustrophobic room, and dozens of scrolls and stacks of parchment littered the floor.

"What in the name of the gods is all this?" Bellaydin said as he stepped over the untidy floor. In the far corner, several framed paintings were stacked carelessly, coated with dust. Seized by curiosity, he pulled out one of the frames for a look. When he realised what he was looking at, he nearly tripped over his own feet.

The painting depicted three figures. The two in the background were cloaked, their faces hidden in the shadow. They flanked a third figure in the foreground who, though wearing a similar robe, had his hood down so his face was visible. Bellaydin had no problem recognising this man. Shortly after Bellaydin had arrived in Wishapton, William Ap'Lydin had pointed the man out in a different portrait. Bellaydin was looking at Alusine Ap'Lydin, his father. The surge of happiness he felt at discovering a new portrait of his father ebbed quickly as he studied the marks on the robe Alusine was wearing. Bellaydin had seen the same, ubiquitous symbol everywhere in Goriinchia and on the bodies of Maria's assassins. It was the mark of the Horned God.

Alusine Ap'Lydin was a follower of the Horned God.

Bellaydin found himself lost for words. Reeling, he stared at the picture, hoping that his eyes were mistaken, and it would turn out that the man in the picture was someone else entirely, but he knew that there was no mistaking it. It was Alusine Ap'Lydin, his father. Bellaydin could even see echoes of his own features in this proud, dark man who stared back from the canvas – the same dark, unruly hair, identical black, sunken eyes. Even the man's stance so reminded Bellaydin of himself that he may as well have been looking at his own reflection.

Maybe it was a trick, a juvenile joke, a puerile attempt at parody of some sort, and Bellaydin's father was innocent of the charges Bellaydin's own mind already wanted to lay against him. Bellaydin cast the portrait aside and started to rummage through the rubbish strewn about the room hoping to find something, anything, that might exonerate Alusine Ap'Lydin. The papers scattered around the room were of no help. Although they may have been written by Bellaydin's father – they were certainly written in his handwriting – they contained nothing of interest, being mainly records of diplomatic meetings, store inventories, and some amateurish poetry.

Bellaydin found a cabinet, pushed up against one wall, and yanked it open, nearly tearing one of the doors off the rusted hinges. Inside was a torn and mouldy cloak, black in colour. Bellaydin pulled it out and his heart sunk as he ran the cloth through his fingers. The clear, unmistakable emblem of the Horned God was emblazoned on it, just like in the painting. The sleeves and hem of the cloak were stained with a dried dark liquid. Was it blood? Bellaydin shuddered at the thought.

There was something else in the cabinet, behind the cloak. Bellaydin reached down and pulled out a small box, sealed with a heavy rusted lock. The lock still held, but Bellaydin didn't think it would be that hard to open. Taking it to his study, he smashed the box on the side of the table and broke the lock open.

The box had housed tattered pages of parchment. At some point in the past someone had attempted to burn them – the pieces were scorched at the sides – but then had thought better of it and rescued the pieces. The writing, again, in Alusine's steady hand, was still readable.

Bellaydin picked up the first page and read the words with dread. "The Journal of Alusine Ap'Lydin, Heir of Lydin."

Bellaydin trembled. It chilled him to realise that the small scraps in his hand could provide the first true insight into his father's mind.

I always knew I was destined for something greater.

The Tears of the Divine

My brother Caradoc was content to follow the path that had been set for him. Happy to walk in the footsteps of the countless Ap'Lydins that had come before, willing to do nothing to set him apart from any of those men.

This would never do for me.

Charcoal obscured the next few lines of text, but Bellaydin continued reading as soon as the writing became legible again.

My father or brother must never know what I have been told. A man came to me, a younger son of an unimportant knight, and explained the future that was mine to take and grasp. I heard of ancient and terrible prophecies. I heard of glorious pasts. I heard of grand destinies. And there, somewhere in the middle of it all, was me. The Heir of Lydin, they said. The final and most perfect messenger of the Horned God.

The next scrap seemed to interrupt Alusine's journal, and, although written in his hand, did not seem to Bellaydin to be Alusine's words. Or perhaps Bellaydin desperately did not want them to be.

REJOICE, ye people of the world, and have FAITH, for the dawning of a new age is at hand. I am the Horned God, King of Kings, God of Gods, Holiest of the Holies. On heaven and earth, who is like thy LORD?

Yea, I shall spread my hand upon the earth, and on my chosen people. I shall PROTECT them from the unbelievers, the blasphemers, and the heretics. They shall be filled with WISDOM and will be given the power to smite their enemies and confound the schemes of the INFIDELS. The Tyrant of the MORTAL world shall be punished, removed from his power and the fruit of his vine will WITHER. Yea, just as his gods are brought low, so shall he.

Yea, even those who doubted me shall see a great light. I shall raise the Heir of LYDIN to the throne of Kings and shall install him at the head of the everlasting kingdom. So shall the DAY OF RECKONING fall upon the land, and the Heir will lead armies in my name against the infidels. And He shall RULE in my name, and his deeds will echo my WILL. He shall endure great HARDSHIP, yea, even shall he lose that which he loves most, but in the end, my CHOSEN will prevail.

And so shall the false gods be cast down, their idols smashed on the floors of the temples, their names wiped from the minds of the people. The world will enter a new age of ENLIGHTENMENT, where my church will guide the world towards perfect utopia, and where the follies of the PAST will be put aside and forgotten. All peoples will acknowledge the one TRUE god, yea, even the HEATHENS who scorn my name.

His head spinning as he tried to take in all the new information, Bellaydin continued reading the pages of his father's journal.

If I am to achieve the destiny that I have been told awaits me, I must join the cult of the Horned God. There is no other way. I must keep this a secret, for the followers of the Horned God are distrusted by Emparians, due to their connection to Goriinchia. This is paranoid nonsense. The Horned God is greater than the petty rivalries between the peoples of these lands. He is greater than all the kings and empires of the world put together. He is the one true lord, the one true master of all, the guardian, the protector, the beginning, and end.

The next few pages were too charred to read, so Bellaydin skipped ahead.

It has taken me years to ascend to the rank and position that I have, but last night I finally had the chance to meet the great leader in person. Simon Enlim, prophet, visionary, harbinger of the future that is to come. I have shared with him my ambitions, my hopes, my dreams, and in return, he asked how far I would go to achieve these. I responded that I would do anything, and he told me that it was just as well, for I would soon be tested.

The path to greatness is littered with sacrifice, both personal and otherwise. Such challenges may break the weak, but I am strong. I will not falter. I will do that which is necessary.

The next piece was written in a more hurried hand as if Alusine was under great stress and torment when he wrote it.

The Tears of the Divine

I have done terrible things. I know that now. I have been soaked in the blood of the innocent - men, women, and children. I'm not proud, but these are things I did gladly, for I had hoped for the destiny they promised me.

But no more. They asked for that which I could not give. My own blood. My mind rebelled, and I realised there were some things I could never do. Have I saved my own soul? Have I ensured that I will escape eternity in the pit of the Underworld? No, I am still damned. My life is forfeit. My former brethren will never forgive my apostasy. But my line will live on.

There was only one piece of parchment left, a small scrap, singed and burnt.

He was my friend. We were like brothers. But they give the order, and he obeys. Oh, gods in heaven above, preserve me. They are coming.

He sat down, exhausted mentally and emotionally. The recent revelations had shaken him to the core. The father he had idolised, and dreamed about a good portion of his life, was not the man he had imagined. After reading Alusine's journal, the old, idealised picture of his father had been shattered forever. From what he'd been told, he had thought his father an innocent victim of the cult, someone who was just in the wrong place at the wrong time, but now it looked less a tragic accident than a deliberate attempt by the cult to punish a man who had once been one of their own. Troublingly, the journal hinted at deaths – or rather, murders – in which his father had been involved. The handsome, romantic hero Saegralanna had fallen in love with was fast becoming a myth, if indeed he had ever existed at all. All this time Alusine Ap'Lydin was living a double life, seemingly kept secret from everyone close to him. Another thought came to Bellaydin – his mother, Eleanor, had also died at the hand of the cult leader Simon Enlim. She was innocent, a mere unfortunate victim of her husband's dark, secret identity. And what of the reference to "his own blood"? What was it the cult demanded that finally caused Alusine to reconsider? The death of a close relative? A parent? A sibling? Or perhaps a

175

child. Polnygar or Bellaydin himself. Bellaydin suddenly felt sick.

He tried to rationalise his father's actions. Surely he wasn't an evil man, merely a weak, misguided one. The thought didn't console Bellaydin. In fact, it made him feel even worse. If so much of what he knew of his father was false, how could he trust anything he'd been told about Alusine Ap'Lydin? Who was this friend his father's journal spoke of? Enlim? Was he really a friend? Or was it someone else? Perhaps Simon Enlim hadn't murdered his parents after all. Perhaps...

Bellaydin shook his head. He did not wish to even entertain the notion that was starting to form in his mind. It would not do to dwell on it. He was jumping to the worst possible conclusions based on incomplete information. He had to put it out of his mind and focus on other things.

***

The next few days passed slowly as Bellaydin busied him with the minutia of his everyday life. Excavation work continued on the ruins below Wishapton, with the workers uncovering more ancient relics, including shards of broken pottery, and twisted pieces of ornamental metal. Carfel kept Bellaydin updated on the progress of the diggings, as well as relaying information of other recent events.

"I want to make sure no one goes looking down in those ruins without my knowledge, Carfel," Bellaydin said, midway between his evening meal.

"Of course, sir. I'll have the diggers erect a barrier around the entrance once they finish for the day."

Bellaydin nodded. "Good. I don't want anything stolen if we can help it, I have a feeling there's quite a lot of interesting things down there. I'd prefer it if I was the one to find them."

"I'll make sure of it, sir."

"Excellent - now, what of other news?"

"The Privy Council continues to debate the matter of the succession and the prospects of a marriage for the Queen."

"Yes, yes," Bellaydin let the irritation show in his voice. "What else?"

"I do hesitate to tell you this, sir since at the moment it is little more than rumour or idle chatter, but I have been hearing some disturbing reports coming through from the Goriinchian marches."

"Rumours? What rumours?"

Carfel furrowed his brow as if he wasn't very confident of the rumour he was about to repeat. "There is talk that the Goriinchians have rebuilt their armies and are once again preparing to invade Emparia."

Bellaydin looked surprised. "Oh, come now. That's ridiculous." He waved his hand dismissively, "Where would they get the numbers? They barely have enough men left to till their fields, let alone to build an army."

"That being true sir, the stories that are circulating are telling of new armies mustering deep in the south. It may be prudent to be cautious."

Bellaydin gave a rueful expression. "I suppose so." He chewed a lip. "It's probably best to keep our eyes open for the next few months."

Though Bellaydin's words expressed concern with the alleged renewed Goriinchian threat, his mind was still obsessively going over the revelations about his father's secret life. Since the discovery Bellaydin had been almost eternally distracted.

"Something on your mind, sir?" Carfel said.

"Oh, no, it's nothing. Don't worry. You are dismissed, Carfel."

***

Later that evening Bellaydin received an unexpected visitor. With far less fanfare than usual, the Duke of Alariat arrived at Wishapton, forgoing the usual honour guard. It was a cautious, low-key visit, but Haakon de Morcor greeted Bellaydin as warmly as he ever had.

"Bela, my boy," Haakon embraced the younger man. "How have you been?"

"Not so well, I must confess." Bellaydin offered Haakon a seat, which the older man accepted, and then took a seat himself.

"I understand my boy." Haakon paused as Carfel approached with two goblets of mead, offering one to each of the men. "Thank you, my friend." Haakon took the drink, watching and smiling as Bellaydin did likewise. "The tragic death of Maria weighs on my mind too, Bela. I feel culpable for the bloodbath in Genio, I can assure you. If I had my time again, I would do things very differently. I was a fool to be so trusting."

Bellaydin closed his eyes to avoid dwelling on painful memories. Haakon's comments did not comfort him. Bellaydin knew deep down, that Maria's blood was on his own hands. Still, it was not just Maria's death that was upsetting him, and Haakon deserved to know the truth.

"There's something else, Haakon," Bellaydin said. "I've found something out about my father. Something I... well, it makes me rethink a lot of my feelings about him."

Haakon raised an eyebrow. "What do you mean?"

"Wait here," Bellaydin dismissed Carfel and rose from his seat before disappearing into his study. He emerged only a few moments later with the box that contained the burnt remnants of the journal of Alusine Ap'Lydin and handed it to Haakon.

"What is this?" Haakon asked. "It's half burnt."

"Just read it." Bellaydin watched Haakon as the old duke read the various scorched pieces of parchment. As Haakon read his face grew darker and the smile on his face disappeared, slowly turning into a frown.

His brow furrowed and creased; Haakon looked up at Bellaydin. "Are you sure these are your father's?"

"It is his handwriting," Bellaydin said. "Don't you recognise it? I'm surprised you never knew."

Haakon looked wistful. "We all have our secrets, Bela." His voice had a weary edge. "But I never dreamed your father kept one like this."

"You never even suspected anything like this? How could you have not known?" Bellaydin felt the anger rise in him, and he practically shouted the accusation.

"Please, Bela, forgive me. I suppose I could never have thought anything like that about my closest friend."

Haakon looked deeply hurt and Bellaydin, slightly ashamed of his outburst, sank back into his chair. "I guess it doesn't matter anymore anyway."

Haakon rose from his chair, and laid a hand on Bellaydin's shoulder, comforting him. "Your father made a mistake in his life, Bellaydin – one single mistake. It doesn't make him a terrible person."

"A single mistake? In his writings he says he's killed many. Men. Women. Children."

Haakon nodded. "That may be. We will never know the truth of it. He repented, though, he knew he was –" Suddenly Haakon cried out in pain, clutching his chest.

"Haakon? Haakon." Bellaydin cried out as the older man slumped to the floor, his face contorted in pain. "Haakon. Haakon. Can you hear me?"

179

Bellaydin cradled the older man in his arms, calling for Carfel.

"Sir, how can I help?" Carfel said as he rushed into the room.

"We need to get the Duke of Alariat to one of the rooms. Fetch the healer."

"Yes, sir." With Carfel's help, Bellaydin assisted the coughing and groaning Haakon to one of the guest rooms and then sent Carfel on to fetch the healer.

"I'm sorry to trouble you, Bela," Haakon said weakly. "Just a bit of a turn. I'm not as young as I once was."

"No," Bellaydin said. "It's much more serious than that. You are ill, Haakon, and you have been for quite some time. These spasms of yours. Something is doing this to you. Some illness, affliction, or the like - it is not natural, nor normal."

Haakon leant his head back on the pillow. "What do any of us know of the normal world anymore? All has changed. I am a stranger in a strange land. My heart weeps for that which has been lost. Wulfric, Wulfric, where is Wulfric?" Haakon, delirious with pain, continued to babble incessantly. Bellaydin patted the older man's hand reassuringly, even though he was quietly alarmed by the sudden turn Haakon had taken.

"He's not here, Haakon, you're in Wishapton," Bellaydin reassured him.

"Wulfric is dead. He died years ago. The man who wears his skin is a stranger, an imposter." Haakon's voice began to fade, as if he was close to losing consciousness. Suddenly, he leant over the bed and coughed violently. He looked half-mad with pain, his eyes wide, the pupils large and black

"Easy, easy, Haakon. You need to rest." Bellaydin caught the older man.

Haakon shook his head, and withdrew something from his clothes, pressing it into Bellaydin's palm before collapsing back on the bed. "Use this – pierce the fog of lies – see the truth..."

Haakon's voice died off as he passed out, exhausted. Within a few moments, the healer arrived and, after a few minutes' examination, decided that Haakon just needed bed rest. Accepting the diagnosis, Bellaydin left the duke in peace, and retired to his own room. As he did so, he opened his hand and saw that Haakon had passed him a spyglass – the same one that Bellaydin had been given by William over a year ago.

Bellaydin was puzzled. Just what did Haakon want him to do with it? He'd said Wulfric was an imposter and that Bellaydin had to "see the truth". What truth was Haakon referring to? Bellaydin put it out of his mind – Haakon was clearly sick, delirious. It was probably a sort of fevered delusion. For now, he would try to do as Haakon, and get some rest.

CHAPTER 12

The next day Bellaydin rose early, eating a light morning meal as he watched the sun rise. Haakon, though conscious, was still not feeling well, and the healers advised him to stay in bed.

"Sir, we have some new arrivals today." Carfel bowed.

"Who is it?" Bellaydin said.

"A battalion of Her Majesty's private guard, sir, led by the Duke of Oldharbour. They are requesting lodging in Wishapton."

Bellaydin looked up at Carfel, surprised. Wulfric Highcrown? What was he doing here? "Tell them I'll be down in a few minutes."

"Very good sir," Carfel nodded and departed.

Bellaydin adjusted himself in the mirror before heading outside to meet the newcomers. He found them below, milling about the courtyard, a full complement of soldiers.

"So glad you found the time to come down and greet us, Sir Bellaydin," the Duke of Oldharbour said as Bellaydin approached. His tone was sarcastic, biting.

Bellaydin noted with interest that unusually Wulfric seemed to be missing his ever-present companion, Kahlaf el-Lahn. Bellaydin shook the duke's hand. "It's always an honour to welcome you to Wishapton, your Grace, but I don't see your Ahktarran bondsman anywhere."

Wulfric raised an eyebrow. "Kahlaf could not accompany me here today. Duties of another nature occupy him."

"What sort of duties might those be?"

"Duties that need not concern you," Wulfric said.

"Yes, well, to what do I owe the pleasure of this visit?"

"The security of the throne, nothing less," Wulfric said.

"What do you mean?"

"Don't be obtuse, Ap'Lydin." Wulfric pointed at Bellaydin, his tone aggressive. "You of all people should have heard of the new armies being marshalled in Goriinchia."

"Those are just wild rumours."

Wulfric frowned. "Don't be so foolish. There are too many reports to discount these stories as mere hearsay and rumour. We need to be certain. We need the truth."

"And just how do you propose we find that?" Bellaydin said.

The soldiers eyed him cautiously as Wulfric stepped aside and nodded at them to bring something forward. The squad of soldiers parted as they led an unkempt man to Bellaydin. The prisoner, a burly bearded man with a tangled mass of red hair snarled and grunted at the soldiers as they yanked and pulled on the chains that held him.

"A Goriinchian?" It unsettled Bellaydin that the prisoner looked at him with hatred in his eyes.

"He was found scouting near the southern marches," Wulfric said. "A forward scout sent by his people, no doubt."

"Well, have you learned anything? What has he told you?"

Wulfric looked at the prisoner, his frown giving way to a thin smile. "Nothing yet. But he will. I have various methods of persuasion. He will talk, or he will die."

"What are you implying, your Grace?" Bellaydin blurted out. "Torture?"

Wulfric ignored the question. "Take the prisoner below the keep. I will see you there, Bellaydin."

As Bellaydin watched, the duke and his men departed with the prisoner to the dungeons of the keep. Bellaydin's mood turned dark. He didn't like the way the duke was treating him; he knew he was being patronised. Wulfric had taken it on his own initiative to torture this prisoner, and he would do it on Bellaydin's property.

"Sorry about all this,"

Bellaydin turned around and saw a familiar face. "Sir Geoffrey." Bellaydin embraced his friend. "What are you doing here? Wulfric didn't rope you into some mission of his again."

"No, I learned my lesson about that," Geoffrey said. Talthas was next to Geoffrey and gave Bellaydin a bow and a smile.

Geoffrey lowered his voice and leant closer to Bellaydin. "I'm here on Her Majesty's explicit instructions. The Privy Council have their concerns about Wulfric's motives and plans. They've sent me to watch over him for them."

"So, you're a spy?" Bellaydin raised an eyebrow.

"Of sorts. Mainly I'm just here to keep him out of trouble."

"Good luck with that. You'll need it." Bellaydin said.

"So, do you believe these rumours about the so-called new armies of

Goriinchia?

"Nonsense," said Talthas. "They've no men left."

"That's about the right of it." Geoffrey laughed. "Let's just say that unless the Goriinchians have turned to recruiting women, children and cripples, I don't know where they've found the soldiers for any armies, new or otherwise."

"I guess they believe the Horned God will provide," Bellaydin couldn't help but smirk.

"Well, the Goriinchians had better hope so," Geoffrey chuckled. "Otherwise, I think Ygarak's next invasion will fail just the like the ones before it." He suddenly stopped. "Perhaps it's just my imagination, but you don't seem to be your normally ebullient self. Something troubling you, my friend?"

Bellaydin forced a smile. "I'm fine. I've just had a lot on my mind lately."

Geoffrey put a hand on Bellaydin's shoulder reassuringly. "Haven't we all, my friend. Don't worry, it builds character."

"Thanks Geoffrey. We'd best go and see Wulfric before he attempts anything you or I are going to regret."

"Don't you mean something that he'll regret?"

"I know what I meant, Geoffrey," Bellaydin said.

***

The keep was dark and cold, the only illumination being the glow of the torches at the far end of the chamber. Bellaydin had never been here before. As if reading his mind, Geoffrey whispered to Bellaydin. "William never liked this place. He found it unpleasant."

"I am pleased that you have decided to join us, Bellaydin," Wulfric said without turning around, "There will be things said here today that you too will need to hear."

Bellaydin approached the duke warily. "Don't be too pleased with yourself. I'm here to make sure you don't go too far."

The duke stood near the Goriinchian prisoner, who had been restrained on a filthy, disused rack. He was sweating profusely and babbling words in Goriinchian. A pair of soldiers flanked him on either side and some distance away a third soldier tended to a burning forge, ominously turning a metal spike over and over in the flames. Bellaydin had little doubt how Wulfric intended to use it.

"I will do what must be done, Bellaydin. No more, no less." Wulfric's face seemed different, almost malevolent, under the flickering light

Bellaydin frowned. The answer did not comfort him in the slightest.

Wulfric lowered his head close to the terrified prisoner and, his words slow and deliberate, switched to the Goriinchian language as he interrogated him. "What is your name, Goriinchian?"

"Connor," the man shuddered as he spoke.

"Very well, Connor," Wulfric said. "There are two ways we can proceed. You can tell me what I wish, and it will all be over in an instant. Resist, and you will be here a very long time. Pain is mandatory, but the quantity and duration are up to you."

The Goriinchian nodded, shuddering as he did.

"Now, what are these armies that your lord has assembled?" Wulfric said.

The Goriinchian shook his head fiercely and answered in Goriinchian. "I don't know the answer you seek."

"Very well, I shall prompt your memory then, shall I?"

Wulfric nodded to the guard at the forge. With a rapid movement, the soldier pulled the searing poker from the fire and thrust the white-hot end against the Goriinchian's chest. The prisoner screamed in agony as his flesh burned. Bellaydin averted his eyes, trying not to look at the grisly scene and hoping to block it from his mind, despite the acrid smell of burning flesh that hung in the air.

"Look away if you wish, Ap'Lydin," Wulfric said as the soldier carried on with the torture. "But what you are witnessing here is necessary. It's the only way."

Bellaydin wanted to yell out a rejoinder, to tell the duke that he was wrong, and that what he was doing was disgusting but a tiny kernel of doubt stopped Bellaydin from saying anything. *Maybe this IS the only way.*

"Stop. Stop," the Goriinchian screamed. "I'll tell you everything."

"Ah, the correct response – finally," Wulfric waved to the soldier to stop.

"It doesn't matter if I tell you anyway. You cannot stop the triumph of the Horned God," the Goriinchian muttered, his voice faint, his eyes distant.

"What do you mean by that? Triumph, how?"

Suddenly, the Goriinchian's eyes went wide, and he gasped in pain, thrashing about on the rack. Bellaydin shouted. "Wulfric, stop!"

"I'm not doing anything." Wulfric seemed somewhat perplexed by what was unfolding by him. Within minutes the Goriinchian seemed to go slack. His eyes rolled back in their sockets.

"Is he dead?" Bellaydin said, after a moment's silence.

Suddenly the prisoner seemed to spring back to life, struggling under his restraints, and babbling in incoherent scraps of Goriinchian.

"What in the name of the Underworld?" Geoffrey said.

"Answer me." Wulfric yelled at the Goriinchian.

The Goriinchian gave an unsettling smile and spoke in a frighteningly calm voice, at odds to the panicked scream from before. "Soon Ygarak will reign over reunited Karlicia, and the Horned God will drive out your false gods. It is inevitable."

"Enough of this nonsense." Wulfric said. "Tell me about the armies."

The Goriinchian cackled like a banshee. "The faithful number like drops of water in the ocean, Enparran. Goriinchia will crush you like insects."

"Your bluster will not work with me, Goriinchian," Wulfric said. "Your strength was decimated by the war. We know that your master can barely muster a single battalion of half-starved peasants and invalids. So, where are these new armies from?"

The Goriinchian laughed again. "You know nothing, Enparran. It is through the powers of the Horned God alone that Ygarak has replaced his armies. The Lord has raised men of bronze and steel from the very soil itself and imbued them with his divine power. They will cut through your soldiers with ease and lay waste to the lands of the infidels."

"He is coming, and you will worship him. He is coming. He is coming. He is coming."

The Goriinchian's words slowly devolved into meaningless dribble, and Wulfric seemed to grow ever more frustrated. Twice more he tried torture as a means of loosening the Goriinchian's tongue, but the prisoner seemed to have lost his mind, and no more information was forthcoming. The vague promises of death, destruction, and religious conversion, coupled with repeated mentions of armies of bronze and steel were all that they could get from the prisoner before he finally lost consciousness.

Bellaydin found the whole experience unsettling and distasteful. Seeing the prisoner in that powerless state, seeing the pain on his face – it had caused Bellaydin's mind to flash back to the moment just before his cousin's death, when he too lay on the rack, tortured by the Goriinchians, and left to die. It was something he never wanted to experience again, and certainly not be involved in. Perhaps Wulfric was right, perhaps it was necessary. Still, it didn't feel right.

Instinctively he thrust his hands into the pockets of his garment and suddenly felt something cold and hard. It was the lens that Haakon had given to him. *Pierce the fog of lies.* Haakon's words rang in his mind. *See the truth.*

Almost on a whim, Bellaydin held up the spyglass to his eye and looked at the scene in front of him. The room seemed much the same. He still saw Geoffrey, just as normal, and the Goriinchian prisoner. When he moved his head to glance at Wulfric, however, he almost jumped back in surprise. He saw the familiar shape of the Duke of Oldharbour just as he expected, but another figure seemed to overlap Wulfric's. This new figure was indistinct. It seemed to occupy the same space as Wulfric, but towered over him in height and possessed a thin, emaciated build. It had an alien, fey cast to its appearance.

Almost immediately, however, the figure vanished, as if it had never been there. Bellaydin removed and then held the lens to his eye again. Wulfric stood alone in front of him, just like before.

The figure did not reappear. Dumbfounded, Bellaydin put the lens back in his pocket. As if sensing his discomfort, Wulfric regarded him with odd interest. "Something the matter, Ap'Lydin?"

"Nothing at all," Bellaydin tried to sound nonchalant. "Just a little tired."

"Same here," Geoffrey interrupted. "Perhaps we should see if supper might be ready."

***

"What do you mean? What did you see?" Geoffrey looked confused.

Bellaydin had finally told Talthas and Geoffrey what he had seen through the spyglass. The trio was at the dinner table, and Wulfric had excused himself. Although they were presently alone, Bellaydin hushed Geoffrey.

"I'm not exactly sure. It was something else, not human. It stood where Wulfric was standing. Almost like an echo."

"How did you see this echo?" Talthas asked. "With your own eyes?"

"Not exactly," said Bellaydin. "With this. Haakon gave it to me." He took the spyglass out of his pocket and passed it across the table. Talthas had a look through it himself before passing it to Geoffrey, who regarded it with interest.

Geoffrey turned the lens over in the palm of his hand. "I remember this. I got it from the Duke of Oldharbour himself. I gave it to William. It's a magical viewing lens of some sort. I don't know how it works exactly."

"Perhaps it helps one see things that are hidden from plain sight." Talthas mused.

"Perhaps," Geoffrey said. "Or maybe it's been enchanted, and Bellaydin just saw an illusion. You can't always trust the things you see, particularly when there's magic involved."

"So, you're saying I should just forget about it?" Bellaydin said.

"I'm just telling you not to jump to any conclusions," Geoffrey said. "Look, I know Wulfric. He can be a cold bastard, but he's not an inhuman creature in disguise. Let's not go chasing after fairy tales. There's enough superstitious nonsense going around these days without the rest of us falling for it."

Bellaydin sighed. "I guess you're right."

"Of course, I'm right, I always am." Geoffrey winked, gulping down his mug of beer.

Bellaydin didn't respond.

"Honestly, put it out of your mind for now, Bela," Geoffrey suggested warmly.

They soon steered the conversation to other topics until all three had had their fill of talking and eating. Bidding Geoffrey and Talthas a fair evening, Bellaydin retired to his own quarters, but not before checking in on the recovering Duke of Alariat. Haakon was still asleep, muttering half-formed words behind closed eyes. Bellaydin decided not to wake the old man and instead continued to his own room, changed into his nightclothes, and slipped into bed for some well-deserved rest.

***

Once again, Bellaydin dreamed. He couldn't recall how long it had been since he had slept well, untroubled by visions. Tonight's vision was a little different, however. He did not dream of Goriinchia. He did not dream of the Heir of Lydin. He did not dream of long dead Fey lords or the machinations of the Horned God.

Instead, he saw a land of sun and desert sands, of incense and swirling robes, of henna and rouge-tinted hair. A man stood before him, a proud, handsome figure in exotic, noble garb. Bellaydin had never seen this man before but felt an instant sense of recognition. Somehow he knew this was the legendary Belial'ad-Dīn, a man from Qardleean fable. Kahlaf had once told Bellaydin about this man; a man cursed by his own blood.

Bellaydin watched as Belial'ad-Dīn went about his life, untroubled by any concern and blessed with wealth, power, love, and success. The idyllic scene suddenly turned dark, and the sky went red as blood. Belial'ad-Dīn collapsed to the ground, cowering before a towering shadow that suddenly emerged before him. The shadow took shape, becoming a dark and terrible figure of smoke and fire. Instinctively, Bellaydin knew this to be Belial, a jinni of the Underworld, and Belial'ad-Dīn's father. Belial set about destroying all that the man held dear and turned Belial'ad-Dīn's life into misery.

The vision abruptly shifted, and Bellaydin found himself standing where

Belial'ad-Dīn had been. Bellaydin saw the scene of destruction and despair through Belial'ad-Dīn's eyes – as if they were his own. The scene shifted again, and the looming, terrible form of Belial shrank to transform into a familiar, human figure.

"Father," Bellaydin said.

Alusine regarded his son with avaricious eyes, with no sign of familial affection.

"Who are you?" Alusine Ap'Lydin asked. His tone was dark, sinister.

"I am Bellaydin."

"What are you?"

"I am your son."

"Yes, and you shall be that which I could not."

With those words spoken, the troubling images and sounds dissolved into incoherence, and Bellaydin would finally drift off into untroubled sleep.

CHAPTER 13

Polnygar yawned.

It had taken their party of four more than a few days over some treacherous terrain but at last, civilisation came into view. As the wagon made its unsteady way over the path and up the hill, she saw a walled town, dominated by an impressive fortress – Wishapton

As they approached the town, Polnygar felt a sense of familiarity. It was not just from a lingering sense of nostalgia from her brief time here as a small child. The buildings that comprised the settlement reminded her of those in Harralin, though they seemed to be of sturdier construction. They were certainly not in the same league as the elegant villas and estates of Aderilund, nor the white spires of Liderial, and struggled to even match the stone wonders of Macrodonia and Ralom, yet they still held a unique charm of their own.

"The Emparians are kin to the men of Skurj and the rest of those northern lands," Aelzandar explained after a few questions from Polnygar. "And though divergent experiences in these lands since their migration thousands of years ago may have created many subtle differences in culture and language, the broad strokes remain the same."

"It seems so familiar to me," Polnygar said. "But it was so long ago that I lived here. In a way, in seems nothing more than a dream now. A whisper of a life lived before."

Aelzandar placed a hand on Polnygar's shoulder reassuringly, squeezing it slightly as he smiled gently at her. "I must confess myself to feeling a strange sense of familiarity too. And something else, I look upon this place and I feel *hope*."

As they passed through the gates of the town, children and adult alike came to gawk at the wagon, hoping to see what exotic wares the newly arrived merchant might be carrying. Within a short amount of time, they had reached the marketplace, and Egbert pulled the wagon to a stop.

"This is where we part ways, friend," the merchant said. "'Twas a pleasure to share the journey with you. If you're interested in any of my wares, well, you know where to find me."

Polnygar, Aelzandar and Hebu disembarked from the wagon, grabbing their possessions, and leaving Egbert to set up his stall in peace.

Hebu sniffed the air. He gagged slightly, and added, "Is it just me, or do humans have real trouble with the concept of proper sanitation?"

"Try to be polite, Hebu," Aelzandar remonstrated. "We're trying to make a good impression, after all."

Hebu raised his eyes to the sky, and then glanced from left to right, "I doubt making an impression will prove too difficult in this mud-soaked collection of hovels."

Polnygar paid little attention to Aelzandar and Hebu. In truth, her mind was elsewhere, still going over the events of the past few weeks. Augustin's death still hurt and she felt an aching emptiness inside her that she doubted would ever be healed. Worse still was a realisation that it was perhaps her own failure that meant the Baron had died, that if she had been quicker, stronger, more skilled, Augustin could still be alive. Knowing that becoming mired in self-pity and regret was pointless, Polnygar tried to push the thoughts from her mind, but time and time again they would return, like unwelcome guests.

"Repent. The end is coming. The time of tribulation and punishment, when the Horned God will wipe away the sinful world and all the depravity that lies upon it."

Polnygar froze. The mention of the Horned God caused a sudden chill to travel down her spine.

"Is that a priest?" Hebu sneered. "He's so filthy. And hairy."

Polnygar remembered the elegant, immaculately clean priests of Macrodonia, their shaven heads glistening in the sunlight. The ragged man in front of them was quite the opposite, dressed in sodden rags, with a tangled mess of grey hair and a filthy beard. Only a tarnished medallion around his neck alluded to his identity as a holy man.

The man grabbed Polnygar's wrist. "You, Saldarri girl. Listen to my words. Listen to me." The man prattled on, making little sense to Polnygar. Eventually a few militiamen, hearing the commotion, came and dragged the man away, apologising to Polnygar and her companions.

"What was that about?" said Hebu.

"Master," Polnygar said. "Did you see the symbol around his neck?"

"Indeed, I did. The Horned God. We should hope that they do not know who we are. It would be best for us that, when it comes to the cult of the Horned God, the right-hand does not know what the left-hand does."

Hebu snorted as the dishevelled preacher disappeared into a guard tower, still ranting, and raving as the soldiers manhandled him. "I think in this case we may be safe. I doubt our friend there knows what his own hand is doing."

"That being said, caution would still be advised," said Aelzandar.

They approached the central structure of the keep, a solidly built stone fortress, likely the destination they had been seeking. Soldiers and labourers milled about the base of the keep; there seemed to be some sort of construction or excavation taking place on the other side of the building. Polnygar wondered what was going on, but from the angle she was looking from, it was difficult to tell.

"I think this is the place," Aelzandar said. "Let me see if I can find someone to help us."

Aelzandar left to talk to some soldiers nearby, and judging from the animated discussion, he was having some difficulty convincing them. Eventually, however, they seemed to relent and Aelzandar returned to Polnygar and Hebu, a smile across his face. "I do believe things are in order now."

"There was a slight misunderstanding, but once he knew he was dealing with the arcane representative of the King of Macrodonia, things changed."

"I remember you taking a leave of absence from that position, my lord," chided Hebu.

"Yes, but they don't need to be troubled with that now, do they?"

A man approached them, bowing stiffly as he greeted them. "My name is Carfel. I welcome you to Wishapton. Please come with me, I will take you inside."

The guards raised the keep's portcullis and, with Carfel leading the way, Polnygar and the others went past the outer walls and barbican, and into the keep proper. They soon found themselves in a comfortable and elegantly furnished sitting room.

"Please take a seat, friends," said Carfel, his hands clasped. "Lord Ap'Lydin will be with you soon."

As Carfel departed, Polnygar turned to Aelzandar. "I have a cousin here. He is about my age. I wonder if this is going to be him."

"Polnygar?" Polnygar's breath caught in her throat as she looked up at the newcomer who had said her name.

Carfel had returned with a somewhat younger man. Despite the unfamiliar garb, the short hair and the scruffy beard, she instantly recognised the man standing before her.

"Bellaydin." Polnygar exclaimed, and nearly leapt from her seat to embrace him. Bellaydin, clearly as shocked and surprised to see his sister as she was to see him, hugged her tightly.

"I see he does know you then," Hebu remarked dryly.

"Ah," said Carfel awkwardly. He turned to Aelzandar, seemingly conscious of not interrupting the reunion in front of him. "May I present Sir Bellaydin Ap'Lydin, Lord of Wishapton. Aelzandar of Macrodonia, and his companions, my lord."

As the siblings finally released their holds on each other, Aelzandar rose from his seat and extended a hand. "My lord Ap'Lydin. It is a pleasure to meet you at last. I've heard great things about you. Your sister certainly thinks highly of you."

"Thank you, thank you," said Bellaydin.

"If it pleases my lord," said Carfel. "Lord Aelzandar understates his own importance. He is not a mere ambassador, but also the Archmage."

"Really?" Bellaydin said, looking towards Aelzandar. "That is impressive."

Carfel nodded, and Aelzandar returned the gesture.

"It's been so long, Bela," Polnygar said to her brother. "So much has changed, for both of us."

Bellaydin smiled. "I know, Pol. We can fill each other in on the last couple of years over dinner."

Bellaydin said a few words to Carfel, and the man bowed his head before leaving the room.

"Come on, Pol, friends," Bellaydin said. "Let me show you around."

With Bellaydin leading the way, Polnygar, Aelzandar and Hebu were taken on a tour of the keep. Bellaydin showed them the studies and libraries, the bedrooms, the dining areas, and much more. He made sure that Polnygar saw the collection of Ap'Lydin portraits, giving his sister a chance to see the image of their father and even of herself at a far younger age. Polnygar was impressed and pleased to be able to see it all. Although not to the level of her brother, she did hold some level of curiosity about her paternal origins, and the things Bellaydin showed her helped illustrate some of the gaps in knowledge of her non-Eldara ancestry, often bringing back into focus long-forgotten parts of her childhood memory.

"It's odd, Bela," Polnygar smiled. "Even after all the talks we used to have, I never thought we'd end up here again. Is it everything you thought it would be?"

"In some ways, it's exceeded my expectations. In others, well…" He sighed. "I'm not afraid to admit that sometimes I miss Aderilund. Even if I didn't feel like it when I was there, it was still home. After all, that's where Mother is."

Polnygar smiled and squeezed her brother's shoulder. "Bela, Bela, Bela. Underneath that manly exterior, you're still that little brother I left behind. I wonder what mother's doing now. I hope she doesn't miss us too much."

"She'll be alright," Bellaydin said of Saegralanna, his mother in all but name. "She's stronger than we realise, you know. Besides, I'm going to visit her again, one day."

"I know. Me too." Polnygar mused.

She looked about the hallway. "Is there anything else I should see? I never suspected that our cousin would have kept all these pictures up."

There were some things that Bellaydin chose not to show his sister. He kept to himself the knowledge of the secret room, the painting of Alusine Ap'Lydin in the garb of the cult, and indeed any details at all pertaining to their father's secret life. He didn't know how to tell his sister such troubling information and wasn't sure how she would react. Could she take it all in? Even now, days after discovering the troubling secret himself it still plagued his mind. He still wondered how he could have misjudged just what sort of person Alusine Ap'Lydin really was. Despite the thoughts clouding his mind as he strolled with his sister and her companions, Bellaydin kept up appearances, and the smile remained fixed on his face.

"Quite an impressive keep you have here, Lord Ap'Lydin," Aelzandar said. "Seems to have been well maintained. Has it been in your family for a long time?"

"Our cousin William lived here before me," Bellaydin said, with a hint of regret in his voice. "Before that, it was our father and my mother. I don't know much of any earlier history."

"A pity," said Aelzandar. "I'm sure it would be fascinating."

***

The group engaged in light conversation before Carfel came to escort the group to the dining hall, where the long table had been set for Bellaydin and his guests. Others quickly arrived to greet them; Sir Geoffrey Keslin, grinning broadly, Talthas, not far behind him, and a pale and withdrawn looking Duke of Alariat.

"My friends, this is the Duke of Alariat; Haakon de Morcor," Bellaydin said, guiding Haakon to the table.

"We are honoured," Aelzandar said, bowing. Hebu and Polnygar did likewise.

Haakon nodded ever so slightly in response, saying nothing as he took his seat. His eyes were distant, unfocused.

"Is the Duke of Oldharbour going to be joining us?" Bellaydin asked.

201

Geoffrey shook his head. "I'm afraid he's still away on whatever interesting diversion he's discovered."

Geoffrey looked at Bellaydin questioningly, as if wanting to be introduced to the other newcomers.

"And this rogue here is Sir Geoffrey Keslin," Bellaydin chuckled quietly, as the knight strolled forward proudly.

"Pleased to make your acquaintance," Geoffrey said, firmly shaking Aelzandar's hand, "We don't see many elves around here these days. Talthas here, being the exception, of course."

The archmage looked the elven ranger up and down and offered the Eldara greeting. "Blessed be Talthas," said Aelzandar. "And honour to your houses."

"Blessed be Aelzandar," Talthas said, returning the greeting. "My family always thought your exile unjust. I am humbled in your presence."

Aelzandar gave a nod and a smile.

Geoffrey crouched down to shake Hebu's hand. "And you, my good gnome."

"Gnome? Gnome?" Hebu's voice rose in tone as he grew more indignant. "I am not a gnome."

Geoffrey stepped back, slightly surprised at the reaction. "Apologies, my good man."

Geoffrey turned his head and noticed Polnygar. "Why, who do we have here?" He smoothly took Polnygar's hand in his. He raised her hand to his lips, and gave her a single kiss,

"Might I introduce Polnygar, my sister," Bellaydin eyed Geoffrey with caution, placing a stress on the word "sister"

"Your sister, you say?" Geoffrey said with interest. Noticing Bellaydin frowning at him, Geoffrey mouthed silently, "What?"

Bellaydin shook his head sternly at Geoffrey, who feigned a scandalised look. If Polnygar noticed the playful exchange, she didn't let on.

As everyone ate, Bellaydin related to his sister and her companions the events of the past two years; of the journey from Aderilund to Goriinchia, of the perilous trek through Goriinchia, including their capture by the forces of Ygarak, and the events of the siege of Wishapton, leading to their cousin's bloody torture and death. Polnygar for her part recounted the details of her own travels, the trip to Macrodonia, the pursuit by assassins, the discovering of a talent for the Art and her training under Aelzandar. She went on to detail the theft of the Tears of the Divine and the pursuit of Ivellios to Skurj, and the devastating battle there, where Augustin perished and Ivellios once again escaped.

If there was any commonality between their tales it was in the figure of the Horned God, who had featured prominently over both siblings' lives. The terrible god and his followers lurked at the edges of both their stories, always in the background, as if orchestrating the entire series of events. The term "Heir of Lydin" had been thrown at both Bellaydin and Polnygar Ap'Lydin.

"It is a remarkable set of coincidences," Aelzandar noted. "The followers of the Horned God seem to have associated you with this semi-mythical Heir of Lydin figure. I wonder what it is that the Horned God considers special about you two."

Bellaydin shook his head. "Whatever it is, it's certainly deeply ingrained in Goriinchian culture. Their ruling class is obsessed with it."

"Amongst other things," said Geoffrey. "The Horned God's not exactly tranquil."

"Bah." Hebu threw down the piece of mutton he was eating, and stood up on his chair, trying to give himself some height. "If these barbarians have such an interfering tyrant for a god, maybe they should go and find other ones more amenable. There's plenty to choose from, after all."

203

"Ah," said Aelzandar, "that's not so simple, my friend. The Goriinchians, if I am correct, only believe in the existence of a single god – the Horned God."

Hebu looked surprised. "One god? That's the most foolish thing I've ever heard. How could one god have created everything? Does one man build a castle? Does one man make an army?"

Aelzandar smiled as Hebu continued his impassioned argument, ranting and raving against what the Nemoi labelled "stupidity, shallowness and lack of imagination", while the others watched on with fascination. Some, like Geoffrey, chuckled at various moments. The conversation then drifted to Ivellios, as they pondered his motives and intentions.

"I knew he hated us, but I never thought he'd stoop to murder or betraying his own king." Bellaydin took a drink of beer.

Aelzandar mused, rubbing his chin. "What concerns me most is what he plans to do with the Tears."

"Why would he bring them here?" asked Polnygar. "I don't think Ivellios would have ever visited these lands in his life. I can't imagine him willingly working for humans, or even with them, for that matter."

"I don't know, my dear," Aelzandar said. "It still seems a great mystery, all of this. And that is what worries me. There's some missing puzzle piece here, I know it. Once we discover what it is, we shall be in a better position."

"Well, I'll do anything to help, you know that Bela," Geoffrey said. "I'd do whatever it takes to keep you safe. You and your family."

"Yes, no one wants you to share your father's fate," said Haakon. For a moment, Bellaydin's heart skipped a beat, but then he realised that the duke probably didn't intend the double meaning.

"His death," Haakon clarified. "And that of your mother's, 'twas a terrible tragedy."

"Polnygar did mention that her father had been murdered by the cultists of the Horned God," Aelzandar said.

"Not cultists," Haakon waved a finger. "Cultist. Simon Enlim."

Aelzandar looked surprised. "I'm sorry?"

"Enlim, Simon Enlim. That was the murderer's name."

"I think you must be mistaken," Aelzandar said.

"Are you saying I don't know how my best friend died?" Haakon demanded.

"No, I'm merely suggesting that there must be a mistake. The cult leader Simon Enlim died centuries ago."

"And you know this for a fact?" Haakon said.

"Yes, I do." Aelzandar looked right at Haakon. "I killed him."

Bellaydin turned to the elf. "You killed Simon Enlim centuries ago?"

"Without a doubt. It was on the plains of Skurj, in defence of the Tears of the Divine and the Genio heir."

"You're sure it was him?" Bellaydin asked.

"Without a doubt," Aelzandar repeated.

"Perhaps it is you who are mistaken, Archmage" Haakon's voice, though weak, was insistent. "Are you sure he was dead?"

"I put a sword right through him," Aelzandar said. "That usually seems to work."

Bellaydin waved a hand. "It must be another Simon Enlim." Aelzandar pursed his lips into a thin smile. He obviously disagreed, but held back out of courtesy. Something about Aelzandar's information troubled Bellaydin, but he was too tired to think about it now. He glanced at Haakon, who seemed angry and confused.

The duke's voice sounded feeble. "If you'll excuse me, my boy, I'm still not feeling particularly well. I think I might retire to my quarters."

"Of course, Your Grace," Bellaydin said. "Have a pleasant sleep."

"Thank you, Bela," Haakon said. "Pleasure to meet all of you. I will see you on the morrow."

Haakon left, and Bellaydin changed the subject. "Well, if everyone's had enough, I think we should retire to the study. I have something to show you, Aelzandar, something I think you might be interested in."

Aelzandar put down his goblet and dabbed the sides of his mouth with a cloth. "Well, I must say that I'm intrigued, Bellaydin."

As everyone finished up, they vacated the table, leaving the remainder for the serving staff to clean up. Following Bellaydin's lead they took a stroll to the keep's study. Though cluttered, the study was large and had enough room for all of them to fit in comfortably.

Bellaydin walked to one side of the room where a shrouded table stood. "Over here, Aelzandar. It's under this blanket." Bellaydin removed the blanket to uncover the tarnished, bronzed armour that Bellaydin's workers had excavated from under Wishapton.

"Well, now I must say, that is an impressive find," Aelzandar said. "Where exactly was it found?"

"We have been digging under the keep. There appears to be some old ruin buried underneath. This was found inside."

"An ancient ruin? Was that the excavation work we saw being undertaken on our way in here?"

"Indeed. Can you tell me what it is? Look here on the inside of the helmet. That's Elven, isn't it?"

Bellaydin grabbed the headpiece and passed it to Aelzandar, pointing out the worn inscription on the inside. "Well, you are correct. The script is

Eldaric," Aelzandar used the elven term for their own language. "But of a remarkably archaic form. Thousands of years old, in fact. Based on what you've uncovered here, I have no doubt that this is the remnants of a Soldara automaton."

Polnygar stepped forward, her eyes wide. "It's true, these are the same as the ones I saw in the temple near Qar Arrid. This automaton is the same as the ones that nearly killed me."

"Automaton?" Bellaydin shook his head in disbelief. "I'm not sure I understand."

Aelzandar placed the helmet down on the table. "An automaton is an artificial construct, animated by the Art. The Soldara used them as a source of labour and as guards for their citadels. There were tales that the most powerful Soldara lords had whole armies of automatons, tireless in battle, able to undertake any command flawlessly."

"And what is a Soldara?" said Geoffrey. "Some sort of wizard?"

"Sort of, yes. They're an ancient elven people," Polnygar explained.

Polnygar reached deep inside her own memories for everything Aelzandar had told her about the Soldara and repeated it for those present. She told Bellaydin and the others everything she could remember – from the Soldara's origins as the original spellweaver caste of the elves, to their growing disenchantment with the direction of elven society, ending with their self-exile in Emparia, and the subsequent mysterious disappearance of their entire civilisation.

Aelzandar smiled proudly. "I couldn't have explained things better myself."

Bellaydin stood for a while, deep in thought. "I wonder if perhaps this means that the Fey of Goriinchian legend are indeed this Soldara. It certainly would seem so, all things considered. I wonder if that means the ruins underneath the keep are also linked to these Soldara."

"It's certainly possible," Aelzandar conceded.

"Wait a minute, look here, at the top of the automaton head," Polnygar blurted out. Bellaydin looked to where Polnygar was pointing.

"This sphere thing attached here." Polnygar turned to Aelzandar. "Don't you think this looks like the object that came out of Augustin's mouth in Ralom? As well as out of the mouths of those brainwashed soldiers in Qar Arrid?"

Aelzandar raised an eyebrow as Polnygar passed him the automaton head. "Now that you mention it, I do see some resemblance. Curious."

Talthas shook his head. "Wait, you are saying that this Ivellios is making people swallow pieces of old Soldara automata? Why in the name of Mother Hydria would he do that?"

"I'm not sure. At least, not yet. We will see in time, I expect." Aelzandar turned to Bellaydin. "You know, I would be quite interested to see these ruins you have uncovered. Perhaps you might show me some time."

"No time like the present, archmage. It's only just outside."

"If you don't mind, Bellaydin," Geoffrey said. "Talthas and I have some things to see to. You don't mind if we give this otherwise thrilling tour of old rocks a miss?"

"Of course not," Bellaydin said. "I'm sure your other duties take precedence."

After Geoffrey and Talthas' departure, Bellaydin led the rest of the group out of the keep to the excavation site. Even in the dying hours of the afternoon light, labourers still toiled within the site, hauling stone, dirt, and other debris from inside the ruins. Large piles of refuse were starting to build up just outside the excavation area. As Bellaydin approached, the labourers saluted him, but otherwise continued with their work.

"You have a lot of men working here," Aelzandar said. "How much have you uncovered?"

"Enough to be sure it is a tomb of sorts. A few corridors, an antechamber or too," Bellaydin said. "Every time we dig out one room, we find another. I don't know how much there is down there. The ruins seem to go on forever."

"Most intriguing," Aelzandar strolled towards the roped off tomb entrance, looking over the uncovered masonry with utmost curiosity.

Polnygar looked at the site with interest. "What's it doing under this village?"

Aelzandar ran a hand over the stonework of the ruins. "I think my dear that perhaps it would be more appropriate to speculate what this village is doing on top of the tomb."

"I assume whoever built the tomb was long gone before Wishapton was settled," Bellaydin said. "From what I recall, the town is barely a century old."

Aelzandar examined some of the carved inscriptions over the tomb entrance. "I think you are correct in such an assumption. This is Eldaric script. But it seems to be gibberish."

"The script is Elven," Bellaydin explained, "but its content is Goriinchian. They seem to use a degraded form of the Eldara script."

"Most curious," Aelzandar said.

"I'd give you a guided tour but it's still unstable inside," Bellaydin offered. "We haven't completed the work."

"Yes, well, it would probably still be a little dangerous to blunder around inside. Perhaps a little later."

Bellaydin suddenly heard someone shouting for him nearby. "My lord!"

"Never a moment of quiet here," Bellaydin muttered under his breath. A soldier approached, puffing and out of breath.

"My lord Ap'Lydin."

"Yes, what is it?" Bellaydin's tone was terser than he hoped.

"The scouts have returned, my lord and they say they have information that can't wait, my lord. You need to hear it now. They're waiting just outside the gatehouse."

Bellaydin and the others hurried with the soldier to the gatehouse where the three scouts were waiting. Grimy and sweaty from their journey, the scouts regarded Bellaydin with weary and grave faces.

Bellaydin got straight to the point. "What is the news from Goriinchia?"

"It is as we have heard, my lord. The Goriinchians have formed new armies. They are advancing towards the Emparian border."

"But that makes no sense. These armies must be minuscule. Ygarak can't possibly have enough men left to form any substantial force."

The scouts looked at each other nervously before answering. "My lord, Goriinchia does not field armies of flesh and bone."

"We saw them with our own eyes, my lord," another scout interrupted. "Great battalions of metal men march under the direction of Goriinchian generals. Bronze soldiers, glinting in the sun, stretching as far as the eye could see."

"Metal men," Bellaydin exclaimed.

"They have crushed all resistance in their way, my lord. Implacable, unstoppable, relentless. And they are coming this way."

Bellaydin felt his heart lurch in his chest and his mouth go dry. Old sensations resurfaced; feelings not felt since the first time he huddled in Wishapton waiting for the inevitable Goriinchian attack. This time his cousin wasn't around to help him.

"Soldara automata," Polnygar said quietly.

"Indeed. From the sounds of this, the Goriinchians seem to have automata of their own." Aelzandar said. "Most troubling."

Bellaydin turned to one of the scouts. "How far away?"

"Four days at the most, my lord. They were moving quickly."

Bellaydin closed his eyes and cursed under his breath. "Give me a few moments," he said to the scouts. Nodding, they departed, leaving Bellaydin and the others alone. He leant back against a wall and let out an exasperated sigh, "Where in the name of the Underworld would the Goriinchians have got their hand on an ancient elven metal army?"

"I think I know," said Polnygar. The others turned to her. "Ivellios. He's a spellweaver, for one, and we know he went to the Temple of the Ancients and saw automata there. Of all people, Ivellios would be one to tell the Goriinchians about the secrets of the Soldara. If anyone could provide them with an army of these things, it would be Ivellios."

Aelzandar nodded. "A most plausible hypothesis my dear. Our wayward enemy has both the means and the motive."

Bellaydin sighed, rubbing his forehead, "Aelzandar, you seem to know about these *automata*. Where do we stand? Do we have any chance?"

Aelzandar pursed his lips. "There is always a chance."

"I want the truth, archmage," Bellaydin said firmly.

"If it's the truth you want, Bellaydin, then I suggest you start to evacuate this town right away."

"And if I don't?"

"Then everyone in this town will be dead in four days."

CHAPTER 14

For the second time in as many years, Wishapton was facing a Goriinchian attack. This time, burned out from the recent war, depleted of men and with the walls still showing the scars of the previous assault, few held out any hope for the town's salvation. The mood only got worse as troubling rumours spread around town that the Goriinchians were leading armies of enchanted metal men, massive and powerful enough to smash Wishapton with their bare hands. Soldiers and militiamen did their best to calm the panicked citizens and re-establish order in the evacuation, but the gathering gloom of night and the relentless rain did nothing to placate heightened anxieties.

Bellaydin walked through the keep, watching as the servants and attendants collected the last of the valuables, ready to be loaded onto wagons and taken from the doomed town. Bellaydin felt a little sad to see the home of his family for generations being stripped like this, but he knew there were few other options. Wishapton was going to fall, and Bellaydin was adamant that no-one he cared for should be there when it happened.

When Aelzandar first explained just how unstoppable the automata were, Bellaydin had raised his voice and in strident tones declared that he and the other brave men of Wishapton would defend their home to the death. But it was an idle boast, and in the face of the archmage's calm, reasoned tones, it soon withered. He meekly surrendered to Aelzandar's arguments, feeling a strange mixture of relief and shame as he began organising what needed to be done.

"Where are the others?" Bellaydin asked his sister. Polnygar was helping a servant remove an Ap'Lydin family portrait from the wall.

"Aelzandar and Hebu are down below, helping the evacuation," Polnygar dusted her hands. "I think Geoffrey and Talthas went with them."

Bellaydin said. "We should probably go help them. The attendants here have things under control." He looked around, furrowing his brow. "You haven't seen Haakon, have you?"

Polnygar shook her head. "Perhaps he's in his room?"

"It'd be strange if he is, given everything that's going on."

"Shall we go look in on him first?" Polnygar offered. Bellaydin nodded.

"Come on," he said. When the siblings reached Haakon's quarters, Bellaydin leant close to the door and called out in a loud voice.

"Your Grace? Are you there? Are you awake? I need to speak to you, Your Grace." There was no answer. Bellaydin became more forceful and direct.

"Haakon?" Bellaydin rapped his knuckles on the door. Again they were met with silence. "Haakon!"

"I don't think he's going to answer," said Polnygar.

Bellaydin tried to turn the door handle, but the door was locked. Bellaydin yelled again, pulling on the handle in vain. He turned to his sister and cautioned her to move behind him. "Stand back, Pol." With a couple of forceful kicks, Bellaydin smashed down the door.

Polnygar blinked, taken aback by the strength emanating from her once scrawny little brother.

"Haakon? Haakon?" Bellaydin called out as he looked around the room, which was an absolute mess. The bed sheets were muddy and torn; they looked as if they had been ripped by wild animals. There was blood splattered on the carpet and on the walls. The drapes on the window fluttered in the wind, wet from the rain.

"What in the name of the Underworld?" Bellaydin whispered.

"What happened here?" Polnygar and her brother looked on the scene of mayhem and destruction.

"I can't imagine. Where on earth is he?" Bellaydin said. Alarmed, he searched the room for some sign of what had happened to Haakon.

"Maybe someone attacked him!" Polnygar looked back at the shattered remnants of the door. "Although, I don't see how they could have got in here. Or, indeed, how anyone could have got out."

Bellaydin looked at the open window and turned back to Polnygar, alarmed.

"You're not saying he jumped out the window?"

"Maybe he was forced to." Bellaydin stuck his head through the window and looked outside. The ground below was soaked and covered with compacted mud and hay. If Haakon had jumped out the window, he must have survived the fall somehow, since there was no sign of a body. "Come on, we've got to find him."

The pair of them rushed through the keep, past soldiers and servants alike. Coming around the side of the building, Bellaydin and his sister came to a halt just below Haakon's window.

"Here, look." Bellaydin pointed to the ground. "The ground is disturbed here. He fell, but on his feet, somehow."

Polnygar drew closer, moving some disturbed hay with her feet. "Look at the footprints. Fairly clear in the mud."

Bellaydin nodded. "Let's follow them."

"Bela, do we have time for this? We need to leave soon." Polnygar asked.

"I'm not leaving without him, Pol."

Polnygar studied her brother's distressed face and said simply, "Let's go then."

They had barely walked twenty feet when they heard Geoffrey's voice calling out for Bellaydin.

"Over here," Polnygar called back.

Geoffrey approached, panting. "We're nearly ready. Aelzandar thinks we should lead the first group out. He sent me to find the both of you." His expression suddenly changed as he looked at Bellaydin. "Wait. Where are you going?"

"Haakon's missing," Bellaydin said. "Something's happened to him. I need to find him."

To Bellaydin's surprise, the knight did not respond with a joke, or a contrary quip, but instead, nodded gravely. "Do you need any help?"

"Pol can help me." Bellaydin gestured to his sister. "You go back and tell Aelzandar to get the first wagons rolling. We'll catch up."

"If that's what you think is best," Geoffrey nodded to both and patted Bellaydin on the shoulder before sprinting off back towards the town proper.

As they followed the prints in the mud, Bellaydin noticed that the length of the gait and the depth of the impressions indicated that Haakon had been limping. Hardly surprising, considering the height he had fallen from. Bellaydin considered it a minor miracle that the old man hadn't broken both his legs, or indeed his spine.

"They lead to the tomb." Polnygar said. The excavation site loomed before them.

"Why on earth would Haakon be going there?" Bellaydin ran towards the tomb entrance. The rope that had served as a cordon to the entrance had been torn off, leading the way open. Muddy footprints disappeared into the darkness. "It looks like he went inside."

"If indeed it is Haakon's footprints we're following," Polnygar said.

"I'm pretty certain they are," Bellaydin said. "But nothing else here makes any damn sense."

"Are we going in then?" Polnygar said.

"Just a minute, let me find something to light our way, a torch or something." He scrabbled through the labourer's equipment that had been left nearby.

"No need," Polnygar said nonchalantly and with a snap of her fingers and a few arcane words, she conjured a small floating sphere of light, enough to illuminate their way in any darkness.

Bellaydin looked at his sister with wonder. "I certainly don't remember you being able to do things like that before."

"I've learned a few things since we left Aderilund." Polnygar flicked her wrist, sending the ball of light forward. Together the two Ap'Lydins followed the glowing ball into the gloom of the tomb.

"Maybe you'd better lead, Bela," Polnygar said as they moved down the tunnel. "I don't really know the way."

Her brother shrugged. "Truth be told, I've never been down here myself either. Keep following the footprints."

The prints themselves were still visible in the dust and dirt of the cave floor, but they were fainter and much less distinct than they had been outside. The tunnel sloped downwards and, as it continued further along the roughly hewn stone walls, gave way to smooth walls covered with faded murals.

"What are these pictures?" Polnygar brought the light closer.

Bellaydin looked at the art on the walls. "I'd say they were put here by whoever built the tomb."

"Goriinchians then," Polnygar said.

"Probably." He took a closer look. "Though I will say they don't look very Goriinchian."

The Goriinchian art that Bellaydin had seen managed to be both dull and abstract simultaneously, but the pictures painted on the walls here were vibrant, colourful, and so full of life they seemed poised to leap from the walls. The figures depicted didn't seem to be Goriinchians either, at least none that Bellaydin had ever met. The female figures were boldly rendered, dancing and twirling around each other – so unlike the dour, silent, hooded women of Goriinchia.

Polnygar pointed below the mural. "There's writing here, too"

"It's Goriinchian. Like the writing on the outside." Bellaydin traced a finger over the cracked and faded inscription. "I think it's a story. The artwork is a narrative of the life of the person buried here. See, here is his birth," Bellaydin pointed to a vividly depicted scene of childbirth. "And here is his early life. He seems to be learning under some sort of priestly figure."

The pictures continued after that. Another one showed the man, now an adult, meeting two more figures, a woman– beautifully depicted in bright and varied colours – and another man, cloaked and mysterious. After that, there were various images of confused looking battles, before a depiction of the titular figure being buried by his surviving followers, with the cloaked figure watching.

"There's a name here, too." Bellaydin said. "It must belong to whoever is buried here. Mael."

"Who's that? Do you know?"

"Somewhat. The Goriinchians call him Mael the Apostate."

They continued moving through the gloom, with only the small light to lead their way. After ten or so minutes of navigating their way down the winding tunnel, the footprints disappeared completely. A few more minutes after that they came across a huddled, shivering figure, slumped against a wall.

"Haakon!" Bellaydin ran towards the man. He tried to pull him from the ground. Haakon moaned in protest.

"Haakon, we have to leave. We must get you out of here. The town is going to be attacked by the Goriinchians. We need to evacuate."

"No, too late. Too late." Haakon mumbled.

"It's not too late," Polnygar said. "But we have to leave now."

"He's here. I know he's here. I saw him. He hides from me." Haakon stared at Bellaydin, his eyes fearful and bloodshot.

"Who's here? Who is it?"

"You don't know – don't know. He's not who you think he is. He wears another's skin. I could not see at first, but I have learned the truth. The truth."

"Who? Who are you talking about?" Bellaydin demanded.

"He's gone mad, Bela," Polnygar said. "I don't think you'll be able to coax much sense from him. We might have to drag him back outside."

"Come on, Haakon, we have to get out of here." Bellaydin pulled the man up from the ground and attempted to put the older man's arm around his shoulder.

Haakon gasped, grunting in pain, and clutching his chest. "No, no. He is here. He must be found."

With strength out of place for a man of his age and condition, Haakon gave a yelp of pain before pushing Bellaydin to the ground. Without so much as a glance behind his shoulder, Haakon disappeared into the tunnels, his footsteps echoing into the darkness. Polnygar helped her brother to his feet, and the pair of them gave chase, but Haakon seemed to have found a hidden reserve of strength and disappeared with such speed that Bellaydin feared that they would not catch him.

"It's like he's possessed," Bellaydin panted.

"Whatever it is, we're going to lose him if we're not careful. Maybe we should just leave him."

Bellaydin said. "He'll die here if we don't help him. I can't let that happen. He saved my life the last time Wishapton was under attack. It's only right I return the favour."

Ahead the tunnel came to a fork, with two passages heading off in opposite directions.

"Which way did he go?" said Bellaydin.

Polnygar looked from left to right. "I don't know. I can't see his footprints."

Bellaydin crouched to the ground and examined the floor. "The dirt is a bit disturbed on this side. Perhaps he went this way?"

Polnygar shook her head. "Your guess is as good as mine."

Bellaydin rubbed his chin. "Maybe we should split up, take separate tunnels."

Polnygar shook her head. "I don't think that would end well. Neither of us is familiar with these catacombs. We'll both end up being lost."

"Good point," Bellaydin said. "Let's go with my hunch then."

The pair of them moved down the passage where the dirt had been disturbed. They continued to move through the catacombs for what seemed like an eternity the passage suddenly opened into a large chamber. Inside, flanked by crumbling stone statues was a large, ornate stone sarcophagus.

"I don't think this is where he's gone," Polnygar said. "Should we keep moving?"

Bellaydin stepped into the chamber, looking about in awe. "This must be the tomb itself." He glanced at the statues. Both were in varying levels of disrepair, but they both clearly depicted the same man – a tall, proud looking figure, bearded and dressed in the manner of a Goriinchian warlord. The statues seemed to stare at Bellaydin with a grim, determined expression.

All of a sudden, Bellaydin thought he heard laughter. He stepped back from the statues, nearly tripping over himself and, as he did, a strange wind howled through the chamber, kicking up dust and dirt. As Bellaydin tried to walk back, the wind only seemed to increase in intensity, nearly knocking him to the ground. A strange mist seeped in from the sarcophagus, mixing with the windblown dirt and dust to coalesce into a vaguely human shape. The ghostly form began to solidify and took on the features of a Goriinchian man.

The peculiar man emitted a breathy sigh, before speaking in indistinct Goriinchian. "Another thief disturbs my slumber. You are too late. The last of your kind took all of the valuables that remained."

Bellaydin was frozen with a mix of terror and shock. He glanced at Polnygar, who seemed equally paralysed at the presence of the spirit before them.

"I'm not a thief." Bellaydin eventually managed to splutter.

"So, they all say. What do you claim to be then? Traveller? Adventurer? I have seen so many of your kind. The last was that fey warlock and his friends. They claimed to be here for reasons no more sinister than curiosity. But then they revealed themselves to be nothing more than common grave robbers."

The spirit moved closer, and in the dim light of Polnygar's spell, Bellaydin saw a similarity between it and the two statues. "Are you Mael the Apostate?" he said.

The spirit laughed. "You must be one of the Horned Thug's minions. It was your people who gave me that title, though I will admit, I never sought to disown it. I considered it a badge of honour. A sign of my freedom."

"I'm not with the Horned God," Bellaydin said. "In fact, just the opposite. He has marked me as his enemy. Just like you."

"Just like me?" the spirit mocked. "Then you should know that the Horned Thug will win in the end. He always has. His enemies always turn on each other, betray each other. Like I was betrayed."

Bellaydin dared a glance behind him and then, keeping the spirit in his gaze, tried to shuffle backwards. "Who betrayed you?"

"The warlock who stood by my side. He promised me greatness. He said I would defeat the Horned God. He told me I was the Heir of Lydin."

At the sound of those words, Bellaydin suddenly felt like he'd been struck with a thunderbolt. Stunned, he could barely get out his next words. "You're the Heir of Lydin?"

"So I was told." the ghost sneered. "But his words were false. My woman was taken from me, murdered by the Horned Thug's zealots. My armies were decimated, and I fled here, with my last followers. I believed in justice and I despised tyranny, so I was doomed to die in exile. In my last moments, he came to me and said that I had failed, that I was never meant to be the one who would free my people. It had all been a lie."

Bellaydin wanted to respond but before the words could form on his lips, another spoke. "It was not a lie, Mael. You were simply never meant to be that person."

From the shadows stepped Wulfric Highcrown, Duke of Oldharbour. His clothes were filthy, stained with mud and sweat but on his face, there was a mixture of amusement and disgust.

"I see you, my friend," the spirit said scornfully, as it swirled around Wulfric. "The skin you wear does not fool me."

"Wulfric?" Bellaydin said, shocked and confused. Polnygar helped him from the ground.

"Come to mock me, have you, Ailill?" The spirit hissed at Wulfric. "Come to see what your treachery has wrought?"

"It was not treachery that did you in, Mael. Your rebellion was doomed from the beginning. All I gave you was hope. That was my only mistake."

"I was promised," Mael said.

"You were promised nothing. And in the end, so are you nothing."

"Wulfric, what's going on here? How does this spirit know you? What is he talking about?"

The spirit laughed mockingly. "So he doesn't know, does he? Oh, how your lies will bring you low, Ailill."

"What are you doing here, Ap'Lydin?" Wulfric said sternly.

"I'm looking for Haakon," Bellaydin hesitated. "You didn't answer my question, though."

Ignoring the question again, Wulfric simply turned around to leave.

Bellaydin called after him. "Wait. Where are you going?"

"Stupid child," Wulfric said. "I am not here to indulge your curiosity."

"What's going on?" Polnygar said.

Everyone was momentarily distracted by a shuffling, groaning noise.

Another figure emerged from the darkness. "I told you. I told you," Haakon said. "He is here. I saw him from my window."

Haakon smiled and limped towards Wulfric. "Where once I was blind, my eyes have been opened. The truth has been revealed."

"He's gone mad," Wulfric said.

The spirit erupted into laughter and streamed about the room. "Or perhaps only in madness does he see. How long have you infested that body, like a maggot in a cadaver?"

"Fools," Wulfric spat.

Polnygar whispered into her brother's ear, "We have to get out of here, Bela."

"Haakon," said Bellaydin. "Calm down. We can help you. Just come with us. We'll get you and Wulfric outside."

Haakon wheeled about, frowning, "But this is not Wulfric. My friend is dead, years past. This is just a creature that wears his skin."

Haakon was muttering nonsense. Bellaydin thought he sounded insane and panicked. But something deep inside Bellaydin's mind told him that there was more to this than he thought. Almost instinctively his hands went inside his clothing and brushed against something cold, angular. He pulled it out – it was the magic lens. Holding it to his eye, he looked towards Wulfric.

The familiar image of Wulfric Highcrown dissolved, replaced with a gaunt and terrible figure, insubstantial as a shadow, with gleaming, red eyes. In shock, Bellaydin dropped the lens, and the figure disappeared, Wulfric Highcrown once again appearing as he did before.

"I must be going mad too," Bellaydin said out loud.

"It is not madness when you see the truth, thief," the spirit taunted. "Only madness when you refuse to accept that truth."

"And what is the truth?" Bellaydin glared at Wulfric, and the old man seemed to harden under his gaze. "*Are* you Wulfric?"

"What is the answer you want to hear?" Wulfric asked gruffly.

"I just want the truth."

"A much-overrated commodity."

"Tell me." Bellaydin yelled.

Wulfric took particular umbrage at the change in Bellaydin's tone. "Who are you to demand such things from me? You are no one. I am ancient. I am the true king of this land. I am the Lord of the Tears. The Master of the Last Citadel. I am –"

His words were cut short as Haakon, with a sudden lunge, leapt in front of him, withdrawing a dagger from his belt. All at once he stabbed the other duke straight through the chest. Bellaydin and Polnygar had no time to stop Haakon. They hardly had time to even fathom what was unfolding before them. Screaming in agony, Wulfric pushed Haakon aside, smashing the Duke of Alariat against the wall, and then slumping to the ground. He was bleeding so fast that it was starting to pool.

Bellaydin took hold of his senses and rushed to Wulfric's side. He cradled the dying man's head as Wulfric muttered deliriously.

Meanwhile, the other duke seemed to be mostly unharmed. Haakon regarded the two Ap'Lydins with sadness. "I'm sorry, but I had no choice." Polnygar started to run to Haakon, but he held up his hands to the light and, twisting a ring on his finger, said only a single word. "Goodbye."

Haakon immediately disappeared before Polnygar's eyes, leaving the astonished girl to wave her hand through thin air in disbelief. "Haakon has disappeared." she announced.

With a triumphant laugh, the spirit of Mael also dissolved into the air.

"Pol, help me," Bellaydin said. By now Wulfric was well and truly lying

225

in a pool of his own blood and appeared to drift in and out of consciousness.

"You fools." The duke blubbered through bloody lips. "You've done nothing except guarantee your own deaths."

"Do you know where Haakon's gone?" Bellaydin demanded, but the duke gave no response except a faint gurgle.

"We need to get him out of here," Bellaydin said to his sister.

Polnygar looked around. "He'll never make it, it's too far."

"There's another way out of the tomb," Wulfric gasped. "Just beyond this chamber there is a dead end. A false wall hides another exit from the tomb."

"Now how could you know that, Wulfric? This place has been buried for hundreds of years." Wulfric did not respond to Bellaydin's question with anything except incoherent muttering.

"He's losing a lot of blood," Polnygar urged. "He's not going to last long."

"Here." Bellaydin tore a strip from his surcoat. "Use this to bind the wound."

Polnygar took the piece of cloth from her brother and working as quickly as she could, tightly bound the cloth around the wound, securing it with the best knot she could manage.

"Now let's get him out of here," Bellaydin said. The siblings pulled Wulfric up, supporting him on either side with his arms slung around each of their shoulders. Bellaydin pointed to the other end of the chamber.

"The other exit should be over here," Bellaydin said as they moved towards it.

"I truly hope for his sake that he's right about that," said Polnygar.

Bellaydin leaned Wulfric against Polnygar. "Here, hold him for a second."

Prodding about the wall, Bellaydin eventually found a section he could depress, so he pushed it with a bit of force. As he did so, the wall rumbled. They could hear the grinding of ancient gears going to work. The entire section swung open, revealing a new tunnel. Light streamed into the chamber from this new passage.

"This looks promising," Bellaydin grabbed Wulfric's other arm again and helped his sister escort the dying man through the passage. After a few minutes, they emerged into the early evening dimness of the surface. The moons were high and bright this evening, providing good illumination.

Together Bellaydin and Polnygar lay Wulfric down on the grass. "Wulfric, can you hear me?"

Wulfric's eyes opened. "What are you doing, you fool?" the old man's voice was weak, and fading, but seemed to have lost none of its fire.

"We'll get you help, you hear? Stay with us."

"You can't help me, boy." Wulfric said. "You shouldn't have interfered. Now you have doomed everyone. I'm dying, and this time I feel it is for the final time."

"Who are you, really?" Bellaydin said. "You're not Wulfric."

The old man smiled, coughing slightly. "That's been my name since your parents died, boy, but I have gone by many names. I am Ailill, the warlock who guided Mael the Apostate. I am Simon Enlim, the right hand of the Horned God."

Bellaydin nearly tumbled backwards in surprise. "You? You murdered my father!"

Polnygar's eye widened. "What?"

Bellaydin repeated his assertion. "This man murdered our father."

Wulfric's blood-spattered lips quivered. "Did I now? What do you really know about the events of that day? Time is short. If the Horned God is to be defeated, one of you must be the one to do it. To that end, I give you these two gifts."

Pushing Bellaydin aside, Wulfric tore the bandages from his chest. Then, with a primal scream, the old man thrust his hand into the wound.

"By the gods, what is he doing?" Polnygar sounded alarmed.

Bellaydin watched in fascinated horror as the duke's hand emerged from his own gaping wound, his fist clenched around something. "This is what you need, Bellaydin."

The duke grabbed Bellaydin's hand, pressed a hard, metallic object into the younger man's palm. Immediately Bellaydin yelped with pain, as he felt a burning pain hit his hand and shoot up his arm. He tried to drop what Wulfric had given him, but the old man held Bellaydin's fist shut with a surprising strength. Bellaydin's flesh sizzled as the pain continued.

"Let me go. What are you doing?" Bellaydin threw Wulfric to the ground and opened his palm to dislodge whatever was there. A small piece of metal dropped to the ground. "My gods, why did you do that?"

Polnygar picked the piece of metal from the ground. It looked familiar to her. "Bellaydin, it's a piece of the Tears of the Divine."

"What?" Bellaydin took the metal piece from her. "Are you sure?"

"Without a doubt. Show me your hand, the one it burnt." Polnygar grabbed Bellaydin's wrist and compared his palm to hers. "The scar. It's the same as mine."

"If this is a part of the Tears, then how did Wulfric –"

The elderly duke was on his back, struggling for breath. "Come close, Bellaydin. Take this."

Bellaydin approached Wulfric, coming close enough to feel the old man's breath on his forehead. "What is it?"

"Knowledge," Wulfric whispered.

As soon as he spoke, Wulfric's eyes blazed with a brilliant radiance, and Bellaydin found himself transfixed, unable to turn away. The light burned brighter and brighter until eventually, everything disappeared in a white light.

In an instant, Bellaydin found himself far from the world he knew. He was spinning through time, experiencing thousands of years of memories in an instant. In the blink of an eye, people were born, lived their lives, and then died. Mountains crumbled into dust, and civilisations rose and fell without end. He saw a tower, the same one from his countless dreams, but this time he was on that very tower, standing with another figure. The figure resembled an elf, though he was monstrously tall, gaunt and had an alien cast to his features. The figure turned to Bellaydin and caught him in a piercing gaze, his silver eyes shining. In a single glance, Bellaydin knew that the figure before him could only be a Soldara Lord.

"They come, Palamius, in their thousands, and Lydin is leading them. Blood will out in the end, after all. Proud of your bastard now?"

"Lydin chose his own path. It is nothing to do with me." These words came from Bellaydin's mouth, but the voice was someone else's – deep, sonorous, and possessed of a strange, discordant tone.

"Perhaps not, but he comes all the same. Their force is vast. The automata will not stop them. Not this time. We have but one chance. We must use the Tears."

The scene dissolved into a blur of images as time seemed to speed up before Bellaydin's eyes. The next thing he knew he was standing somewhere else, in the shattered remains of a tower, the other Soldara towering over him in rage.

"Give me the Tears, Palamius. Or I shall take the power by force."

Pain gripped Bellaydin, but he realised it was the pain of another, a mere memory.

"You shall never have the Tears, Nahirios, for I shall seal the power inside with my own blood, and the blood of my line."

More memories flashed past in an instant, and soon his surroundings changed. He was now the warlock Ailill, advising Mael the Apostate in his betrayal of Ygarak. Strange sensations abounded. He could feel the white-hot metal of Kaltban against his skin as he forged the blade with his bare hands. He heard the sizzle of flesh as he burned the symbol of the Tears of the Divine into Mael's outstretched palm and could almost feel the agony of Mael's soldiers as they were routed by the Horned God's in a tremendous, bloody battle.

Once again, the vision changed, and now Bellaydin found himself lying in the snow, a biting cold wind blowing about his head, chilling him to the bone. Touching himself, he felt blood on his clothes, and a deep wound to his stomach. Curiously, however, he felt no pain, even when he brought himself to his feet. He looked down at himself. He was dressed in black and grey, his clothing giving little idea as to his present identity. A man came towards him, dressed in the garb of a cultist of the Horned God but, instead of coming in anger, the cultist approached in reverence. "My lord Enlim. You live."

As the realisation dawned that he now wore the body of the infamous Simon Enlim, Bellaydin's hands went around his neck. Hanging around it was a single piece of the Tears of the Divine, the same piece given to him by the dying Wulfric. As he touched it, the vision changed again.

Now he was in more familiar territory – Emparia – the city of Genio. He saw Hotar Citadel, the residence of the Earls of Genio. A door was in front of him and, from behind it, he could hear voices, scuffling. He opened the door and saw two men locked in a fight to the death. One was robed; a hood covering his face. Bellaydin saw the other man's face and recognised Alusine Ap'Lydin, his father. He wanted to shout out, tell his father who he was, but he could not. He was not here; Bellaydin was merely living another man's memories.

He tried to rush towards the two fighters, hoping to save Alusine Ap'Lydin's life, but before he could reach them, the hooded man stabbed Alusine Ap'Lydin through the stomach, murdering him in cold blood. Feeling taken over with rage, Bellaydin leapt at the man, wrestling him to the ground. Blood smeared from the murderer's hands on to Bellaydin's clothes and arms.

A voice cried out, and Bellaydin looked up, only to see Wulfric Highcrown standing in the doorway. The duke looked much younger, so much so that Bellaydin barely recognised him, and his face was contorted with shock and horror. Before Bellaydin could say a word, Wulfric was after him in a fury.

The scene changed again and now Bellaydin found himself lying in the snow, acute agony running through his body. His legs were broken and twisted, and nearby he saw Wulfric lying motionless on the ground. With a tremendous roar, Bellaydin felt himself tear the piece of the Tears of the Divine from around his neck. He then thrust the piece of metal into the comatose body of Wulfric Highcrown. It was then he heard a voice, and it was calling his name.

"Bellaydin."

The voice was familiar.

"Bellaydin."

He opened his eyes.

"Bellaydin." Polnygar eyes were wide and her voice frantic. "Are you alright?"

Bellaydin stared at his sister for a few moments, feeling dazed and confused. He stumbled over his words. "I'm fine, yes. Where are we?"

"Just outside Wishapton, remember?" she said. "Are you sure you're alright?"

Bellaydin tried to stand but felt so giddy he almost fell again. Polnygar offered her arm in support. "I feel dizzy. What happened, Pol?"

"Wulfric grabbed your head with his hands, and you went into convulsions and then blacked out. You were lying there for an hour. I tried to rouse you, but you just kept muttering things and wouldn't wake."

"Muttering things? What things?"

"I don't know," Polnygar said. "Just names, words. It didn't make much sense."

Bellaydin sighed. "Well, we need to tell the others we're safe. They're probably looking for us. Has anyone come for us?"

"No," Polnygar said. "But I can still send a message regardless."

"Magic?" Bellaydin asked. Polnygar nodded in affirmation. "Do it quickly, Pol. Time is of the essence."

Polnygar threw her head back and retreated within her mind, hoping to far-speak with Aelzandar.

"Polnygar? Is that you? Where are you?" The archmage's voice was clear and urgent.

"I'm not sure. A lot has happened. We're safe. But the two dukes are dead."

"What? What happened precisely?"

"I'll explain when we see you. We're going to try and find you."

"Come quickly. We cannot wait forever. The refugee convoy must start moving or the Goriinchians will kill us all."

"Understood. If we are not there in an hour, leave without us."

"Done. They know we're coming, but they won't wait long." Polnygar surveyed their surroundings. "Look, Bela. We've got to get out of here. We're behind the refugee convoy as it is. If we wait any later, we'll never catch it."

"Wait, what about –" Bellaydin wheeled around, looking to the ground. "Wulfric."

The duke was clearly dead. His eyes were cold and staring, and his flesh cold to the touch. The torn, blood-stained robes and the gory mess that marked his chest seemed to glint in the moonlight, like a macabre message to Bellaydin.

"We must cremate him," Bellaydin said.

"There's no time," Polnygar said. "And I think it's fairly clear that building any sort of pyre would just attract attention."

Bellaydin sniffed the air. "What attention? We haven't seen any Goriinchians thus far." As if on cue, an arrow screamed past Bellaydin's head, embedding itself in a nearby tree.

"Satisfied?" Polnygar said.

Leaving Wulfric's body, Bellaydin and Polnygar tried to make an escape as more arrows flew their way. One particular arrow tore close by, almost carving a groove in Polnygar's left cheek, causing her to cry out in pain. Bellaydin stopped, turning to his sister, trying to see if she was harmed. As he did, he noticed shadowy figures emerging from the undergrowth behind them. Turning around, he saw more in front of him, closing off their escape. As they came into view, he recognised them from their familiar tartan clad garb.

"Saldarri," Bellaydin said.

"Do not move, Heir of Lydin." One of them aimed an arrow at his neck. "We have you surrounded. Put your hands in the air."

Bellaydin raised his hands, followed by his sister. The Saldarri scout looked surprised and, motioning to his fellow Saldarri to take up positions, approached the two Ap'Lydins.

A Saldarri looked confused as he examined the pair of them. "Two marks?"

"What did he say?" Polnygar asked her brother in hushed tones.

"Something about two marks," Bellaydin whispered back. "He's pointing at our hands."

The Saldarri went from Bellaydin to Polnygar in turn, rubbing a finger on each one's scarred hand, as if to see if the either of the marks was faked.

"Two marks." the lead Saldarri said again in Goriinchian.

The other Saldarri moved closer, murmuring things to each other.

"What's going on?" Polnygar asked her brother.

He eyed the Saldarri wearily. "I'm not sure. But it doesn't seem good."

"You both bear the mark of the Heir." The Saldarri walked back and forth in front of them. "And I was instructed to find and bring the Heir. So, I will do as asked."

The Saldarri leader shouted out a few commands to his fellows; immediately Bellaydin and Polnygar were grabbed roughly.

"Where are you taking us?" Bellaydin asked.

"To Goriinchia."

CHAPTER 15

Aelzandar watched the horizon, illuminated by the last feeble tendrils of sunlight. "An hour has passed. I am beginning to think Polnygar and Bellaydin have been further delayed."

The archmage was seated in the wagon, Hebu beside him. Soldiers and common folk milled about, preparing the other wagons. Talthas stood nearby, looking about the crowd of people, before signalling to a soldier walking their way. As he did, Geoffrey came up beside the group.

"Sir Geoffrey! Any sign of them?" Talthas asked.

"I'm afraid not," Geoffrey said. "I've checked every wagon from here to the end, and I can't see either of them anywhere."

Hebu wrinkled his brow. "I'm sure they'll turn up," he suggested.

Talthas nodded in assent. "I do hope they're both alright. It's probably too late to turn back to find them now."

"True," Geoffrey said. "We're probably only a day or so ahead of the Goriinchians by now."

Hebu fixed Geoffrey with a beady glare. "Yes, dear knight. But given we seem to be dragging so much –" The Nemoi glared pointedly at the sluggishly moving wagons, filled with farmers and labourers. "–weight, it won't be long until that army closes the gap."

Aelzandar raised a conciliatory hand. "Yes, Hebu, your point is well-taken. There is a danger that the Goriinchian army will overtake us. The decision, however, has been made, and we must deal with the situation as best we can. Polnygar did tell us if they were delayed any further that we should leave without them." *That's not all she said in that mind message she sent, either.*

Geoffrey sat back, feeling troubled. He was worried for Bellaydin and Polnygar's safety but the knowledge that the Duke of Alariat and the Duke of Oldharbour were now dead also weighed heavy on him. How had they died? Was it an accident? Was it murder? Who could have killed them and why? There were several possibilities, none of which comforted him. It also made Sir Geoffrey the ranking noble in this caravan of refugees, another fact which did nothing to comfort him. Fighting battles was one thing, being responsible for the safety of hundreds of common folks was another. The thought of what would happen once the Goriinchians caught up to them chilled him to no end.

Talthas spoke to Geoffrey. "I'm going to have a look at the rear end of the column. See if they haven't turned up amongst the stragglers at the end there."

Geoffrey nodded and waved the elf off. A few moments later, the wagon came to a halt. "What's going on? Why have we stopped?" Geoffrey leapt from the wagon, and walked up the path a little, hoping to see the source of the disturbance. He found one of the wagon drivers. "You there. What's the hold-up?"

"Sorry, Sir Geoffrey, but we've been stopped by a patrol."

"Goriinchians?" Geoffrey's mouth went dry.

"No, sir. Emparians. They bear the colours of the Duke of

Oldharbour."

"But he's dead." Geoffrey thought the words but didn't say them out loud. No one needed to know that yet. He didn't want to cause panic.

A single soldier marched towards him. He wore a green and purple surcoat with the twisted snake of House Highcrown. "Are you Sir Geoffrey Keslin?"

"Yes," Geoffrey said. "What is this about?"

"Our commander wishes to speak with you. Come this way sir."

Geoffrey nodded and followed the soldier. A few feet away, he found more of the Oldharbour soldiers standing at attention. Their commander, a familiar green figure, stood nearby.

"Sir Geoffrey," Kahlaf el-Lahn said, "Surprised to see me?"

"Kahlaf. What are you doing here?"

"Obeying the instructions of my master." The Ahktarran's voice was as gruff as always. "These men are part of his ducal guard. The duke gave me strict instructions to meet you here. He told me to expect to you to be leading this procession."

"Then you know."

"That you have evacuated Wishapton? That the Goriinchian forces are on the move? Yes."

"But how did the message get to you so quickly?" Geoffrey said.

Kahlaf only grunted in response.

"And what sort of answer is that?"

"A short one, Sir Geoffrey. Such information is to be shared only between myself and my master."

"Your master," said Geoffrey. *He doesn't know yet, does he?* "Yes, and where is the Duke of Oldharbour? Is he with you? He left us days ago without any sort of farewell."

The Ahktarran paused, mouth open and fangs displayed, before giving a curt response. "He is presently occupied with matters that do not concern you. Is the Duke of Alariat with you?"

He doesn't know that either, Geoffrey thought. *Makes sense.* "Ah," he said out loud, as if to drown out what he was actually thinking. "No. He's also occupied with something else. Something that does not concern you." He felt an odd sense of satisfaction in throwing the Ahktarran's own words back at him, even if they weren't exactly true.

Kahlaf ignored Geoffrey's retort. "We need to get the refugees through the pass. Then you and I have work to do. We are going to make sure that these refugees make it through by engaging the Goriinchian force in battle."

Geoffrey laughed. "Is that all? Will it be just you and myself, my scaly friend, or are we going to perhaps invite someone else along?"

"This is serious, knight," Kahlaf said. "We shall need every able-bodied man who can bear arms."

"Bear arms? What good will that do any of us? From what I've heard, these automata are nigh invincible."

Kahlaf snorted, and drew close to Geoffrey, intimidating him with his bulk. "You are correct, Sir Geoffrey, they are all but invincible but they have a weakness, one which we may exploit."

"A weakness?"

"Follow me," Kahlaf instructed. Geoffrey complied, trailing the Ahktarran towards the rear section of the battalion. Amongst the soldiers Geoffrey could see Talthas, his hope to find Bellaydin and Polnygar amongst those in the rear of the column unsuccessful. The elf gave Geoffrey a nod of acknowledgement.

Some distance away, flanked by two guards, was a canvas-covered wagon. Kahlaf led Geoffrey straight to it. "The automata cannot be harmed by ordinary weapons of steel or iron. Their metal hides are impervious to almost any material. Only one thing can penetrate their skin."

Kahlaf pulled back the canvas, revealing the wagon's contents: a large collection of finely made weapons, all fashioned from the same bluish-silver metal. Eyes wide, Geoffrey picked up a sword from the wagon, and held it up in the light, marvelling at how the blade reflected the light almost as much as a mirror.

"What in the name of Kytilas are these made of?"

"Skymetal." Talthas had come to stand close to Geoffrey, his face hardly hiding his surprise. "It is rare, difficult to work with, and beyond the skill of an ordinary smith. Each of these weapons is worth a king's ransom. These are Eldara-made, make no mistake."

Geoffrey turned to Kahlaf in disbelief. "Is this so? Who would have been generous enough to provide you with these?"

The Ahktarran's face betrayed nothing. "My lord the Duke of Oldharbour."

"Where did he acquire Eldara-made weapons?" Talthas asked. "Did he not tell you?"

"I did not ask," Kahlaf said. "It is not my place to do so, nor is it yours."

"We are trusting our lives to these weapons," Geoffrey reasoned. "Surely you could make an exception, just this once."

Kahlaf straightened his back. "My lord has my undying loyalty. And even if I were not his bondsman, he would have earned that loyalty a thousand times over."

"Ah, well. Worth a try." Geoffrey peered at the collection of weapons in the wagon again.

"I only see weapons for hand-to-hand combat here," he said. "What are we going to do if they shoot arrows at us from a range?"

"The duke has provided us with a quantity of skymetal-tipped arrows and crossbow bolts. They should be enough for our purposes."

"I'd like to believe you." Geoffrey said. "But I have my doubts about this, even with these weapons. How likely is a victory?"

"I will not mislead you, knight," Kahlaf said. "Our chances are slim. If you continue your journey with the refugees, however, there is no doubt that the Goriinchians will catch you and if they take you by surprise, you are all dead."

"That's putting it rather bluntly," Geoffrey said.

"I do not believe in lying to spare a man's feelings, knight. When I tell you now that if you do not stay and fight then the refugees will die, I do not exaggerate for effect."

Geoffrey sighed. Things seemed to be going from bad to worse. He was now forced to choose between letting thousands of innocents die or sacrificing his own life. For a moment his natural cowardice and sense of self-preservation threatened to reassert themselves, but in the end, he knew there was only one option.

"Very well," Geoffrey said. "Let's hand out these weapons and organise a defence. The refugees can continue on ahead without us." Sometimes he hated being a good man.

***

Bellaydin struggled to stand up.

The Saldarri had taken no chances with either Ap'Lydin sibling and had bound and gagged both, no doubt prompted by stories that one of them could use the Art. In truth, Polnygar had felt too stunned and surprised to remember the incantations of any useful spell, and by the time her mind was focused, they had already tied her hands and covered her mouth with the rag. Once satisfied both siblings had been properly restrained, the Saldarri had driven the pair on a forced march from Wishapton deep into Goriinchian territory. For days they had kept up a punishing schedule, only stopping periodically to give Bellaydin and Polnygar minimal food and water. By now both siblings were thirsty and hungry and exhausted from lack of sleep.

"Do not tire yourself, Heir," the leader Saldarri ranger told Bellaydin. "There is no need to struggle."

Bellaydin tried to yell out a response, but his words were muffled by the gag. The ranger patted his shoulder. "Do not fear, Heir, we will not harm you. You have been asked for, by the Seeress." Underneath her gag, Polnygar tried to speak, Bellaydin wondered if she was asking who the Seeress was.

For the past few days, the Saldarri had repeatedly reassured Bellaydin that he was in no danger and that they were taking him to the Seeress. Bellaydin did not trust their words. In his view, it was just as likely that he was being taken directly to the Prophet-King Ygarak and the priests of the Horned God. Besides, even if they were telling the truth, Bellaydin had only met the Seeress once, and that was certainly not an experience he wanted to relive. Polnygar couldn't understand Goriinchian, and Bellaydin wondered whether for Polnygar if ignorance was bliss, or if fear of the unknown was just as overwhelming.

The lead Saldarri's name was Caelwych. Bellaydin had heard the other Saldarri referring to their leader by name as they walked. Their captors revealed little else of their identities, though, and most of the journey was taken in silence.

Hours passed, and just when Bellaydin thought he might collapse with exhaustion, his Saldarri captors came to a stop. "We are here, Heirs of Lydin.".

Spread across the hill in front of them was a collection of huts and tents, interspersed with the occasional campfire. Saldarri men and women gazed at Bellaydin and Polnygar in wonder as if sizing up their strange appearance. Caelwych led them onwards along a path that led up a forested hill. Bellaydin remembered the path. Other memories of that day – nearly two years ago now – came back to him. Morgan. Was she here somewhere? Would he see her again? He had neither heard nor seen the girl since their escape from her uncle but she had always been in his mind, lurking in the back of his thoughts.

When they reached the cave entrance, Caelwych removed the gags from both Polnygar and Bellaydin, and then untied both their bonds. "Do not attempt to flee, Heirs. Despite your importance we have no qualms about shooting you where you stand." As if to emphasise his point, Caelwych fingered the wood of his longbow.

Bellaydin nodded, and, after a quick translation, made sure his sister also understood the situation. "I wasn't really contemplating any escape anyway," she said. "It's not like we have any idea how to get back to Wishapton."

"It's somewhere to the north," he said. "But that's as much as I can guess."

As Bellaydin and his sister spoke to each other their Saldarri captor had lit a torch from his belt and illuminated the way ahead. "Move."

With Caelwych pushing them forward, Bellaydin and Polnygar entered the cave tentatively. Polnygar seemed unsure of what to expect, whereas Bellaydin, his last visit clear in his mind, knew exactly what awaited them. He dreaded what was to come.

"Take a seat," Caelwych led Bellaydin and Polnygar to the table and chairs that stood in the middle. He placed the flaming torch in one of the wall sconces. "The Seeress will be with you soon."

Within a few minutes of Bellaydin and his sister sitting down, the

Seeress entered the chamber. She seemed older than Bellaydin remembered. Hunched over and supported by a cane, she shuffled towards the table. Caelwych came to the old woman's assistance and helped her into her chair.

"So," the Seeress said, her voice cracking with age, "the Enparran has returned."

"You speak Emparian?" Polnygar seemed glad to finally be able to understand someone.

"I speak all the tongues of men and beasts, Enparran. Your brother knows this." The Seeress turned her gaze towards Bellaydin.

"Wait, wait, how do you know I'm her brother?"

The old woman gave an enigmatic smile. "Visions, Enparran. In my dreams I have seen you both. I knew that you would find your way here in the end."

"Find our way here?" Polnygar said. "Your men kidnapped us."

The Seeress glanced at Caelwych, who shrugged. "Caelwych is enthusiastic, but he meant no harm. In truth, the Saldarri have saved your lives this day. You were sought by another one, the followers of one who would do you great harm – The Horned God."

"The Horned God seeks the Heir of Lydin," Polnygar said.

"Indeed, he does. Indeed, he does."

"And which of us is this Heir?" Bellaydin said.

The Seeress smiled, fixing Bellaydin with a crazed stare. "Both of you."

"What? How can that be?"

"The Heir of Lydin will only become apparent when the blood of Lydin has thinned to its last drop. While both of you survive, there will be no Heir. To make sure the prophecy comes to pass, the Horned God will continue to prune the line of Lydin until only one of you remains."

Bellaydin looked at his sister, who looked just as ashen. He felt the blood drain from his own face and was certain he looked the same. "You said continue. How long have the Horned God's followers being killing our family?"

"For as long as the Horned God has reigned over Karlicia, the sons of Lydin have been his prey. Your family's blood calls to him, enraging him like a red rag to a bull. The Horned God murdered your father. He slaughtered your mother, killed your cousin. And now only three remain."

"Two," Bellaydin pointed to himself and Polnygar.

The Seeress seemed unsure. "In my visions, I have seen a girl, a child of noble blood, her parents both gone."

Bellaydin sighed. "That would be Maria. She is gone. The Horned God's followers killed her."

"That is something I have not seen in my dreams. If what you say is true, then the Horned God is closer to his final prey than ever before."

Polnygar's brow wrinkled. "Can we not escape? Flee from this place? Bela, let us leave this god and his wretched followers behind."

The Seeress shook her head. "You cannot escape his reach, child, even if you fled to the very edges of this world. The deepest ocean, the highest peak, the darkest forests, he will find you anywhere."

Bellaydin wanted to argue otherwise. He wanted to call the Seeress out on her lies and tricks, but in his heart, he knew she spoke the truth. The Horned God's followers had found them in Aderilund, they had found him in Emparia and Goriinchia, and they had chased his sister through Macrodonia, Ralom and Skurj. If the Horned God's tendrils extended that far, there was no telling how distant a place he would hunt them. "What do we do then? Fight?"

The Seeress nodded. "Yes. You must fight."

"You want us to fight your god?" Polnygar said. "Why? Isn't that blasphemy for your people?"

The old woman fixed them with a defiant stare. "I am not one of the Horned God's slaves, however much his priests and warriors might wish it. I stand apart, dreaming the words of the prophecy that even the Horned God himself cannot stand against. The Saldarri, for their part, serve the Horned God as their Karlician overlords demand, but have not done so willingly. And those that know their heart know that they chafe under the Horned God's yoke. They profess words with their mouths that which they reject with their souls."

Caelwych stared at Bellaydin, his stare firm and unrelenting, as if to emphasise what the seeress had just said. "The Goriinchians may believe the lies of their lord, but only because of the very sickness that Ygarak has planted in this people." The Seeress raised her hands above her head. "Young men strut and preen, and kill and rape and holler and shout over the so-called occupied Karlicia, where the Enparrans rule, but why do they care? They've never been there. They do not know that land, the land where Enparrans have lived for a thousand years. Ygarak and his lord have painted an illusion, and his slaves believe it because they are offered nothing else. Their memories are short, and they know little of the world. The Saldarri remember the past. They remember it all too well."

"Are you Saldarri?" Bellaydin said. "I don't see any pointed ears."

"I am of a long bloodline of Seers, Enparran, and yes, so my forefathers were of Saldarri stock. But since those days the blood of Saldarri and Karlician has often mixed and sometimes, as in my case, little trace of the fey remains." The Seeress leant closer. "Let me tell you a story, Enparran. The way you choose to respond to this story is up to you. There once was a place – Karlicia – a peaceful and tranquil land where people worked and played under the gods of their forefathers. We Karlicians were protected by the spirits that first delivered the Karlician people from the yoke of the Lords of the Fey. But things changed with the coming of Ygarak and his master. The land descended into darkness, and we all became slaves of the uncaring so-called true god."

"Then we are allies, against a common foe," Polnygar said urgently. "You can help us; we can help you."

"More than you imagine." The Seeress' aged eyes twinkled in the torchlight. "The Saldarri will follow the Heir of Lydin, whoever that might be. But first, you must do something for us. I would have you right a wrong that had its roots in our first meeting, Enparran. You remember my Gariníon, Morgan Culainn? Your meeting had a profound influence on that one. Morgan was always devoted to the faith she was raised in, and the Horned God was her entire world. Events, however, seem to have shaken her resolve. Her father's death set her on a different path, one of doubt and disbelief." The Seeress leant over the table and pressed something into Bellaydin's hand.

"Morgan's medallion, the symbol of the Horned God," Bellaydin said. "Why are you giving me this?"

"Her faith steadily dwindled since the last time you spoke, Enparran, until the day when it dwindled into nothing. Unfortunately, the Horned God is a jealous god and possessive of his slaves. He cannot abide to release even one. The penalty for apostasy is —"

"Death," Bellaydin finished. "Is she —"

"No," the Seeress said. "She still lives. Even the Prophet-King and the High Priests would not dare to end a Karlician life without the proper procedure. She is to be subject to the tradition of her people and given time to repent of her apostasy. If at the end of this period of clemency she has not repented of her apostasy, she will die on a heathen's pyre."

"It's my fault," Bellaydin said. "I planted that doubt in her head."

"Then you must atone, Enparran, and save her life. Do this, and you will have proven yourself to the Saldarri."

246

Polnygar turned to him. "I'm with you, Bela," she said, laying a hand on his. "Let's do this."

Bellaydin smiled. "Thank you, Pol."

"Morgan is being held at the temple a day and a half by horse to the south." The Seeress said, "Caelwych will guide you there."

Caelwych nodded. "You will not walk alone, Enparran. I will bring ten of my finest men along with us."

Bellaydin looked up and thanked him. Caelwych acknowledged the thanks with a curt nod. "For the honour of our ancestors, we will prevail."

Bellaydin looked grim. He certainly hoped they would.

***

They set off as soon as possible. The Saldarri had been as good as their word, and both Bellaydin and Polnygar had been provided with fresh horses and ample supplies. Once he was sure that they did not plan to escape, Caelwych also made sure that the siblings received new weapons, a sword and bow each. The blades may have been dull, but they were well-made and would suffice for their purpose.

"So, do you pray to the Horned God? Or to someone else?" Bellaydin asked Caelwych, as the three of them rode out in front of the following Saldarri.

"With my lips, yes, with my words, yes. But in my soul, I speak only to the Triple Goddess. That is the Saldarri way." He replied in heavily accented Emparian, understanding that while Bellaydin understood the Goriinchian tongue, Polnygar did not.

"And the other Goriinchians don't know?" Bellaydin asked.

"We Saldarri are always treated with suspicion. Saldarri blood is considered to bestow a tendency to heresy, and the priests of the Horned God are ever vigilant for what they see as signs of betrayal. Still, we are

247

useful to Ygarak and as long as we follow his orders, for the most part, we have been left in peace. But now the great warchiefs, who have ruled Karlicia since the War of Pacification, are in decline. The high priests and the church are rising to take their place, and Karlicia is becoming a far less tolerant place. The war chiefs were mostly concerned with the reconquest of occupied Karlicia. Theological matters bored them. But now men such as Cathan Culainn have absolute authority, and they wield it with a righteous fury."

"I've met Cathan," Bellaydin murmured. "He's not a pleasant man."

"There is worse. I have heard tales that Ygarak has summoned a new figure to join him in the highest echelons of rulership. A foreigner."

"An Emparian?" Bellaydin said.

"No. If the tales are true, this new lord is not a man, but a fey lord, ancient and terrible, and able to harness the powers of the Underworld."

"Ivellios," Polnygar said, staring straight at her brother.

"Are you sure about this?" Bellaydin said.

Caelwych shook his head in uncertainty. "I can't vouch for it. As I said, they're just tales."

Before long they had reached their destination. A craggy hill rose seemingly out of nowhere, the land surrounding it barren and devoid of any vegetation except for a few skeletal trees. The temple of the Horned God was an ornate keep, decorated in the macabre fashion of the Goriinchian faith. A tall, spiked wall surrounded an open courtyard and within it stood a solemn grey tower, like a single fingerbone pointing into the sky.

"We are here," Caelwych said. "We must approach with caution."

"Will we be that noticeable?" Polnygar said.

"Saldarri squads often come and go with few words," Caelwych said. "But they very rarely ride with non-Saldarri."

"Humans, you mean," Polnygar looked at her brother.

"We'll try to pass ourselves off as Saldarri," Bellaydin said. "Give Polnygar your cloak."

Caelwych undid his tartan cloak and passed it to Polnygar.

"We'll have to disguise my ears," Bellaydin tore a strip of cloth from his clothes and wrapped it around his head, tying it tightly. "How do I look?"

Polnygar laughed. "It doesn't suit you. But it should at least fool them."

"Well, I hope so. If any of them recognise me it's going to get very messy out there. Maybe the beard will help." He rubbed the hair on his chin, thinking of the time that had passed since he had last been seen by Goriinchians. He hoped that they would find little to recognise in his face. With their spontaneous disguise sorted, Caelwych led them towards the temple.

Bellaydin was surprised at the ease with which they gained entry. He had expected a fierce questioning, and consequently a frantic attempt by the Saldarri to hide Bellaydin and Polnygar's identities. But nothing even close to that occurred. Instead, a few bored looking Goriinchian warriors opened the gates for them as soon as they saw them approaching.

"Well, that seemed easy."

"Yeah," Polnygar said, "A little too easy."

Bellaydin nodded. "Keep your eyes open."

They rode through the gates and into the open area past the walls. A large crowd had gathered in the centre of the enclosure, shouting, and yelling in response to events that were occurring on an elevated wooden platform near the temple proper.

Several Goriinchian priests stood on the stage, dressed in the grey and black robes of the Horned God. One of them, taller than the rest, wore a grotesque yet ornate horned mask, probably in emulation of his god.

"Loyal sons of Karlicia, honoured slaves of the Horned God." The high priest's arms were wide and his voice shrill. "We are here today to do the Horned God's work. We are here today to deal with those who oppose His will. We are here today to punish those who make themselves the enemies of God."

With each word, the priest's voice seemed to whip the crowd into a maddening frenzy. They were chanting now, repeating the priest's words, and raising their fists in the air as some sort of salute. "Behold the worst of all criminals and traitors, the apostates. Those who heard the blessed voice of the Horned God yet spurned it."

The crowd jeered and hollered as a downcast group of men and women were pushed onto the wooden stage. Dressed in ragged grey clothes, the prisoners were chained together and judging by their anguished shuffling and limping, had clearly been physically mistreated, if not outright tortured. "Each of these will be consigned to the flames, like the basest infidel, their souls consumed by the fire. Take them."

Soldiers grabbed the prisoners, taking them from the stage to the ground below where a large pyre had been constructed, with several tall stakes. One by one, the prisoners were unchained from each other and tied to the stakes.

"There. It's Morgan," Bellaydin said.

"How do we get to her?" Polnygar said. "Look at all the soldiers."

Caelwych looked from Polnygar to Bellaydin. "We need a distraction. Any ideas?"

"Pol, can you use your magic?" Bellaydin said.

"I can try," she said. "What sort of distraction do you want?"

"Surprise me." Bellaydin rode slowly towards the chanting crowd, trying to look inconspicuous. The soldiers were moving towards the pyre, burning torches in their hand. Bellaydin quickened his pace. Morgan was tied to the furthermost stake, and he moved closer towards her. As he did, the high priest removed his mask and revealed his face, and Bellaydin nearly froze. It was Cathan Culainn, Morgan's own uncle. Bellaydin tried to blend into the crowd, hoping that Cathan wouldn't recognise him.

Suddenly Bellaydin was rocked by the sound of a huge explosion and nearly toppled off his horse. Around him, the chanting crowd started screaming and scattered in a panic. Bellaydin looked up. Above him, etched in the sky, was the spectral image of the Transcendent Court of Aderilund. Bellaydin silently thanked his sister.

As the crowd pushed and jostled, one of the soldiers dropped the torch he was carrying, directly onto the pyre. The flames shot up as the kindling was quickly consumed. Bellaydin's horse reared.

"Whoah. Careful." As soon as he had spoken those words, he realised his mistake. Someone near him yelled out, "Enparran." Soon the whole crowd was screaming the word.

High on the stage, Cathan was furious, and his voice called out above the din. "Light the pyre. Kill the Enparran!"

A soldier ran towards Bellaydin but then collapsed, an arrow sticking from his back. Bellaydin glanced back towards his sister. She had drawn her sword as the Saldarri let off arrow after arrow. Bellaydin calmed his horse and urged it forward, riding past Morgan. The fire was coming close to her, and smoke clouded the area, only serving to panic the crowd even further.

More soldiers poured out from the temple, archers and black-cloaked priests coming with them. Bellaydin would have to move fast. He pushed his horse forward again, and with a massive leap, cleared the fire, cutting Morgan's restraints and pulling her onto the horse's back. He looked at the other prisoners and for a moment hesitated, but then; resisting the urge to flee, he freed them as well.

"Get him. Get him!" Cathan yelled out.

Clearing the pyre, Bellaydin rode on, one arm holding tightly on to Morgan, the other holding his sword as he slashed at the soldiers who got in his way.

"Bellaydin?" Morgan's voice was distant, as if she couldn't believe what she saw. "You came."

"It'll be fine, Morgan. I've got you." Suddenly Bellaydin's horse reared, and he toppled from it, hitting the ground with a thud. His sword clattered next to him. Looking up, he saw his horse fall to the ground, an arrow sticking from its neck. Half of the Saldarri that had come with them were also dead, their bodies lying battered and bloody in the dirt. The cloth slipped from his head.

Polnygar called in alarm. "Bela!"

"Get Morgan out of here, Pol." Bellaydin picked up his sword and fended off an attacking Goriinchian.

"What about you?" Polnygar said.

"Go!" Bellaydin ordered.

He parried another blow, kicking his attacker in the stomach. More soldiers ran to engage him. He looked up, and caught the gaze of Cathan Culainn. A flicker of recognition passed over the high priest's face. "Soldiers. It's him. The Heir of Lydin!"

Nearby, Polnygar pulled Morgan onto her horse and looked on in dismay. "Come on, we have to save him!" The other Saldarri were engaged in battles of their own, their horses long since toppled under them.

"It's no good," Caelwych let off another arrow, skewering a Goriinchian through the neck. "There are too many of them to fight. Is there some spell you have, perhaps?"

"There's no time, and if I did, I'd end up hurting Bela as well." Polnygar said.

"We must retreat!" Caelwych yelled.

"Wait, we can't leave Bela," Polnygar said. The Goriinchians had surrounded her brother.

"It's too late. Either we leave him, or we all die." Caelwych said. "And I don't intend to die here. Morgan must be returned. That was what you promised." Without another word, Caelwych turned his horse behind and left before Polnygar's eyes.

"Wait, no! You can't do this." She could no longer see Bela through the throng of Goriinchians.

Ashamed, and feeling cowardly, Polnygar turned her horse and followed Caelwych, not even daring to turn back for a final glance.

CHAPTER 16

Geoffrey desperately needed a drink, and with every minute that passed, his thirst seemed to grow stronger. He had been fine but that was before Kahlaf informed him that he had to stay and fight an impossible battle against an army of magical walking statues that had so far smashed everything in their path.

As was usual with his preparation, Geoffrey tried to find some ale, beer, or any sort of alcohol to build some courage with, but Kahlaf had been insistent that Geoffrey keep sober. In the end, the Ahktarran drank an entire keg in front of Geoffrey, a spiteful move that was made worse when Kahlaf explained that the Ahktarran capacity for alcohol consumption meant that drinking the entire keg had no more effect on him than drinking a similar amount of water.

Geoffrey cursed Kahlaf, but not too loudly. The Ahktarran was, after all, standing right next to him. "This strikes me as a very bad idea," Geoffrey said to no one in particular.

Kahlaf heard the knight's mutterings and rolled his eyes in disgust. "You should keep your opinions to yourself, knight."

Geoffrey and Kahlaf stood in the centre of the line of Emparian soldiers. Some were well-trained men-at-arms, brought by Kahlaf from the Duke of Oldharbour's own private guard. Others were militiamen from Wishapton, who had tearfully sent their own wives and children on ahead with the wagon train before joining this likely suicidal attempt to delay the Goriinchian force. On the other hand, Geoffrey reasoned, if there was a place suited to one glorious last stand, where he was standing was probably it. A narrow pass between two mountain ranges, the peculiar funnel-like shape of the corridor might serve to even the odds, if only slightly. It even had a name: Cutthroat Pass. Geoffrey hoped the name wouldn't prove prophetic.

"I see smoke on the horizon," Geoffrey said.

Kahlaf nodded. "The Goriinchians are taking no chances this time. They are destroying everything in their path. It is likely there is no Emparian alive between us and the Goriinchian border."

"Bellaydin and Polnygar are still out there," Geoffrey said.

"We must hope that they have found their own way out of Wishapton," Kahlaf said.

"We should have gone back." Geoffrey had always regretted leaving the Ap'Lydins in the town.

"If we had turned back, we'd all be dead," Kahlaf said. His tone was coldly factual.

"So you keep reminding me," said Geoffrey.

Behind the line of infantrymen was a ridge upon which the Emparian archers and crossbowmen had assembled, with Talthas standing in the very centre. Again, they were a mixture of seasoned troops and militiamen, but even so, the Eldara's bowmanship would inspire them to greater heights.

At the back lines stood the archmage Aelzandar and his Nemoi companion, Hebu. The soldiers had moved the remaining wagons between the infantry and archers, hoping to protect the bowmen from rush attacks by the Goriinchians.

From his own position, Geoffrey could see the elven archmage reading through various scrolls and pieces of parchment that Aelzandar kept passing between himself and his small assistant.

"I hope he's got some big, powerful spell planned," Geoffrey said. "Or this battle is going to be over very quickly."

Geoffrey had placed his usual sword in one of the wagons behind them. Instead, he was now wielding one of the skymetal weapons that Kahlaf had brought with him. Geoffrey had chosen a mace, figuring it to be the most suited for combat with what amounted to a walking suit of armour.

It was not long before Geoffrey spotted the first ranks of the Goriinchian army making their way over the horizon. Even at such a distance, the automata were recognisable, marching in perfect symmetry, their metal legs clanking and the burnished bronze of their skin shining in the afternoon sunlight.

"Here they come," Geoffrey clutched the mace tightly. He felt a tightness in his chest and a bad feeling he was about to go into battle for the last time. He whispered a small prayer. "Kytilas protect me."

Next to him Geoffrey heard the Ahktarran muttering something in his own language, a bizarre sibilant tongue. He wondered if Kahlaf too was praying to one of the gods, despite the Ahktarran's assured display of self-confidence.

The army drew closer. In between the ranks of automata, Geoffrey could see Goriinchians marching. They were mostly archers, but, in a curious twist, there seemed to be very few Saldarri marching with them. An unusual sight, given previous Goriinchian invasions heavily relied on the skill and courage of the elf-blooded longbowmen. Perhaps something had happened that limited their availability. Certainly, many of them must have died in the previous incursion, but by that token, the deaths would have been evenly spread across the whole Goriinchian military.

"Archers!" Talthas barked, as the Goriinchians came within range. "Loose Arrows!"

The Emparian archers fired off a round of arrows. Geoffrey watched as the Goriinchians, seeing the volley, move back behind the automata. Most of the arrows bounced off the automata harmlessly, producing an audible metallic "ping" as they did, but the skymetal-tipped arrows punctured through the automata armour. Still, the automata were stronger than Geoffrey had hoped and though quite a few were hit and sustained damage, only one fell to the ground, and it had been hit half a dozen times.

"They're returning fire," Geoffrey said. "Take cover!"

The Goriinchian archers fired a volley of their own arrows towards the Emparians. Luckily, most of their shots missed their targets. Only two Emparians suffered wounds, and neither of those wounds was fatal. Geoffrey noted with relief the vast gulf in skill between these archers and the Saldarri bowmen he had faced at Wishapton.

Once the archers had finished, they retreated behind the automata once more, ready to withstand another barrage of Emparian arrows. After the Emparians had returned fire, the process started again, and Geoffrey watched the back-and-forth between the two sides with vague disinterest, his mind dwelling instead on the full battle yet to come. It was the sound of strange words being recited behind him that brought him back into reality.

Aelzandar.

Geoffrey did not understand a single word being said by the old elf, but he did recognise the Draconic tongue when he heard it. The harsh, angled consonants and carefully enunciated vowels seemed to evoke an air of mystery and ancient power, just like the dragons that were supposed to have spoken the language. As Aelzandar's voice reached a crescendo, the ground in front of Geoffrey seemed to shimmer and inexplicably turn a dark, greyish black. The automata continued to march forward, seemingly oblivious to what was happening, until they reached the blackened ground. Then, one by one, they seemed to falter. Some halted, their legs shaking, and their feet apparently stuck to the ground. Others started to flail about almost comically, as their feet seemed to be unable to grip the ground below. Some lost their footing entirely.

The Emparians let out a cheer. Geoffrey felt inclined to join in, but he shot a glance towards Kahlaf, and the Ahktarran seemed disapproving. In any case, they weren't out of the woods yet since some of the automata had made it through the magical swamp and were almost at the Emparian line.

"They're here," Geoffrey said, adopting a defensive stance. "Stand by."

The automata loomed within striking distance, their metal faces cold and impassive. Once they were close enough, each of them swung their metal fists in perfect synchronisation. Two soldiers were killed instantly, their bones and flesh smashed into a bloody pulp. Geoffrey only narrowly avoided a similar fate himself, by dodging out of the way. Kahlaf managed to take the automaton on its own terms, deflecting the fist with his own weapon and then striking it return, smashing through the metal shoulder and sending it crumpling to the ground.

Geoffrey fell backwards as the automaton came towards him, the metal statue cranking and grinding as it attacked him with amazing speed. He moved to the left and right rapidly in succession as the automaton's fist smashed into the dirt on either side of him. Just as it was pulling back for another blow, Kahlaf seemingly appeared out of nowhere and with an immense blow, severed the automaton's head from its body. Geoffrey got to his feet just in time to see a ray of lightning spark from Aelzandar's finger towards the enemy, electrifying several of the automata in a continuous arc. Three of the great metal men toppled to the ground, and Geoffrey quickly moved closer to his surviving comrades to plug up the gaps.

"They're faltering," Geoffrey said.

"Keep your mind on the task at hand, Sir Geoffrey." Kahlaf scolded. "There will be time for celebration when and if we survive."

"Will do," Geoffrey punctuated his words with a crushing blow to the side of an automaton.

Despite Kahlaf's caution, Geoffrey could see that the Goriinchians were starting to see the tide of the battle turn against them. They appeared shocked and dismayed by the stout defence the Emparians were putting up. The automata, though powerful enough to kill men in a single blow, were also stupid, somewhat clumsy creatures, able to do little else in battle except charge straight for the nearest enemy. With skymetal weapons and Aelzandar's magical support, the Emparians dealt with the metal warriors far more effectively than their untrained and unprepared counterparts the Goriinchians had clobbered through across the ground of southern Emparia.

Before long the last of the automata were disabled and the Emparians, though bloody, battered and down to a quarter of their original number, gave a cheer. The surviving Goriinchians soon surrendered and were taken into custody.

"Seemed a lot easier than I expected," Geoffrey flipped his mace over, wiping it clean of blood and black grease. The strange black slime had wept from the wounds of the automata, and Geoffrey guessed that it was to the automata as blood was to humans.

"I too have my suspicions," Kahlaf said. "It seemed to be far too small an invasion force."

"Maybe some got lost along the way," Geoffrey said.

Kahlaf gave him a withering look and turned around to the prisoners, who were currently being assembled in a makeshift enclosure. "It may serve us well to question these prisoners."

"Good idea. What are you waiting for?"

"You are the one who speaks Goriinchian here, Sir knight," Kahlaf said.

"Oh, right," Geoffrey put his mace away and approached the captured Goriinchian soldiers, holding his hands up in a conciliatory fashion. "Look," he said, switching to Goriinchian. "I just need to ask you a few questions."

"We will tell you nothing, Enparran dog." A soldier spat at Geoffrey and the other Goriinchians nodded, muttering in agreement.

"Is that so? That's alright then, my friend. You don't have to tell me anything. Instead, I'll turn you over to my tall, green, friend over here." Geoffrey pointed to the hulking figure of Kahlaf, who was busy deconstructing the remnants of an automaton with his bare hands. As Geoffrey watched, the Goriinchians' eyes widened as they stared at the Ahktarran, their eyes lingering on Kahlaf's large, sharp teeth, and wicked, curved claws, some of which were still stained with the blood of their comrades.

"Demon!" the earlier Goriinchian soldier cried out.

"I'll just go get him, shall I?" Geoffrey offered.

The Goriinchian let out a terrified stammer. "No, wait! We shall tell you what you want, infidel."

"That's better," Geoffrey folded his arms. "Is this the entire army that crossed the border from Goriinchia?"

"No, Enparran. As instructed, the war leaders divided the army into six separate groups after the destruction of Wishapton."

Geoffrey shivered. The force that they had faced today, the army that had nearly annihilated them, was only one-sixth of the Goriinchian forces that had crossed the border. "Why?"

"There was talk that the priests were after something or someone. They expected to find him in Wishapton, but the town was abandoned. Hence the war leaders were told to divide their forces and send them in different directions to search for this missing man."

"Who was the man?" Geoffrey pressed the Goriinchian for answers.

The Goriinchian's breath came in ragged gasps. "I don't know. Only the war leaders did."

"Where is your war leader?"

"Gone. He died in the battle."

Geoffrey's shoulders slumped. "Where were the other armies? Where were they headed?"

"I don't know." The Goriinchian seemed nervous and agitated. "All they told us is that we would meet up again at the infidel capital, the great city where their whore of a queen holds court."

Geoffrey called the Ahktarran over. Kahlaf's eyes fixed on Geoffrey's face. "What have you learned?"

Hurriedly, Geoffrey repeated what he had learned from the Goriinchians, taking care to emphasise the small proportion of the Goriinchian armies they had already faced, and that the armies were planning to eventually reach the Emparian capital.

Kahlaf bared his fangs and let out a small hiss. "Then there's not a moment to lose. We must continue on our way, and hope that we will reach Emperor's Palace before they do." With so much as another word, Kahlaf stomped off to the wagons, leaving Geoffrey alone with the prisoners.

"Is that all, Enparran?" the Goriinchian said.

Geoffrey turned around. "Ah, let me think. Oh yes, one more thing." With one swift movement, he swung at the Goriinchian, connecting his fist with the prisoner's face, and sending him to the ground. "That's for calling Her Majesty a whore."

***

The Tears of the Divine

Polnygar wept.

It wasn't quite the triumphant return she had in mind. She had brought back the Seeress' granddaughter, Morgan Culainn, but at the same time, she had lost her own brother, the brother she had only just reunited with after years apart. It hardly seemed any sort of victory at all.

The Seeress greeted them as they entered the camp. "Morgan."

"Seanmháthair," Morgan said, tears streaming down her face. She embraced the Seeress and sobbed freely.

The Seeress held her granddaughter tightly, turning her eyes to Morgan's rescuer. "You have returned, Heir of Lydin. But where is your brother?"

Polnygar stared at the ground and did not answer.

Caelwych answered for her. "He was captured by the priests of the Horned God. There was nothing we could do."

Polnygar shot an angry glance at him. "You *could* have done something, but you turned and fled."

Caelwych frowned. If the accusation stung him, he made no sign of it. His face betrayed not even the slightest flicker of emotion. "No, we were outnumbered. To try to save your brother would have only led to our own capture."

"Better that than leaving him there to die." Polnygar insisted.

"Your brother is not dead," Caelwych said.

"And how can you be sure of that?" Polnygar shot back.

"Caelwych speaks the truth, my Enparran child." The Seeress's tone was comforting. "The Goriinchians will not harm your brother while they know you still live. If they kill him, they risk making you the sole and final Heir of Lydin. Since your brother is the one in their custody, it would be in their interest to force the mantle of Heir onto him, something that can be accomplished only with your death."

Polnygar calmed somewhat. "So, you are sure my brother will not be harmed?"

Caelwych looked grim. "I did not say that. What I said is that he will not be killed."

Polnygar straightened her back. "I'm going to rescue him."

"Did you not hear what the Seeress said?" Caelwych asked. "It's you they'll be after now, not your brother. Going to rescue him would be exactly what they want you to do."

"I don't care." Polnygar's expression didn't change. "I'm not leaving him with them."

The Seeress held up a hand. "Peace, Caelwych. The girl loves her brother. That is not a crime."

The Saldarri grumbled. "She could endanger us all."

"The girl has made her decision. And since she has helped us, and saved my precious Morgan, we shall help her." The Seeress placed a hand on Polnygar's shoulder. "The time has come. The Saldarri will ride with you, Heir of Lydin. We shall rise up against the slaves of the Horned God and reclaim the land of Karlicia that once was."

The Seeress thumped her staff on the ground; chanting words in Goriinchian, she then raised the staff above her head as a salute. All around Polnygar, Saldarri emerged from their dwellings, and echoed the salute, crying out into the night air.

"All around the lands of Karlicia, the Saldarri will answer our call, Heir of Lydin. Ygarak will fall, and the Horned God will know fear." The Seeress beckoned for her to come closer. "There is one more thing, Heir of Lydin. We have a gift for you." The Seeress nodded to one of the Saldarri and he passed to her an object covered with a tartan piece of cloth. "This was recovered from a river, near the cairn of Aonghus Culainn. Before that, it was borne by William Ap'Lydin." The Seeress pulled back the cloth.

Underneath was a magnificent sword, with a brilliant gold-inlaid hilt and a blade that seemed to shimmer with blue light.

"This is Kaltban, Sword of Destiny," Caelwych's tone was reverent. "The sword of your forefathers. It was destiny that the Heir of Lydin would bear it. That is why we once believed your cousin to be the heir, until he fell during the war."

Polnygar looked at the Seeress. "William was the Heir?"

"So we thought," the Seeress responded. "But now another possibility has presented itself." She looked at Polnygar, her eyes urging. "Go on, take it."

Obeying the Seeress, Polnygar grasped the sword's handle and carefully took it from the old woman. With a flourish, she held it above her head. Such theatrics seemed appropriate, even if they made Polnygar redden a bit with self-consciousness. The Saldarri that had gathered around her seemed to appreciate the gesture, though, and they gave off another mighty roar.

"See now the words of prophecy made flesh," the Seeress called out. "See now the awakening destiny of the world. See now the Horned God's own power turned against him."

The Seeress dropped to one knee, bowing before Polnygar. As the old woman bent down, the other Saldarri followed suit.

"No, please, don't," Polnygar said, flushing again. "This isn't necessary."

Morgan stood up and approached Polnygar. "You would rescue your brother?"

"I won't leave him with those brutes." Polnygar said. "I've looked after him all my life, and I'm not about to stop now."

"I want to help," Morgan said her voice wavering.

"Morgan Culainn," Caelwych said. "That is not wise. The Seeress has not given you permission to leave."

The old woman laughed out loud. "The Seeress has not said anything either way yet, Caelwych."

"You've been a prisoner of those people, and now you want to go back there? Really?" Polnygar said.

"Yes," Morgan said. "I can help you. I can help you save Bellaydin. I owe him my life, and more. He opened my eyes to a wider world. He showed me that there are things greater than priests, and temples, obedience and gods."

Polnygar was sceptical. "My brother showed you that?"

"You don't believe me." The girl's eyes were wide, earnest. "I scarcely believe it myself. I realised I'd walked in darkness for so long."

Polnygar gave Morgan an appreciative look. "You are brave to defy your own uncle."

Morgan shook her head. "Cathan is a wicked man and hides his evil with a cloak of righteousness. Even if I had stayed true to the Horned God, my uncle would have found a way to make me suffer." Morgan took Polnygar's hand, grabbing it with a sudden swiftness that surprised Polnygar. "Please, my faith may have dwindled into disbelief, but I still know right from wrong. And now I see clearly, without the clouds that have darkened the sky since the day of my birth. I would ride with you, Polnygar, if you will have me."

Polnygar looked at the girl's eyes brimming with fresh tears, and nodded. "It'd be an honour, Morgan."

"This is ridiculous," Caelwych said. "Morgan is not a warrior. She's a woman."

Polnygar raised an eyebrow. "Pray tell, what's the difference?"

The Seeress chuckled. "Indeed. If the Heir of Lydin here is both a woman and a warrior, then I don't see why Morgan can't be either."

Polnygar smiled, taking Morgan's hand. "You're more than welcome to come, Morgan."

Morgan nodded and could not help but smile herself, emboldened by Polnygar's courage and her grandmother's words of support.

Caelwych was clearly irritated but he had no desire to second-guess the seeress. Instead he called out to everyone gathered around him. "We must prepare. The Saldarri will gather, and we will make plans." He touched the hilt of the sword. "Tonight marks the beginning of the end for Ygarak and his master."

***

Bellaydin opened his eyes.

Still groggy, he tried to look at his surroundings but found himself unable to turn his head. Heavy ropes restrained him, and his flesh, black and bruised, seemed to ache like hell with every movement he made.

A voice tinged with cruelty dragged him from his stupor. "The infidel wakes."

Cathan Culainn, high priest of the Horned God stood in front of Bellaydin, attired in the ceremonial finery of his station. The grey robes were covered with dark stains – blood, Bellaydin reasoned – and the large symbol of the Horned God emblazoned on Cathan's chest seemed to burn itself into Bellaydin's vision.

Bellaydin stammered. "Where am I? Where's my sister? How did I –"

"You were quite tenacious, infidel," Cathan said. "It took half a dozen of my soldiers to bring you down."

Bellaydin's voice was weak. "Why haven't you killed me?"

"Now, now," Cathan's voice was slick. "The Horned God is a god of peace, infidel. He wants his children to approach him of their own free will. That is why you are being given a choice."

267

Goriinchian soldiers approached. Bellaydin tried to move his head to watch, but the pain made it difficult. The warriors came to flank Cathan on either side, watching the high priest with awed, reverent faces. When they glanced at Bellaydin, their stares turned cold, unfeeling. Cathan came closer, so close that Bellaydin could feel the priest's putrid breath on his face and see the caked dirt and filth in Cathan's beard. "Your friends are in great danger, especially your sister."

Bellaydin flinched but said nothing.

"Oh yes. I know about your sister. The Horned God has revealed many things to me. She and her Saldarri friends, including the Culainn whore, should fear for their lives. They have sinned against the Horned God, and the penalty is death. You can save them, infidel. Your life for theirs."

"You're wasting time," Bellaydin said. "You'll soon be dead, and this place in ruins."

"If you are expecting the Saldarri and your sister to mount some grand rescue, then rest assured, we are quite safe here. The Horned God knows of their plots, and they will be dealt with. Again, I tell you. This need not be. Accept the Horned God's grace, and you can save your friends, faithless though they may be. The Horned God is the all-forgiving father of us all."

"You'll get nothing from me," Bellaydin said, but his voice was wavering.

"Don't be a fool, infidel. Death is inevitable."

"So, kill me."

"The death I speak of does not come for you alone. I have thirty thousand automata, ready for orders, able to leave at any time. If I give the word, they will attack the Saldarri camps, and leave no one standing, including your sister. Is this really what you want for your own flesh and blood?"

Bellaydin's mind swirled. He couldn't think straight. One part of him

268

wanted to defy Cathan, to spit in the smug Goriinchian's face, but a more cautious part pleaded with him to think rationally. Perhaps Cathan could exterminate his sister and the Saldarri with a single word. Perhaps the high priest would refrain from doing so if placated. Could he be trusted? Unlikely, but what choice did Bellaydin have? He was trapped, a prisoner. The others had likely no idea where he was. Would there even be a rescue party? How could there be? Despair played at the edges of his frazzled mind. His resolve began to weaken.

"What is your offer?" Bellaydin's voice cracked.

"So, you are interested?" Cathan eyes' glinted.

"I haven't agreed to anything except to hear this offer."

"Cautious to the end. The Horned God sees potential in you, infidel," Cathan said. "Why, I do not know, but the ways of heaven are inscrutable. Nevertheless, he is willing to accept your obedience and servitude if you submit. Become a slave of the Horned God, infidel, and not only will you save your own life, but so will you save the lives of those you care for."

Bellaydin laughed. "Your god wants me as a worshipper?"

Cathan frowned. "Do not mock the Horned God, infidel. He was the god of your birth, the creator of all existence. Just as he was at your beginning, so shall he be at your end. He is the one true lord, and you are his lost sheep. In the end, all return to their true master. Do not forget, your sister's life is at stake. As is your own."

Bellaydin tried to think, hoping to find a third path away from the unpalatable, terrible choice given to him.

"Your freedom or your sister's life," Cathan said.

Both. Gods, give me both. He wanted to scream. He knew Cathan would never accept such an answer, so he pushed his mind through the alternatives. He couldn't let his sister die, but how did he know Cathan would keep his promise? Servitude to the Horned God was a horrible, chilling future, but at least it offered the opportunity for escape. He would keep his life, if Cathan was truthful, and, in the end, hadn't Morgan herself broke free from a lifetime of indoctrination? For someone there unwillingly, the chains would be even weaker.

"I accept. Spare my sister's life, and the lives of Morgan and the Saldarri, and I will submit."

Cathan's face relaxed. "It is done." He raised his hands. "Bellaydin is no more. Gwydion is born into the Horned God's radiance."

Bellaydin was confused, but before he could ask what Gwydion meant, the two soldiers grabbed him, preventing him from struggling even to the slight extent possible in his bonds. Cathan opened a pouch on his belt and, slipping his hand inside, withdrew a small, oddly shaped metal sphere.

"Behold: Truth." Cathan forced the sphere down Bellaydin's throat, making sure that Bellaydin swallowed the object. Bellaydin felt the guards unhand him and before he knew what was happening, a heavy blow knocked him into unconsciousness.

All went black.

For a while, he drifted in his own thoughts, floating aimlessly. Then, a sharp pain catapulted through his senses, tearing his thoughts into pieces with agonising strokes.

His eyes fluttered open. He was somewhere else, a room with stone walls and a ceiling, ancient and crumbling. A thin stream of sunlight came in through a high window. Bellaydin lay on a flat uncomfortable cot, and the clothes he wore were not the ones he remembered. Instead, he was garbed in a long, grey tunic, and as he raised his arms to his face, he spied the symbol of the Horned God on his sleeves.

Without warning, he experienced a sudden painful lurch in his chest. It was as if his heart had suddenly seized up. After a few seconds of agony, the pain subsided, and he was left clutching his chest, sweating profusely.

"The change is often hard to bear," said a voice. "Rebirth is not an easy path."

"Haakon?"

In the dim light, Haakon de Morcor was only just visible. The Duke of Alariat looked older than he ever had before, his once kind, jovial face now taut and pale. He no longer wore the clothes of an Emparian noble. Instead, he was garbed in the robes of a high priest of the Horned God.

"Yes Gwydion. It is I." Haakon's eyes flashed in the darkness.

Bellaydin turned his head, his neck aching and pain still coursing through his head. "I'm not Gwydion. I'm Bellaydin."

"You will be Gwydion soon enough, my boy." Haakon said. "You have given yourself to the Horned God, and he has accepted your servitude."

"Where am I?" he said.

"They call this the supplicant's chamber. It is where those who are undergoing the change wait until they have fully received the Horned God's grace. It will not be long till you too hear the Horned God's blessed voice."

Haakon came closer and stroked the younger man's hair. "Gwydion, you have done nothing wrong. You have acknowledged the truth, just as your father did."

"My name is not Gwydion," Bellaydin insisted. Yet against all sense and judgement, he felt a seed of doubt sprouting in the depths of his mind. Perhaps his name *was* Gwydion.

He tried desperately to hold to the fraying strands of his sanity. "You betrayed us, Haakon. Why?"

"As always, I had to heed the word of the Horned God, my true master."

"And your loyalty to him trumped your loyalty to us?"

Haakon blinked. "Of course, my boy, he is my lord and master. And I have served him even longer than you have lived."

Longer than Bellaydin had lived? An image suddenly flashed into the young man's head – the painting of his father, Alusine Ap'Lydin, and another member of the Horned God's cult.

"You were the other man in the painting with my father," Bellaydin reasoned.

"Gwydion, I was your father's closest friend. We did everything together. When he entered the Horned God's faith, so did I. But I stayed true, where he faltered. So, the Horned God ordered he be punished for his apostasy."

A memory flooded Bellaydin's mind, but it was not a recollection of his own life. It was a shard of the memory of the being that had possessed Wulfric Highcrown, a memory of the death of Bellaydin's parents. He had been told that Simon Enlim had been responsible for the murders, but when he experienced Wulfric's memories for the first time, he knew this was not the case. Now the memory reappeared in his mind, clearer, and more vivid, despite the pain Bellaydin was wracked with; Alusine Ap'Lydin lying in a pool of blood, his wife screaming, the murderer taking down his hood to reveal the face beneath.

"You." Bellaydin shouted, pointing to Haakon. "You killed them."

Haakon's voice held an unfathomable sadness. "A divine command. I had to obey."

"No, you didn't. You had a choice."

Haakon drew himself up, his face proud and uncompromising. "No. I had to do it."

"No, you didn't!" Bellaydin yelled.

Haakon's face softened. "You don't understand the Horned God's power, he —" Suddenly Haakon fell to the ground, clutching his chest, wheezing, and grimacing in pain. "No, my lord, no. I will serve."

Bellaydin watched as Haakon knelt on the ground, his hand tightly against his chest, his skin lined with sweat, and his face contorted with pain and discomfort. It was a sight that Bellaydin had seen many times over the past two years, and whereas before he had put it down to Haakon's advancing age, it was beginning to seem that there was something else at work.

Haakon stood slowly. "When one does not obey the Horned God's voice, punishment is swift. That is a lesson that you will learn just as surely as I have. You speak as if your father was a blameless man, Gwydion. His robes were stained with just as much blood as mine."

"Why does the Horned God want me?"

Haakon smiled faintly. "The Horned God believes in you, Gwydion, and he always has, even if you have not believed in him. He believes that you can help unite these lands and end the pointless strife and conflict. With the Horned God's power, we shall elevate you to the throne of your people. We shall wed you to the Emparian queen, unite the bloodlines, and bring the voice of the Horned God to all the people of Emparia. So shall then the Goriinchians and Emparians be one. United under one king, and one god. And you, Gwydion, will be his voice in this world."

Haakon's eyes were wide, a grin fixed on his face. It was becoming clear to Bellaydin that whatever sanity remained in Haakon de Morcor was quickly evaporating. A new fear formed within him, and Haakon's presence no longer reassured him. Instead, he felt just as fearful as he had with Cathan Culainn.

"I don't want any of that," Bellaydin said. "I just want to go home."

"You cannot go home yet, Gwydion," Haakon said. "The Horned God has one final task for you before he sends you home. You are the Heir of Lydin. You hold the key. You are the key." Haakon reached into his robes, and drew out a trinket, sparkling as it caught the light. "The Tears of the Divine, Gwydion. Just as it was said, the Heir of Lydin can unlock their secrets. The Heir of Lydin can complete the prophecy of the Horned God and restore him to his place in the heavens."

Bellaydin's hand instinctively went to his neck. Haakon must have taken the Tears when he retrieved Bellaydin from Cathan's clutches. A sickening feeling bubbled through Bellaydin as he realised what this meant. All the pieces of the Tears of the Divine were now in the hands of the followers of the Horned God.

"What are you doing with that? Taking it to your master?"

"No, not yet" Haakon said. "Without the key, without you, my great lord cannot unlock the full power. You bear the mark, Gwydion, just as was foretold. You have submitted to the Horned God, just as was foretold. And all that remains is for you to be the last of the Ap'Lydin bloodline. I have no doubt that will soon be the case."

Bellaydin was stunned and inwardly furious. He'd trusted them. "No! Cathan Culainn promised me. He told me that if I submitted, they'd leave Pol alone."

Haakon turned to him, looking at him with a sympathetic, almost mournful face. "I'm sorry, Gwydion, but in all things, we must sacrifice to achieve greatness. And this is the final step for the Heir of Lydin. He must sacrifice that which he loves most. Only then will he come into his inheritance. This was where your father failed. This was where his courage left him." Haakon sighed. "I hope you are of stronger mettle."

CHAPTER 17

Inside Castle Emparia, the great nobles of the Privy Council squabbled amongst themselves. Recent events had drastically reduced their numbers. The Earl of Genio had died over a year and a half ago at the Battle of Wishapton. The Duke of Emperor's Palace, the most senior Duke in the realm, had died under suspicious circumstances, with no legitimate son to succeed him. Now rumours had reached the capital of even more losses – of the death of the Duke of Oldharbour and the defection of the Duke of Alariat.

The last was most troubling of all. The Duke of Alariat was a close relative to Her Majesty the Queen, and for the monarch's own cousin to betray her was a serious blow to the confidence of the crown. There had been many such blows recently. Goriinchian armies had appeared from nowhere and ravaged the southern border of the realm. In addition, riots had broken out in the major cities and boroughs, seemingly linked to the exponential growth in the church of the Horned God.

"We have sinned, your Graces," Archbishop Garamond intoned, looking at the assembled nobles. "We erred by allowing this heathen faith to take root in our lands. Now it threatens to consume all we hold dear."

"I do not fear these fanatics, your Eminence," one of the earls said.

"They will fall to cold steel like any other man."

Some of the other nobles murmured in agreement, but a few objected. "Turn our blades against our own people," said one. "Have you gone mad?"

"Desperate times call for desperate measures, my lords," the archbishop said.

"But– "

The Earl of Tyronsville thumped his fist on the table. "Enough of this. We must take action!" Alfred Bauer was usually jovial and positive, but his mood had taken a dark turn with his brother Augustin's death. The younger Bauer had been killed by followers of the Horned God in far-away Skurj and now the earl wanted nothing more than revenge on those he believed responsible for the tragedy.

"My lords, I assure you that the situation is under control." The Duke of Georgeton folded his hands. Widely believed to be a stiff and unimaginative dullard, Oswin Zalltor was enjoying his position of pre-eminence solely by virtue of being the last remaining duke at hand.

"Gods-damn-it, Georgeton," the Earl of Tyronsville swore. "You and I both know that is not true. Your former sworn sword was found to be working with the Goriinchians, who knows what other traitors we have in this realm."

The Earl of Warding spoke up. "I agree with Tyronsville." Such decisive rhetoric was unusual from Anson Mainstream, who most believed to be little better than a coward. "Something must be done. The reports of Goriinchian armies need to be followed up on, and the rioters need to be properly dealt with."

"There are no Goriinchian armies, you blithering idiots," the duke said. "You're letting yourself get fooled by fairytales. Hah. Phantom armies. Magic walking armour coming down from the highlands to kill us all, do you really believe any of that?"

The two earls looked slightly embarrassed. The Earl of Tyronsville stammered out a reply. "There may have been exaggerations, but the threat is real. Your Grace, have you forgotten what happened to your grandson?"

The duke's voice went quiet. "Do not bring Tancred into this."

"I'm sorry, your Grace. Nevertheless, I believe –" Bauer's words were cut off by the sound of shouting and yelling coming from outside halls.

The duke stood up, turning towards the doorway. "What in the name of –"

Three guards staggered through the door, engaged in a scuffle with another man.

"What is going on here?" the duke demanded.

"Forgive us Your Grace," one of the guards said, "But he wouldn't take no for an answer."

The man, a scruffy blond knight dressed in tattered, bloody armour, straightened himself up and attempted to wipe some of the mud from his chain shirt.

"Who are you?" the duke demanded.

The knight gave a bow. "Sir Geoffrey Keslin, Your Grace. And I have news for the Privy Council."

The duke sat back down, a smirk on his face. "Keslin. Weren't you attached to the Earl of Genio?"

"Yes, I was, Your Grace," Geoffrey said. "Though lately I have been tendering service to the crown, and then to the late Duke of Oldharbour." He reached inside his tunic and withdrew the ducal seal of Oldharbour, placing it on the table in front of the nobles.

"You have our attention, Keslin. Out with it."

Geoffrey hesitated. "If I may, Your Grace, my lords, I'd like to bring in my companions. They can explain the situation far better than I."

The guard looked at the Duke of Georgeton, who, sighing, nodded his agreement. One of the guards left and returned with four new figures in tow – a short, squat creature carrying a bunch of scrolls, an elderly elf dressed in robes and a younger elf garbed in the manner of a scout. The last newcomer was the strangest of all, a hulking and bestial looking Lizardman. The duke's face curled in disgust, and the two earls seemed to echo his disquiet.

Geoffrey stammered out an introduction. "I'm sorry, Your Grace, my lords, this is Sir Talthas of Goriinch Hill, Kahlaf el-Lahn, Hebu of Jagoncoilis, and Aelzandar, Lord Archmage and Chair of the Council of Nine."

Mention of Aelzandar's name spurred immediate reaction from the nobles. The duke raised an eyebrow, and the Earl of Tyronsville coughed.

The Earl of Warding was far less subtle. "Oh, surely not," he remarked.

"You have heard of me then, gentlemen?" Aelzandar said.

The duke seemed hesitant to admit so, but he responded, "An elf named Aelzandar was said to have served as court wizard to the King of Emparia, but that was two hundred years ago."

"Really?" Aelzandar feigned surprise. "I must say it doesn't seem like it's been that long, but time does tend to catch up on you, eventually."

"Don't try to swindle us," the duke scoffed. "I'm not some easily impressed swineherd, elf."

"Nevertheless, Your Grace," the Earl of Tyronsville cut in. "That is the Staff of the archmage he bears, is it not? He is entitled to the respect that the Emparian crown offers to such an august office."

"*Foreign* office," the duke said. "This is Emparia, not Macrodonia."

Aelzandar's tone changed, as if he was explaining things to a particularly dim child. "Your Grace, decades before you were even born, I had already left my mark on this kingdom. I served under Alusine the Great. I tutored his daughter, Ellinda, the first Countess of Genio, in the ways of the Art. You have history books, don't you? *Look me up.*"

The Duke of Georgeton turned a shade of crimson. "Very well." He pointed to Geoffrey and Aelzandar. "You two take a seat. But I'm afraid your manservants will have to remain standing."

"Manservant." Hebu muttered in disgust. Aelzandar silenced him with a wave, and so the Nemoi resorted to pouting from behind the archmage's chair.

"Alright, Keslin, out with it," the duke said. "And this better be good."

***

Polnygar shivered.

The cold, dry air of the foothills gave her uncomfortable reminders of Skurj, and thinking of that land caused her to dwell once again on the death of Augustin Bauer. The agony over losing the first man she had ever loved still wounded her deeply. Only the frenetic pace of events since her arrival from Skurj had prevented her obsessing over the loss until this point.

Ignoring the sinking feeling in her stomach, Polnygar cleared herself of any distracting thoughts, and concentrated on the task at hand. Ahead of them, the gentle hill rose higher, coming into the base of a craggy and foreboding mountain range. A dark and mysterious tower stuck out from the mountains, like a horrid scar on the horizon.

"Is that it?" Polnygar said, turning to Morgan.

The Goriinchian girl had been silent for most of the trip, apparently lost in her own private thoughts. Polnygar had barely exchanged four words with her since they left the camp of the Seeress.

"Yes," Morgan said finally. "That is the Forbidden Tower, the abode of the Prophet. That is where we will find Bellaydin."

"I gather that the Prophet is waiting for us in there." Polnygar moved her horse and looked with a mixture of wonder and dread at the beckoning tower.

"Ygarak rarely leaves his fortress," Caelwych said. "He rode with his armies in the last drive to the occupied lands, but this time he has chosen to remain here."

"To what end, I wonder," Polnygar mused. "Did he know we would come?"

Caelwych scratched his beard. "Although the Prophet-King can divine the threads of the future, just as the Seeress does, he can only see the many possibilities that the future may bring. It remains hidden to even his eyes which one of these futures will come to pass."

"His soldiers will await us," Morgan said. "As will my uncle."

There was no trace of familial loyalty in Morgan's voice as she spoke of Cathan Culainn. Polnygar had heard the tale of her father's murder, and she had no doubt that Morgan held her wicked uncle solely responsible. Knowing little else what to say, Polnygar gave Morgan a sympathetic look and then nodded to Caelwych.

"Let's go." Polnygar rode onwards towards the so-named Forbidden Tower alongside Caelwych and Morgan, with the other Saldarri soldiers following behind. "Hold on little brother, help is coming."

As they came closer to their destination, the challenge up against them became clearer. A thin and rather treacherous path wove up the mountain to the base of the tower and a sturdy wall separated this path from the outside wall, patrolled by Goriinchian soldiers. Rather than a portcullis, a large stone gate was situated in the centre of the wall. It was radically different construction, and to Polnygar's eyes, it must have predated the rest of the wall. Most likely the Goriinchians had repaired the ruined remnants of the fortifications that they had found there.

Dismounting from their horses, Polnygar and her companions took stock of the situation from a safe vantage point – a small, sheltered alcove on a rocky escarpment.

She moved across to a ledge, which offered a clear view of the Goriinchian defenders. The fortifications were only lightly defended, and barely a dozen soldiers patrolled the walls. "Is that really it, do you think?" Polnygar was unimpressed. "I was expecting it would be better guarded."

Caelwych peered towards the enemy, his gaze steely and uncompromising. "If the forces arrayed against us here are weak, then you should offer a prayer of thanks to the Seeress. She has kept her word, and as promised, the Saldarri people have revolted against their taskmasters. Now Ygarak's men struggle to fight the Enparrans as well as extinguish a thousand rebellions across their own lands."

"I hope they know what they're doing," Polnygar shook her head. She had a funny feeling that inspiring this rebellion had condemned most of the Saldarri to a pointless, bloody death. She didn't like that idea.

"They know, Heir of Lydin." Morgan's voice seemed almost reverent. "They know that they fight for freedom and not just ours, and the freedom of the countless thousands yet to be born."

Polnygar smiled and clasped Morgan's hand tightly. In many ways, the Goriinchian girl was still an enigma to Polnygar, and difficult to read. Bellaydin had spoken of Morgan's once strong dedication to the Horned God, but now, as far as Polnygar could see, no trace of that devotion remained. There was no hatred, no resentment, however – merely nothing. It was as if part of the girl's soul had died along with her faith.

"So, what do you think? Can we take them?" Polnygar rested her hand on Kaltban's hilt. The sword, as always, was cold to the touch. Behind her, Saldarri archers strung their bows and moved into position. They looked at

Polnygar expectantly.

"The gate will prove difficult," Caelwych said. "We have no means of breaking through it."

"Don't worry about the gate. I have a few surprises in store. Just keep the defenders occupied."

"Our bows are ready." Caelwych said. "You only need to give the word."

Polnygar did nothing for a few tense moments, waiting for the Goriinchian soldiers to move into range of the Saldarri longbowmen. Then she nodded to Morgan and Caelwych, and the three of them mounted their horses and moved out quietly. A few other Saldarri warriors rode with them, but the bulk remained behind, moving into position for the coming barrage of arrows.

"Now."

The sky darkened with the arrows of the Saldarri as Polnygar rode towards the gate, her mind focused on the power she was building up from within herself. It was easier now, easier than she could ever remember, the easiest since she took those first few tentative steps in Macrodonia under Aelzandar's watchful gaze. Her fingertips crackled with power, and a thrilling, intoxicating sensation raced through her body as she carefully moved her lips to the words of the ancient arcane language. She raised her hand into the air, her palm open, and facing towards the gate.

"Ferouth-Ha-Kalim!" The gates exploded with a tremendous blast; twisted pieces of metal, brick, and stone hurtled through the air all around her. Goriinchian soldiers were flung to their deaths, some smashing against the cliff-face, and others plummeting to their deaths with agonised screams.

Caelwych pulled his horse to a stop beside her, momentarily shocked and awed by the sheer destructive power Polnygar displayed, but the Saldarri quickly regained his wits and, with a war cry on his lips, he led the other Saldarri horsemen through the gap in the wall, quickly overwhelming the surviving defenders. Before long, Polnygar joined them, barely getting to swing Kaltban before the battle was over.

None of the Saldarri said a word as Polnygar approached them, sword in hand. Most tried to avoid her gaze, by looking at the ground, or elsewhere. Caelwych, a concerned look on his face, grabbed Polnygar by the arm and whispered a warning into her ear. "Be careful, Enparran. Our men have their superstitions. Your talents, though they may have proved useful, smack too much of witchcraft for their liking. The lessons of the Horned God are not that easily overturned."

"Would you have not used these powers considering what we're up against?"

"I advise only caution and prudence," Caelwych said.

Polnygar turned to look at the Saldarri soldiers, who stood apart from her, muttering and whispering to each other.

"You're safe for now," Caelwych said, patting her briefly on the shoulder. "They're too awed by that display to challenge you openly, even were you not the prophesised Heir of Lydin. In time, their views may change."

"Is that a threat?" Polnygar's face felt hot. Stressed and irritable from the battle, she certainly did not appreciate being questioned over the way she had brought victory.

"No, merely a caution," Caelwych repeated and went off to talk privately with the other Saldarri.

"You have a gift," Morgan said, coming close. "You should not let it go to waste."

Polnygar smiled. "Thank you. I'm glad someone sees it that way."

"Don't let the words of others offend you," Morgan said. "In truth, it wasn't that long ago when I would have joined in their cries, and damned you as a witch, or a demon-lover, or idol-worshipper."

"But now?"

Morgan chewed her lip. "I think I've begun to see a wider view of the world."

Polnygar nodded, thanking Morgan again for her show of support.

Suddenly, an unfamiliar wailing sound reverberated in Polnygar's ears. A long, mournful note carried on the wind. It was coming from some distance up the path, towards the tower. Morgan turned around. She had heard it too.

"What's that sound?" Polnygar asked.

"Bagpipes," Morgan said warily.

Caelwych drew his sword. "A war band approaches from the tower. You hear that song? That dirge? That's the hymn of the Horned God. A High Priest will be among the warriors."

As the horrible lament continued, Polnygar felt uneasy. The appearance of a large force of Goriinchian soldiers coming down from the mountains only made her feel worse.

"Loose arrows." Polnygar said, but even as she spoke those words, she thought she may have acted too soon. Most of the arrows flew off target as the high ground worked in the Goriinchians' favour.

A tattered black and grey banner fluttered above the Goriinchians, with a simple Horned symbol emblazoned on it. The Goriinchian priests frowned on idol-worship and holy icons, but they were not totally blind to the power of symbols, particularly on the field of battle. The banner certainly had a demoralising influence on the Saldarri, as many of them found their old fear of the Horned God resurfacing, making their fingers tremble and causing their courage to flee them. Polnygar too felt the urge to turn tail and run, even though her feet seemed to be frozen in place.

"It's High Priest Cathan Culainn," Caelwych said.

Polnygar looked towards Morgan, and the girl looked shocked and panicked by the sudden appearance of her uncle. As the soldiers marched closer, the sputtering arrow fire of the Saldarri little more than a nuisance, Cathan Culainn was not difficult to spot. He wore the full black and grey robes of a Goriinchian cleric and, in imitation of his divine patron, Cathan was crowned with a magnificent horned helm.

It did not take long for the Goriinchian soldiers to stream down the mountain and surround Polnygar's band. Goriinchian and Saldarri soldier eyed each other warily, as centuries of mutual suspicion and distrust finally reached its pinnacle.

"Your arrival comes as no surprise," Cathan growled, moving out from the crowd. "An infidel leading apostates to holy ground, while their brethren revolt against their masters. Did you really think this would go unnoticed?" He was speaking in heavily accented Emparian, and by his tone made it very clear he was speaking the language only by sufferance.

"I want my brother."

"He is ours now, little infidel girl," Cathan spat. "And you are hardly in a position to make demands." He turned his eyes towards Morgan. "Especially after taking something that belongs to me."

"Morgan's not yours, Cathan, she never was. You're not getting your hands on her." Polnygar was firm.

"You dare to defy the Horned God?" Cathan said. "Your blasphemy will bring about only your own doom. Kill them!"

Polnygar felt an instinctive surge of power and her experiences at the Battle of Harralin flashed into her mind. Without prompting she threw up a protective shield around herself, Morgan and the Saldarri. Arrows bounced off the invisible barrier, prompting cries of surprise from the Goriinchians.

"There you have it. Witchcraft," said Cathan. "What more evidence do you need? Destroy them, in the name of the Horned God!"

The Goriinchians gripped their weapons tightly and with war cries echoing on their lips, they pushed forward with speed and aggression. Just as in Skurj, the shield would stop arrows and other projectiles but was easily penetrated by the full force of a human body. The Saldarri moved to engage the Goriinchians and though still tired from their previous battle, fought with surprising tenacity to hold off the Goriinchian assault. The Goriinchians themselves battled with the fire of men who knew that they were on the side of gods, fighting creatures damned by the heavens. Goriinchian axes sliced through Saldarri flesh, Saldarri swords spilt Goriinchian blood.

Polnygar fought with Kaltban, marvelling in the sword's perfect balance and supernatural speed. The blade seemed a natural extension of her arm and her moves felt fluid and practised. She eluded the attacks of her foes with ease and exploited every slip in their concentration. Like a whirlwind of death, Polnygar cut a swath through the Goriinchian ranks and she could almost feel the moment at which their morale started to falter.

"Forward you fools. Now." Cathan waded into the melee himself. The High Priest wielded a tremendous claymore and judging by the short work he made of a Saldarri foe, was more skilled in the use of the weapon than Polnygar could have imagined.

"I am the right hand of the Horned God." Cathan's sword ripped through the Saldarri like a scythe through wheat. "And I shall carry out his will." In the blink of an eye, Cathan was before Polnygar, sneering as he slashed his blade down towards her. Polnygar retaliated, and their swords clashed, again and again, as the two warriors, evenly matched, became locked in a fight to the death.

The sounds of battle continued around Polnygar but slowly her mind filtered them out, until all she could hear was the sound of her own breathing, and Cathan's guttural, hate-filled voice. "You're a fool, infidel, if you think you will save your brother. He has a grand destiny in front of him. Your death will set him on that path." Cathan reached back to deliver a killing blow, but Polnygar was too quick, moving to his left, and riposting with a blow of her own. Cathan counterattacked, mocking her as he did. "You are tiring, are you not, infidel? I can feel it. Your fear, your anger, your hate for me. These emotions are weakening you. You cower before the Horned God. And it is right that you do, for his power guides the fates of all of us."

Polnygar ignored the taunting and continued to fight back against the High Priest when a dying Goriinchian fell next to her, knocking her aside, and causing her to drop Kaltban to the ground. She tried to reach for the falling sword but at that very moment, Cathan kicked forward, his boot slamming into her head, and sending her tumbling backwards.

Cathan smirked triumphantly, revelling in his moment of victory. Polnygar tried to scramble to her feet, but Cathan's sword was already above her head, ready to come down at any moment. He savoured his victory, spitting his words like venom. "For the Horned God."

Polnygar braced herself, anticipating the blow.

Nothing happened. She looked up. Cathan stood frozen in place, his face contorted in utter surprise, before toppling to the ground, the blade of a shortsword embedded in his back. Amazed at her good fortune, Polnygar quickly stood up to see who had delivered her lucky escape.

Morgan.

The Goriinchian girl's eyes were red, but her face otherwise showed no trace of emotion even though she had just killed her own uncle. It was clear to Polnygar that whatever kinship Morgan may have once felt for Cathan Culainn had long since vanished. Polnygar grabbed her sword, giving Morgan a quick embrace and word of thanks, and then went to rejoin the battle.

With Cathan's fall, the battle was all but over. The Goriinchians, seeing their leader's death, lost the heart for fighting and many shouted that they had been abandoned by their god. Some fought on with fanatical fervour but for the most part, Goriinchian resistance collapsed, with the survivors fleeing the victorious Saldarri. Panting, and relieved at their stroke of luck, Polnygar let the Goriinchians run. With the battle over, she had other things to focus on.

"Morgan, are you –"

"I'm fine." The girl refused to look Polnygar in the eye. "It's nothing."

"Are you sure? That couldn't have been easy."

"I said I'm fine. Let's just continue on." Morgan turned away, going to walk up the path. "This way, to the tower."

Polnygar shook her head. "Wait, let's not rush on off ahead before we know what's facing us up there."

"I agree," said Caelwych. "There might be more off the Horned God's thugs nearby. It'd probably be best if we tried to avoid blundering into any more ambushes." Caelwych barked a few commands to his subordinates, telling them to scout out the surrounding area. The men did as asked, disappearing off in different directions.

"Why do we delay?" Morgan said. "Your brother's in there, and we have no time to waste."

Caelwych grabbed Morgan's wrist. "There's no telling what awaits us in that forbidden place. We must be prepared and proceed carefully."

Polnygar looked towards the tower that menaced before them. She had a feeling this would not be easy.

***

The Duke of Georgeton was not impressed. "Is this really necessary?"

Aelzandar turned to the duke, a slight smile on his face. "It would raise the people's morale significantly if they saw evidence that their sovereign was going to stand by their side and face the same dangers as they do."

"But Her Majesty has never been in battle."

"It's in her blood," Geoffrey stated. "After all, her father was a great warrior king."

The nobles of the Emparian Privy Council had only reluctantly agreed to the plan, and that was mainly on the strength of the archmage Aelzandar's arguments.

Queen Amaryllis of Emparia, second monarch of the House of de Morcor, entered the antechamber with her two attendants. She was dressed in highly ornate and customised armour, engraved with her family's crest and polished to an astonishing degree. From her facial expression, it wasn't exactly something she was comfortable in, or even familiar with.

"This isn't going to work," the duke said.

"I say we give it a try," the Earl of Tyronsville said. "With your Majesty's permission, of course."

The queen nodded, giving her approval.

"I still think this idea is ridiculous," the duke said. "What should happen if she were injured in battle?"

"Her Majesty need not enter the fray herself, your Grace," Aelzandar explained. "We merely need to give the public the impression that she is willing to do so."

"Propaganda, in other words," Hebu stood on the tip of his toes, as if doing so would make him better heard.

"So, just what do we face out there?" asked the Earl of Warding. "These tales you've spun for us, I'm not quite sure I believe a word of it."

"These are not tales, my lord," Aelzandar said, "but ancient history. Long before your ancestors first claimed this land, a noble yet terrible race of elves ruled over it. The Soldara. The last legacy of the Soldara marches towards this city as we speak. An army of automata, nigh-invulnerable."

"Why should we believe you?" the duke demanded.

"You can believe me, or you can wait until the proof of my words shows up in front of this city's gates."

There was silence as the three nobles looked at each other. "Your point is well taken," the Duke of Georgeton said. The two earls merely smirked at their superior's capitulation.

"You know what doesn't make any damn sense." Geoffrey rubbed his hands against the sides of his head. "If Ygarak has had an army of magical automata all this time, why did he not simply set them against us to begin with? Why bother with troops of flesh and blood when he could have simply flattened us with warriors of metal?"

"The automata may be creatures of the Art, fashioned through the arts of the arcanist, but they are powered by something else," Aelzandar said. "Souls. The Soldara always used the souls of living and thinking beings to power their creations, souls they harvested through their own fell magic. Ygarak must be doing the same."

"You mean this whole conflict until now has just been some sort of sick and twisted mustering for that bastard?" said Geoffrey incredulously.

"In a manner of speaking," said Aelzandar. "And it points to something more troubling. If Ygarak can master the arts of the Soldara, he is much more than some barbarian general. His command of the arcane might match, or even exceed, my own."

"We *can* win, can't we?" Geoffrey said, his very question betraying the uncertainty he felt.

"There is always hope," Aelzandar said. "And at the very least, we have had the chance to plan ahead."

"I do hope your plan for our defence consists of something more than simply parading Her Majesty around the battlements, though." The Duke of Georgeton's tone was curt.

"But of course, your Grace," Aelzandar nodded. "I believe Kahlaf would be the best one to explain that to you."

The duke took a seat, and the earls followed his lead. "What assistance can you give, lizardman?"

"Sir Geoffrey and I have brought with us a small quantity of weapons fashioned from skymetal. Only these weapons can damage the automata. Steel cannot penetrate their armour."

"So what are you waiting for? Get our soldiers armed."

"We don't have enough weapons to outfit the number of soldiers required for the city's defence. We must, therefore, turn to other methods."

"You *just* said these things were invulnerable to everything else." The Earl of Tyronsville sounded exasperated.

Aelzandar cut in. "Ordinary weapons may not be able to harm them, but they will still be vulnerable to massive damage, whether by the Art or from siege weapons."

The duke shook his head. "I still don't agree with the decision to keep Her Majesty here. The automata are not yet laying siege to the city. We could get the queen out now, and take her somewhere safe, like Oldharbour, or Georgeton, far out of the way from this invasion force."

Aelzandar argued his point. "The Goriinchians will soon control the routes away from the capital if they don't already. Send messages to the other lords and barons of the kingdom. We will need their troops in the battle to come."

"Nevertheless, as the senior member of the Privy Council here, I make the decisions, and what I think is that –"

"Georgeton, stop," said the queen. "I will not have it said that I cannot face the same dangers as my people. I will stay and fight, just as Sir Geoffrey and his friends have."

The Earl of Tyronsville said, "Her Majesty has made her decision, your Grace. Now we must abide by it."

The duke sighed. "You're all mad. Very well, Lizardman, show me these weapons of yours."

***

Who am I?

The words floated in the young man's head, his mind a seeming void. His identity, whatever it had once been, seemed to have melted away, leaving little in its wake.

I am Gwydion.

Was that his name? Is it even a name? It wafted aimlessly in his mind, devoid of context, of history.

Something within him latched on to the name and from it reconstructed some semblance of self-awareness.

I am Gwydion. I am the slave of the Horned God.

He felt a pang as these assertions formed in his head. *I had another name once. What was it?* Any attempt to answer that question by shreds of a previously life was quickly quashed by the emergence of his reborn self. He quickly got to his feet and looked about his surroundings.

"Where am I?" Gwydion wondered.

A voice whispered to him. *"This is the last Citadel."*

He turned around but saw no one. The voice was emanating in his own thoughts.

"How did I come to be here?" Gwydion asked the voice.

The Tears of the Divine

"You came here of your own free will, as I knew you always would."

"Who are you?"

"I am your one true master. I am the beginning and the end, the first and the last. I created the world of angels, the world of demons, and the world of men that sits between. I was there at your birth, and so shall I be there at your death. You know my name. It was the first name you ever whispered."

"The Horned God," Gwydion said.

"That is correct. I have a task for you, slave."

"I obey my lord."

"A great power was stolen from me many years ago and sealed away. I have foreseen that it is your blood that can unlock this power and return it to its owner."

"What must I do?"

"When the time comes, I will send for you, and you will reunite the last piece of the Tears of the Divine. The circle will then be complete, and the power denied to me returned. I shall be reborn into my full power."

The mention of the Tears of the Divine sparked some sort of vague feeling of recognition deep within Gwydion, but he shrugged it off, and once again nodded his head. "Yes, my lord. I will do as you command."

The voice left him, and for a moment Gwydion felt a sudden, biting pain as if an invisible hand were squeezing his heart and lungs. It passed quickly, however, and Gwydion soon felt as if the pain had never happened.

"Gwydion." A man entered the room. "What are you doing? You should be resting." The man was old and grey and had a weary, resigned look to his features. His eyes seemed to speak of sadness and loss.

"Yes, I do feel tired." Gwydion said. "Who are you? You look familiar."

The man looked at Gwydion sympathetically. "I've heard that the change could affect the memory, my boy, but I had never seen it myself. I

293

am Haakon. I am your oldest and most loyal friend, and your only family left in this world. That should be enough for now." Gently Haakon took Gwydion by the arm and led him back to the cot. "We can speak more of this later. For now, you need your rest. By tomorrow we shall know where things stand."

Lying back down Gwydion rambled. "But the Horned God gave me a task."

Haakon stroked the younger man's hair. "I know, my boy. We can take care of this later."

Lulled by Haakon's presence, Gwydion fell asleep, his rest dreamless and comforting.

CHAPTER 18

Polnygar looked up.

The first thing she noticed about the tower was its sheer size. It reached far into the sky, and almost without hyperbole, Polnygar felt she could say its peak brushed the clouds themselves. The fortress dominated the landscape for miles around, and despite not taking seriously the Saldarri claim that it was a cursed place, Polnygar acknowledged that even she felt awed in its presence.

The next thing she noticed was the dilapidated state of the structure. The Saldarri had said the building was ancient, built in the earliest days of their ancestors, and Polnygar saw nothing to doubt their claims. The white stone that the tower was built of was weathered and crumbling from countless centuries of neglect. Whole sections of the structure seemed to have crumbled into nothing. Attempts at repair had been made by the Goriinchians, but most of these later additions did not match the artistry of the original structure.

Another thought struck Polnygar the longer she looked at the tower. Its style of architecture, its great age, as well as the type of material used in its construction all made Polnygar doubt that it had been built by

Goriinchians.

As if sensing her thoughts, Caelwych came to stand next to her. "This place is all that remains of the legacy of the Fey Lords. Our ancestors went to war with the Fey and this was the last of their accursed strongholds to fall. For centuries after that it was forbidden to us, a taboo site that would remain empty to remind us of the folly and evil of the past. The story was that just before the rise of Ygarak a group of foreign warlocks took up residence there. Eventually, their lust for power caused them to fight one another until only one remained, a warlock that would later join with Mael the Apostate and put him on his path to damnation."

Polnygar walked closer towards the tower. Two great doors, nearly identical to the gates below, were the most noticeable features of the front of the tower. The doors were made of bronze, and inscribed with sigils and stylised representations of tall, otherworldly-looking figures.

"This script is Eldaric," Polnygar traced her fingers over the doors. She looked to her left where a broken statue lay amidst other rubble. At first, she gave it only a cursory glance, but when her eyes caught the statue's face, she was intrigued by an element of familiarity. She quickly ran towards the statue, examining it up close. Though old and weathered, it was not part of the original tower; still, it pre-dated the Goriinchian construction in the area. "The face looks familiar." Moving about the statue's pieces, she discovered what must have been its base, a small stone plinth with a few words inscribed in Draconic. "Grey Mage," she said, reading the inscription. "Grey Mage Cassian."

"There's no time for us to look at old rocks, we have to get inside," Caelwych said.

Polnygar took a final look at the half-destroyed statue of Cassian, her thoughts lingering back to Aelzandar's tales about his old master. She wondered if Cassian was one of the warlocks that the Goriinchians believed had once lived here. Caelwych coughed loudly and Polnygar returned to the gate.

"Give me a hand here. Morgan, Caelwych, you lot there." There was only about ten of them altogether now, but their collective strength was enough to force the doors open, the hinges groaning and grinding as they did. The interior of the tower was dark, and Polnygar felt a shiver of anticipation as she stepped inside.

She suddenly realised that she seemed to be standing by herself. "Aren't you coming?" she said, turning back to Caelwych.

"This tower is forbidden," Caelwych said. "And cursed. The men refuse to step foot on it."

"What? We've come this far and now you want to turn back?" Polnygar said. "I thought you said they didn't believe in the Horned God?"

"They believe in his power, and they certainly believe in the evil of this place. I'm sorry, Heir of Lydin, but we must remain outside. We'll watch to make sure that Goriinchian reinforcements do not arrive here. We'll protect your escape route."

Polnygar's eyes darted from the tower to the Saldarri and then back again. "I can't go there alone."

"I will go with you," said Morgan. "I do not fear the tower, nor the Horned God."

Polnygar eyed the rest of the group critically. "I'm glad to see someone here has courage."

If Caelwych and the Saldarri were embarrassed about seeming cowardly next to the two women, they did not show it. Instead, with Caelwych's guidance, the Saldarri took up positions outside the tower entrance, ready for any Goriinchian that might arrive.

Caelwych nodded to Polnygar. "We'll see you two when you return."

Without another word, Polnygar and Morgan stepped inside the tower, unsure as to what awaited them.

Realising they would need some light Polnygar whispered a few words to create a small gleaming ball, letting it illuminate the space from over her right shoulder.

Morgan seemed both surprised and impressed at Polnygar's power. "I've never met a real witch before. Our people lived in deathly fear of your kind."

Probably with good reason. Polnygar thought. She looked around. They were in a large, stone antechamber, lacking in any sort of furnishings and decorations, except for a few faded images painted on the walls. For the most part, the room was empty, though portions of the floor were covered with rubble and debris. At least one of the great pillars that held up the roof had collapsed.

Moving the light closer, Polnygar studied the painted images. They bore some similarity to the pictures she and Bellaydin had seen in the tomb underneath Wishapton. She wiped off the thick layer of dust and cobwebs. As before, these pictures had been created by ancient Goriinchians of strange, foreign wizards and barely recognisable alien, lordly figures. *The Soldara.* Polnygar thought.

"There are stairs here, leading up," Morgan pointed to the other side of the room.

"Only way is up, I guess." With each step, the darkness seemed to abate ever so slightly. Polnygar saw light streaming down from the next floor.

"I don't think the next level of this tower is abandoned," she whispered to Morgan. "Let's be careful."

As they reached the top of the stairs, Polnygar heard voices. Motioning for Morgan to stop, she waited, back against the wall, as she heard two men talking to each other in Goriinchian. After a few moments, they stopped talking, and she heard their footsteps fade away.

"Who were they?" Polnygar whispered to Morgan. "What were they saying?"

"Two priests. They didn't speak of much. There were comments about some new servant of the Horned God's. A Fey Lord placed above all the priests of Goriinchia. The priests were not taking it well."

Polnygar did not need the Goriinchians to mention a name to know who they were speaking about. It could only be Lord Ivellios, traitorous spellweaver and thief of the Tears of the Divine. After Ivellios' true allegiance was revealed, Aelzandar reasoned that the renegade would make his way here. From the sounds of it, the archmage was right.

"Do you think they have gone now?" Morgan asked.

"By the sounds of it," Polnygar said. "Let's keep moving."

Polnygar led the way up the ancient set of steps, with Morgan following closely behind. Uncertain of what to expect, she took every step with a great sense of trepidation. As she neared the top, her heart leapt when she came face to face with the object of their search.

"Bellaydin," Polnygar cried out. She ran to embrace her brother, but he shrank from her, moving away as she approached.

"That is not my name." Bellaydin's gaze was distant, unfocused.

"Bellaydin, wait, what's wrong?" Polnygar's voice quickened, her tone alarmed.

"I am not Bellaydin. My name is Gwydion. And you should not have come here."

"Gwydion? But what – how?" She looked around the room, and then back at her brother. His eyes, a grotesque milky white, looked unpleasantly familiar. She had seen such eyes before, in the city of Ralom, when Ivellios had bent Augustin Bauer to his will, and then again in Qar Arrid, with the brainwashed guardsmen. Had the same thing happened here?

"Bellaydin, what have they done to you?"

299

"I have been shown my true destiny." Bellaydin's voice was twisted and strange. "I have been shown the true power of the Heir of Lydin."

"No." Polnygar grabbed her brother by the shoulders. "They've done something to you like they did to Augustin. You've got to snap out of this."

Bellaydin shoved Polnygar aside with a disdainful glance. "The Horned God speaks to me now, and finally I see."

"See what?" Fear gripped her, and she took a few steps backwards.

"Answers. Everything. The totality of existence. The final great truth of this universe." Bellaydin smiled, but the expression did not cheer Polnygar. It only unsettled her further.

"The high priests have done this to him," Morgan said to Polnygar. "As they have done to others."

Taking a breath, Polnygar extended a hand. "Bela, please, let me take you away from here. I can get you help, find someone to remove this spell from you, we can –"

Bellaydin merely stared at her, the smile disappearing from his lips. "There is no escape. The Horned God sees all things. The end is near."

A figure emerged from the shadows. Polnygar drew Kaltban from its scabbard and held it in front of her warily. In the murky gloom, she glimpsed a familiar face, but not one she had expected to see here. "I know you. You're the Duke of Alariat. What are you doing here?"

Haakon ignored her question. "Why are *you* here, girl?" His voice was scarcely more than a whisper.

"I'm here to save my brother."

"Your brother is no more," Haakon said. "There is only Gwydion. The true Heir of Lydin and instrument of the Horned God's will."

"What have you done to him, you monster?" Polnygar demanded. Her face twisted in anger.

"I have done nothing. It was his choice." He stepped into the light, and Polnygar gasped as she saw the man's appearance. The ragged, unkempt appearance of his hair, the unfamiliar robes emblazoned with the Horned God's symbol, this was not the man she had met at Wishapton.

"He would never have willingly made such a choice," Polnygar said.

"Ah, but he did," Haakon said. "All of those who come before the Horned God come of their own free will, and Gwydion had more reason than most. He had hoped that through this, you might be spared, but in coming here you have only thrown away your own life. I too had hoped that you would be spared, that the prophecy might be fulfilled another way, but as it was said, so must it be. The Heir of Lydin must sacrifice that which he cares about most - the nearest in blood." Haakon drew a sword from his belt, a thin, grey bladed weapon that seemed to glimmer with an unholy black sheen. "I'm sorry. I wish there was another way." Haakon passed the sword to Bellaydin, who took it without emotion, turning it over in his hand as he looked from Polnygar and then back to the sword in his hands.

Bellaydin glanced at Haakon, his expression unsure.

"It must be done," Haakon said, his tone gentle but firm.

"It must be done," Bellaydin repeated in a monotone.

Polnygar stepped back, shaking her head. "No, no. Bela, don't do this." Tears streamed down her face as she reached down with her hand, her fingers grasping the hilt of her sword.

"You are the will of the Horned God, Gwydion," Haakon exulted. "The will made flesh."

Bellaydin looked at Polnygar, his eyes hard, but still did not move. "What of the other?" he said, looking towards Morgan.

"She is no of importance," Haakon said. "You may leave her..." Suddenly Haakon howled and doubled over in pain. "No mercy, no." he cried, "I obey my lord, I obey." He straightened up. "The apostate must die as well," Haakon said, his voice weak and weary. "The Horned God commands it."

"Yes," Bellaydin repeated monotonously. "The apostate will die too." His eyes reflecting a will not of his own, Bellaydin took a lurching step towards Polnygar and Morgan.

Tears in her eyes, Polnygar steeled herself for the inevitable. She drew her sword just in time, as Bellaydin brought his own blade down on his sister. She blocked his attack without a moment to spare.

"Morgan, help me." Polnygar said as she fended off Bellaydin.

The Goriinchian girl was already moving, however, running towards Haakon with her weapon drawn.

"That is not wise," Haakon said as Morgan hurtled towards him. "Like it or not, you are still a slave of the Horned God, the one who has given power to me, power over all his dominions." Haakon extended a hand towards Morgan and clenched his fist. Morgan suddenly came to a dead halt, frozen in the air and unable to move a muscle. "And power over his slaves." With barely a glance as Morgan crumpled to the ground, Haakon turned his gaze back to the Ap'Lydin siblings, still locked in mortal combat.

Polnygar struggled. Her brother's moves were stiff, forced and utterly predictable, but unlike Polnygar, Bellaydin was not holding back. The power that Haakon and the Horned God exerted over Bellaydin was such that even though Polnygar did not want to hurt her brother, it was clear he would not return the favour. The cold dead stare in Bellaydin's eyes stirred painful memories within Polnygar. It took her back to Ralom, where she had seen the same unfeeling look in the eyes of Augustin Bauer. Thinking of Augustin awakened the feelings she had for the man, the pain she had experienced at his death, and the burning rage she now felt towards the Horned God and his followers for trying to take away yet another person she loved.

With a triumphant yell, Polnygar brought her own sword up, catapulting

Bellaydin's sword out of his hands, and sending it clattering to the ground below. Before her brother could react, she smashed the hilt of her own sword into his jaw, sending him tumbling backwards. Bellaydin stirred on the ground, groaning, but did not stand. His dazed expression remained fixed on his sister.

"No, no, no." Haakon said, his voice rising with anger. "Get up. A slave of the Horned God does not surrender. Get up."

Bellaydin made no move but merely continued to stare at Polnygar.

"Get up." Haakon yelled. "Get up. Get –" Haakon cried out in sudden pain and anguish, clutching his head, and crouching to the ground. His face was a mask of pain, lined with sweat and fear. "But my lord. I have done as you asked."

Polnygar tried to keep both the prone Bellaydin and Haakon in her field of vision.

"But what is it you wish, my lord?" Haakon muttered. There was a brief silence and then Haakon slowly stood. "But, my lord, he is the Heir – you said –" Haakon clutched at his chest but persisted. "No, my lord, I cannot." Haakon flinched in pain again and tottered unsteadily on his feet before righting himself. He panted, fighting back tears. "Please, my lord, he – No. No! I refuse." Haakon barked the words with adamance and defiance that shocked even Polnygar. In a sudden show of strength he tore the medallion of the Horned God from his neck, throwing it to the ground.

For a moment Haakon almost smiled, relief slowly drifting across his face, but almost immediately his features distorted with agony as he clutched his chest, staggered backwards and finally collapsed to the ground

He spoke for the last time. "Free. At last."

Simultaneously the power holding Morgan in place seemingly disintegrated, leaving the Goriinchian girl once again free to move. Polnygar looked from Haakon to Morgan, and then back to Bellaydin.

"We need to help him," Polnygar remembered Aelzandar's clearing of Augustin's mind and tried to picture the words that the old archmage had spoken that fateful day, more than a year ago.

Her brother stared at her, his white eyes bereft of feeling or compassion. Polnygar approached him without fear, her mind focused only on the words of the spell, the words she had heard Aelzandar chant, the words she had read in the books and the archmage made her study. Those very words now blazed brightly in her mind, as bright as the stars in the night sky.

She began the incantation, chanting the Draconic words as Morgan stood nearby. Morgan showed little reaction, but due to her cultural antipathy to what the Goriinchians considered witchcraft she occasionally flinched involuntarily. As Polnygar's words became louder and faster, Morgan's eyes widened, and she even took a step backwards, as if afraid of what might happen at the conclusion of the spell.

Polnygar said the last word of the spell and then looked at her brother. For a moment, nothing happened, but slowly, Bellaydin's head slumped forward, then backwards again. He let out a low groan. The madness began to clear from his eyes.

"Bellaydin!"

Bellaydin shook his head and got to his feet groggily. Eyes darting from left to right, he seemed confused and bewildered at his surroundings. "Pol?"

Polnygar, overcome with relief, embraced her brother, pulling him tightly to her. Bellaydin did not resist the hug but seemed surprised at the gesture, and indeed at his surroundings.

"Where am I? What happened?" He turned around, his eyes wide in wonder. "Morgan!" Bellaydin and Morgan embraced, and he planted a kiss on the Goriinchian girl's cheek.

"How did you both get here? I remember –" He turned once more and then stopped, his smile turning into a frown as he came to look at the crumpled body that lay in front of him. "Haakon." His voice carried a mixture of sadness, regret, and resigned acceptance.

Polnygar came to stand beside him and put a hand on her brother's shoulder. "After what he did to you, he deserved everything he got."

Bellaydin knelt and looked at Haakon, whose face was oddly calm and serene, the tortured circumstances of his death seemingly wiped away. A glint attracted Bellaydin's eye. Around the old man's neck was the piece of the Tears of the Divine. Why had he kept it, rather than delivering it to Ygarak or the Horned God? Bellaydin removed the piece from Haakon's sorrowfully and placed it back on his own.

"Maybe," Bellaydin said. "I don't know."

"It's over, Bela," Polnygar said, "He's dead now."

"No," Bellaydin said. "Haakon died a long time ago, the same time as our father. And this isn't over yet. There is another who serves the Horned God. He waits for us, for the confrontation he knows is coming."

"Who?" Morgan asked.

Bellaydin and Polnygar, exchange knowing looks. Only one name came to Polnygar's lips. "Ivellios."

"The name is not familiar to me," Morgan said.

"You may not know him by name," Bellaydin said. "But there's no doubt in my mind that he's the Fey Lord of which your people have spoken."

Morgan blinked. "You know him then? You have encountered him before?"

Polnygar gripped the hilt of her sword. "Let's just say that Ivellios and I have a history together."

***

305

Bellaydin moved forward, with Morgan and Polnygar following. As they went deeper into the seemingly endless maze of corridors and stairways, a curious sensation came over Bellaydin. Though he had never been to this place before, and remembered little of the short time he was imprisoned here under Haakon's power, there was a strange sensation of familiarity about it. It was as if some part of his mind could recall the layout of this place intimately.

But it goes beyond that, Bellaydin thought, as he walked past crumbling and faded murals. The memories he had of this place were not of how it was now, but how it had been in a distant time, long since past. In his mind's eye he could see gleaming walls and proud murals, banners depicting crests of glorious noble houses long since extinct. He glimpsed shadows out of the corner of his eyes, walking mirages that resembled the walking men of metal the Goriinchians had sent against Wishapton. *Automaton.* The name came to Bellaydin's head, but the images he saw were again, from another time, and the automata he had dug from Wishapton seemed crude and badly constructed compared to the gleaming upright figures that once patrolled these halls.

"Bellaydin, is something wrong?" Polnygar looked at him with concern.

"No, no," Bellaydin said. "It's just that, well, how can I put this? I know where to go."

Morgan blinked. "Is that a problem?" The Goriinchian girl seemed puzzled.

"It is, because I've never set foot here before."

"Perhaps Haakon showed you –"

"No. I saw little during my imprisonment. This memory is not recent. It's almost as if…" He trailed off without completing his thought.

"Almost as if what?" Polnygar said.

"I can remember things that happened before I was born, *thousands of years* before I was born. I can see this place the way it was when it was young."

"But how?"

"I don't know," Bellaydin said. "But I think you'll agree when I say I don't think it bodes well."

***

"Soldiers." Geoffrey barked. "Attention."

Geoffrey looked at the soldiers assembled in front of him with a weary glance. *This is not going to be enough men.*

Though the weapons and armour that Kahlaf had provided would at least allow them to damage the automata, they still found themselves outnumbered and, to put it one way, outmuscled by the giant metal thugs currently marching their way. Whatever plan Aelzandar and Kahlaf were cooking up, Geoffrey hoped it was a good one, for all their sakes.

"Trusting my life to a wizard and a giant lizard," Geoffrey muttered under his breath. The unexpected rhyme caused him to smile and forget his troubles for a moment. Of course, he would have never made a comment like that if Kahlaf had been within earshot.

The soldiers had taken to their new weapons and armour with some scepticism, clearly distrustful of both the elven wizard, and the lizardman warrior that had procured said weapons for them. Not to mention, they were unfamiliar with the exotic craftsmanship that had gone into the forging of such strange equipment. Eventually, however, most of them accepted what they had been given, a sentiment helped by the fact that the weapons and armour were well crafted, lighter than they looked, and superbly balanced.

"There are fewer soldiers at hand that I remember," Talthas said, echoing Geoffrey's earlier sentiment.

307

Geoffrey gave a grim nod. "The war has taken many."

"Time for one last stand then," said Talthas.

"Well, here goes nothing," Geoffrey mumbled to himself. He raised his voice and announced. "The Duke of Georgeton." The duke arrived, dressed in ceremonial regalia, and accompanied by his personal guard.

"Thank you, Sir Geoffrey," the duke muttered. "You may stand down."

"As you wish, Your Grace," Geoffrey shuffled to one side.

"Men of Emparia." the duke announced. "I shall be very frank with you, with all of you. No doubt you have heard tell of what approaches us this day, of what foul sorcery and perverse magics the Goriinchians have used to vex us. Where their own soldiers failed against the courage and honour of Emparia, now they seek to pit men of steel and sorcery against us, nightmarish abominations forged from some hellish anvil. I tell you that the rumours are true and such foes are bearing down on us even now."

Most of the soldiers tried to suppress whatever emotions and doubts were welling up inside them, but a few betrayed what they were feeling with an unsteady gait, a quivering arm or leg, and furtive, darting movement of the eyes.

"But I say take heart. Remember that you are men, the finest of the divine creation. And you are Emparians, the finest of all men. Never forget that those you fight are alone. They have no one who loves them, while you take with you the fondest wishes and desires of all men and women in this great land. What you fight today are soulless creatures, powered only by dark magic. The gates of paradise are closed to them, so you should not fear them. Instead, only pity them, for the oblivion that awaits."

The soldiers erupted into enthusiastic cheers and hoots. Geoffrey turned towards the duke. "Nicely done, your Grace."

"Sometimes I surprise even myself," the Duke of Georgeton said. "Now, you should go see that archmage friend of yours. He's been asking for you."

"No rest for the wicked I guess," Geoffrey sighed.

***

When Geoffrey and Talthas got back to the keep, they found Aelzandar in the company of Kahlaf and some grim looking Emparian officers.

"Ah, Sir Geoffrey, Sir Talthas," Aelzandar greeted the duo, "I hope the soldiers are prepared for the task ahead."

"As well as can be expected, archmage." Geoffrey said, looking around the room distractedly. "You still haven't told us exactly how this is all going to work."

"All in good time, my dear knight," Aelzandar said. The archmage laid a hand on Geoffrey's shoulder and smiled mischievously. "Please, both of you take a seat."

Geoffrey looked surprised but did as asked with no real protest. Talthas followed suit.

Aelzandar said, "I believe I may have found the secret weapon we could use against the automata. Hebu. The scroll please."

The Nemoi rushed towards the archmage, a papyrus scroll in hand, and placed it on the table, unfurling and smoothing it out for others to see. *"The Properties and Enchantments of Homunculi and Golemcraft,"* Aelzandar read aloud. "Some of my own research that by a remarkable stroke of fortune touches on the principles of Soldara golemcraft. From what I have here, I believe it may be possible for me to fashion a counterspell."

"A counterspell?" Talthas said, "What will it do?"

"The automata have no minds of their own," Aelzandar said. "These ones are controlled by an individual, probably deep in Goriinchian territory and close to Ygarak himself. In essence, they are nothing more than puppets dancing on some unseen puppet master's strings. This spell, to put

309

it bluntly, will cut those strings."

Geoffrey looked sceptical. "How can you be certain?"

"The Horned God has been having his slaves ingest pieces of these automata to control them. When they attempted to do the same to the Baron Augustin Bauer, I ended the control by retrieving the automaton piece from Bauer and learning the exact form of the Art used."

"Impressive," said Talthas. "When can you cast it?"

"I need time to properly form the correct incantations and prepare the correct material components."

"That is where we come in, knight," Kahlaf grunted.

"Oh, I don't like where this is going," Geoffrey said.

"Kahlaf, Talthas and yourself will be instrumental in buying us the time we need, Geoffrey," Aelzandar said. "You need to lead the soldiers in holding off the automata."

"I see," said Geoffrey. "I hope you don't need us to hold for long."

"I will be at your side, Sir Geoffrey," said Talthas. "Until the end."

"Yes, I'd hoped that wouldn't be necessary."

"We must all do our part," Kahlaf grunted. "Together we shall try."

"Or die," Geoffrey said. He sighed with resignation. "Let me get into my armour."

***

He heard voices. Strange voices – speaking in deep, inflected tones – seemed to hover in the air about him, dusty with age. These were voices that had not been heard for millennia, words of the ancient beings that once lived here.

"Soldara," Bellaydin said aloud.

310

"What?" Polnygar said.

"Huh? Sorry?" Bellaydin responded.

"You said Soldara." Polnygar said, "What about the Soldara?"

Laughter seemed to surround him. Laughter, as well as distant shouts and screams.

"What was that?" Bellaydin said.

"What?" Polnygar said. "What was what?"

"I don't hear anything," Morgan agreed with Polnygar.

Bellaydin looked around in the darkness warily. "It must be in my head."

Polnygar looked at her brother with concern. "Here," she said, handing Kaltban over to him. "Let's swap swords. Kaltban should give you more light."

Bellaydin passed the weapon given to him by Haakon to Polnygar and took Kaltban in return. Just as his sister had promised, the glow from the sword's ice-blue blade provided more illumination. "Ahead," Bellaydin said as strange images swirled in his memory, distant, unfocused. "We need to go forward to the great antechamber."

"Why?" said Polnygar. "What's there?"

"It is where the Soldara lords Nahirios and Palamius fought over the Tears of the Divine. That's the place where they quarrelled and set upon each other, and where Palamius destroyed himself rather than let Nahirios take the power of the Tears."

Polnygar blinked. "How in the name of the Underworld do you – "

Bellaydin gripped his throbbing head in frustration, as pain seemed to etch deep furrows into his mind. "I don't – I don't know." Still clutching his head, he collapsed against the wall, losing his footing.

"Bellaydin!" Morgan cried in distress.

"I'm fine now. The pain, it seems to be subsiding."

These memories, the strange thoughts in his head. Where were they from? Haakon? The High Priest Cathan? *No, not there. Where then?* Another face appeared in Bellaydin's mind. *Wulfric Highcrown. Actually no, not Wulfric.* He corrected himself. *The creature who wore Wulfric's skin.* He had gifted Bellaydin with knowledge and memories of a thousand lifetimes, memories of this place, of the ancient Soldara, of the Tears of the Divine, and the Horned God and his followers. *But why?*

"Let's keep moving," Bellaydin panted.

They continued down the hall, Bellaydin's sword illuminating the faded murals and inscriptions on the wall.

"What are these images and writing?" Morgan said. "Do they tell the story of this place?"

Bellaydin looked back towards Polnygar and Morgan and nodded slowly. "These tell of the exile from the elven kingdoms, of the Soldara using the Art to enchant portals that would take them far across the sea, this land over here." He waved Kaltban over another section of the wall. "Here it's written that the Soldara raised great citadels to dominate the people in these lands, great magical towers where the Soldara would be lords unchallenged. The humans toiled in the field, their wealth going to their spellweaver overlords." He stepped forward and pointed ahead of them. "And that wall has the tale of how it all came to an end. How the ancient Karlicians rose up under leaders such as General Lydin, and made war upon the Fey, tearing down all the great towers, except for this one, the Last Citadel."

"You didn't even read that last one," Polnygar pointed out. "Yet you could describe it with such confidence.

"I didn't read it. You're right. But I knew," Bellaydin said, puzzled.

"Where is this antechamber that you mentioned?" Polnygar asked.

"Straight ahead," Bellaydin said.

Presently he heard a deep, chilling voice that shook him to his core. *"So, come then, Heir of Lydin."*

"Who's there?" Bellaydin shouted.

"I don't hear anyone, Bela," Polnygar said.

"Just as was foretold you will come before me, for the final time. Just as Lydin rose up against me, so shall the last of his blood submit."

"No, I will not. I will not," Bellaydin said.

"Who are you talking to, Bela?" Polnygar pressed in panicked tones.

"No one," he said. "No one."

Before long they reached another corner, which had Bellaydin led them around, and soon they found the darkness lifting as they entered a large, ornately decorated room well-illuminated by glowing jewels embedded in the walls. A large arch dominated the other side of the room and under it, a single shadowed figure walked towards them.

"Careful," Bellaydin readied Kaltban. He motioned for Polnygar and Morgan to follow and they did, their own weapons at the ready.

Lord Ivellios had changed in the years since Bellaydin last saw him. Gone was the haughty, proud, and handsome spellweaver lord of Aderilund; in its place was a hunched, sinister figure with a deathly pallor and black robes. The symbol of the Horned God dangled from his neck as he twisted a lip to sneer at Bellaydin.

"Here you have come, as predicted. So I hoped, so I expected, from Lydin's heirs," Ivellios said. The Eldara noticed Morgan. "You should not have come here, apostate. You should have been content with the fate that the Horned God had given you."

"I no longer serve the Horned God," Morgan said, her voice only wavering slightly. "Not while he punishes the just, and rewards the evil."

Ivellios gave a short laugh and turned to Polnygar. "You foolish girl. Have you come to throw your life away like that fool who shared your bed?"

Polnygar ignored the taunt. "I see you have regrown your hand." Her words dripped with scorn.

Ivellios gave a smug smile. "The powers of the Horned God are great. I am now stronger than I have ever been. This expedition of yours is futile. The Tears are already with my master, as you will be too. All that remains is to separate the wheat from the chaff." Ivellios turned his gaze, and pointing a pale finger in Bellaydin's direction, chanted in the language of the arcane.

"No!" Morgan dropped her weapon and ran towards Bellaydin, grabbing on to him. Bellaydin himself felt himself unable to move as Ivellios's spell weaved about him. The piece of the Tears around Bellaydin's neck began to glow and spark with a violent ferocity.

Polnygar looked on in shock as both her brother and Morgan disappeared entirely from where they had been standing.

"What have you done, you monster?" Polnygar said.

"They have gone through the Soldara gate. On to meet their destiny," Ivellios said. He regarded Polnygar's desperation with some amusement. "They're not dead, if that's what you fear, but they soon will be. Your brother was foolish enough to bring the Tears with him here, close enough for the Horned God to sense its presence. The girl was too blinded by her own feelings to let him go. They are with the Horned God now, just as was prophesied."

"Your counterpart Haakon believed in prophecies," Polnygar said with venom. "And now he's dead."

"Haakon was a fool. He was too bound by old loyalties, by the feelings he still felt for the infidels of his youth. He didn't realise that sometimes the hand of fate must be forced, that sometimes obstacles block the way of what must be. I have done so and become the living embodiment of the Horned God's will. Now all that remains is one final impediment. *Your continued existence.*"

"You've tried to kill me before," Polnygar was defiant. As she spoke, her mind focused on spells of protection and warding. "And you've failed every time."

"Your survival was essential until this moment," Ivellios mocked her. "Those previous attempts on your life were merely to shape your actions in the way the prophecy required, to mould either yourself or your wretched little brother into the Heir of Lydin. Now that the role has been filled, your own life is forfeit, and you will face the full breadth of a spellweaver's powers." Ivellios roared in anger and threw a blazing fireball towards Polnygar, but Polnygar had prepared for a moment like that, and immediately threw up a shield. The flames, though enveloping her in a sphere, did not come anywhere near her body.

"You have learned much, Mal-halyth, but your little parlour tricks are no match for a master of the arcane." Throwing his hands in the air, Ivellios caused the room to shake and tremble, unbalancing Polnygar from her feet. She toppled to the ground as all around her cracked and crumbled.

"This is my domain." Ivellios yelled in triumph. "I can harness the energy of the last citadel of the mighty Soldara. I can bind its power to me, and unleash the strength of the ancients. You, girl, are nothing but an insect caught in the storm."

Polnygar's sword tumbled from her grasp, and she fell backwards, as the room continued to shake.

Ivellios looked down at her with disdain, his gaze baleful and full of venom. "Nothing more than mongrel slime. How dare you attempt to wield the power of the Eldara masters. You, with your impure blood, are not fit to lick the mud from my boots. Time to die." Electricity crackled about his fingertips, and he flung a bolt of lightning at Polnygar.

Quickly she raised a hand, spoke a few words, and strengthened her shield. The lightning reflected off it, bouncing back to strike the wall with a tremendous thunderclap, leaving a blackened and scorched mark behind.

"Do you see now? Do you see how fate is inevitable? We are all helpless before the Horned God's power. We are all instruments of prophecy. You have served your purpose, and there is nothing more to you." He held out a hand and spoke a few words of Draconic. As he did, a glowing blade of energy materialised inside his grip. As he held the conjured sword tightly, he turned to Polnygar. "No more games, little Mal-halyth. This ends. Now."

CHAPTER 19

Geoffrey squinted into the gloom.

A gleaming point of light appeared on the horizon. Soon after another appeared, then another. "The signal fires." He turned to the soldier next to him. "Sound the horn." The man nodded, running off. In short order, trumpets started to blare.

Geoffrey called out. "They're here. To arms!"

Long ago, when the Emparian capital had been a much smaller town, the Garns Fortress had been built to protect it. Now, many centuries later, it was the nexus of the defence for the sprawling metropolis of sixty thousand souls that lived astride the Garns River. If the fortress fell, the city would be doomed, but if it stood, the enemies would never set foot in the city streets.

If it was any mortal enemy walking towards them, Geoffrey would have been confident. But the Goriinchian-commanded automata striding towards them was a most implacable foe, and Geoffrey's pessimism threatened to overwhelm him. It was all he could do to remember his training and stay at his post.

All around him, soldiers scrambled for position, taking up their places. Archers lined the walls, Talthas stood among them, while spearmen and militia assembled behind the gate, ready to handle any that broke through the gate. Geoffrey would feel safer if he knew that Aelzandar was joining him in this fight, but the archmage was holed up inside, desperately trying to prepare the spell that might permanently disable the automata army.

"The air is cold, it thins the blood," Kahlaf said as he approached Geoffrey. "A good day to die."

"I can't say I agree with that."

"There are things more important at stake than our lives," Kahlaf said, licking his fangs.

"All the same, I think I'd prefer to keep mine."

Oddly, the Ahktarran did not come back with a biting reply, but merely glanced at Geoffrey and gave a gruff, short chuckle. "Fight well, Sir Geoffrey."

Geoffrey smiled, in spite of himself. "You too, Kahlaf."

The Ahktarran nodded and turned his eyes to the horizon. Geoffrey, after a moment's thought, did likewise.

The great nobles of the realm emerged from the fortress, resplendent in their battle garb. The Duke of Georgeton, as ranking noble, led the way, followed by the Earl of Tyronsville and the Earl of Warding and finally, the queen herself, mounted on a magnificent white mare.

"Emparians, your Queen," the Duke of Georgeton announced.

In a single unified motion, every soldier and noble dropped to one knee and bowed. The young queen, looking uneasy and nervous, acknowledged them with a nod and a smile.

"My dear subjects," she began, her voice occasionally trembling in spite of her best efforts. "All of you here are doing your duty, defending your homeland, your family, your freedom, and your lives." As she continued, she seemed to gain strength, buoyed by the patient attention of her subjects. "My father, Henry, had tremendous love for this land, and great dedication to his subjects. When the time came, he would not shy from his duty, and would lead his men into battle." Soldiers around murmured softly in reverent memory of the late monarch. "I may not be the warrior my father was, but I am your queen, appointed by the gods, by divine right, by blood, and I intend to fulfil my duty here today. Follow me, and I will lead you to victory." The queen fumbled slightly as she attempted to draw her sword from its scabbard. With persistence, she succeeded and held the sword high upon her head.

All around, the soldiers of Emparia stood back up, gazing towards their queen, their voices united in a singular roar as they proclaimed, "Long live freedom. Long live Emparia. Long live Queen Amaryllis."

Geoffrey wanted desperately to be bolstered by the show of valour before him. In any other circumstances he'd have found the Emparians – and indeed their young queen's – bravery inspiring. But he knew what lay ahead and there was the persistent reminder that most of them might not live to see another day.

Almost on cue, Geoffrey felt a clawed palm on his shoulder and a deep, breathy voice in his ear. "Sir Geoffrey," Kahlaf said. "They come."

Sure enough, a veritable sea of silver and grey started to appear over the edge of the horizon, slowly moving towards the walls with an inhuman, relentless gait.

"The automata," Geoffrey breathed.

***

Bellaydin opened his eyes.

In the dim light, he could perceive the faint outline of the chamber, a dusty, cobwebbed room that had not seen use for centuries. Out of the corner of his eyes, he glimpsed faint, ghostly figures here and there. Some seemed to be human wizards, dressed in fashions centuries old, others seemed to be Soldara spirits, haughty, vain, and wearing ornate robes thousands of years old. The ghostly forms ignored Bellaydin's presence and merely milled about the chamber, echoing actions from their own long-departed lives.

He felt Morgan touch his leg. "Where are we?" He could hear the fear in her words. She trembled as her eyes darted about the room.

"I don't know," Bellaydin assessed their surroundings. There was no sign of Polnygar. In the darkness, he glimpsed ancient statues and dormant automata standing on the walls. He waited for them to spring to life, but nothing happened. They were as dead as the rest of the ruin.

In front of them was an eldritch sculpture that honestly looked like a massive meshed dish to Bellaydin. The details on the sculpture were ornate and nigh incomprehensible though. Adorned on its sides with diamonds, the central piece was a dark crystal. Bellaydin realised he had seen a similar structure under Goriinch Hill. That one was clearly broken, and its crystal had been shattered to pieces. This crystal, however, was glowing green, its pulsating light illuminating the chamber they were in.

"You have come. As I knew you would."

Bellaydin felt Morgan jump back in fright. She evidently heard the voice too, deep and echoing throughout the chamber. It was not simply in his head this time.

"Who is there?" Bellaydin demanded. "Show yourself."

"A slave is in no position to demand things of his master. Not now, not ever. You are my creature, Gwydion. You always have been."

"I'm nobody's slave."

A deep, sinister laugh reverberated through the room. Morgan held on to Bellaydin even tighter, her eyes wide.

320

"On the contrary, you were the most perfect of slaves. Everything that has happened, has happened because I have willed it so. The death of your parents, the circumstances of your birth, your journey through these lands and back again, all were but a part of my plan. You are mine, Gwydion, you belong to me, and it has been that way since the day you were born. The prophecy will be fulfilled. You will complete your destiny."

A shadowy figure emerged out of the gloom, coming closer to Bellaydin and Morgan. Shaking nearly as much as Morgan was, Bellaydin held Kaltban in front of him, readying himself for who – or what – might emerge from the shadows. The darkness parted, and a giant figure manifested before Bellaydin, encased entirely in armour.

"Ygarak," Bellaydin said.

The armoured man's face was obscured by a helmet. Beneath it, black sinister eyes glowered at Bellaydin and Morgan. Though silent, the contempt radiating from the figure was palpable. A chain dangled from its neck, and clinging to the chain were the other pieces of the Tears of the Divine.

Bellaydin moved to take the Tears. As he did so, the figure raised a hand, and Bellaydin and Morgan found themselves thrown back three feet and slammed into the wall. Groaning, they both clambered to their feet.

"Do not defy the Horned God again. You will not survive." There was silence for a moment as the figure stared at them, its eyes dark and cold.

"Blasphemy," declared Morgan. "You are the Prophet, yet you speak as if you are the Horned God himself."

The figure did not respond but merely turned around, facing away from Bellaydin and Morgan. The voice said, *"And who are you, apostate, to question the will of the Horned God? You know so little. Have you forgotten, apostate? The Horned God and his prophet are one."*

"The Horned God and his prophet are one," Morgan mouthed the words she had learned as a child. The words stirred something deep in the recesses of Bellaydin's memories.

The Horned God and his prophet are one.

Bellaydin found his head being assailed by visions from a different time from someone else. He saw a small farming village, from centuries ago, and a young Goriinchian tending to his sheep. *Ygarak*, he thought. Barely more than a boy. This was the age at which the Goriinchian holy book claimed he first received his visions, the age at which he first saw his god and received the sacred words.

The Horned God and his prophet are one.

Bellaydin now saw the young Ygarak plucking something from the fields. At first glance it looked like a gold coin, but it was actually a broken medallion. Bellaydin realised with awe that he was looking at Ygarak discovering a piece of the Tears of the Divine.

The Horned God and his prophet are one.

The boy was now tying a string around the gold piece. Bellaydin was struck by how innocent he looked. Young Ygarak put the medallion around his neck and looked at it admiringly before he was seized by agony. He clutched at his head and clawed at the medallion around his neck before falling limp to the ground. Mere moments later, he rose back, none the worse for wear.

The Horned God and his prophet are one.

Centuries ago, a boy named Ygarak died alone in a field, and the world never knew.

Back in the chamber the armoured man moved with slow and deliberate precision, his hands reaching for the helmet on top of his head.

Bellaydin was terrified of what he was to see, his fear freezing him in place. The great helm was removed, and it became apparent it was not the helmet that was horned. In truth the horns were attached to the head of the figure himself. The being turned to face Bellaydin and Morgan.

Bellaydin felt his stomach twist in fear and revulsion. He recognised the Goriinchian face that looked upon him; Ygarak. This face had once been human, but little remained of that little boy who tended sheep in his idyllic village. Instead, there was an infernal, demonic cast to the face, from the horns that erupted from the once-human skull to the great fanged teeth that crowded the disfigured jaw. Patches of red hair on the scalp and chin vied with darker hair, hair that seemed to belong to another. Strange bones and growths covered Ygarak's face. It was almost as if there were two faces, both trying to impose themselves on the same head. *One human, Goriinchian in fact, and the other —*

Bellaydin's eyes honed in on the jagged, deformed, but clearly elven ears.

Soldara.

The figure's voice echoed in the recesses of his mind. *"Mortal flesh does not easily support such great power. But I endure."*

Ygarak flexed his muscular arms as if in exultation, and a pair of ragged black wings unfolded from his back. Morgan whimpered in terror; Bellaydin was too shocked and repulsed to say anything. Now he could see the great lie, the great fraud that lay at the dark heart of the Goriinchian nation.

Ygarak was not the great prophet of the Horned God. In fact, *Ygarak was the Horned God*, and the Horned God was Ygarak.

Bellaydin now understood what he had seen in the memories of the being that had possessed Wulfric Highcrown. At one point in his many lives he had led, the being was a Soldara named Palamius. His rival, Nahirios – himself a powerful Soldara – had attempted to use the Tears of the Divine to destroy their enemies, the Goriinchians. In a bid to thwart Nahirios' efforts, Palamius sealed the Tears' power with his own blood. Bellaydin couldn't be certain how it transpired but the ensuing conflict led to both Soldara being trapped within the shattered pieces of the Tears.

It was not a benevolent, loving god that had found the poor Goriinchian boy in the fields so many centuries ago, but Nahirios, trapped in that particular piece of the Tears of the Divine, lying in wait for a unsuspecting soul and mind to prey upon. The real Ygarak had to die that day so a spirit of dark genius and malevolence could take the boy's body, wearing it as a wizard might wear a robe, and using that form to set the Goriinchians on the path they now tread.

"It was all a lie." Bellaydin said finally. "You lied to these people. You masqueraded as a prophet, so you could lead them to worship you."

"You speak as if you believe you are my equal. You are not. You are a mere mortal."

"You are not a god, Nahirios."

"A meaningless name. A meaningless statement. What is a god? The only difference between the gods of your kind and the one you see before you is that you know I exist. The Horned God endures. Your gods do not."

Bellaydin felt a twinge of doubt, as the Horned God's words struck him. It was true, he had never seen the gods of Emparia, nor the gods of the Eldara, nor the gods of any land. Were they frauds too, like that of the Goriinchians?

"You can't keep the Goriinchians ignorant forever. They'll discover this lie."

"This lie, as you call it, is all that unites the people of this land. If they destroy it, they would destroy themselves. The slaves live to serve the Horned God. They know no other way. It is their nature."

"Not so," Bellaydin said. "There's Morgan. And others, too. They are your slaves no longer."

"This apostate is not free. Once a slave of the Horned God –" The Horned God raised a hand and clenched his fist. Immediately Morgan tumbled backwards, and with a strangled gasp, choked. *"– always a slave of the Horned*

God."

"Morgan." Bellaydin wanted to help her, but he was hopelessly outmatched. "Stop it. Leave her alone."

Ygarak squeezed his fist tighter. *"Your words have no sway here, Heir of Lydin."*

"Tell me what you need." Bellaydin screamed. "I'm clearly the one you wanted this whole time."

The Horned God lowered his hand and Morgan's lifeless body fell limply to the ground. *"This form does not befit me, but I am trapped, shackled to this plane. Leashed by Palamius to this mortal frame, god incarnate in flesh, denied the power in the Tears of the Divine. My power. Only the blood of Palamius can unlock this. The remaining power of his legacy is contained in your blood, the sole branch of Lydin's once thriving tree, pruned for generations by my will."*

The Horned God's words cut deep. Here was the reason behind all the deaths in Bellaydin's family– his parents, his cousin, William, William's daughter Maria – all to make him the last Ap'Lydin.

"You're wrong. I am not the last Ap'Lydin." Bellaydin said.

"Your sister will pass soon enough. She too must embrace her fate."

***

Lightning crackled throughout the chamber as Polnygar and Ivellios battled. They were causing utter pandemonium. Fireballs exploded through their fingertips, scorching the walls and ceiling. Unearthly creatures appeared out of nowhere due to their magical summons, and then disappeared just as quickly, banished back to their own realms. The sheer power and destructive energies of a wizardly duel was on full display.

"You are weakening, Mal-halyth," Ivellios taunted as he directed a torrent of magical energy towards Polnygar. "I can feel your willpower unravelling."

Polnygar paid no heed to his words, instead concentrating on deflecting the energy bolt Ivellios had hurtled her way. Raising an energy shield around himself Ivellios walked towards Polnygar.

"Why do you fight?" he taunted. "Your brother would certainly have submitted to the Horned God, and I have no doubt that Goriinchian girl has likewise returned to her master. You fight alone."

Polnygar held the sword out in front of her, gripping it tightly with both hands.

"That weapon belongs to the Horned God," Ivellios said. A sinister smile crept across his face. "You should return it."

"You want this sword?" Polnygar said as Ivellios came towards her. "Come and take it." She swung down on the spellweaver. Her sword sliced through the magical shield, but Ivellios conjured his energy blade up to block it. Arcane sparks flew as their weapons clashed.

Time and again the two struck each other, with neither taking any appreciable advantage. Ivellios fought with a savage frenzy, the cool and calm spellweaver Polnygar had known in Aderilund long gone. Polnygar's own prowess surprised even herself, and she found a skill and resilience she never knew she had. She thought of those who had fallen, those whose lives the spellweaver had stolen, and used these thoughts to push her assailant further. When her thoughts went to Augustin, she felt a pulse of rage go through her body and smashed her blade across the spellweaver's body, her pain only having increased her strength.

Shocked, and bloodied, Ivellios stumbled backwards as blood spattered across his robes. He touched his chest in disbelief as if he found the idea of injury impossible. His eyes narrowing, he swung his own weapon in a parabolic arc, cutting a deep gash in Polnygar's arm. As she stumbled back, Ivellios wheeled about, and smashed her in the face, sending her toppling to the ground.

"Pathetic Mal-halyth." Ivellios' face was smeared with sweat and blood, and his eyes were cold and unforgiving. "How *dare* you spill Soldara blood."

Polnygar, her body aching all over, pulled herself to her feet. Despite the gravity of the situation and her own exhaustion, Polnygar could not resist laughing at the spellweaver. "If you think you are Soldara, you are seriously deluded. You are no more Soldara than I am."

"How dare you! Vile filth, you have no comprehension. The Horned God has favoured me. He has seen the purity of my bloodline. He knows that I, above all others, have kept the ideals of the Soldara alive. That is why he has chosen me to rule this world as the new dawn comes. Once the mistakes of the past are no more. The unbelievers, the weak, the impure. All shall be swept aside."

"Words, nothing more." Polnygar said.

"You know nothing. While your brother submits to his new master, the infidels of Emparia will be destroyed by the automata, creatures which I brought to life, thanks to the secrets the Horned God kept in these halls." He held his hands above him, conjuring a great cloud of magical energy about him. "We are the awakening destiny of the world. And you, you are the last relic of the old order, soon to be forgotten."

CHAPTER 20

"Here they come." Geoffrey yelled.

The automata marched towards the walls relentlessly, stopping for nothing.

Talthas' voice cried out over the din. "Loose!" The Emparian defenders unleashed a hail of arrows. Other defenders threw boulders or boiling oil. The automata shrugged off all manner of attacks, continuing in their straight march.

"Soldiers at arms," the duke called out.

"Steady," Kahlaf called.

Below them, the automata reached the walls crammed together in a torrent of sheer force as they attacked the gate by smashing into it repeatedly.

"The gate. The gate," Geoffrey yelled, rushing to assist the defenders. Kahlaf followed, bringing with him any of the remaining melee fighters from the top of the walls. "Reinforcements, to the gates!"

The automata hurled themselves at the metal girders of the portcullis, ramming the metal bars with their shoulders. The gate buckled under their repeated attempts.

"They're coming through," Geoffrey warned.

"Hold, Hold," Kahlaf growled. The gate collapsed into pieces of twisted metal; an automaton rushed through, crushing one soldier's windpipe with a lunge, and smashing the skull of another defender against the wall. Other Emparians rushed to fill the gap, and the automaton was disabled by a skymetal mace to the chest.

The victory was short-lived, however, as other automata rushed into the breach, rending and maiming the defenders with ease. Elsewhere along the wall, more automata, unfazed by arrow fire or boiling pitch wore down the stone through pure physical effort. As they charged the wall, yet again, a web of cracks began to form in the masonry. The situation looked desperate.

"Back! Fall back," Geoffrey called.

"Retreat! Retreat to the fortress," the duke ordered.

The automata swarmed through the opening, trampling any soldiers in their way.

"Regroup! Regroup!" Geoffrey's cry was frantic as all about him, the defenders were overwhelmed. The automata were relentless as they pushed forward but curiously, they ignored any soldier not directly in their path. Geoffrey nearly fell to the ground in surprise as one automaton pushed past him as if he wasn't even there.

"What in the name of the Underworld?" Geoffrey said. "Are we all suddenly invisible?" He watched as the automata lumbered past him, their metal heads not even giving him a fleeting glance. Whatever they were after, they were single-minded in their pursuit of it.

A deep and terrible realisation dawned on Geoffrey. He had made a terrible mistake. These automata were not seeking to kill or to take land -

they were seeking a prize that would win them the war without a campaign, a prize that Geoffrey himself had served up on a silver platter.

"Protect the queen!" He struck the nearest automata to him with his mace, felling the creature with a blow, and then ran to join up with the rest of the fleeing troops. "Come with me!"

But most of the soldiers seemed in no hurry to do so, the Emparian lines breaking like waves on the shore. Soldiers scattered before the oncoming automata, deserting their posts in fear of their own lives. Geoffrey looked for the other commanders in vain. Only the duke, his head above the crowd of men, was in sight, though he was sorely pressed as the great mass of men pushed towards him, retreating before the automata.

"Hold! For the love of your country, for your duty!" the duke commanded. Three automata moved towards him with unusual speed, their eyes aglow. The duke pivoted on his horse, turning towards his assailants, but one of the automata swung wide, smashing a metal fist into the horse's flank. The horse reared violently, throwing the duke to the ground. The automata attacked again, and soon the horse itself toppled to the ground, out of sight.

The duke cried out, pulling himself to his feet, "To the Underworld with you." He moved to defend himself, but the automata had already moved past him, suddenly treating him as no real threat, much to his shock.

Geoffrey ran towards the duke, avoiding fleeing soldiers and rampaging automata as he did.

"Your Grace, we must –" An automaton smashed past Geoffrey, knocking him to his feet. The duke, crouching down, helped the knight up. The duke looked at the raging battle that was now taking part behind them and cursed. "In the Sun King's name, they shall not take this city, not while I still take breath."

Geoffrey ran beside him. "Your Grace, they don't want the city. They want the queen. We must get her to safety."

331

The duke yelled. "I told you we should have never risked this in. Back to the fortress."

"It won't hold for long," Geoffrey said.

"It's all we've got. And it'll give us some time," the duke said.

The duke and their knight fought their way through the crush of attackers back behind their own lines. Despite the great numbers of automata, moving past them seemed relatively easy, as their single-minded advance left them effectively blind to any defenders coming up behind them. The Emparian defenders were retreating to the fortress, and Geoffrey saw a trio of knights leading the queen inside far ahead of the advancing line of automata. He breathed a sigh of relief.

"It's not over yet," the duke said. "But if your elf friend doesn't show his face soon, it might as well be."

Geoffrey said nothing, looking around at his troops. He raised his sword, hoping that this proof of his own life would help the soldiers regain morale so that the retreat to the fortress might be more orderly. A few weary cheers greeted his gesture, and Geoffrey knew that they would not last longer.

"Come on, Aelzandar," Geoffrey whispered, "We're nearly out of time."

***

Polnygar stumbled back.

Her body was tiring, battered and bruised by the relentless assaults, both magical and physical. Ivellios had taken an enormous amount of punishment himself, perhaps even as much as or more so than Polnygar, yet the zealous fervour in his eyes had not dimmed at all. Clearly, the spellweaver was drawing power from elsewhere.

"While the Horned God reigns, I cannot die," Ivellios boasted. "But you are alone, little Mal-halyth. None of the false gods of the Eldara or Human nations will hear you. Not here."

Polnygar tried to hold her sword, but her strength was fast fading, and the weapon felt heavy in her grasp. It clattered to the ground.

"You would have never defeated me," Ivellios said, his tone quiet, almost apologetic. "The impurity of your blood made certain of that. Nothing lies in your future, except for death."

Polnygar's eyes flitted from Ivellios' hands to his face and back.

The spellweaver chuckled. "I don't need a sword to kill you, Mal-halyth. With the power I wield my bare hands are more than sufficient."

Flames flickered at the end of the spellweaver's fingertips as his eyes gleamed maliciously. "The Horned God is victorious on all fronts." Ivellios raised his hands. "You are no longer needed."

As flames engulfed her, Polnygar's last conscious thoughts were of agonising pain and the horrible realisation that she had gambled all.

And lost.

***

"Hebu," Aelzandar called out. "Attend to me."

"Yes, master," Hebu remarked, scurrying towards the archmage. "What is your wish?"

"I think we're done here," the archmage said, closing the book and grabbing a few pieces of parchment.

"You have the spell?" Hebu asked.

Aelzandar gave the Nemoi an odd look. "Something like that. Staff." The Nemoi obliged and Aelzandar, staff in hand, looked straight ahead with determination. "It's time. To the very top of the tower. We need to have a good view of the battlefield."

As they hurried past, a soldier saluted and, spotting the parchment in the archmage's hands, went to alert his superiors. "At arms, men. Make way for the Lord Archmage."

Not far away, Geoffrey heard the cry and sprang into action. "Hold the line."

"There's too many of them." a soldier cried, as the brawling automata threatened to break through the shield wall. Masonry dust and chunks of stone littered the ground around them.

"Fight on anyway," Kahlaf ordered, his hands a rapid blur as he swung and parried against the clumsy aggressors.

"Just a moment more." Geoffrey dispatched one of the automata with a crushing blow. "Help is at hand." His voice was calm and assured as he did all he could to hide the panic within.

"My lord, look!" shouted one of the soldiers, pointing above them, to the tower ramparts.

Framed against the setting sun stood the archmage Aelzandar, his robes fluttering in the afternoon wind, his staff aloft and his other hand outstretched.

"Help has arrived," Geoffrey breathed.

Aelzandar recited words in the ancient language of the Art. "Hezula Efherem Mulius, Akaris."

In an instant, the automata shuddered to a halt, frozen mid-step just as they were about to breach the Emparian line. Soldiers looked about them, in a mixture of wonder and relief. A few even touched the motionless statues

"They've stopped." Geoffrey said, "We've done it." He looked around, scarcely believing what he could see. "Oh, my gods, we've done it." He lifted his sword, and all around him, soldiers let out a triumphant cheer.

Emparia was saved.

***

Fear gripped Bellaydin.

The Horned God loomed above him, a triumphant look upon his hellish features.

"Yes, yes. I feel it now. Your sister, the penultimate Heir of Lydin...she has passed...her life essence no more. You, Gwydion, are the last."

Bellaydin felt his blood turn cold; a shudder and sense of sorrow filled him.

The Horned God had to be lying. To make Bellaydin lose hope, to make him lose himself to despair.

His heart pounding, Bellaydin tried to back away from the menace before him, looking vainly for a place to run, or even hide. But the Horned God saw all, and no matter where he tried to go, the walking corpse that was once Ygarak stood before him.

"Do not run, mortal. Why fight when you cannot win? Why delay the inevitable? Why will you not embrace your destiny?"

"You don't know my destiny," Bellaydin said, moving backwards.

"But I do. You will surrender the Tears, as was foretold, and the power will be unlocked. Then, you will surrender your mortal frame to me, and I shall leave this crumbling form, and take yours. I shall live for millennia more. You shall become one with me. You shall be part of my Will, just as one day all will."

"No," Bellaydin shook his head.

"You should consider the power arrayed against you, Heir. I could incinerate you with a word."

"Then this body would be worthless to you."

"No matter. Your sister's is ready and waiting to be possessed. Though I do not relish the form of a female, the power would still be there. There is much I would endure

335

for my destiny."

"No," Bellaydin tried to move away, but he was wrenched from the floor and flung through the air with great force before being smashed against the wall with a crunch. Pain shot through his body, the torture slowing time to a standstill for him. In agony, Bellaydin slumped against the wall. He felt his ribs, cracked and broken, and tasted blood in his mouth.

"Give me the Tears and yourself. There is no other way." The Horned God reached out his hand. *"It is your destiny."*

Cornered, Bellaydin trembled. His hands, smeared with blood, reached for the Tears around his neck.

"Yes," the Horned God whispered. *"As it was written, you shall deliver to me the power that is mine by rights."*

"Why would I?" Bellaydin stammered through blood-flecked lips.

The Horned God pressed a finger against Bellaydin's forehead. *"Let me give you a vision of the future. The future you and I will create."*

Bellaydin screamed. His mind swirled with new thoughts. He saw himself returning from Goriinchia a hero. He saw himself named a duke, and a member of the Privy Council. The queen herself became Bellaydin's bride – how could she not? And he became ruler of Emparia in all but name, and father to a line of great and powerful kings.

But it was not him accomplishing these things. The Horned God lived within him and pulled his strings. In Bellaydin's name Emparia would be transformed, as the old faiths were replaced with the new. In Bellaydin's name tyranny would descend upon the land and all Emparians would become slaves of the Horned God.

And it would not stop with his death. Bellaydin's sons, grandsons, his entire line would be vessels for the Horned God, shells he could inhabit, jumping from one to the next as each body aged and died. Each body bred from the line of Lydin, and so delivering the Horned God the full power of the Tears of the Divine.

From Emparia, other lands would follow, as a line of god-kings spread the Horned God's faith by the sword, forcing submission where it was given, and dealing death to those who resisted. Finally, there was nought but an Empire of the Horned God. An eternal world of slaves.

The Horned God's mind pressed into his like a torrent, threatening to engulf him. He struggled against it, trying to resist, but he could feel his resolve crumbling with every moment. The Horned God's mind gave off a feeling of exultation as it sensed its moment of triumph drawing near. But then another's thoughts pushed forth from Bellaydin's mind, throwing the Horned God back in confusion.

This one is mine.

Palamius. Or as Bellaydin had known him, Wulfric.

The two Soldara minds battled, with both evenly matched. Wulfric was all cool reason, his mind honed for centuries for this exact moment, but the Horned God was raw fury, utilising all his willpower to snatch the prize he desired.

Wulfric was weakening. The Horned God would soon overwhelm him. With his own mental strength fading, Bellaydin collected his thoughts and pushed back against the Horned God. He sensed the Horned God's confusion, and with Bellaydin's mind working in concert with Wulfric's, the pair pushed back and overwhelmed the Horned God, forcing him out of Bellaydin's mind.

Bellaydin looked up, as the Horned God seemed distracted and saw the Tears of the Divine dangle from the chain around the creature's neck.

Fighting back pain, Bellaydin steeled himself. It would be the only opportunity he would get, and even if he failed, he knew it was his only chance. He reached out for the Tears.

"What are you doing?" the Horned God demanded. *"WHAT ARE YOU*

337

DOING?"

With unabiding fury, the Horned God pulled Bellaydin into the air and flung him from one side to another, crushing him against one wall and then the other.

"Submit. Submit!" The Horned God released him, and Bellaydin dropped to the floor, his battered body slumping on the stones. *"You cannot defeat me. You cannot –"* The Horned God stopped mid-sentence, and eyes wide, he brought a clawed hand to feel the chain around his neck. The Tears were gone.

"What have you done? What have you DONE?"

Bellaydin stirred and opened his fist to reveal the three missing pieces of the Tears. As the Horned God thundered with rage and moved towards Bellaydin with a furious speed, Bellaydin pulled the final pieces of the Tears from around his neck, and, bringing it together with the others, closed his fist. A blinding pain seared through him, and he thought he heard the voice of Wulfric Highcrown. *"It is done."*

His senses were alive, reaching out in a manner he had never felt before. The light blinded him, but Bellaydin could see everything as if he were existing in all places and all moments, looking down upon himself from afar. Power burned in Bellaydin's veins; power greater than he had ever felt. All things seemed possible. He was the blazing sun, the eternal stars, the energy that bound existence together.

Ygarak thundered towards him, and Bellaydin instinctively held up a hand to shield himself from the inevitable blow. It never came. Instead, the Horned God was lifted into the air and thrown backwards against the wall, just as Bellaydin himself had been.

Astonished, Bellaydin stood, and looked at his hands. A radiant glow enveloped his palms and fingers, emanating from the Tears themselves, and suffusing his entire body.

"No!" Ygarak raged. *"The power is mine. You shall not take it from me."*

His fury shook the very walls themselves. Ygarak summoned a sphere of pure energy: a crackling ball of lightning and flung it towards Bellaydin. Bellaydin raised a single hand, and the sphere dissolved harmlessly into mist. With the power, came knowledge, wisdom beyond any mortal, and Bellaydin felt a confidence unlike anything he'd experienced. He would deal with this false god.

"Automata." Ygarak ordered. *"Destroy."*

The previously dormant automata on the walls lurched into life, their ancient metal bodies creaking and clanking as they moved towards Bellaydin. His entire body now surrounded by the glowing energy from the Tears, Bellaydin raised his hands above his head, forcing the power outwards into a circular shield. As the automata crossed the line they dissolved into nothingness. Bellaydin turned his gaze towards Ygarak who stared back, his eyes dark with fury. As he did so, Bellaydin felt a burning sensation within him. Clutching his chest, he realised that the power was corroding him from the inside out.

"What now, mortal? You cannot control this power. It was never meant for one such as you. You should have submitted. As with those you brought here, you face annihilation rather than victory. You have brought only death."

"No." Bellaydin said, "You bring death. I bring life." He channelled the energy consuming him towards Morgan's body, searching for her heartbeat and willing it back into being. He felt a throb in her heart, then another, and her chest rose and fell with ragged gasps.

"But how many can you save before the power consumes you?" Ygarak taunted.

Bellaydin's mind burned, but he fought through the pain and found his sister. So close to death, and yet he could save her. The power of the Tears could do so, just as it had Morgan.

***

Polnygar gasped as she felt an invisible force pull her out of what had felt like a sea of fire. The flames that previously consumed her had been spontaneously doused. She was disorientated, if only momentarily. Above her Ivellios' thin-lipped smile turned into a frown, his eyes filled with confusion. From the corner of her eyes, Polnygar spotted the sword she had dropped earlier. Without much thought, she reached for it, rose to her feet and thrust the sword upwards, burying it into the spellweaver's chest.

The sword had cut through flesh and bone and reduced Ivellios' final words to a pathetic gurgle. The spellweaver fell to the ground, blood rapidly pooling about his corpse, the puzzlement he felt in his last moments etched permanently on his lifeless face

Polnygar allowed herself only a moment of respite and concentrated on the next task at hand. She had to find her brother.

The words that Ivellios had used to transport her brother and Morgan to the Horned God's domain stirred in her memory. It was her only hope of finding them, even if it meant travelling to the lion's den itself.

With practised fluidity she weaved the spell, speaking the incantations and performing the ritual from memory. Within a moment the room around her was gone, and a different chamber formed around her. Before she could take in her new surroundings, she was blinded by an immense light. She heard a roar and a scream of agony.

Squinting against the dazzling brilliance that surrounded her, she could see Morgan huddled up against the wall, and two figures, locked in mortal combat. Shadows against the light, their features were obscured and indistinguishable, save for the menacing horned profile of one, and the golden, glowing eyes of the other.

"Bela!" Polnygar called out. She hoped in desperation that Bellaydin could somehow hear in all in the mayhem. If he was there at all.

One of the figures thrust its sword through the chest of the horned one. The horned figure roared in fury and dissipated into an explosion of light and energy. Polnygar was thrown back against the wall.

The remaining figure turned towards her, and she saw her brother's face, his eyes blazing like twin suns, his mouth agape in a silent scream.

"Oh, Bellaydin," she whispered. "What have you done?"

"THE HORNED GOD IS NO MORE. THE SHADOW IS LIFTED BY MY WILL." The words tumbled from Bellaydin's mouth in a voice that was not his.

"Bellaydin?"

"I AM NOT BELLAYDIN. I AM NOT GWYDION. I AM THE TRUE MASTER OF THE TOWER."

"Then depart whoever you are," Polnygar shouted. "And give me my brother back."

"NO." For a moment, the room went dark, but just as suddenly the light flared back into existence.

"IT IS NOT ENOUGH. ALL MUST BE CLEANSED." Bellaydin held a hand towards her, pulling the threads of energy that permeated him towards his fist, coiling them like string. Light danced on his fingertips.

Polnygar had seen what had become of Bellaydin's last opponent and she had no desire for that fate. Her brother was in there somewhere, buried under these alien thoughts and desires. She only had to reach him.

Long ago Aelzandar had taught her how to use the Art to share thoughts with another. She had never considered that she might use it to try save her life. Clearing her mind as best as she could, she pushed herself forward into Bellaydin's mind. Her brother's presence was not difficult to find. It was like a blazing star in the middle of a void. Once she had established a link, she tried to feed him reminders of who he was.

She sent him an image of the two of them as children, Polnygar's young self draping a protective arm over her little brother, who she had just pulled away from a scuffle with an Eldara boy. "They're too stupid to realise how amazing you are," the voice of young Polnygar reverberated around them.

Other images from their life together flashed by, of their shared laughter and hardship, of the moments spent with their mother, of their recent reunion. In the midst of these warm memories, Polnygar thought she heard Bellaydin's voice, struggling to be heard.

But the mind controlling her brother fought back, trying to blast her thoughts with concentrated energy, trying to force the memories back to her own mind. But she persisted until her brother could finally find his voice and let out a primal scream. There was an explosion of light, and then everything went dark.

CHAPTER 21

Polnygar awoke to gloom and silence.

As her eyes adjusted to the dim light, she caught a glimpse of her surroundings. The walls of the room were scorched and blackened; here and there she saw the twisted and melted remnants of what must have once been automata.

Suddenly, the floor and walls shuddered. Cracks appeared in the stonework, and dust and detritus fell from the ceiling. Any stability the ancient ruin had was crumbling quickly. They had to get out of there. And fast. She heard sobs and turned to see Morgan, her face bruised and burned, crawling towards her.

"It's done," Morgan whispered.

Polnygar checked the girl's life signs. She was injured but would live. Ignoring her own aching limbs, Polnygar pulled Morgan to her feet and slung Morgan's arm over her shoulder. "Here, lean on me." Polnygar said. "We have to find Bellaydin and get out of here."

"Bela?" Polnygar called out. "Bela?" She heard a soft groan. Bellaydin's clothes and skin had been burned, but he still lived. "Bellaydin."

"Polnygar," Bellaydin said groggily. "Is that you?"

"Bela, can you get up? Can you walk?"

"What happened?" he said. "Can't feel my legs or arms..."

"Morgan, can you help me get him up?"

The Goriinchian girl nodded, and using the wall as support, they brought Bellaydin off the ground, and supported him on either side.

"Ow." Bellaydin opened his palm. The Tears of the Divine were still there, the gold untarnished, unharmed by the events that had taken place.

The room shuddered and shook again. Polnygar steadied herself. "Come on, we'll have to deal with that later. We must get out of here. Morgan, hold on to him while I cast the spell."

In an instant Polnygar's spell had returned them to the archway above and, with Morgan and Polnygar supporting Bellaydin on either side, they made their way through the ruin as it seemed to crumble around them.

The surviving priests and warriors made no effort to stop the trio, most of them being more focused on escaping the collapsing structure themselves. Those who were more pious stood transfixed as their most sacred and holy place collapsed about them, seemingly taking the religion of the Horned God with it.

Outside the temple, Caelwych and the Saldarri were waiting for them. "What happened in there?" Caelwych said as the three stumbled out of the ruin, but he didn't wait for an answer, instead waving them forward. A crumbling piece of stone toppled from the tower, hurtling to the ground a few feet away. "The whole place is about to collapse. We'd best move quickly."

"Please," Polnygar said. "My brother needs help."

Caelwych called for a few Saldarri to strap the injured Bellaydin to one of the horses. "Come, we must move. The Seeress will be waiting."

The journey back was unimpeded. The Horned God's followers seemed to have lost their will to fight and did not put up any resistance. The group passed ransacked temples, razed towns, and the aftermath of pitched battles. Everything they saw pointed to a disintegrating power structure. Polnygar wondered if perhaps by ending the reign of the Horned God and his priests they had doomed Goriinchia.

When they stopped to make camp for the night. Caelwych examined Bellaydin's injuries.

"The wounds will heal in time." As grateful as Polnygar was to hear that, she could not help but wonder if Goriinchia's wounds would heal as quickly. She never thought victory would feel hollow

Later that night, they sat around the campfire with the other Saldarri soldiers. She relished the taste of her first hot meal for a long time.

"You and your brother have helped us more than we ever dared imagine," Caelwych said. "No more will the Saldarri scrape on bended knee to the will of others. We are free, at last. For that, we thank you."

Polnygar nodded. "Use that freedom well."

"We will, outsider," Caelwych said. "You should have no doubt of that."

***

For the first time in what felt like an eternity, Bellaydin slept comfortably. His slumber was peaceful, even if it was not without dreams. In fact, he dreamed of his father. Unlike the nightmares of the past year, though, these were not disturbing omens of a future that was to come. Instead, the thoughts were comforting.

He saw his father's face warm and smiling, eyes sparkling. "My son," he said. "You've become the man I couldn't. I'm proud of you."

"I didn't do it alone," Bellaydin said to the spectre. Its eyes bore into him, full of an infinite sadness.

345

"Of course. Polnygar, my darling child. I am proud of her too. You must tell her for me."

"I will, father."

"The two of you have done what I never could. You have redeemed our line. Thank you, my children. Thank you."

Bellaydin reached out to his father, and for a moment, it felt as if they were embracing, but soon the dream ended, and he awoke to discover morning had come.

The dream was still on his mind when he rose and walked about the camp. For years both his nights and waking hours had been plagued with prophetic dreams. With the fall of the Horned God, would these dreams now end?

Gradually the others awoke and in short order they packed up and set off early for the journey back to the Saldarri camp. On their arrival, they were greeted by the Seeress, who met them at the camp entrance with other Saldarri.

The old woman smiled, extending her arms. "Greetings to you, Heirs of Lydin," the Seeress said. "Tales have already begun to reach us. We have heard of your exploits at the Tower of the Magi. "

"Bellaydin slew the Horned God," Polnygar said. "He is the true Heir."

Bellaydin blushed. "After you led a Saldarri attack, rescued me, drove the Horned God from my mind and defeated Ivellios. And dragged my unconscious body from the tower while it collapsed around us. I think it's clear which of us is the real hero here."

The Seeress smiled. "You are both equally Lydin's Heir. And equally heroes of our people."

"I didn't expect that," Bellaydin said.

The Seeress nodded. "Fate and destiny are never simple matters. I understand you have returned with the Tears too?"

"Yes," Bellaydin said, opening his hand and offering the Tears.

The Seeress gasped and recoiled. "I will not touch it, Heir of Lydin," she said. "I sense that great power still resides within. There are others who can help you with it, who understand its powers more. You will see them soon."

The Seeress held up her arms and called out loudly. "Behold, no longer must we tell only the tale of Mael the Apostate, for now, we have a new story to tell: Gwydion the Apostate, Slayer of the False God, and Polnygar, Witch of the North, Liberator of the Saldarri.

The Saldarri cheered loudly at the words of the Seeress.

"Thank you," Bellaydin said, "We should get back to Wishapton."

"We have prepared for your journey north. Saldarri rangers will take you to the border. Once you are within Enparran lands, you should be safe. In the meantime, we would be honoured if you would stay and help us celebrate the downfall of the Horned God."

"We wouldn't want to impose," Polnygar said.

The Seeress laughed. "Now how could the guests of honour possibly impose?"

It was only a short time after that that the celebrations began. The Saldarri lit bonfires and brought wine for their guests. Then, one by one, the Saldarri joined in dancing around the fires, re-enacting with shadows the tale of the Heir of Lydin and the Horned God's fall.

A smiling Caelwych held a hand out to Polnygar, urging her to join the merriment with a nod of his head. Though initially shy, Polnygar soon found herself laughing and dancing with them as best she could. Bellaydin watched nearby, a smile creeping across his lips, and he found himself clapping as his sister moved about with the Saldarri, re-enacting her battle with the spellweaver Ivellios.

On the other side of the fire, he caught Morgan looking at him. As his eyes met hers, she turned away for a moment but then glanced at him again. She was smiling, which for Bellaydin was still a novelty to see on her face. A glorious mane of flame red curls bounced loosely over her shoulders, unbridled by any hood. He felt like he was looking at her for the first time in his life, a sentiment that made his stomach tighten.

He moved around the fire, dodging the revelling Saldarri, refusing their invitations to join them while he made his way to the Goriinchian girl.

"Morgan," Bellaydin said. "You disappeared after we reached the Seeress' camp. I thought I must have offended you in some way."

"No," she said. "Nothing like that. I just needed some time to think, that's all. The last few days have been a lot for me to take in. I met a god. And I saw a man kill that god."

"Well, I –"

She smiled and placed a finger on his lips. "I wasn't asking for an apology."

"I wonder," Bellaydin mused. "If the girl I met all those years ago outside her father's camp had known this was where our story would lead, would she have ever freed me from that cage?"

"Maybe not," Morgan admitted. "But that girl is gone. She died with her father."

"A pity," Bellaydin said. "I was rather fond of her."

"How interesting," Morgan said archly. "She hated you."

Bellaydin shot her an inquiring look.

Morgan smiled playfully in return. "At least that was what she kept telling herself. But beneath the hate something else burned, I wager."

"So, she was consumed by the flames then," Bellaydin said. "And then, like the phoenix of old, Morgan Culainn was born anew."

Morgan tucked some stray hair behind her ear. "I like that."

Bellaydin grinned. "Me too."

They heard singing from the bonfire. Polnygar's voice, merry with wine, rose above the din.

"You are not going to join your sister?" Morgan asked, coming up beside him.

"A bit too sore," Bellaydin said, rubbing his arms. "Though I could use a walk."

Morgan gazed at him and smiled, reaching down to take his hand. "Come," she said, pulling him away from the crowd, "Let's take that walk then."

"Where to?" Bellaydin asked.

"You'll see," Morgan responded. She led him to a hill that looked over the Saldarri camp. The bonfire and the flurry of movement from the revellers looked like embers dancing on midnight sand. Bellaydin found the sight comforting.

"You have done so much for us," Morgan had turned towards him. "For me. And yet there's been no reward."

Bellaydin shrugged. "I never really expected one."

"I know," Morgan said. "But who said the reward was for you?"

She leant close and kissed him. Bellaydin was surprised, but he did not resist, and after a beat, he returned the kiss with urgency. He pulled away, but only for a moment. "I thought you didn't like us heathen Enparrans."

Morgan feigned ambivalence. "Perhaps I changed my mind."

He kissed her again, then turned back to look at the bonfire. "We should probably get back. The others might notice us gone."

Morgan grabbed his wrist playfully. "Not quite yet, hero." She pulled him down with her to the ground. It was much later when the two of them finally fell asleep in each other's arms, exhausted but contented.

***

Bellaydin's thoughts drifted back to Wishapton, and then to Aderilund. So much had happened in the years that had passed that he scarcely recognised himself as the boy who had left that land so long ago. He had been through the crucible, and he had survived.

At dawn's light, they prepared to leave. But it would only be him and Polnygar.

"Are you sure?" Bellaydin said to Morgan. "You're more than welcome to come with us. At least for a visit, I mean. After last night, I thought perhaps –"

Morgan smiled and shook her head. "My place is here, Enparran, with my people. We must rebuild. They need me."

"It wouldn't have to be a long visit," Bellaydin said.

"I'm sorry, Bellaydin," Morgan said. "This is goodbye. May our paths cross again." She kissed him on the cheek, then turned and left.

Polnygar approached, smiling widely.

"What?" Bellaydin said.

"Nothing." Polnygar continued to grin. "We should get going, yes?"

"I suppose so," Bellaydin said.

Shortly thereafter, they departed for Emparia, with their Saldarri escorts leading the way. The marchlands of northern Goriinchia were strangely peaceful, and it did not take long for them to reach the borders. Bidding farewell to their escorts, they continued alone.

It was a bit more than an hour later before Polnygar spoke. "Where are we?"

Bellaydin looked about. "If I'm not mistaken, we're near Wishapton. Or what remains of it."

As they crested the hill, the burned out remains of Wishapton came into view. Bellaydin brought his horse to a halt, surveying the town he had called home the past year.

"It'll be alright, Bela," Polnygar said. "We can rebuild. Life goes on, little brother." She paused. "Are my eyes playing tricks on me, or are there soldiers near the town?"

"No, no, I see them too. Emparian," Bellaydin said. "It looks like the royal banner."

Bellaydin and Polnygar urged the horses onwards. As they got closer, they saw that the Emparian troops were working in teams throughout the ruined city, hauling rubble, scouring through the broken and burned embers. The soldiers were focused on their task but as the Ap'Lydins approached, one of the men snapped to attention.

"Hail, travellers," the soldier said. "I'm sorry, but as you can see, you won't find any lodgings here tonight. Wishapton is no more."

Bellaydin returned the soldier's salute. "Understood soldier. I was Baron of this town. My name is Sir Bellaydin Ap'Lydin."

"Oh, my lord Ap'Lydin," the soldier stammered. "I apologise for not recognising you, my lord."

"Forgiven, soldier," Bellaydin said.

"We're to look for any or all survivors, my lord," the soldier explained. "We're not having much luck."

"Well, your luck just changed."

"Sir?"

"Survivors. You're looking at them. Take us to whoever's in charge."

***

Bellaydin and Polnygar were led up the hill to a makeshift camp. Their escort brought them to one of the larger tents and called to whoever was inside.

"Sir, we've found someone, finally. Two survivors. In fact, they asked to see you specifically."

There were a few muttered words from inside, and an armoured knight emerged from the tent, an Eldara by his side. Both men said the same word simultaneously. "Bellaydin?"

"Geoffrey!" Bellaydin exclaimed. "Talthas!"

Geoffrey extended a hand towards Polnygar. "Polnygar? By all the gods. We thought you were dead."

"We came pretty close," Polnygar chuckled.

"You must fill us in on everything that has happened," Geoffrey said. "Just let me fetch the others."

"Others?" Bellaydin said.

Polnygar heard a familiar voice. "I believe he is referring to us."

"Master," Polnygar blurted out almost instinctively. "Sorry, Aelzandar," she said, somewhat self-conscious. "Force of habit."

"Not a problem my dear," Aelzandar said as he crested the hill. "I'm just glad to see you alive and in one piece."

Hebu scurried across the grass to join his master, and bringing up the rear was the Ahktarran Kahlaf el-Lahn, his clawed feet moving at a leisurely speed.

"Ap'Lydin," the Lizardman growled. "You are alive. Alive and well, in fact."

"Nice to have one where we all return alive, isn't it?" Geoffrey beamed. "Makes for a change."

"The gods are kind," Aelzandar said.

"Well," Geoffrey said, "I'd best make myself useful, and get our cook. I think a celebration is in order, after all. Come, Talthas!"

"Hebu, perhaps you might assist as well?" Aelzandar suggested.

"Yes, we could use someone to carry the wine," Geoffrey said.

"You grubby human," the Nemoi sounded angry. "I speak eleven languages, have taught in the finest academies, and designed tombs and palaces for kings and queens. And you want me to carry your wine?"

"Hebu," chided Aelzandar.

"Oh, very well," the Nemoi grumbled and left with Geoffrey and Talthas to organise the celebratory meal.

Aelzandar smiled at Polnygar. "Would you care to walk with me, my dear? There is so much about your journey I'd like to hear."

Polnygar looked to Bellaydin, who smiled and nodded towards his sister. "Of course, Aelzandar," she said.

"We shall see you at supper, my boy," Aelzandar told Bellaydin.

As the others left, Bellaydin and Kahlaf were the only ones to remain on the hill. "So, Ap'Lydin," the Ahktarran said, "We are alone together again. We have come full circle."

"I never took you to be the sentimental type," Bellaydin teased.

The Ahktarran let out an uncharacteristic chuckle. "A most astute observation. It is done then? You recovered the Tears? The Horned God is no more?"

Bellaydin nodded in affirmation. "Maybe we'll get some peace and stability in these lands yet."

"You have done the right thing, Bellaydin," the Ahktarran said. "But do not delude yourself. Peace and stability? Emparia will take decades to recover, if it ever will, and those here who followed the Horned God will find themselves hated and ostracised by their own family and friends. But these are small matters to the events that will take place in the marches. Without the unifying influence of the Horned God, Goriinchia will fragment, and tear itself apart. For all we know, nothing of that proud nation will remain in a hundred years."

"You make it sound like Goriinchia is destroyed. And that it's all my fault."

"You did destroy Goriinchia. And who else do I blame then? Was it not you who struck down the Horned God? Who killed their priests and warlords?"

"But I had no other choice. You said I did the right thing."

The Ahktarran's lips curled into a fanged smile. "That I did. It was the correct choice. But the consequences remain."

"Why are you telling me this?" Bellaydin did not hide the annoyance in his words. He had been in good spirits until now.

"There is something you need know, Ap'Lydin," the Ahktarran said. "How you choose to react is your own choice. You may believe you should have been told it earlier, but in truth, the time was not right. I tell you now because the time has come."

"What? What is it?"

"The last message of Wulfric Highcrown."

The Ahktarran bent down to Bellaydin's level and, moving his lips close to Bellaydin's ears, Kahlaf whispered, "Maria Ap'Lydin lives."

"What?" The blood drained from Bellaydin's face. "What do you mean? HOW?"

"Your cousin did not fall to her death. She survived."

"I don't believe this. Are certain? Why would you keep this from me? Where is she?"

"Yes, I'm certain," said Kahlaf. "I did all as I was instructed for victory."

"For victory? Damn you." Bellaydin clenched his fists. "These are people's lives you're talking about."

"I did what had to be done." The Ahktarran stiffened. "Your cousin's daughter fulfilled the role that was required of her. That role did not necessitate her death, but there was a need to make it appear as such to our enemies."

"Where is she?" Bellaydin asked again. "Tell me now."

"She is safe, far from here. It would be best for all concerned if you never saw her again."

"Best for all concerned?" Bellaydin huffed. "How can you say that?"

"Your family has enemies, Ap'Lydin, and has for centuries. These enemies have pruned the branches of your family at every opportunity. They murdered your grandfather, your parents, and your cousin. Maria would have been killed too eventually, had we not intervened to make it appear they had succeeded in their first attempt."

"But the Horned God is gone now. The danger has passed."

"I thought you understood me, Ap'Lydin. It is not over. The Horned God's minions remain and for some of them, the death of their god will not end their vendetta against the Ap'Lydins. Do you really imagine they will go quietly into the night? No, none of them will rest until the last Ap'Lydin is gone. If you care for Maria Ap'Lydin at all you will not seek her out, you will not attempt to find her, you will not mention her. If you keep this secret, she will be safe. If not, her life will be forever in danger."

"Why tell me then?" said Bellaydin. "Why tell me if I can't ever see her

355

again? When I can't see for myself that she's alive and well?"

Kahlaf shrugged. "You needed to know the truth. You needed to know that you did not fail your cousin, William. You needed to know that you kept your promise. You loved William Ap'Lydin, did you not Bellaydin? Then ask yourself this: What would he have wanted?"

"His daughter safe."

"That is why I'm telling you."

EPILOGUE

Spring, Year 236 of the Third Epoch

The city of Aderial was in a festive mood.

There was much to celebrate: King Talan's recovery, the demise of the usurper Ivellios but especially the defeat of the Cult of the Horned God, whose very presence had disrupted the idyllic Aspen Kingdom in the first place. As the focal point of Aderilund, it was only natural it was in Aderial that Eldara of all castes and from all walks of life had converged to thank the gods for their deliverance.

Banners festooned the dwellings and buildings of Aderial, and the spellweavers created a wondrous display of lights and colours in the skies above.

A magnificent parade wove its way down the main boulevard of the Eldara capital, and the people recreated the fall of the Horned God in colourful and imaginative detail.

The Hall of the Ancients, in the city's heart and hence the centre of any celebration, hosted the loftiest of the celebrations, and word soon spread that the king himself would lead the proceedings. Eldara crowded around

357

the building, peering through the great arched windows, hoping to catch a glimpse of their beloved monarch through the crowds of gentry within.

Bellaydin stood where he thought he never would again – in the presence of the Eldara councillors and nobility. Unlike the last occasion he did so, he was here as an honoured guest, rather than a barely tolerated interloper. His sister Polnygar stood by his side, offering quiet words of encouragement to her nervous brother.

He rubbed the scar on his palm absent-mindedly. It still itched occasionally, though not as badly as before. Ever since he had returned the Tears to Aelzandar, who had, in turn, resealed them in an enchanted receptacle, Bellaydin had found the pain in his hand slowly residing. Now it was nothing more than a dull ache, one that he only noticed in times of stress.

"Bela for the last time, relax, would you? We were invited, remember?"

"I know," said Bellaydin. "It still feels strange, though. They're all staring at me."

"What do you expect?" Polnygar said, grinning. "They're elves. They've never seen a real hero before."

"Still feel uncomfortable," Bellaydin grumbled.

"Well, look around. You're not the only one."

Nearby in the chamber stood Sir Geoffrey Keslin, newly named Emparian ambassador to the Aspen Throne. The knight looked astonished at his surroundings and kept fidgeting with his clothes in a vain attempt to feel comfortable.

"Honoured Lords and Ladies of the High Council, distinguished guests, would you please rise for their Majesties, King Talan li'Karn-Raka and Queen Talina li'Aderias."

All present rose and bowed their heads with respect as the king and queen's procession made its way into the Hall of Ancients. The two monarchs looked even more glorious and radiant than Bellaydin remembered. The queen was stunning to behold, her beauty only enhanced by the jewels and gown she was wearing, reserved for occasions of high state. The king, having completely recovered from the illness Ivellios had inflicted upon him, stood tall, looking strong and noble.

"We thank you, our subjects, and honoured guests. Please, be seated," King Talan said warmly, waving his hands.

"It is indeed a joyous day and one most fitting for us to hold court in this land. For today we commemorate the anniversary of the fall of the Horned God and the end of the cult that once tore the Aspen Kingdom apart. The treason of Ivellios will long stand as a dark chapter in the history of the Eldara, and the damage he has done will take many years to heal from."

"But that is the past, and now, with Ivellios gone, it is time to look forward to the future. With that in mind, it is fitting that we recognise the efforts of those who have done so much and asked for so little in return."

"Would Bellaydin and Polnygaranna Ap'Lydin step forward?"

Nervously, Bellaydin took a step forward and, raising his head, looked towards the king, if a little hesitantly. His sister Polnygar showed no such reticence and looked forward proudly.

"Aderilund is your home, just as it is home to the Eldara. You have been denied this because of the hatred, jealousy, and bigotry of one who is now gone. Therefore, under the authority granted to me as monarch and occupant of the Aspen Throne, we hereby rescind, in perpetuity, the edict expelling you from these lands. This land will always be open to you. Any further talk of excluding the Ap'Lydins from the Aspen Kingdom will be considered treason. You will always have a home here. Furthermore, you will never want for anything. The property and belongings of the now deceased Lord Ivellios will now be deeded to House Aelsar. Naturally, as descendants of the house you shall share in the bequest."

"Thank you, Your Majesty," Polnygar said.

"I am humbled, Your Majesty," said Bellaydin.

"Good. Aelzandar li'Ellthiros li'Geihnos, please step forward."

Aelzandar obliged, tapping his staff on the marble floor as he did.

"Old friend," the king said warmly, "I find myself once again in your debt. And I also find myself in need of a new Lord Paramount Spellweaver —"

"With deepest respect, Your Majesty, I must —"

"No is not a word for princes, Aelzandar," the king teased.

"Then it seems I must agree," Aelzandar replied, his eyes twinkling.

"I thought you might." Talan grinned.

Aelzandar acknowledged the king with a respectful bow.

"Sir Geoffrey Keslin," the king exclaimed. "Please step forward."

Geoffrey looked surprised, and shuffled forward, his eyes stuck to the ground.

"How can we reward one of Emparia's finest knights?" the king asked.

"Well," Geoffrey said. "I hear you make some fine wine."

"Indeed, we do. The vineyards here are without compare."

The king paused a moment, deep in thought. "Take as much as you need when you go home. It will make you a very rich man." The king paused again. "Or at the very least, a happy one."

Geoffrey laughed nervously and then, bowing his head, took a step back.

"Would Lady Saegralanna li'Saegras please step forward?"

Bellaydin looked over as the woman who had raised him for twelve years looked around, surprised, and then, stepping forward, bowing before your king.

"Your majesty," Saegralanna said, "I am honoured by your attention, but I was not among those whose deeds we celebrate today."

"Not in person, my lady," Talan said, "But you raised these two fine young heroes for most of their lives. You turned them into the people they are today. If we are to honour their heroism, then surely I must honour the woman who prepared them for such a task."

Saegralanna's eyes glistened with tear and her cheeks flushed with pride. Sneaking a glance at her smiling children, she bowed even deeper.

"We are also in need of a new Lord Speaker here in Aderilund. I do recall early in my reign a rather effective Speaker named Saegras," the king said with a smile. "It is natural for his only daughter to take up where he left off, is it not?"

"Your majesty, I am deeply honoured."

"The honour is mine, my dear lady. Rise, Lady Speaker, and take up your responsibilities. You shall help us forge a new beginning for our kingdom."

Saegralanna rose, beaming from ear to ear. Bellaydin had never seen her so happy.

Bellaydin, despite his nerves, found himself laughing, the depth and sincerity of his laugh caused Polnygar to join in the mirth too. Forgetting himself, he pulled his sister in for a warm embrace, kissing the top of her head. Polnygar lay a tender hand on her little brother's cheek. He dared say she was proud of him. He realised King Talan was looking at him, and that made him feel slightly sheepish at having been so candid with his emotions. But the king nodded, a kind smile gracing his face and Bellaydin found himself at ease again. He looked around from Saegralanna to his sister, to

Aelzandar, and Geoffrey, and the happy faces of the assembled Eldara.

It was true, he thought.

Everything is beautiful in Aderilund.

Everything.

APPENDIX

CHARACTERS

In order of appearance

Polnygar Ap'Lydin: Half-elf, apprentice to Aelzandar, sister of Bellaydin Ap'Lydin.

Augustin Bauer: Brother to the Earl of Tyronsville, former Royal Ambassador

Aelzandar: Archmage, Royal Wizard of Macrodonia, and Lord of the Nine Orders

Hebu: Royal Scribe of Macrodonia

Sir Holger Keller: Knight of the Order of the Crux Caruillin. Nephew to Sir Agmar

Sir Agmar Keller: Grand Master of the Order of the Crux Caruillin

Gerd von Genio: Burgomeister of Harralin.

Vaerath: Eldara spellweaver

Laerosanna: Apprentice to Vaerath.

Talina li'Aderias: High Queen of the Eldara. Wife to High King Talan.

Talan li'Karn-Raka: High King of the Eldara. Husband to High Queen Talina.

Ivellios: Lord Spellweaver of Aderilund

Pallios: Spellweaver

Odo Aelfling: Half-elf labourer at Harralin

Bellaydin Ap'Lydin: Baron of Wishapton, brother of Polnygar Ap'Lydin

Amaryllis de Morcor: Queen of Emparia

Sir Geoffrey Keslin: sworn sword to the Countess of Genio

Sir Talthas li'Lyros: Eldara ranger, now knight of Emparia.

Haakon de Morcor: Duke of Alariat, cousin to Queen Amaryllis

Kahlaf el'Lahn: Ahktarran bondsman of the Duke of Oldharbour

Wulfric Highcrown: Duke of Oldharbour

Carfel: Steward of Castle Wishapton

Foril: Foreman at Castle Wishapton

Maria Ap'Lydin: Countess of Genio, daughter of the late William Ap'Lydin

Sir Dallen Withers: Former Sworn sword to the Duke of Georgeton

Lothar: Captain of Gerd von Genio's personal guard.

Egbert: Emparian trader

Connor: Goriinchian prisoner

Mael the Apostate: Long-dead Goriinchian warlord and enemy of the Horned God.

Caelwych: Saldarri ranger

The Seeress: Mystic prophetess of Goriinchia

Cathan Culainn: High Priest of the Horned God

Morgan Culainn: Niece of Cathan Culainn. Daughter of deceased warchief Aonghus Culainn

Archbishop Garamond: Leader of the Emparian branch of the Church of Ralom

Alfred Bauer: Earl of Tyronsville

Oswin Zalltor: Duke of Georgeton

Anson Mainstream: Earl of Warding

Ygarak: Prophet-King of Goriinchia

Saegralanna li'Saegras: Head of House Aelsar, mother to Polnygar Ap'Lydin and foster mother to Bellaydin Ap'Lydin

NATION STATES AND REGIONS

Aderilund: Southern Land. Part of the Aspen Kingdom – the realm of the Eldara.

Caruillin: Vast empire dominating the north of Carurlonia. Major provinces include Skurj, Lerid, the Heartlands and the Vallistian Marches.

Emparia: Northern Kingdom populated by Emparians. It borders Goriinchia, with whom it has a long history of conflict.

Goriinchia: Southern neighbour of Emparia, inhabited by the Goriinchians and the Saldarri. Ruled by the religion of the Horned God.

Infinite Caliphate: A religious empire ruled by the followers of the Infinite Faith. Qarld is the most powerful province, and the Sultan of Qarld serves as Caliph of the empire.

Lerid: Large province to the south of Skurj. Ruled by the Grand Duke of Lerid.

Macrodonia: Hot, desert kingdom to the north of Aderilund. Ruled by a King known as "Pharaoh", and home to Macrodonians and Nemoi.

Mokeria: City-state to the south of Aderilund.

Qarld: Exotic sultanate to the north-west of Macrodonia and largest province of the Infinite Caliphate. Known for its desert mystics and proud Bedouin tribes. Home to Qardleeans, Nemoi and Ahktarra.

Shadrish Archipelago: Island chain off the western coast of Carurlonia and a province of the Infinite Caliphate.

Skurj: Frigid land in the extreme north. Borders Alfheim. Home to the Knights of the Crux Caruillin.

Tarken: The so-called "Hermit Kingdom", reclusive and secretive realm ruled by "Dragonborn" Emperors.

Thulia: Legendary frozen land somewhere north across the sea from Skurj, believed to be the origin of the Thulian race.

Vallistian Marches: Southern lands of the Empire of Caruillin that share a border with the Infinite Caliphate.

SETTLEMENTS

Aderial: Capital of Aderilund.

Alariat: City in Emparia. Seat of the Duke of Alariat and the Archbishop of Alariat

Drakeford: Small town near the border of Emparia and Goriinchia, seat of Sir Edric Keslin, Baron Drakeford.

Emperor's Palace: Capital of Emparia. Seat of the monarch and of the Duke of Emperor's Palace.

Genio: City of Emparia. Seat of the Earl of Genio.

Georgeton: City in Emparia. Seat of the Duke of Georgeton.

Gorin: Capital of Goriinchia.

Oldharbour: Large port city in Emparia. Seat of the Duke of Oldharbour.

Harralin: Major settlement in Skurj.

Korfar: Goriinchian settlement near the Emparian border.

Liderial: Ancient city of the Eldara. Situated just north of Skurj. Seat of the elven monarchs and capital of the Aspen Kingdom.

Oldharbour: City of Emparia, seat of the Duke of Oldharbour.

Qar Arrid: City of Qarld, home to the Great Library

Qar Dal: Former capital of the Caliphate, site of the defeat of the archmage Ralur almost two and a half centuries ago.

Qar Udel: Prominent city of Qarld, and seat of the Sultan.

Ralom: The Holy City. Centre of the Triune faith of the Church of Ralom.

Tower of the Magi: Ancient ruin in Goriinchia. Sacred temple to the Horned God.

Tyronsville: Emparian city. Seat of the Earl of Tyronsville

Wishapton: Emparian town. Close to the Goriinchian border and southern-most city of the Earldom of Genio.

Warding: Emparian city. Seat of the Earl of Warding

NATIONALITIES AND ETHNICITIES

Ahktarra: Lizardmen from the land of Qarld.

Caruillani: Humans from Caruillin

Emparians: Humans from Emparia.

Goriinchians: Humans from Goriinchia.

Eldara: People of the Aspen Kingdom. Known to outsiders as "Elves" or "Fey".

Leridians: Humans from Lerid.

Macrodonians: Humans from Macrodonia

Nemoi: A diminutive people from the land of Macrodonia.

Qardleeans: Humans from the land of Qarld.

Saldarri: A Goriinchian tribe of mixed human and Eldara blood. Expert trackers and archers.

Sarrisite: Follower of the Infinite Faith. Named for the Prophet Sarrius, founder of the Infinite Faith.

Soldara: Ancient ancestors of the Spellweaver caste. Believed extinct.

Selvara: Nomadic cousins of the Eldara. Named for Selvaros, who rejected the founding of Liderial by Lideros.

Skurjans: Humans of Skurj.

Shadrish: A dark skinned sea-faring folk from the Shadrish Archipelago, western province of the Infinite Caliphate.

Tarkenese: Humans from Tarken.

Thulians: One of the three ancestor races of humanity, believed to be the common ancestors of Skurjans, Emparians, Goriinchians and Caruillani, among others.

MAGIC

Art, The: The term for magic, most commonly used by humans and the Eldara.

Automaton: Animated metal construct in the shape of a human. Created by the Soldara through unknown techniques.

Draconic: The script used for recording knowledge of the Art. Purported to be the language of dragons.

Far-speaking: The ability used by practitioners of the Art to speak to others over long distances.

Kaltban: Magical sword recovered by Sir William Ap'Lydin during the siege of Ralom. Lost by his grandson, Earl William, after being captured by the Goriinchians at Wishapton

Lich: A practitioner of the Art who has succumbed to magic addiction and become a creature sustained only by the power of the Art.

Moon-seer: An individual who can use the Art to perceive the future or grant visions.

Sablium: Black, oily mineral, believed to be crystalline form of Nether. Renowned for its ability to resist the Art.

Sakkaru: The so-called "Flame of Justice", the sword of the archmage Cassian, now wielded by his apprentice Aelzandar.

Sending: Visual message sent via the Art from one mind to another. Similar to Far-speaking, but less precise and commonly manifests as vivid dreams.

Spellweaver: An Eldara Mage.

Skymetal: Extremely rare substance, used in the manufacture of weapons enchanted by the Art, such as *Kaltban* and *Sakkaru*. Believed to be a crystalline form of Ether

Tears of the Divine, The: An ancient magical artefact. Broken into four pieces and scattered around the known world.

Tome of Divine Metaphysics, The: A theoretical work by the archmage Ralur, written after he captured the Tower of Magi in Goriinchia. It is believed to contain Ralur's discoveries into the methods by which a mortal might attain divine power.

RELIGION

Bahamut: Messenger of the Infinite Faith, considered to have passed the words of the Infinite to the Prophet Sarrius.

Celestial Architects, The: Religion of the Nemoi, centred on the book *Nemoinomicon,* and without priests or places of worship.

Divine Martyr, The: Also known as Kytilas. God of chivalry, self-sacrifice and valour. Worshipped by the Church of Ralom, centred in Ralom.

Heir of Lydin, The: Prophesised messiah figure in Goriinchian mythology.

Horned God, The: The deity of the staunchly monotheistic Goriinchians. Followed outside of Goriinchia in secretive, subversive cults.

Hydria: Mother Goddess of the Eldara.

Infinite Faith, The: State religion of the Infinite Caliphate, based on the teachings of the prophet Sarrius

Realms of Righteousness, The: The heavenly realm believed to exist by followers of the Church of Ralom.

Sarrius: Founding prophet of the Infinite Faith.

Silver Lady, The: Also known as the Queen of Light and Life. The wife of the Sun King and mother to the Divine Martyr. Goddess of childbirth, women and the home. Worshipped by both the Church of Ralom.

Sun King, The: God of the Sun, Light and Nobility. Worshipped by the Church of Ralom, centred in Ralom.

Transcendent Faith, The: Religion of the Eldara, centred of the worship of Hydria, "The Great Mother", and her children – the so-called "Firstborn of Hydria".

Triune, The: Worshipped by the Church of Ralom, the Triune is the collective name for the Sun King, the Silver Lady and the Divine Martyr.

Underworld, The: The hellish netherworld believed to exist by followers of the Church of Ralom and the Infinite Faith.

CULTURE AND HISTORY

Alarion I: First king of the unified Emparian nation.

Alusine the Last: Final king of the Ran-Tyron dynasty. Died at the Battle of Goriinch Hill

Ancient Ones, The: Founding heroes of Macrodonian civilisation, revered by later generations as divine figures. One of them, Aldion the High, is counted as first of the archmages.

Black Talons, The: Rebel group during the occupation of Macrodonia by the Caliphate. Later resurrect as a secret police by Pharaoh Jagontay II.

Cassian: Archmage and vanquisher of the Night Dragons. Aelzandar's master.

Eldaric: Name given to the script and spoken language of the Eldara.

Emparian Civil War: The three decade conflict between House Tyron and House Morcor over who was the rightful monarchs of Emparian. It began with the death of Alusine the Last at Goriinch Hill.

Fostering: A tradition whereby young members of noble houses are raised in the households of other families to forge bonds of friendship and amity.

Great Fostering, The: A form of fostering specific to the royal court.

Knights of the Crux Caruillin, The: Chivalric Order headquartered in Skurj and dedicated to the Divine Martyr. Led by Grand Master Agmar Keller.

Mal-halyth: Eldara pejorative to describe a human or one of human heritage.

Night Dragon, The: Legendary creature that terrorised Macrodonia. Defeated by Cassian and Aelzandar

Tragedy of Belial'ad-Dīn, The: A folk tale from Qarld that describes the tragic and sad life of a man born the son of a demon and a human woman.

Tyron: The "Last Davorean", founder of one of the proto-Emparian kingdoms. Ancestor to Alarion I.

Zohra: Legendary beauty of the Infinite Caliphate.

ABOUT THE AUTHOR

Aidan Hennessy lives in Canberra, Australia. He is married with three children and a full-time job. Like everyone else he, blames his delays on the pandemic.

theaplydinchronicles.wordpress.com

www.ingramcontent.com/pod-product-compliance
Lightning Source LLC
Chambersburg PA
CBHW050918030726
47503CB00007BB/2352